The Vote

The Vte

A novel

SYBIL DOWNING

UNIVERSITY OF NEW MEXICO PRESS ❧ ALBUQUERQUE

LIBRARY OF CONGRESS CATALOGING-IN-PUBLICATION DATA

Downing, Sybil.

The vote : a novel / Sybil Downing.

p.   cm.

Includes bibliographical references.

ISBN-13: 978-0-8263-3857-0 (pbk. : alk. paper)

ISBN-10: 0-8263-3857-7 (pbk. : alk. paper)

1. Women—Suffrage—United States—Fiction.

2. Suffragists—United States—Fiction.

3. National Woman's Party—Fiction.

I. Title.

PS3554.09348V67 2006

813'.54—dc22

2006008283

DESIGN AND COMPOSITION: MELISSA TANDYSH

This Book Is Dedicated

To My Husband

Contents

Acknowledgments

The list of people who offered their expertise and support is long. Among them are Karen Gilleland, Margaret Coel, Ann Ripley, Lesley Kellas Payne, Donald deKieffer, Elizabeth Downing, Robert Williams, Jennifer Spencer, archivist at the Sewall-Belmont House, Washington, D.C.; Sam Daniels and his staff at the Library of Congress Photography Department; Peter Penzer, author of *Washington Past and Present*; the staff of the Western History Collection and the Government Documents departments of the Denver Public Library; Patricia Johnson at the Pueblo, Colorado Public Library. Thanks also to Adam Kane, Lincoln Bramwell, Lydia Lennihan, and Luther Wilson for his belief in the project.

Chapter 1 ⟶ ❧

Kate Brennan heard the taunts of the crowd milling about the White House gates and slid across the taxi's leatherette seat to see what was going on. She had a train to catch, but at the sight of the twelve women lined up along the wrought iron fence, she asked the cabbie to pull over.

Leaning out the open window, she studied the women. Most seemed to be in their twenties, her age. Their shoulders back and heads held high, they looked like bareheaded warriors in white linen dresses. Motionless beneath the hazy June sky, they held purple-and-gold-edged banners that read, "How Long Must Women Wait for Liberty, Mr. President?"

Kate remembered the photo on the front page of the *Philadelphia Inquirer* last year, showing suffragist picketers being hauled off to jail. Yet here they were, different women, of course, but carrying the same message. She sensed the danger heightening around them and felt a twinge of something close to envy.

Months before the country had entered the war, when her brother Tom had enlisted and wangled his way over to France, she'd hit upon the idea of quitting school and joining the nursing corps. She would have, too, if she hadn't been so queasy at the sight of blood. Or was that just a handy excuse?

Kate rested her arms gingerly on the cab's hot windowsill. Behind the women and the wrought iron fence was the drive, lined with beds of roses, leading to the stately colonial pillared portico. From here, in the shade of the arching sweet gum trees, the White House looked cut off from the world, isolated. And she thought of the president inside. Two years ago, she'd heard him speak about keeping the country out of the war. A slender man with a sharp nose, squinting through his pince-nez in the bright Colorado sun, he'd stood at the rear of the train's observation car decked out in red-white-and-blue bunting and made promises he hadn't kept. But her parents forgave a fellow Democrat anything.

The crowd's taunts became jeers, edged with the threat of violence. To Kate's relief, four men in the stiff black caps and high-necked dark blue uniforms bearing the insignia of the District Police came through the gate next to the White House guard post and took up positions near the picketers.

A shout rose from the crowd as a skinny boy in filthy knickers and a ragged shirt hurled a tomato at one of the women, narrowly missing her. Raw laughter erupted. A second tomato found its mark, the blood-red juice trickling down the woman's starched white dress as she stood unblinking, like a marble statue. All the while the policemen never moved a muscle.

Two sailors advanced on a dark-haired girl—five feet tall, if that—cursing her as they snatched at her banner and shoved her to the sidewalk. Three more men surged around her, like circling wolves, seemingly ready to tear her apart as the crowd and the policemen looked on.

Outraged, Kate pushed open the door, and dodging the oncoming cars and those that had pulled over to watch the goings-on, ran toward the policemen. Even as she grabbed the nearest man's arm and pleaded for him "to do something," she saw the woman who had been thrown to the sidewalk, being hoisted above the heads of the mob and tossed from man to man, like a captured trophy.

The next instant the crowd seemed to move as one, surging forward, sweeping Kate into its midst. Bodies slammed into her, crushing her as they carried her along. She had visions of being trampled to death. Hands clawed at her clothes and purse. She gasped for air that reeked of sour sweat. A man's heavy shoe stomped on her left foot, and she cried out in pain. A woman near her in a dark dress screamed. Kate shoved her elbows against a fat man's chest, twisting away from his groping hands, fighting to keep her balance, to find a way out when whistles pierced the air.

The crowd quieted, but Kate had the feeling the quiet was like an animal biding its time, ready to spring again if the opportunity showed itself. She caught her breath. Her hat was gone, but somehow she'd managed to hang onto her purse. Uneasy, she looked around to get her bearings and saw she was next to the fence with several of the picketers who were gathering the remains of their banners. Instinctively, she went to help them, only vaguely aware of the hush behind them until she heard a man say, "Okay. Leave that stuff where it is, ladies. You're comin' with us."

Kate shot a glance over her shoulder.

"You heard me," said a cop wielding a billy club. "Get a move on."

A tall woman with a thick mass of red hair piled on top of her head eyed Kate and said, "If you're wondering what's going on, we're being arrested. Thus, the paddy wagon waiting at the curb."

Kate followed her gaze to a black wagon, its rear doors standing open like a monster's maw. She started to turn away when a large hand clamped her shoulder and yanked her toward the line of women. Indignant, she tried to break lose. She pleaded for help from the bystanders she passed but they merely gawked at her as they might a wild creature in the zoo until she was standing behind the paddy wagon. Her blood pounding in her ears, she tried to catch her breath. Another officer shoved her up the two steep iron steps, and she stumbled as she stepped up over the sill.

"Move over a smidge, Julie," a woman's calm voice said. Two hands firmly pulled Kate down onto a hard wooden bench. Slowly, her eyes adjusted. Faces emerged from the shadows. They were looking at her.

"Are you okay?" the woman next to her asked.

Kate looked closely: the red-haired woman.

"I'm sorry you got caught up in all this."

"That makes two of us," Kate said.

"My name's Lucy. Lucy Burns."

Kate nodded absently and glanced away, the perspiration beading along her hairline, as she peered around the small space until she found the windows little more than barred slits near the roof. Once, when her mother had locked her in a closet for lying, the walls had closed in on her as if she'd been buried alive. She'd been sure she'd suffocate before her mother let her out.

"I'm Kate Brennan," she finally managed, more to hang on to that fact than share it. If she hadn't gone sightseeing with her friend, Millie, yesterday and they hadn't taken a detour by the White House, she might not be in this fix.

The door slammed shut, a padlock snapped in place. Gears ground. The paddy wagon lurched, throwing the women against one another as it started forward. Exhaust fumes filled the space, and Kate choked, unable to breathe. She felt a powerful urge to pee. She was afraid she might go in her pants, and in this heat it wouldn't be long before the stink gave her away. Beyond her misery, she heard Lucy talking to the person next to her. Incredibly, they had breath enough to discuss legal matters: rights and fines and sentencing.

After what seemed like an hour but was probably no more than fifteen minutes, the paddy wagon slowed, came to a stop. The women shifted expectantly. The clank of the padlock being unlocked was followed by the door swinging open. Kate's spirits rose at the sight of the sky. She pulled in a deep breath, struggled to her feet, and waited her turn to escape.

Lucy Burns leaned toward her, said casually, "Just so you'll know, we are about to be booked, brought before the magistrate, and charged with whatever they decide on. Today will make our third foray."

"You've been through this three times?"

Lucy's bright blue eyes danced as if pleased with herself. "I guess you could say it's getting to be a habit."

The cop at the foot of the steps slammed a nightstick against the steel steps, startling them. "Cut the gab and get a move on, you two. I ain't got all day here."

"Lucy, wait. I hate to bring this up, but I have to use the bathroom."

"We'll see what we can do."

Kate followed close behind her down the steps and through a metal door held open by a cop into a windowless corridor.

"After we're—charged, what happens?" Kate asked, breathlessly, not sure what she felt was fear or anticipation, now that she was free of the van.

Lucy glanced over her shoulder. "The judge will hear the cops' side, let us have our say, then give us a choice—pay a fine or go to jail."

"Well." Kate smiled and felt a flush of relief. The day wasn't a complete loss. She had forty dollars in her pocketbook, and she could telegraph her father for more if any of the suffragists were short. She might not catch her train, but her father would forgive her. She'd missed trains before. Her mother was another matter. "That sounds reasonable enough."

Lucy Burns turned again and looked at Kate for an instant.

"I mean, it's not as if you're automatically going to be thrown in jail," she said, feeling an urge to explain.

"Or you either," Lucy said, never slowing her pace.

Kate reddened and trotted after Lucy, so anxious to make amends she almost overlooked the door with the sign that said, "Women." Before she could decide whether to go in or ask permission, Lucy had hailed the policeman behind them. "Officer, some of us need to use the ladies' room."

"That so?"

"Urinating is one of those bodily functions you can only put off for so long. Therefore, we'd appreciate . . ."

The cop mumbled something crude about women who couldn't hold their water as he pushed open the restroom door and Kate moved past him, the first to enter.

Finally squatting over the cracked toilet seat, Kate surveyed the names and curses etched into the sides of the filthy wooden stall.

A banging on the door reminded her that the cop had wanted to come in with them. But Lucy had barred his way, waving other women inside as she'd smiled and appealed to his sense of chivalry, as if she expected nothing less. The stalls had no doors. And Kate had panicked at the thought of a strange man, any man, watching as she sat on the toilet. At home in Denver she'd never shared a bathroom with anyone but her little sister. In college, she planned her days around the times when she'd have the best chance of having the bathroom on her floor to herself. Her roommate had called her obsessive. All Kate wanted was privacy.

She heard Lucy and the three other women leave and she finished, left the stall. Walking across the room to the sink, she imagined the feel of the cold water on her face and neck, the taste of it. But the faucets were missing. Even as the cop stood in the doorway, she stood staring down at the two empty holes as if she could will faucets to appear.

Lucy had waited for her, and, a policeman at their heels, feeling like a dog on a leash, Kate followed her into the main part of the station toward the other picketers, who had lined up in front of a chest-high counter. One by one, the women stepped up to the cop in charge, gave their names and addresses, dates of birth, stated whether they were single or married, their father's name if single, their husband's name if married. By the time it came Kate's turn, she had recovered enough from the monkey business and humiliation to be mad clear through. "Officer, listen here. There's been a mistake. These women were just—"

"That's what they all say." He gazed up at her with blood-shot eyes, yawned. "Let's have it. Name, address. You seen how it works."

"I demand to—" she began, then gave in. Raising a ruckus with this man would be a waste of time. The judge was the one to talk to.

6

She glanced past the policeman asking the questions and saw men clutching the bars of jail cells, heard their curses. The stench of the place, the heat, the din, the people—white, Negro, men and woman, old and young, some handcuffed, cops—everywhere. It was as if she had entered a Hell she had never imagined.

Lucy Burns touched her arm and Kate followed her past battered desks where tough-looking, unshaven men sat in rumpled suits, shirt collars unbuttoned and ties askew, talking on phones, eyeing the women with smirks as they went by.

What passed as a courtroom was small, with a magistrate's bench on a raised platform, a desk and chair off to one side, and a half-dozen or so wooden benches, all but the first two occupied by Negroes.

Kate slid in next to Lucy at the end of the front row where the women sat, tried to calm herself. She ought to put her mind to how best to explain the circumstances to the magistrate. But all she could think about was how much a cigarette would help. Her mother didn't approve of women smoking. At college, a student could be kicked out if caught smoking, which may have been why Kate had taken up the habit. Yet there was something about lighting up and inhaling that always soothed her nerves.

She wondered if police stations in Denver were this bad. Certainly, there wouldn't be as many Negroes. She couldn't remember seeing any downtown, at least not on Sixteenth Street or along Sixth Avenue, where her mother shopped for groceries and meat. The only Negro woman she knew was Nancy, a heavyset woman with pendulous breasts—Kate had never heard her last name mentioned. Nancy worked for Mrs. Finley in the big, old house at the end of the block. And there were the waiters at the Denver Athletic Club, every one of them Negro, but dignified looking in their immaculate, starched white jackets and always smiling.

A person didn't have to know much to know the Negroes in this place were a bad bunch. Their eyes had a flat, sullen look, except for a skinny woman with a red cast to her skin and an old felt hat pushed back on her nappy hair who winked at Kate. She was reminded of an article she'd read in the *Post* yesterday about a knife fight between two drunken Negroes in a place called Scott's Alley across the street from the Senate office building.

Overhead, wooden blades of a large electric fan circled slowly in the stifling air. Kate glanced at the clock hung on the streaked, ochre-colored walls behind the magistrate's bench. Four o'clock. By now her train was on its way to Pittsburgh. Only God knew where her suitcase was—probably stolen. Even if the cabby was honest and had returned it to the garage for safekeeping, she'd have to go through the nuisance of retrieving it.

A door behind the magistrate's bench opened. The cop pushed to his feet. "All rise." Feet shuffled. Someone coughed. When everyone was standing, a small, compact man, wearing steel-rimmed glasses and a black, flowing robe, strode in, sat down, and began to thumb through the stack of file folders on the bench. Several moments passed. Finally shoving them to one side, he looked over at the policeman behind the desk. "Well, sergeant . . ."

The cop got to his feet again. "As you see from the paperwork, Your Honor, first up is the ladies. Picketing, obstructing a public sidewalk, and disorderly conduct."

Kate sat forward, straightened, trying to catch the magistrate's eyes. "Your Honor . . ."

He ignored her, lowered his chin and surveyed the row of women facing him over the top of his glasses. "Here you are once again. I must say I am truly disappointed."

Kate cleared her throat. Once he got sidetracked with the picketers, she was afraid she'd lose her chance to explain her situation. She raised her hand. "Your Honor . . ."

The magistrate shot her a fierce glare. "You'll have your chance." He glanced at the sergeant. "Who're the arresting officers, sergeant?"

"Maguire and Stillman, Your Honor." He nodded toward the rear of the room, and the magistrate waved the two men forward. Wasting no time, the bailiff swore them in, one at a time, each giving the same story: the women had disobeyed the District ordinance against obstructing a public sidewalk and had contributed to a riot.

When the police had finished, the magistrate leaned his arms on the bench, arranged the sleeves of his robe, and laced his fingers. "Now it's your turn, ladies." He looked toward the far end of the bench. "The young woman at the end . . ."

The small, dark-haired girl who had been knocked to the sidewalk rose to her feet.

"Olivia Melburn."

"And how do you answer the charge?"

"Not guilty, Your Honor."

The magistrate pushed his glasses in place. "Haven't I seen you before in this court, young woman?"

"You have, Your Honor. Last fall."

He nodded. "I thought so. Never forget a face."

The petite woman stepped forward. "Your Honor, as of March first, according to a decision made by this very court, National Woman's Party members, henceforth, had the right to assemble peacefully outside the White House gates. Which they did yesterday and the day before. Yet today, we are arrested for doing nothing more than petitioning our country's president for redress." She turned to the other women. "The banner, please."

Instantly three women produced one of the frayed banners that had fluttered so bravely earlier and held it above their heads.

"'How Long Must Women Wait for Liberty?' A fair question, wouldn't you say, Your Honor?"

From the back of the room feet stamped. The magistrate banged his gavel. "Order in this court." He glared at Olivia Melburn. "I will not tolerate grandstanding."

"Your Honor, since we have not been accorded an attorney, I must testify in my own defense. From noon until we were arrested by the officers, we were standing next to the White House fence, doing nothing more than holding up this banner you see before you and others like it. We were set upon by an unruly crowd. We addressed

9

our president today, as we have before, with the demand for the ballot in no narrow or selfish spirit, but from purest patriotism and as a glorious example to the nations of the earth. We, like you, Your Honor, are American citizens of a democratic nation."

Kate listened, hypnotized by the brave words.

"Miss Melborn, I am a busy man. We have all been through this before. If you ladies had kept moving . . . But you didn't." He shifted his gaze to the bench. "Who's next?"

One at a time the others stood, gave their names, and proclaimed their innocence. When it was Lucy's turn, she rose with a quiet dignity that sent shivers of admiration through Kate. "Sir, I, too, am innocent. Miss Melburn presented the facts. Yet you dismiss them out of hand. We were not arrested because we obstructed the sidewalk, but because we were pointing out to President Wilson that he is obstructing the progress of justice and democracy. We—"

Again, the gavel thundered. "Sit, Miss Burns."

For a few moments the steady tick of the clock on the wall behind the magistrate was all that interrupted the silence as he shuffled through the files until, as if almost an afterthought, he read Kate's name.

She rose to her feet, barely able to control her trembling, and blurted, "Your Honor, Miss Burns is right about the crowd—and the police."

"Indeed," he said coldly without looking up from the papers. "How do you plead, Miss Brennan?"

"Your Honor, I am not a member of the National Woman's Party. I was a bystander. When I saw men attacking these women, I tried—"

He glanced over the top of his glasses that had settled halfway down his nose. "But you were there in the thick of it, were you not?"

"It turned out that way, yes. But—"

"So I ask again: what is your plea?"

"Not guilty," Kate said in a voice tight with anger.

"Very well. That does it then." He straightened in his chair with the air of someone glad to have finished an annoying task, surveyed the women before him, and gave another brisk rap to his gavel. "Having heard the evidence, I find these defendants guilty as charged for obstructing a public sidewalk and disturbing the peace in violation of police regulations and the Act of Congress. Therefore, I impose a fine of twenty-five dollars or—" He hesitated for an instant as if trying to make up his mind. "Or fourteen days in the Occoquan Workhouse."

Kate felt Lucy stiffen.

The magistrate leaned forward, glanced to his right. "I'll start with you Miss Melborn. Which is it to be?"

She stood. "Jail, Your Honor," she said, calmly, and sat down.

One after another, each woman stood, professed her innocence and chose jail. Finally, the magistrate nodded toward Kate.

"It appears you are the last of the lot. Miss Lennon, is it?"

"Brennan. Kate Brennan," she said, rising.

"Fine or jail?"

She hesitated. Yet what was there to hesitate about? She had the money to pay the fine. No one expected anything more of her. These women weren't family or friends. She had no duty toward them. She hardly knew them. They wouldn't care one way or the other what she decided. Kate gazed up at the magistrate. Pie-faced, button-eyed, he didn't give a hoot what had actually taken place this afternoon in front of the White House. She was no expert on the law, but anyone could see these women were being railroaded. She was being railroaded.

"Well?"

Her throat tightened. Her mouth went dry. She felt as if she were on the edge of a cliff—she, who was terrified of heights. "Jail, Your Honor," she said, and sank down on the bench again.

The black-robed judge snapped the file folder before him closed and nodded to the bailiff.

"Kate, don't be stupid," Lucy whispered. "Stand up and tell him you've changed your mind, that you'll pay the fine."

"It's too late." And, without looking at Lucy, she rose and joined the line of picketers to be led back the way they came. Past the desks of detectives whose hooded eyes undressed them as the women paraded past, along the twenty-foot length of windowless hallway, the cracked, grey concrete floor, hard beneath their feet, the click of their heels the only sound, out to the paddy wagon, up the black iron steps, through the narrow door, and into the suffocating heat.

After they'd found places along the two benches, Lucy leaned toward Kate. "I appreciate your gesture, if that's what it was, but you made a very bad decision."

The door slammed shut, and the paddy wagon jerked forward. Someone asked Lucy a question, diverting her attention, and Kate was grateful to be off the hook. How to put into words her reaction as she'd listened to them, so brave, so eloquent? Anything she'd say would sound foolish.

The heat was sucking the breath out of her as she stole a glance at the women around her. She knew their names now and whether they were married or single. Straight-backed, hands folded in their laps. They sat with the self-assured grace of women with purpose. No wonder they'd flustered that pitiful excuse for a judge. The prospect of being in jail with them for fourteen days excited Kate and, at the same time, scared her to death.

After a blessedly short trip, Kate stumbled down the steep stairs of the Black Maria and followed the women being led by two cops to the lower level of Union Station and into the only passenger car of an RF&P train. Lucy Burns gestured to Kate. She wants me to sit next to her, Kate thought, with a feeling of gratitude. Yet once the cop at either end of the car shoved the door shut and she was sitting on the ancient rattan seat in the dark, breathing in coal smoke, she had to fight against tears. A whistle sounded. The car jerked, began to move through a tunnel until it reached daylight again, chugging steadily across a bridge and the Potomac, past Alexandria, and into the Virginia countryside.

The day was fading into evening, and Kate relaxed a little at the sight of the trees, the flowering shrubs. She'd graduated from Bryn Mawr, outside Philadelphia, and had spent Thanksgivings with friends in Virginia. Yet the jungle of red maples, crabapples, pink blossomed flowering chestnuts, beech, black walnuts—the wild azaleas in pinks and virginal white—so different from home, still amazed her. In Colorado, with its dry air and treeless expanses, the azaleas would have to be nursed like babies in a hot house, and even then most wouldn't survive.

She dug in her purse for the slender box of Lord Salisbury Turkish cigarettes she'd taken to smoking, opened it, and held it out to Lucy, who shook her head and eyed the cop guarding the door.

"Thanks, but if the gentleman at the door sees you have cigarettes, he'll take them away."

Kate nodded, closed her purse, shifted her attention to the other picketers sitting in front and behind her. Olivia and Lydie were talking in low tones, but the others were gazing out the window, seemingly lost in their own thoughts. The nine Negro women— two looked like children—who had been brought to the station in another paddy wagon now sat behind the picketers, separated by several rows.

Bathed in the soft light of early evening, the passing farms and pristine houses in the midst of the lush landscape held a benign look. Kate found it unimaginable that a prison was only a few miles to the south. But looks could be deceiving. Back in her college days, some of the nastiest people she had known managed to convince the world that they were just this side of sainthood. For one, the captain of the lacrosse team and darling of the Bryn Mawr faculty. Her last name, ironically, was Sweet. Lisbeth Sweet. Blond curls like a halo. With a smile that melted hearts, the one who'd ratted on Kate about smoking and then professed innocence when Kate had confronted her.

Wiping cinders from her cheeks, she began to chew on the inside of her mouth, a habit she had licked years ago. She tried to make sense of the situation. She had been on the way to Union Station to catch the train home. Instead she was in a railcar rolling toward a prison notorious enough to have made the headlines and frighten the unflappable Lucy Burns. If she'd told the cabbie to go on, she'd be about to make her way from the Pullman to the dining car, where a white-coated Negro would usher her to a table covered with white linen and take her order for Maryland cracked crab. And as she ate, she'd gaze out at the western Pennsylvania countryside, wondering what she might do between trains in Chicago tomorrow afternoon.

"So why did you do it, Kate?" Lucy asked.

Kate started, looked at her. "I guess because I was mad."

To Kate's chagrin, Lucy's eyes sparked with amusement.

Wanting to redeem herself and because it seemed a logical way to work into an explanation, Kate said, "You see, a few years ago my mother was active in the suffrage movement at home and I—"

"And home is where?"

"Colorado."

Lucy regarded Kate, the hint of amusement still in her eyes. "So you're going to jail because of your mother."

Kate bridled, blushed. "No, it was how the judge never listened to a word any of us said."

"Oh, he listened all right. That was part of the problem."

Kate looked carefully at Lucy, uncertain of her meaning. So she shifted the subject to the Occoquan Workhouse.

"Where to begin?" The amusement in her eyes gone, Lucy considered Kate and arched an eyebrow. "First, you should know that where we have been sentenced, without benefit of a trial by jury or representation by an attorney is not a jail like the one you saw at the police station. It is a prison. There are those who say Occoquan Workhouse is a model, the last word in prisons, as prisons go. But it is a prison, nonetheless—and no model of any kind, much less of kindness, believe me." She wiped the perspiration beaded along her hairline with an index finger. "Actually, the judge choosing

Occoquan is the result of orders from the White House, which, as you can imagine, will make our attorney's job of securing our release all the more difficult."

"But how—? Why?"

Lucy gave a faint snort. "It's about politics, neither plain nor simple. That's why we're here. Oh, there may come a day when you'll look back and count the next two weeks as one of life's more interesting experiences. But now, you have every right to be frightened. Just know that you're going in there with good company. Olivia, the others—Jean Bowles and Paula Jakobi in front of us there. Lydie Street, the girl with the blond hair and extraordinary dark eyebrows, across the aisle. Katharine Hepburn—the tall one with all the hair who looks like a duchess—comes from an old Philadelphia family. Her husband's a pediatrician with a budding practice in Connecticut. Every one of us has been through this before, so take our lead."

Kate nodded, twisting the middle button of her cotton suit jacket around and around. Whatever bravado she had felt as she sprang from the cab was long gone. "I will. Thanks."

The train rolled on, and Kate concentrated on the purple streak that cut across the nearby crimson field to the sun glaring on the horizon. Lucy Burns had given her no particulars about what lay ahead, but her tone had implied dungeons straight out of the Middle Ages, a place where prisoners rotted away their lives. Even if it were true, their sentence—and Kate's, too—was only fourteen days. And, as Lucy had said, the other women had been sent there before and had come out, apparently none the worse for the experience.

The train slowed. Ahead was a small white clapboard depot. Two trucks were parked next to the side door that said "Freight." Four men wearing brown uniforms with holstered pistols hanging from their belts leaned against the trucks, smoking, watching the train.

Behind her, Kate was aware of a stirring in the car. She looked around at Lucy and the others for clues. But they seemed to have drawn inside themselves and didn't respond to her questioning glance. The train stopped with a jerk. Steam shushed out between the wheels, billowing past the half-open windows. The cop at either end opened the door, motioned the women to get out.

The Negro women were loaded in one truck, Kate and Lucy Burns and everyone else in the other. The sun was low, but the air still hot. They sat on boards laid across the truck bed. A guard, a rifle in one hand, climbed in. The women moved away from him, keeping their eyes on the floor. A shiver of apprehension ran down Kate's spine.

They drove along a dirt road beyond the outskirts of the little town into farm land, past orderly rows of corn and cabbages, blue and low to the ground. The truck with the Negro women was ahead of theirs, and its dust blew into their eyes and noses, made them cough.

The truck slowed. Paula and Katharine and Jean held hands, but for only a moment. The truck stopped. Lucy Burns, sitting across from Kate, winked at her. Kate tried for a smile. The back of the truck was lowered, the guard jumped down. One by one, the women scrunched down on the truck floor, then jumped down, awkward in their skirts.

Finally, it was Kate's turn. She hit the ground hard, nearly fell. Straightening, she stared at a three-story, red stone, fortress-like building. She caught in her breath. Fear squeezed her tight like a vise. Out of the corner of her eye, she could see rows of neat white clapboard buildings that might have been housing at a summer camp, except there were bars on the windows. Just behind them were brilliant green fields and grazing cows, hills in the distance, too perfect to be real, like a stage backdrop.

Four hard-eyed women in dark gray uniforms—presumably guards—billy clubs stuck through the belts around their waists, approached. Every instinct told Kate to turn and run. Instead, she followed Lucy and the others toward an open door.

Chapter 2 ꧁

Her head high, Lucy Burns swallowed all feeling and stepped inside the large room, the receiving room as it was called, and wiped the sweat from the back of her neck. She could handle fourteen days. And, if she went at it in the right way, she might convince the superintendent it would be in his political self-interest to treat them as political prisoners, which would make their stay somewhat more bearable. She glanced at Kate, her eyes wide with a look of terror and confusion. Lucy understood. Given a mirror, she'd have seen her own face the first time she was led in chains into London's Old Bailey. Kate's age or a little older, four years out of college, and a graduate student at Oxford, she had been lured to the call for women's rights by the fiery words of Emmeline Pankhurst in a drafty Manchester hall.

Lucy glanced around the room. It had been painted a bilious, pale green since last fall. Given the filing cabinet, the desk, and wooden chair, it could well be a company office. But, beyond public view, through the door at the far end was something else. There, generations of cockroaches had come and gone since Lucy's first visit. Another generation was waiting. And rats. The cots and cells would be filthy; the guards tough.

The risk of being thrown back in Occoquan had always been there, she knew. But she had hoped it wouldn't happen. The other women lined up, waiting for her to make the first move. They had taken the risk willingly. Veterans, they knew what lay ahead, knew the ropes, what to do. Except Kate. A girl who just happened by the wrong place at the wrong time, who had no idea what she'd gotten herself into. She should have paid the fine. Lucy felt no responsibility for her.

The Negro women, heads hung low, were being led out by two guards when the round-faced matron seated at the desk motioned to her. Pop-eyes with a hard mouth. Lucy knew her as Mrs. Herondon. "Well now. We meet again."

"So we do." Of all her jailers, Lucy feared her the most.

"Okay. You know how it works. Name and personal effects."

"I don't think so," Lucy said, planting her feet on the gray-tiled floor. "We are political prisoners and demand to be treated as such. We want to see the superintendent."

The matron fixed her with a cold stare. "You know better than that. The super ain't none of your business."

"On the contrary," Lucy said. "We intend to wait until he shows up." She turned toward the women behind her. "It seems Mr. Whitaker may be delayed."

They nodded, calmly as if they were in a railroad station waiting room, except there were no benches or chairs, and the women sank to the floor, cross-legged, arranging their skirts about their legs.

The matron's face flushed beet red, and she pushed to her feet. "Hold on just a minute. There's rules here."

"Don't I know," Lucy said, because she did. The inflexibility of those rules was exactly what would give her time to take a stand. "Nevertheless, we are waiting for Mr. Whitaker." Lucy sat with her back straight, hands on her knees. It was almost worth spending the next days in solitary just to annoy Herondon, who had once beat her black and blue.

"You'll sit here all night without no food."

"If that's what it takes, that's what we'll do."

An hour went by. Another matron—skinny as a pole—appeared; and her eyes widened when she saw the women still in the room. Frowning, she scurried over to Mrs. Herondon, who stood. The two women put their heads together, whispered for a few minutes, occasionally glancing toward Lucy, before they finally nodded as if they'd agreed on a plan. Lucy dared to hope it entailed contacting the superintendent and urging him to show up.

After the skinny matron left, Mrs. Herondon leaned back in her chair, folded her arms again, apparently prepared to settle in. Paula Jacobi started to get to her feet, and the matron instantly ordered her to sit.

"I wish to use the bathroom," Paula said, quietly.

"Register then." The matron settled back in her chair. Paula slowly sat down.

A clock on the wall over Mrs. Herondon's desk said twenty minutes after eight. Beyond the windows on either side of the entrance, the soft evening light slipped into full darkness. Lucy changed her position, rubbed her lower back. Creeping up on forty as she was, sitting on a hard floor had its limits. After awhile, the pop-eyed matron pushed herself to her feet and turned on the overhead lights. In another part of the building, in what was called the dormitory, the prisoners would be settling down for the night.

Lucy smelled the unmistakable odor of urine and knew Paula had wet herself. Lucy scanned her little group: most hunched forward, resting their heads in their hands, the picture of perseverance, no less than she expected. Only Kate sat by herself, still looking dazed. Lucy couldn't remember ever being that young, that innocent.

She rolled her head to loosen her neck muscles and wondered how long it would take the superintendent to make his entrance. He could have been here in a matter of minutes after the word got to him that the picketers had arrived. But he had to show them he came at no one's beck and call, least of all picketers. Since he was in charge, he could afford to play the cat-and-mouse game as long as he chose.

From the very first, even as she'd sat in the paddy wagon, she'd been sure Alice Paul—her cohort in crime, so to speak—or someone else at headquarters with its good view of the White House, would have seen and heard the ruckus, would have immediately called their attorney, Doug O'Brien, to alert him he was needed at the police court. When he hadn't come, she'd reasoned he might have assumed this Sunday's picketing would be no different from the last four or five demonstrations that had gone without a hitch and he'd taken his family on a Sunday drive. Yet, surely, by now, he would have been contacted. Which meant that, at best, it would be tomorrow before he'd be able to get in touch with a federal judge, apply for a writ of habeas corpus, which she knew all too well would take days. Intimidating the Superintendent was her only alternative.

Out of half-opened eyes, Lucy noticed a guard slip in from the hallway. Behind him came another man, then another, until there were six. She drew in a steadying breath, remembering a French horror story she'd read of the reverse: men assembled in a large room who disappeared one at a time. One instant a man talking, the next gone; the space where he'd stood empty. She had the uneasy feeling an order from on high had been given and something was about to happen. Maybe she'd misjudged the situation.

It was time to move. She swallowed hard, got to her feet stiffly, smoothed her skirt. *Audaces fortuna iuvat*—never venture, never win—in the words of Miss Ehlers, her dear old Latin teacher. She caught Marie deLuca's eye, gave her an imperceptible nod. Every picketer rose.

"All of you sit," commanded the matron.

No one moved. Lucy began the litany again. "We demand to see Mr. Whitaker. We have a right to consult our attorney. We are political prisoners, not criminals."

A guard with a black stubble of a beard spat, barely missing the toes of her shoes. "In here, you ain't got no rights."

Then from another room came the sound of a door opening, and a tall, gaunt man nearly bald, rushed in. "Here now. What's going on?"

The matron shot to her feet, relief written across her ruddy face. "They been causin' a fuss and won't register, Mr. Whitaker."

Lucy stepped clear of the other women. "We demand—"

"You demand nothing in here," the superintendent said.

From the corner of her eye, Lucy saw two broad-shouldered guards step forward. She shifted to another tack. "We have a right to—"

Mr. Whitaker gave a nod, and the men seized her. Lucy struggled to break free of their hold, but they twisted her arms cruelly behind her back, held her firm. Half-dragging, half-carrying her, they shoved her down the hallway, out a door and across a courtyard toward a smaller building she knew housed the detention cells. A yellow halo of gnats swarmed around the light that hung over the door held open by another cop as she was hauled inside and thrown in a cell with such force her head struck the iron bedstead. The last thing she remembered was falling to the floor.

Chapter 3

The Colorado sky was pure blue as Mary Daly poked her head out the window, gazed past the string of faded blue work shirts and overalls pinned along the wire clothesline. Not a cloud to be seen, but by afternoon the winds could shift and there'd be a downpour. June was like that. From behind her came the sound of Gino's snores, rough and irregular from the booze.

She turned, sighed as she surveyed the mess of clothes strewn on chairs, the shoe beneath what served as a kitchen table. The good Lord knew she had enough picking up for a lifetime with the likes of Gino Franchetti. But she couldn't help herself. Arms akimbo, she gazed at him, on his back, spread-eagled across their bed, naked as the day he was born, his member lying limp, his mouth open, a dark shadow of beard that nearly hid the scar which ran along one cheek. Nothing faintly resembling what the world would see in a few hours, once he'd slept off the booze and waltzed out of here, washed and shaved in a starched white shirt she'd ironed, like some magnificent Italian god.

A door slammed. The shrill voice of the widow who lived

downstairs ordered her daughter, Rosa, to come back inside. Mary heard Gino stir. She glanced at the watch she'd bought herself as a birthday present last month when she'd turned thirty. Seven ten. Not enough time to get a pot of coffee going and still catch her streetcar. She took her black straw hat from its hook on the back of the door, went over to the mirror by the sink.

"Where d'ya think you're goin'?"

"To work. Not that you'd know about such," she said, securing her hatpin. She glanced over her shoulder, saw Gino slowly sit up, hold his head in his hands. "You'll have to get your own coffee."

He glanced up at her, one eye closed. "Oh, now, Mary, darlin'."

"Don't give me that phony blarney."

"I need twenty bucks."

"Not on your life." And before he could make a move toward it, she snatched her purse from the table, opened the door, and left. Was it in the blood of Irish women that they put up with lice like Gino? Her Da had always said she had lousy taste in men. But then look what her Mom had put up with.

Outside, dew glittering like crystal beads still clung to the strip of grass that ran along the lilac hedge, planted years before the house had been broken up into apartments. Mary tucked her white blouse into her shin-length, dark blue skirt as she strode along the uneven sidewalk, waved at the kid who lived across the street, probably on his way to Wyzowotsky's grocery on the corner for his mother's daily order of ice.

No fancy refrigerators in this part of town, that was for sure. Once, she'd thought the smoke from the trains over on the north side where she'd grown up was bad, but around here the stink from the smelter could rot a person's lungs. If this weren't Gino's stomping grounds, she wouldn't go near the place. May Father John forgive her, but God and the bankers along Seventeenth Street didn't give a damn about the people who lived here as long as they showed up for work.

The number forty streetcar was nearly full, mostly with women she recognized, in their sixties, on the way to clean downtown hotel rooms or houses on Capitol Hill. She'd done the same until the war began. But now women had higher-paying jobs in munitions plants. Some drove streetcars. A good hired girl was scarce as an honest butcher. A year ago Mary sized up the situation and made a deal with Mrs. Griffin, who headed up Mile High Employment, the best agency in town. In exchange for the fee paid Mrs. Griffin by prospective employers, Mary would inspect the fine ladies in their big houses who wanted good help. A few tried to bribe her by passing her as much as a fiver, but Mary had her standards. No exceptions. Only if Mary had given her okay would Mrs. Griffin send a girl out to be placed. If not, they were out of luck. The system worked so well, Mrs. Griffin didn't dare object to being hooked up with the union Mary had started. The Domestic Workers of America, she called it. Added up, she made more money by twice than what she ever made before.

At Broadway and Tenth streets, she rang the streetcar bell, got off, headed up the hill, turned left on Pennsylvania. A quiet neighborhood. Founders' Row, some called it. Old money and the power that went with it. The kind you couldn't buy your way into, not even with political favors. The Brennans in the big red sandstone. Next door, the Dennis place. Across the street, Senator Shafroth's tan brick, then the Millers. And on the corner the Kramers in their gray stone monstrosity complete with turrets, where Mary had worked as the upstairs maid and had to put up with the judge's groping hands for four miserable years.

Climbing the stone steps to the porch, Mary straightened her shoulders, took a peek at herself in one of the long living room windows, tucked a strand of her dark hair back in place. Satisfied, she walked over to the heavy carved door. But before she could put a finger to the bell, it opened and there was old lady Kramer herself, all smiles, asking her in as if she were company.

"Mary Daly, why I hardly recognize you. Look how tall you are. And you've let your hair grow. How old were you when you worked

for us? Sixteen, seventeen?" the bony woman gushed as she surveyed Mary top to toe. "Come in, won't you?" She stood aside and
Mary walked in, looked around. The same gilt-framed portraits
of ancestors with big noses hung on the wall, the same little table
where the downstairs maid put the day's mail was at the foot of the
stairs. She glanced in the dining room, noticed that the silver tea set
needed polishing.

"Well, now, Mary. Please come in and sit down. Goodness knows,
I don't have to show you around the house. There isn't an inch of
it you don't know." Mrs. Kramer's face spread into an eager smile,
revealing her yellow teeth.

Mary settled in the French chair with the blue satin upholstery
that she knew Mrs. Kramer was partial to, smoothed her skirt. "You
said you're after a cook?"

Mrs. Kramer perched on the edge of the couch, nodded. "But a
cook who wouldn't mind doing a little housework, too." She glanced
vaguely around. "The house is a lot bigger than I'd realized."

Mary hid a smile, got her pencil and the small black-leather covered notebook where she kept her records out of her purse. "There's
a lady registered with us last week who might be interested. Ida
Kuhlman. Mrs. Kuhlman. Her husband passed last year."

"Kuhlman. Isn't that German?"

Mary gave Mrs. Kramer a level look. "You don't like Germans?"

"I'm sure she's a lovely woman."

Mary arched an eyebrow. "Still, it all depends."

"Depends on what?" Mrs. Kramer clutched her hands tight
and looked so anxious, Mary almost—but not quite—felt sorry
for her.

"One word from Mrs. Kuhlman that the Judge has been up to his
old tricks and we report him to the police."

"I don't know what you mean!" said Mrs. Kramer indignantly.

"Sure you do. That's why I started the union. You need my members, they need you. Only now we negotiate the terms." Mary
returned her pencil and notebook to her purse.

"What do you mean, a union? Mile High never said a word about a union."

Mary shrugged, gave her a tight smile. "Times are changin', Mrs. Kramer."

❦

Late that afternoon, one eye on the darkening sky, Mary hurried back to the dilapidated three-story house, her head down against the wind, doing a bit of a jig now and again as she dodged the bits of trash that skittered along the sidewalk. Just as she pulled open the front door, a clap of thunder echoed through the thick air, and she breathed a sigh of relief that she'd made it inside before the rain hit.

Standing at the top of the stairs in front of the door to her room, she fished in her purse for her key. Any hairpin could open the lock. But a key gave the place a certain respectability, as if it were more than another way station in her life that had been full of them.

She opened the door, unpinned her hat, placed it on its hook, and looked around the room. Gino was gone, probably on the prowl, playing the part of the big union tough, hitting pals up for drinks as though he were doing them a favor to let them pick up the tab. As was his habit, Gino probably wouldn't show up until the wee hours.

She closed the window against the spattering of rain. The day had gone okay. No, better than okay. She'd passed on the remark about Germans to Mrs. Griffin, and saved Ida Kuhlman from old man Kramer, the letch. As it turned out, Mary had lined Ida up with a doctor's family who lived in one of the newer places out on East Seventh. Nice wife, three kids who shook Mary's hand when they'd been introduced. Ida would have a big room and a bath all to herself, with both Thursdays and Sundays off.

Against all her good intentions, Mary picked up the shoe still under the table, found its mate beneath a pile of Gino's clothes. If she added what was there to the things in the pillow case she used as a laundry bag, she might just go down to the cellar and do some wash as soon as the storm blew over. By then the clotheslines would be free, and there'd be all night for the clothes to dry. In the meantime, she'd fix herself a bit of supper from whatever Gino had left in the cooler, probably a bit of sausage.

The light was fading by the time she washed up her dish and glass, picked up the pillowcase full of Gino's dirty clothes, and headed to the cellar. There never was a time when she came down here that the cool air, the damp smell of the dirt floor and stone walls didn't make her imagine she was stepping into a cave. In the dim light from the hall at the top of the stairs, she could see well enough to find the chain dangling over the two zinc tubs with the ringer attached. To be on the safe side, she glanced around toward the coal shoot and the furnace for whatever might be lurking in the shadows. But all she saw was the assortment of boxes covered with dust and a kitchen chair with a leg missing stacked beneath the stairs.

She gave the hot water spigot a twist, let the water fill one of the tubs. Adding a handful of the soap powder she'd brought with her, she dropped in Gino's shirts and underwear and socks. Soon, her back bent over the soapy water up to her elbows, she became lost in the motion, up and down, her hands moving across the ridges of the washboard, scrubbing at her worries.

Worries about Gino and why she couldn't seem to free herself of her addiction for him. She was no better than a hophead. What she felt for him had nothing to do with love and all to do with the ache in her groin each time he beckoned to her, the electricity that ran up the insides of her thighs when he touched her, when he slid inside her.

Worries about the union and what would happen to it once the war was over. Hundreds of women would be thrown out of work when the boys returned, looking for work, maybe willing to take anything again. The only hope was putting teeth in the labor laws and passing the woman's right to vote amendment. She'd joined the NWP a couple of years ago because she'd thought that if any bunch had a chance to push the old boys into doing what was right and paying women decent wages, they could. But now she was having her doubts.

With a sigh, she pulled the plug, let the soapy water drain, then refilled the tubs with rinse water. She'd done the work so many years it came as second nature: putting her back behind the handle of the ringer, all the while an eye out for a shirt that might get caught up wrong, toss the clothes into the basket, finally to lug the wet mess up the steep stairs to the clothesline.

Once back up in the room, she glanced out the window, admiring her handiwork—Gino's shirts white as snow, socks lined up like so many soldiers, underclothes hung just so. Wash on the line always gave her a satisfied, housewifely feeling. With a little breeze, it would be dry in an hour. Maybe she should have done up some of her own. She went to the chiffonier, pulled open the top drawer that was hers, relieved to see two pair of underdrawers and a shift. She took them out to refold them and her hands grazed the slender black box tied with a faded purple satin ribbon.

Aside from the gold cross she wore around her neck, what lay inside the box were her only other memories of her mother. With care and reverence she removed the box, untied the ribbon, lifted the lid. On top was the holy card with the picture of St. Catharine on one side. She picked it up, about to turn it over and reread the familiar words in memory of her mother when she realized nothing else was in the box. Her mother's tiny gold earrings were gone.

Mary controlled her breath, which was starting to come in shallow gasps. She took everything from the drawer, shook each piece out. Nothing. She searched the drawer beneath it. No luck. Sliding the drawers closed, she tried to imagine what could have happened. And she thought of Gino.

He'd pawned everything she'd owned at one time or another, but this was an all-time low. The sorry, pitiful, son-of-a-bitch. Stealing a dead woman's gold earrings that wouldn't bring five bucks.

She'd been on the move since she was twelve, when her Da had palmed her off as older on account of her height, at first to wash dishes in the back of a saloon, then as a hired girl, only coming home on her days off to hand over her wages. She learned to take care of herself. And she traveled light, leaving nothing behind she cared about, people or things. She squared her shoulders. Then she retied the ribbon around the slender box and slipped it into her purse. It only took a few minutes to pack her few belongings in her battered valise. She was about ready to go, where, she didn't know, but what did it matter?

Finally, she pinned on her hat, left the key on the table. The rent was due on Monday. But that was Gino's problem.

Chapter 4

Transfixed with fear, Kate watched the remaining guards line up behind the superintendent.

"There now," he said, fixing the women with a steady glare. "Let that be a lesson to you." He glanced toward the heavyset woman at the desk. "Matron, are you ready to register these prisoners?"

"Yes, sir."

The superintendent gave an impatient wave of his hand "All right. Step forward."

The tiny Olivia took over. "We repeat our demand, sir, that we be treated as political prisoners and be represented by an attorney." There was no mistaking the steely resolve beneath her southern accent.

The superintendent's face colored a bright red. "Shut your mouth," he snapped.

Olivia ignored him and began to repeat herself even as the superintendent gestured to the guards and shouted, "Lock them up, and be quick about it!"

As the nine brawny men moved in, Kate instinctively moved toward Paula, desperate to avoid them, only to be seized and shoved backwards. Somehow one of her arms caught in the handle of Paula's purse, and as Kate struggled to pull free, the handle broke loose, throwing both women off balance. Guards grabbed them before they hit the floor, and herded them along with the other picketers toward the hallway and down steps. The heel of Kate's left shoe became jammed in a crack, broke off. Hobbling, she followed Paula in a daze out a door, across a yard, through another open door, down a short flight of steps to a bank of cells, their barred doors yawning wide, waiting for them.

Separating the women into groups of two or three, the guard shoved them into cells no more than eight feet square. Kate fought for breath, shaking until she realized she was with Olivia and a woman with wheat-colored hair whose name escaped her, as she tried to get her bearings. The only light came from a row of bare bulbs protected by wire grating fixed into the ceiling along the corridor outside the cells; the only beds were two narrow, stained mattresses—one on a metal frame, the other on the concrete floor. An open toilet was fixed against the far wall. Next to it was a wooden water bucket. No chair. No sink. The window was little bigger than a slit covered by a metal shutter, too high to reach even if she stood on the bed on tiptoes.

Kate shivered as the cell doors clanged shut, keys turned. Silence. Waiting for what, she wasn't sure, she glanced at Olivia and the other woman, watched them as they tucked in their blouses, smoothed their hair, surveyed the surroundings. Their foreheads knit with scowls of distaste, they reminded Kate of seasoned travelers who found themselves in an unacceptable room of a rundown hotel. She moved toward the wall, out of the way, trying to blot out the toilet's stink. Something black scurried across the mattress on the floor. She narrowed her eyes, looked more carefully. A cockroach. A shudder ran through her. Where there was one, there were bound to be others.

Olivia turned toward the cell door. Grasping the bars, she looked to the right and left. "Lucy, dear, are you there?"

A stubby guard with the pasty, smashed-in face of a prizefighter appeared, frowned at her in a threatening way, and Olivia stepped out of reach.

"Right here," came Lucy's familiar voice. "Who've you got in there with you?"

"Lydie. And Kate Brennan."

Kate sensed the roll-call was the next part of the routine Lucy had led the women through in the reception area.

"Paula?" Lucy's voice again.

"Here, Lucy." This time the voice came from the left. "Katharine's with me."

The guard strode in that direction. "I said to shut up!"

But more names were called until, suddenly, there was a stifled cry, followed by an abrupt silence. Kate flinched, caught the worry on Olivia and Lydie's faces.

"I warned you people." The guard strode along the line of cells. "Any more of this and you'll get the same as your friend."

Olivia and the girl named Lydie turned from the cell door, their eyes red-rimmed, and looked at Kate, as if seeing her for the first time.

"Are you all right?" Olivia asked.

Kate nodded, offered a weak smile. She couldn't let them see how close she was to hysterics. "Fine," she said. "But what about Lucy?"

"We'll hope okay." Olivia's tone was dry, matter-of-fact. "Don't worry." She touched Kate's shoulder as if to reassure her and glanced about the cell. "Not exactly the Ritz, but it will have to do. Two mattresses and three people. I guess we better flip for who gets the floor tonight." She glanced at Lydie who fished a change purse out of one of her skirt pockets. Coin in hand, Olivia looked at Kate. "Your call."

"Heads," she said as the half dollar rose and fell onto the stained mattress on the floor.

Olivia looked down, squinted. "Heads it is."

Kate hesitated for an instant, remembering the cockroach, but then straightened her shoulders. "I'll take the floor."

Lydie said she was a good sport, and Kate smiled. Maybe she was. Her mother used to tell her friends she was, but that was after Lizzie was born. Before that she'd been Tom's cute, spoiled, six-year-old sister, the apple of her father's eye. Then, just like that, she disappeared into the middle to become the steady one, the kid who didn't sulk or have tantrums, the good sport. Kate pulled in a deep breath, put her hands on her hips. "I figure someone has to keep an eye on the wildlife."

Lydie giggled. Olivia grinned. Kate grinned back. That tiny bit of bravado had been dues enough.

"Whoever wants to use the toilet, I'll stand guard first," Lydie said. "Our friend out there has the only handle to flush it, and my guess is he'll only do it once, if at all."

So Kate took her turn on the toilet, pretending Lydie's back was a stall door, and she drank some rust-flavored water from the communal ladle. That done, Olivia and Lydie lay down on the mattresses, Kate on the bare floor—all of them fully dressed. Someone with a New York accent beseeched the guard to flush the toilet. After the gush of water subsided, the low voices from the cells gradually faded into silence. The dim light from mesh-covered bulbs in the corridor cast eerie shadows along the wall as Kate settled on her side, resting her head on her arm so that she could keep an eye out for cockroaches.

She adjusted her position, vainly hoping the concrete would magically soften. The stays of her girdle dug into her ribs and she pushed her fingers between the waistband of her skirt and the girdle, but it didn't help. She curled into a fetal position, resigned to a miserable night, when she heard what sounded like tiny legs skittering along the concrete. She tensed, raised her head. Staring back at her was a rat, big as a small cat, poised by the water bucket. And Kate gasped.

"Throw a shoe at him," Lydie whispered.

Kate fumbled for her blue and white pump with the broken heel, took aim, and almost hit him.

The legs of a chair scraped the concrete. The pasty-faced guard glowered through the bars. "Keep it down," he ordered, and she gave him an innocent look.

His back turned, Kate looked back at the rat, his long, hairless tail trailing behind him, his little eyes like glittering chips of coal. He hadn't moved. She'd heard their little teeth were sharp enough to chew off fingers and toes. She got to her feet, kicked at it. The rat retreated into the shadows. And she retrieved her shoe, put it on. With no hope of sleep, she sat down, leaned against the wall, and drew her legs up beneath her skirt. Wrapping her arms around them, she closed her eyes.

Once Kate had been a believer: from Santa Claus to fairies who slipped nickels under her pillow after she'd lost a tooth to those who left a new party dress on her bed when last year's still fit. Eventually, she grew out of good fairies and took to crossing her fingers for luck. So that's what she did. And she let her mind wander to more pleasant times, imagining her mahogany sleigh bed, its mattress covered by crisp sheets, not too soft but enough to sink down into. She wore a summer cotton nightgown, light as a butterfly against her skin, still holding the faint scent of lavender from the sachets Christine made and placed in drawers and closets during spring housecleaning. On a night like this at home she would need only a sheet over her. Then later she'd draw it up over her shoulders against the cooling breeze that puffed the glass curtains out like a ship's sails. And as she settled her pillows, anticipating tomorrow's tennis game, she would hear the gentle coo, like a lullaby, of the dove perched in its favorite spot on the roof of the garage.

Kate drew in a long, shaky breath. She guessed it must be close to midnight, already another lifetime since she'd sat next to Lucy Burns on the train and raged about the smug magistrate. Kate had made her choice all by herself. Now she had another choice. She could go to pieces. Or, being a Brennan, she could keep a stiff upper lip, which had the dubious advantage of leaving the lower lip handy to bite.

A hand touched her shoulder lightly, and a soft, southern voice said, "Reciting the Psalms sometimes helps."

"Thanks," Kate whispered, though the only Psalm she could remember was the Twenty-third that she'd heard at funerals. Not what she needed. She pulled her skirt down around her ankles to guard against the cockroaches. Thirteen more nights to go.

⁂

Kate roused at the sound of heavy footsteps and glanced up at the slit that served as a window, saw the morning light. Beyond the cell door, two guards had joined the man she remembered from last night. One of them strode down the line of cells, unlocking the cells' doors, ordering the women to move out. Kate shot a glance at Lydie and Olivia, and when she saw them get to their feet, followed their lead. One by one, every cell door opened, all except Lucy's. No one spoke. The guards ordered them to line up. And Lucy gave each of them a smart salute as they passed by her cell in single file.

Once outside, blinking in the bright light, Kate followed Olivia as they crossed the courtyard toward another building and asked in a whisper why Lucy had been left behind. "They think she's a trouble-maker and they're right," was the answer.

Remembering the accounts she'd read of suffragists fasting in protest, Kate was about to ask if that's what Lucy would do next when the guard suddenly shouted an order to halt, and two matrons appeared.

Kate leaned closed to Olivia. "What now?"

"I'd guess we're about to shuck our clothes and don prison garb."

"Then we'll go back to our cells?"

"Don't think so. If it's like last time, Lucy will be the only one with private quarters, if you can call it that. We're just the hoi polloi, so we get put in with the other prisoners like one big, happy family. You'll be given a job, maybe in the laundry or the kitchen." She glanced over her shoulder at Kate, gave her a wry little smile. "'Busy hands make model prisoners' is the motto around here. You'll see what I mean soon enough."

"No talking," the taller of the two matrons barked as they entered the fortress-like building Kate remembered from last night, walked down a long corridor, and into a large, dimly lit room. The smell was dank, sour-smelling. Showers, minus curtains, lined one side. The only windows were near the ceiling, their small panes opaque with grime. Four large piles of clothing were arranged on a long, wooden table.

One of the matrons—beaky and hollow-boned like a great wading creature—motioned with her billy club toward the table. "Awright. Listen up. Take one of everythin' here, includin' a towel, strip down and shower. Then get dressed. And be quick about it."

Olivia stepped out from the line. "We are political prisoners, not criminals. We refuse to wear prison uniforms."

With a quickness Kate wouldn't have expected from a woman of her size, the matron drew back her thick arm and slapped Olivia across the face with such force she staggered backward and fell. Lydie broke ranks and ran over to her. As she stooped to help Olivia up, the matron struck Lydie in the back with her billy club, sending her sprawling.

Kate sucked in a quick breath, watched as Lydie and Olivia slowly struggled to their feet.

"Anybody else?" The matron surveyed the silent group. "Didn't think so," she said, with a tight-lipped smile, and she went over to the showers and turned them on, the streams of water more like dribbles. "Now get started."

Kate hung back as the picketers matter-of-factly removed their dresses and underthings. She didn't think herself a prude, but she'd grown up in a household that believed nakedness was reserved exclusively for newborns. Aside from her younger sister, she'd never seen anyone in her family without their clothes. All through college, she'd managed to undress and dress in the closet. So she waited until the last stocking was on the bench before she turned her back, and, pretending the other women weren't around, took off her clothes. In the shower, she hunched her shoulders so as to partly hide her breasts, and passed on the sliver of soap. The threadbare towel was nearly useless. Still damp, she eyed the clothes she was to put on— bloomers, a shift, a gray-and-white striped dress, and a dark blue apron—all of heavy muslin. No shoes. She would have to wear her own broken pair.

Paula Jakobi leaned toward her, said in a low voice, "Just the thing for hot summer days, wouldn't you say?"

Kate glanced at her, perplexed, and then saw the hint of a smile on Paula's mouth.

"If you're worried about your things, they tell us we'll get them back," Lydie said. "Don't make a show of it, but try to keep whatever you have in your pockets."

Kate remembered a handkerchief as she saw others tuck coins, stubs of pencils and bits of paper behind the waistbands of their aprons. One girl—Sylvia, Kate thought her name was—had a comb, and it was passed around, then hidden.

The brown-haired matron ordered them to line up. Stripped of their identity, they listened as the other matron read their names and what their duties were to be. Dazed and confused, Kate caught her name among those who were to scrub floors. The last to leave the shower room, hobbling because of her missing heel, she was tempted to grab hold of Lydie who was in front of her so she wouldn't be left behind.

❧

As it turned out, Kate was thrown to the wolves—that's how she thought of it. Alone, no Lucy or Olivia or Lydie or Paula, not a one of the picketers to show her the ropes, she was handed a heavy bucket of soapy water and a wood-backed scrub brush. Following a gaunt, grim-faced matron along a windowless corridor, Kate passed women on hands and knees, already scrubbing. Negro women in patched shifts, their dark skin pearly with sweat, worked off by themselves. The white women if they looked at her at all, stared at her with dead eyes. One with open sores on her thin arms sat back on her haunches and peered at Kate through an opening in her long, tangled black hair. Kate looked away, swallowed hard, kept going.

Up ahead, a white girl suddenly scrambled to her feet, toppling the bucket by her side, sending filthy water to spread across the concrete floor. No more than fourteen or fifteen years old, judging from her slight build and small breasts, she ran toward a nearby door, hurled herself against it until, miraculously, it opened and she ran outside.

The matron at the end of the hall shouted for guards and dogs. Without thinking about it, Kate went to the open door. Instead of the forbidding courtyard she expected was a large vegetable garden cut by a well-beaten path leading to a high fence topped with layers of barbed wire and fields beyond. There was no sign of the girl. Madness, this place which claimed to be a model—whatever had driven her to try to escape—must have been beyond bearing.

Unable to move away from the doorway, Kate knew, without turning, the women on their hands and knees were watching her, perhaps waiting to see if she would be the next to bolt, not knowing that she didn't have the nerve.

An order to get to work made her turn, pick up her bucket, and walk toward the stairs she was to scrub, the sound of distant barking ringing in her head.

The day wore on. Kate's knees, back, arms: everything ached. Her hands were raw from the harsh soap. She would have sold her soul for a bottle of Jergens hand lotion. If it weren't for the cockroaches and the guards, she'd lie down on the cool concrete floor and sleep forever.

There was no break for lunch. Afraid to ask for permission to use the bathroom, she was growing desperate when she overheard another woman ask to "go pee" and Kate got to her feet, and said she needed to go, too. But one at a time was the rule, and the matrons never took her eyes off them as each took her turn squatting over the bucket for urinating at the end of the hallway.

Time passed. She became obsessed to know the hour, and when she dared, she'd look down the hall to the nearest mesh-covered window, hoping to see a bit of sky, the sun. But all she ever saw was haze. The possibility that they might have to work until dark occurred to her. She bit her lip and leaned over her scrub brush again.

❀

So stiff she could hardly walk, Kate finally followed the other prisoners on the scrub detail into a mammoth, high-ceilinged room, reeking of cabbage and reverberating with the clatter of people eating. Looking for Olivia and Lydie, she surveyed the women sitting on benches on either side of long, wooden tables, all of them hunched over bowls and stuffing their mouths, and found Olivia and Lydie seated next to each other across the room. Just as she moved toward them, a matron pointed to the table closest to the door and told her to take her seat.

She held the skirt of her dress up enough so she could step over the bench and sat down. Directly in front of her on the table were a metal spoon, a tin plate, and a cup. The woman next to her handed her a bucket filled with what looked like a yellowish green soup. Kate gave the soup a closer look, sniffed, didn't like its rancid smell, and passed it on.

Her stomach was rumbling so loud she was certain it could be heard even above the clatter of spoons against bowls. She was about to ask for the bucket to be sent back her way when a prisoner plunked a platter of thick slabs of brown bread down on the table within easy reach. Kate glanced at it. The bread seemed to have raisins in it. And she took two pieces.

Her mouth watering at the thought of food, Kate was about to take a bite when she noticed something unusual about the raisins. She took a closer look, realized that she was staring at shriveled insects, tiny legs and all, and dropped the bread in the bowl before her. She glanced toward the bucket now at the other end of the table, on the verge of reconsidering the soup, when a whistle blew, and, without a word, the women around her pushed to their feet, climbed over the benches, formed a line, and she followed them into the corridor.

The room they entered was as large as the dining hall with the same high ceiling and long narrow, mesh-covered windows. But in place of tables were rows of cots, giving it the deceptive look of an immense dormitory. Except that instead of housemothers, there were matrons with billy clubs, and mattresses covered not with sparkling white linen but narrow lumps of stained ticking so filthy looking that Kate almost gagged. Desperate, she searched for a familiar face and saw Lydie and Olivia, standing by a row of empty cots near the windows.

To get to them Kate had to step over the legs and feet of prisoners, seated on their cots, talking in low voices, eyeing her with suspicion as she passed. As she came closer to the windows, she saw they were open at the bottom. She tried not to look out, but the temptation was too great, and she allowed herself a moment to gaze past the steel-mesh screen at a scene that might have been a painting—it was that far beyond the reality of where she stood—the fields, orderly as a checkerboard, the greens and yellows fading in the shadows, the dark woods beyond.

"Hey, there, girl!"

Kate started, blinked back unwanted tears, looked behind her.

"Stop your lollygaggin' and get yourself a cot."

Kate moved on toward Olivia who saw her, gave her a tired smile, and pointed to an empty cot nearby. Kate wanted to talk to her, to tell her about the day, but with the matron nearby, she didn't dare.

The light from the oversized bare bulbs affixed to the wall above the matrons' desks cast an eerie glow over the room as Kate stood by the cot Olivia had pointed out and watched as her two friends removed their aprons, and folded them into makeshift pillows. Next, they took off their dresses and spread them over the stained canvas. Then, dressed only in their bloomers and shifts, they lay down. And Kate did the same.

Kate shifted around on the thin mattress beneath her sweat-stained dress, trying to find a comfortable position and thought of the matter-of-fact way the picketers had gone about the business of settling down for the night. As if after their three stints here, the routine was second nature. Yet nothing about what Kate had seen today was something a person could get used to. Once they knew what it was like, how could they find the courage to risk returning?

Kate turned on her side, aware of the sound of heavy shoes on the floor nearby, and opened her eyes to see a matron, rhythmically smacking her nightstick against the palm of her other hand, moving down the next aisle, and she closed her eyes again, pretending sleep. Quiet gradually settled over the room until someone started to cough—a persistent, wracking cough that went on for minutes and quit apparently out of pure weakness and lack of breath, only to start again. A woman near her kept grinding her teeth. All the while, Kate lay tense and miserable, listening when what she yearned for was sleep.

Hours passed. Conscious of every new noise, Kate opened her eyes and finally saw the gray light of dawn beyond the mesh covering the windows. She supposed she'd slept, but it seemed as if she'd been awake all night. The room began to stir. Under the sharp eyes of matrons, prisoners sat up, shuffled toward the buckets reserved for urinating, returned to their cots. The matrons resumed their patrol. Kate sat up, glanced at the crushed black-and-white striped dress she'd used as a mattress cover, and wondered how she could bear wearing the thick, rough cotton through another sweltering day.

In the dining hall, she managed a place next to the windows, next to Olivia. Instead of the two eggs, a strip of crisp bacon, two slices of buttered white toast and strong coffee she'd eaten yesterday in Millie's kitchen, she saw a pail half-full of what looked like porridge and another platter of thick slices of brown bread.

Without a moment's hesitation, Olivia reached out, slid the pail closer and dumped a ladle full in her bowl. "Delicious looking, isn't it?" she whispered as she stirred the grayish mixture with her spoon. "Yet I fear not without its surprises." Grinning, she held up a spoonful for Kate to inspect. "You see it?"

Kate shook her head.

"Of course you do," Olivia said, poking a finger into the mess. "There it is: weevil number one. Note the milky color, the tiny, brown snout. Lovely little thing, isn't it? Meal weevils, they're called. Close cousins to the boll weevils that wiped out most of Daddy's cotton crop ten years ago." She dropped the viscous glob back in her bowl.

Sickened, Kate slid the pail toward the woman next to her. "How can you be so . . ."

"Cavalier?" Olivia shrugged. "Complaining to the chef certainly wouldn't help, now would it? So. . . ." She dipped her spoon in her porridge again. "Presto! Weevil number two." The count continued. Olivia was up to twelve when the platter of bread reached them.

Kate gazed at slices for a moment and contemplated the innocent-looking black specks. She had two alternatives to starvation: the bread or the porridge. Choosing the former, she put a piece on her plate, dug out the maggots, and ate what remained.

Kate had hoped to be with at least one of the picketers today, but when she watched them go one direction while she was handed a bucket and told to go another, she knew it was not to be. On her hands and knees, scrubbing the endless halls, she tried to empty her head of all thought. But another day of plunging her hands in harsh soap soon turned them into what looked like two pieces of raw meat. By the end of the day she couldn't bear to touch them, to dry them on her apron. Famished, she was willing to try the soup at supper, but how would she grasp the ladle? As she watched the bucket being passed along, she considered asking the woman next to her for help. The bucket came closer. Tonight, the liquid had a greenish cast with several cabbage leaves floating in its midst but no sign of meat. Kate had never liked cabbage much, but it would have to do. And she gingerly picked her bowl up between the palms of her raw hands and lowered it into the bucket until it filled. It wasn't until she was lifting it to her mouth, soup dripping from the bowl onto the wooden table, that she noticed the other women's stares, and she merely grinned at them between gulps.

⁂

Two days passed, then another. Kate no longer had trouble sleeping. Except for meals and just before lights out, she rarely saw Olivia or Lydie or any of the others. By day eight, Kate's hands had toughened. Her prison clothes were stiff with sweat. She could no longer smell her stink. Her scalp itched. She was certain she'd picked up lice. Yet, a little to her surprise, she'd survived.

The women she had worked with over the last few days must have seen her as a new audience, because stories, whispered in snatches, filtered her way. Like the girl, so slender a breeze might blow her away, who had been in Occoquan since she was eight for no other reason than because her mother, sentenced to five years for petty theft, had had no one to leave her with. And the woman with the matted brown hair who had come to Occoquan six months pregnant and had her baby taken away before she even knew its sex.

A tall, gangly woman with hands as large as a big man's asked her what she'd done to be sent here, and Kate stretched the truth, saying she had been picketing the White House. The slender girl made a crack about how some people didn't have the sense God gave them. Heads nodded, rueful chuckles moved through the group. Yet Kate caught the looks of admiration in their eyes.

Day nine dawned hot, sultry. The sun burned through the haze like a great yellow ball as Kate, bareheaded, marched behind a dozen white women—new to her—and out the doors toward the fields that stretched around the prison. She hadn't been outside for over a week. She wished she had a straw hat like the other women wore, ratty as they were.

In the distance, a half dozen uniformed guards in khaki-colored jodhpurs and long-sleeved shirts and beige, broad-brimmed hats were on horseback, rifles balanced across their horses' withers, patrolling the barbed wire perimeter while others, closer in and also on horseback, stood watch over the prisoners working in the fields.

Dirt spilled into Kate's shoes—by now, both heels were gone—and rubbed against her bare feet as she followed the women moving with a slow, loose-limbed gait toward rows of bright green shoots and a thicket of beech trees beyond. Heads down, they talked among themselves in tones too low for Kate to catch more than an occasional word. Just ahead, waiting for them, were to two guards on horseback, with oversized canvas water bags hanging from either side of their saddles. Each carried a riding quirt, flicking it lightly against their gleaming walnut-colored riding boots with a certain lazy menace that sent a shiver of fear through Kate.

The woman at the head of the line, who seemed to be a kind of boss, was small and sturdily built with full breasts and pale hair tied back from her tanned face by a piece of string. She reminded Kate of the German woman—Ilsa, her name had been—whom her mother hired to do the heavy, spring cleaning.

The shorter of the two guards, with a badly pockmarked face, beckoned to the woman, and she left the others and went closer.

"Liable to be a scorcher today," he said.

The woman only squinted up at him.

Leaning forward, the guard stroked the water bags as he might a woman. "You ladies behave yourselves, hoe them onions just so, and I might just let you have some of this."

"We'd be much obliged," she said in a flat voice.

The guard shot his partner a glance, grinned. "See there. Train 'em right and they're almost good as a dog." He and the other guard guffawed, wheeled their horses and trotted off along the row toward the thicket of trees.

The women straddled the row, and Kate watched as they hiked up their skirts, stooped, holding the tender sprouts out of the way with one hand while they grabbed the offending weeds low with the other to be tossed between the rows. There was an easy rhythm to how they moved. They made it look easy, and Kate tried copying them. But three times out of five, onions came out with the weeds. Bare spots began to appear. She prayed neither of the guards would stir from where they were lounging under the trees to come over and inspect.

An hour went by, maybe two. The sun beat down on her bare head. Her mouth puckered with thirst. She imagined the water bags, suspended from a tree branch. Soon she became obsessed with the thought of water swishing around in her mouth, the feel of it running down her chin and between her breasts. The screech of a bird jolted her out of her daydreams. She straightened. Sweat trickled down her forehead and into her eyes as she looked at the women around her who were still weeding. They had to be as thirsty as she was. She stepped across to the next row where the German-looking woman was working.

"Pardon me . . ."

The woman glanced around, her pale grey eyes expressionless.

"I was just wondering when the guards will bring us the water."

The woman rubbed her lower back, eyed Kate.

"I'll bet it's close to noon and we haven't had a drop."

"Nor for quite a spell more neither, I'd wager," the woman said.

"What if I go over and ask if I can bring a couple of those bags back?"

"Wouldn't if it were me."

Kate shifted her gaze to the guards, hunkered in the shade, smoking, their horses tied to nearby tree limbs, and tried to weigh the risks.

"They best not see you standin' around, college girl," the woman said as she drew a dirty hand across the back of her thick neck, hitched up her skirt as if to return to work.

Kate nodded. *College girl.* She wondered if Olivia and the other picketers had been given names and what they were. Just as she started to turn back to her place at the far end of the row, she gave another look at the guards by the thicket of trees. What more could they do but say no? And she started toward them.

"What you doin,' girl?" a voice asked. "Come on back here now. You'll get us put on report," another called. But Kate walked on.

By now the guards had seen her and were getting to their feet. It was too late to go back. The smaller man, feet spread apart, hands planted on his hips, eyed her "Damned if I remember sayin' you could stop work."

Kate tried to swallow. Her voice came out high as a little girl's. "I've come to ask if we might have some water—sir."

A little smile worked at the edge of his thin lips. "It's in there." He jerked his thumb toward the break in the trees, daring her to come closer.

Fear raced through her. The water bags were so close. Maybe he wanted her to beg. Yet the desperate pleas of the women behind her rang in her head, warnings. And, she dropped her gaze to the ground and mumbled something about how she was new and didn't know the rules, and she retraced her steps.

Hours crept by. The undercurrent of talk had stopped long ago. A guard finally came by with a bag of water. Each prisoner was allowed a mouthful and no more. Kate's hands were raw, her face on fire, her mind unable to focus on anything but the feel of water sliding down her throat.

The sun was low in the western sky before the guards lined the women up and they shuffled back down the rows to the looming brick building. Up ahead, one of the guards who had patrolled the fields stood waiting for them, his eyes making a mental check mark on an invisible list as each woman passed.

A sudden sense of foreboding came over Kate as she came closer, and she kept her eyes on his dust-covered boots with their broad toes, sucked in a quick breath. She started past him when he ordered her to step out of line. Another guard appeared, grabbed her by the arm, took her down a short hall new to her, unlocked a door, forced her down a flight of steps, unlocked another door, shoved her inside, into a cell, turned the key and left.

For a moment she simply stood where she was and glanced around the windowless space no more than five by nine, saw the cot and its rusted springs but no mattress, the slop bucket in the corner. And she listened. For rats and for sounds of people moving about beyond the cell door. Nothing. She had been put in solitary. Like Lucy. And like Lucy, her crime was daring to speak up.

Would they keep her here for a day or . . . Five days remained of their sentence. She hoped that by some miracle word would get to Olivia and the others of where she was. She turned toward the cell door, pressed her face up against the small, barred opening, and saw a guard—a paunchy man with thinning hair—sitting at a small desk reading a magazine. On the slim chance someone might be in an adjoining cell, she called out a "hello." But no one answered, and the guard told her to shut up.

She lay down on the cot, the coils digging into her back, and thought of Lucy again, alone in another cell somewhere, thought of her courage, her smile as she had saluted—even Kate, as if she'd been one of them. Now she'd have a chance to prove it. Pulling in a shaky breath, Kate closed her eyes. At least, she wasn't out in the heat.

Kate was disappointed but not surprised when she wasn't released the following day—or, at least, she presumed it was the following day because without a window and no watch, she had no way to know. To keep up her spirits and pass the time, she established a routine of walking back and forth the length of her cell one hundred times then napping. And watching a resident rat. So far, two slabs of brown bread on tin plates had been shoved through the oblong opening at the bottom of the cell door. Two days worth of breakfast and supper. Each time she slid it back where it came from, uneaten, as Lucy would have done.

45

Two more days went by. At first, she worked long division and multiplication problems in her head. But, lately, she found she couldn't concentrate and she had lost all track of time. The thought that she had been forgotten and might be abandoned terrified her.

She was in the midst of a complicated dream when she heard a voice bark her name. Keys jangled. She opened her eyes and saw the cell door open. She sat up, and a guard with a pencil mustache ordered her to step out. She looked at him carefully, searching for something in his expression that would give her a hint of what to expect, but she saw nothing.

Once out of the cell, the guard barked directions. She felt light-headed as she walked, sometimes forced to reach a hand out to the wall and steady herself. When she reached the door at the top of a short flight of stairs, the guard unlocked it, waved her on, and she saw the soft, gray light of early morning. Gulping in the humid air, she crossed a barren yard into the main prison building where the guard handed her over to a matron and left.

Steeling herself against disappointment, Kate tried not to hope for too much as she followed the matron's order to move along. Even when they entered the large room she remembered from the first day, recalled its smell of mold and she saw the row of showers, the clothes on the bench. Even when the matron ordered her to strip and wash, when she was drying herself with the threadbare towel the matron had tossed her.

Not until the light silk of her slip touched her skin and she struggled with the buttons on her blouse did she become convinced that she was about to be released. Her legs were no longer shaky as she walked into the hall beside the matron. At the far end of the hall was a door and she dared to run toward it.

Kate stood in the entrance to the sunlit reception room, blinking, letting her gaze travel from one woman to the next: Olivia, Lydie, Paula, everyone. Lucy. Paler, her eyes puffy, but Lucy, nonetheless.

Like an Athena with red hair. Their smiles met hers and Kate felt giddy with pride.

"Well, now, Kate," Lucy said with mock seriousness as she came around a long table that had been covered with white linen and was set with silverware. "Rumor has it, you did yourself proud. They almost extended our sentence because of you."

Kate's smiled wavered.

"But as it is, we're all being released today." Lucy put an arm around Kate's shoulders. "In fact, the superintendent, not wanting to appear a complete monster, has arranged for us to have a real breakfast before we go."

The door opened, and four Negro prisoners came in, carrying trays filled with bowls of boiled eggs, white toast, butter, pots of coffee, and a pitcher of cream. As if in a final gesture of protest, not one woman made a move to pick up a fork or spoon. Except for the coffee, which Olivia started around, the food remained untouched.

The Negro prisoners gone, Lucy tapped a spoon against her empty cup. All business, she informed them in a raspy voice that their attorney, Doug McBride, was to accompany them on the train back to the city where they were to appear in federal court. "And, unless the White House decides to put more pressure on, the judge has indicated to Doug that he will overturn the earlier decision to send us here and expunge the misdemeanor charges from the record."

"What took him so long to get us out?" Paula asked.

"Just as last year, the problem was not so much securing a writ of habeas corpus, but of serving it. It took until yesterday for Doug to finally track down the superintendent, ever the artful dodger."

Katharine whose husband was a doctor asked if reporters would be present.

"That's my understanding," Lucy said. "I'll be the official spokesman, but anyone who feels so disposed is welcome to add her two cents—as long as you check with me first." At which, laughter erupted. And, though she didn't quite understand what was so funny, Kate joined in.

The next moment the entrance door opened. Chair legs scraped the wood floor. The picketers stood, and Kate followed them outside. Standing off to the side, she cupped a hand over her eyes and squinted against the brilliant light toward the fields, hoping to pick out the small, sturdy figure of the German woman. But, at this distance, the prisoners were indistinguishable, and Kate turned away, impatient to leave.

Chapter 5

Lucy Burns leaned a shaky hand on the doorframe of the Packard touring car parked in front of three other cars, ducked her head, and climbed into the back. Her crumpled white dress felt wonderfully light. Even in the prison hospital where they'd taken her to force-feed her, she'd had to wear the infernal black-and-white striped get-up. She exchanged smiles with Olivia and Katharine, reached over to the front seat to give Melanie Stevens's shoulder a pat, and sank back.

Doug climbed in behind the wheel. The engine revved, and the car moved slowly along the dirt road, the other cars behind, past guards holding the gates open, past the high wire fence and the fields, until the prison was behind them. At first, they drove in silence, each woman lost in thought, the car swaying as Doug steered around the ruts. The air against Lucy's face was warm as she gazed at the passing landscape, its details etched against the opaque light. The orderly stalks of corn, each crowned with golden, silky tufts, the chipped slats of a red shutter that hung from the window of an ancient farmhouse, the bony shoulders beneath the tattered shirts of two boys trudging barefoot along the side of the road. She remembered reading a translation of Dante's *Inferno*. Like him, she wasn't sure she could trust her first glimpse of Heaven.

Back in Washington, it was a fifteen-minute drive from Union Station to the courthouse. Once inside the buff-colored marble building, Lucy took Doug McBride's arm and walked down the wide hall into the courtroom where the hearing would take place. Leaning on a man for support went against the grain. She felt like an old woman, but today it was that or risk falling on her face.

The instant they entered the high-ceilinged room, heads turned, faces broke into smiles. Lucy nodded to those she knew as she passed and sat down next to Doug at the mahogany table. He opened his briefcase and slid several papers toward her. On the way from Occoquan he'd assured her that the hearing was just a formality. No judge, he said, would throw them back in prison. But she'd become too jaundiced to take even Doug's assurances at face value.

A red-faced cop, carrying a two-inch stack of file folders, took a seat on the bench across from her. A clerk entered from a side door and sat at a small desk below the judge's bench. The scene was set. Dabbing at the sweat running down the sides of her face with her handkerchief, Lucy forced herself to lift her chin. She leaned forward for a better view of Olivia, the others—and Kate—hands in their laps, composed. Soldiers as brave as any on the Front.

Ten years ago, she'd never dreamed of what lay ahead, and a good thing she hadn't. Her doting parents had called her a child prodigy— entering college at sixteen, graduating at nineteen to begin graduate work, then a teaching job. But she'd had itchy feet. Her plan had been to attend the University of Berlin, to study under a specialist in linguistics. But a holiday in England had convinced her to transfer to Oxford's new women's college, Lady Margaret Hall.

After Christmas, the weather turned cold and dreary, and she began to regret her decision. What few friends she had in England lived in London. And, as pleasant as the other women at the college were, they tended to stick to themselves, ignoring a lonely American. So she'd put on a heavier sweater against the humid cold, buried herself in work.

Then, one morning Lucy threw open the shutters and looked out at—sunshine. The sight took her breath away. Without warning, May had burst over the landscape. Carpets of daffodils, golden against brilliant green, beds of deep maroon and white tulips, as elegant as a sixteenth-century painting, swaths of small snowy, lily-shaped flowers that, when she stooped to touch them, bent their heads like demure maidens.

Striding along the path to the library, she inhaled the scent from the milk-white blossoms of the plane trees, and she felt vibrant and free. Unable to concentrate on even so simple a chore as brushing her teeth, she'd packed a stout pair of walking shoes, a change of clothes, and taken a train west to Wales to sate her appetite for color and the out-of-doors.

Two weeks later, she'd returned to her hotel from a day of tramping around Ludlow Castle and was dining alone in the hotel's restaurant when Fate, with a book under her arm, walked through the door.

Slender, with a narrow face partly hidden by wispy brown ringlets, and bright, intelligent eyes, Winnie Lyford glanced Lucy's way, smiled. Lucy stood and walked over and asked her to share her table. By the end of the evening, Winnie had invited her to spend the weekend at the country home of distant cousins, Emmeline and Richard Marsden Pankhurst, on the outskirts of Manchester. Their daughters, Sylvia and Christabel, planned to be there, and Lucy might find them interesting.

Thinking about Winnie's typically English understatement still made Lucy smile. Though Emmeline Pankhurst had been born and bred an English lady who was expected to spend the rest of her life being charming and entertaining, she was fluent in five languages, including Greek and Latin, and could hold her own with her father in a debate about politics. And she had a vitality about her that Lucy admired from the moment they met.

That first evening—Richard Pankhurst at the head of the table, Emmeline seated at the other end—their two daughters began the conversation by regaling Lucy with a story about their being caught in a freak snowstorm the previous fall while hiking with cousins in the Alps, and ending up in a tiny village where they'd had to sleep in the loft above a farmer's cows. By dessert, when the topic shifted to Mrs. Pankhurst and her daughters' plan to shame His Majesty's government into granting English women the right to vote, Lucy hadn't been surprised. What had surprised her—stunned her—was their announced intention to use rebellion and violence if necessary. The method had worked for men quite effectively, they'd said. There was no reason to believe it wouldn't do so for women.

Lucy remembered staring at her and wondering what had happened to the idea that women in polite society minded their manners, asked quietly and said please. They certainly didn't resort to violence. Or did they? Once in her head, the question had stayed there until a year later when she met Alice Paul.

A slight movement caught Lucy's eye, and she glanced up from the documents in her hands to see the door to the left of the judge's bench open. The bailiff ordered everyone to rise. Doug gave her hand a pat. A trim man with gray hair, in a judge's black robes—not the judge who had sentenced them—entered.

Once seated, he surveyed the courtroom with piercing, brown eyes, behind silver-rimmed spectacles. Lucy liked the look of him. Wasting no time, he called the hearing to order, signaled to Doug McBride to begin.

Lucy watched him walk toward the bench. Given the slight paunch beneath the tan summer suit, the apple cheeks and guileless blue eyes, Doug had no resemblance to the fierce, courtroom bulldog he was. First thanking the judge, Doug introduced each of the thirteen women in that slow, courtly manner Lucy associated with the South. He explained in detail how the women came to be sentenced to the Occoquan Workhouse, a facility used to house criminals. He then described how they were treated. Next, he lifted five statements from men and women who had witnessed the melee in front of the White House the day of his clients' arrest out of his briefcase, and handed them to the judge.

"Your Honor will note the affidavits that the crowd attacked my clients: clear evidence that their right to protection under the law was violated, rather than the other way around." He paused as the judge read each statement. "Further, though no record of the original hearing and sentence was kept, my clients can attest under oath that at no time were they represented by an attorney. Grave injustice has been done, Your Honor, and I respectfully ask the Court to invalidate the sentences as well as the original arrests."

Five minutes went by, only the sound of breathing broke the silence as the judge reread the witness accounts. Out of habit, Lucy laced her fingers, rubbed her thumbs together as she watched his eyes travel each page, occasionally frown, then go on to the next.

Finally, the judge looked up, adjusted the sleeves of his robe, and gazed around the courtroom. "After due consideration of the facts and the evidence, this Court finds that because the most fundamental civil rights of the defendants were violated, their original arrest as well as their sentence are invalid." He looked down at the front row of women. "Ladies, you are free to go." Then, with a sharp rap of the gavel, he declared Court adjourned.

For a second or two, no one moved. Then, as if a switch had been pulled, bedlam broke loose. Lucy sprang to her feet, grinning, hugged Doug McBride, who blushed clear up to his hairline. Olivia rushed over. More hugs. Smiling women surged down the aisle toward Lucy, offering their congratulations.

Reporters in their boaters and fedoras, notebooks and pencils in hand, swarmed around, eager to get quotes from Doug McBride. A few interviewed Lucy, dutifully scribbling the words she doubted would appear in tomorrow's editions. She told them as glad as she was to be out of prison, nothing would deter the efforts to secure the women's vote, not even if it meant another jail sentence.

Spectators lingered for a while then wandered off. Gradually, the courtroom emptied. Glancing around to see who of her group remained, Lucy noticed Kate, talking to a tall man, his dark hair gray at the temples. She studied the two. The man looked to be in his late forties and bore a strong resemblance to Kate—the same hair coloring, shape of the face and nose. Her father, no doubt. He had an arm around her shoulders, and he was smiling down at her.

Lucy had worked with a great many women for a long time. She liked to think she had an instinct for who would stick and who would go back to act out the life the world had decided appropriate for them. Thinking back on the Kate of two weeks ago, the innocent with wide-eyed terror, Lucy hadn't expected the courage that had emerged. She had even convinced herself that Kate would join the fight for the vote in Washington. Now, as she watched Kate embrace her father, Lucy had to admit her instincts weren't infallible. By nightfall, Kate would be on a train back to—Colorado.

Chapter 6

The courtroom emptied as the last of the women hugged one another and said good-bye; Kate and her father were the last to leave. She'd had to blink twice before believing her eyes when he'd come up to her after the judge's decision. That her father would make the long trip to Washington had never occurred to her. More to the point, how had he known she had been in prison? She was glad to see him, but she was anxious to get to work. Still, now that he was here, the least she could do was go back to his hotel with him for a good visit.

Once in the back seat of the cab, awkwardness settled between them. Her father held her hand as if she were a China doll and reached for conversation—observations about the terrible heat and the humidity, the difficulty of travel in wartime. She wanted a cigarette, desperately. Instead, she asked about Mother and her sister,

Lizzie. And Tom. Until, finally, the cab drew up to the curb in front of the Hay-Adam with a view across the park to the White House, and they got out.

As she waited for her father to pay the cabby, Kate gazed up at the entrance, thinking how little it had changed from when she had stayed here as a child. She'd been five, and her family had come to attend William McKinley's inauguration and help her grandfather celebrate his election as the junior senator from Colorado. But all she remembered of the occasion were the elephants in the zoo.

Her father took her by the elbow, and they walked by the white-haired, uniformed doorman, who touched the bill of his stiff cap and held open the door. The small lobby had an intimate feel, elegant with mahogany paneling, the domed ceiling edged by delicately colored terracotta tiles in the Italian style. They stepped into the waiting elevator and rode to the third floor, silent in the presence of the uniformed Negro operator.

Her father led the way down the carpeted hallway, lined with gilt-framed reproductions of English country scenes until he reached room 324. With a hand that Kate noticed was trembling, he slipped the key into the lock, turned the knob, opened the door.

"Phew-w-w! It's hotter than the hinges of Hades in here!" he said as they stepped inside. "What we need are fans and lots of them."

Kate smiled as she gazed around the large, sunny sitting room. The Chippendale love seats covered in dark green silk, the graceful occasional chairs, the leather-topped desk, the large bouquet of roses on the small dining room table at the far end of the room—she'd almost forgotten such rooms existed. And she felt it draw her in.

"It's lovely," she said. In another moment, she would be seduced, and she turned toward her father. "Daddy, why did you come?"

He dropped his boater onto the closest chair, came over, and hugged her again. "Oh, Katie, for heaven's sake, you're my daughter. You're mother and I have been frantic. And then when we discovered you were in prison. . . ." He kissed the top of her head and, for a long moment, she basked in the security of his arms.

Finally, pulling back, smiling up at him, she met his searching eyes. "What?"

"I was thinking . . . If only I hadn't agreed to let you take the train alone . . . It's all my fault." He scowled, concern in his eyes. "Are you sure you're all right? Maybe I should have a doctor take a look at you."

"Daddy, it wasn't your fault and I don't want you worry about me. I'm fine."

"You're so thin."

Kate had to laugh. "You sound like mother now." She glanced toward the bedrooms. "If you really want to know what I'd like most in the world at this moment, it's a long soak in the tub, a shampoo, and clean clothes."

"Then we'll talk." Her father eyed her. "Which reminds me, where's your suitcase?"

"Lost, I'm sure. I left it in the cab, before I was arrested."

"It doesn't matter. We'll figure something out so, at least, you'll have what you need to get you home." Her father smiled down at her, love in his brown eyes. "I always said you were a tough kid." He took off his suit coat and arranged it over the back of the desk chair. "Though you have to admit that what you did was more than a little thoughtless."

"Daddy . . ."

As if he'd heard the determination behind her protest, he held up his hands. "Okay. We'll leave it for now. You can tell me all about it later. We'll have three days on the train. Fact is, I thought I'd see about tickets for tomorrow afternoon, though I think a stateroom's out." He paused. "That is, unless you want to rest up a little more first."

Daddy: always the protector—trying so hard, as if she were an invalid recuperating after a serious illness that had affected her mind. How would he ever understand? "Can I have a bath first?" she asked, smiling, and he seemed to brighten.

"And then lunch. Here in the room. How does chicken salad and iced tea appeal to you? Strawberries, if they have any?"

"Perfect." Kate went over to him, hugged him tight around his waist, breathing in the pungent scent of the special tobacco he smoked. He was the compromiser in the family, proud of his liberal attitude toward women, particularly when it came to the women in his family. But she knew he had his limits.

"Your room's the door to the right over there. We share a bath. Use my robe, if you want. The lunch will keep, so take your time."

The bedroom was in shades of blue. Subtly striped, pale blue wallpaper, a deeper blue floral bedspread, and matching drapes. The off-white carpet felt soft as down against her bare feet. She shrugged out of her filthy suit, then the underthings. Naked, she stepped into the gleaming, white-tiled bathroom and laughed when she caught herself checking for cockroaches. Thick, white towels and several face cloths hung over glass rods. She picked up a brand new bar of Pear soap that had been placed on a shell-shaped soap dish, breathed in the scent. The bathtub was almost big enough to swim in, and she turned on the faucets.

Waiting for the tub to fill, she remembered her cigarettes—for some reason the only thing the matrons hadn't stolen from her purse. The box was crushed but the two remaining cigarettes looked smokeable. She took one out, found a slender box of matches on the bedside table, carried them into the bathroom, and laid them on the floor next to the tub, and turned off the water.

The feel of the warm water as she stepped in sent shivers of ecstasy through her. She took her time sitting down. Because her hair was caked with dirt and grease, she started with a shampoo, then worked down, taking special attention to her wrists, soaping and rinsing until the water was so filthy she had to drain it and refill the tub. Finally clean, she retrieved the box of cigarettes, tapped one out, and lit it. Tossing the match box aside, she took in a deep drag, leaned her head back against the porcelain, and stretched full-length. She closed her eyes and blew the smoke toward the ceiling, let the water lap gently over her body. Her neck muscles relaxed; the pain in her back eased. She took another drag. Her mind seemed detached from her body, floating aimlessly, like a leaf on a pond, free of thought. In a moment, she'd fall asleep, and she opened her eyes and slowly stood up, flicked her cigarette into the toilet. Toweling dry, she felt the strain of the past two weeks ease off her body, and she slipped into her father's gray-and-white stripped silk robe, wrapped it around her.

As she padded barefoot into the sitting room, her father was directing a slightly built Negro waiter where he should place the lunch plates and glasses. Once all was in order and the man wheeled his cart out the door and closed it behind him, her father looked over at her and grinned. "I must say you look a tad better," he said, and pulled out a chair for her.

"I feel a tad better, too." Spreading the starched, white linen napkin over her lap, Kate surveyed the heavy, gold-edged china plates covered with crisp lettuce, thick chunks of chicken, and slivered almonds. Two glass bowls were filled with plump strawberries. Sweating glasses brimmed with iced tea. The veritable feast she had only dreamed about in prison.

As she picked up her fork, she felt her father's eyes, and she looked up.

"I hope the salad's okay."

She stabbed a piece of chicken, put it in her mouth.

"Well?"

"Ambrosia," she mumbled with her mouth full. She wasn't sure, but she thought she tasted a hint of curry.

"I swear I ordered hard rolls," her father said, eyeing the napkin-covered plates.

"If they were meant for me, I don't think I could eat them. What's here is more food than I've had in two weeks." Kate took a sip of tea, holding the soothing cold in her mouth for an instant before she swallowed.

Her father looked at her. Kate thought she saw his eyes mist, but an instant later he looked down at his plate, and they busied themselves with eating. Somehow the timing didn't seem quite right to tell him about her plans, and she asked more about Tom.

"As far as I know, he's still flying out of Villeneuve," her father said.

"Not in those same flimsy French planes, I hope."

"Afraid so." He put his fork down on his plate. "When you didn't come home, your mother and I thought you'd been kidnapped. I telegraphed that friend of yours, Millie, but she didn't know a thing. So I telegraphed the district police to report you missing. And then when I didn't hear back from them, I got in touch with the Shafroths."

"Why the Shafroths?"

"Can you think of anyone better than a senator to know how to cut through Washington red tape? Fact is, he personally called the station and had the police check their records. That's how we learned you were in prison." He sat back heavily. "If it weren't for John, you still might be in that place."

"I think the attorney for the NWP—the National Woman's Party—had something to do with it, too," she said quietly.

"Could be," he said in that noncommittal tone he used to avoid argument. "But enough of that for now."

"Daddy, I . . ."

"Later. After you've had a good rest." He pushed his plate aside. "But before you lie down, I want you to make out a list of what you need to see you through the trip. I'll give it to the head of housekeeping. She'll get right at it." He dug into his back pocket drew out his money clip, removed three twenties, and put them on the table. "What do you think? Will sixty dollars cover it?"

"And then some." Kate sighed as she folded her napkin, stood, leaned over and kissed him on the forehead. "Now if you'll excuse me, Daddy, I'll take the nap you offered."

❧

A car's horn wakened her from a sleep so deep Kate felt as though she'd been drugged. She stirred, opened her eyes, and stared into the darkness. Her shoulders tensed, and she jerked her head to the side to see where the guard was before she realized that she was wearing her father's bathrobe. She looked toward the window where the glass curtains hung, unmoving in the still, hot night air. She'd been asleep for hours.

Raising up on one elbow, she peered toward the door, but saw no line of light that might hint her father was awake in the sitting room. She lay back, still groggy with sleep, and thought of her father and her mother, what lay waiting in Denver if she went home. A short stay in the mountains to recuperate, maybe. But, after that, the good works, the luncheons, the expectations of marriage once the boys she'd grown up with came home from France.

But in the last two weeks she'd found what she'd been looking for. She had a purpose. Walking into that courtroom this morning, she knew nothing would deter her.

She'd been brought up in a family that prided itself in standing up for what was right, what was fair. And nothing about the treatment of women in this country qualified.

She sat up, threw her legs over the side of the bed, and went to the window. Looking down, she saw the treetops of Lafayette Park across the street from the White House, where it had all started. Just on the other side, she knew from the talk on the train, was NWP headquarters. And, though Kate couldn't see the house, she felt its pull, its power over her.

She groped her way back to the bed, fumbled for the cord on the bedside table lamp. The filthy clothes she'd left in a pile on the floor were gone. Then she remembered her father saying he would arrange for new ones. Looking in the closet, she discovered a long-sleeved white lawn blouse with a shawl collar, a pleated navy linen skirt. A shoebox was on the floor, and she opened it to see a pair of white leather high-heeled shoes with fashionably pointed toes, which, she was certain, would be in her size. On the shelf above, encased in tissue, she found a pair of silk stockings, silk underpants and slip, a garter belt.

As she examined them, she thought about how best to tell her father she wasn't coming home. She could wait for daylight and face the fatherly inquisition—how was she to support herself, where was she planning to live—but she already knew that no amount of talking would weaken her resolve. And her father hated arguments. So she dressed and, having no hairbrush, smoothed her hair with her hands, slipped on her new shoes, picked up her purse, and, ever so carefully, opened the **door** to the sitting room.

Guided by the light from the bedroom, she went over to the desk, snapped on the lamp, pulled open the drawer and removed several sheets of hotel stationary, a pen. She dipped the pen in the inkwell on the desk and began to write how it had been the day she'd first seen the picketers, the confusion of the arrests, the denial of her most fundamental rights, the unfair sentence, and about Occoquan.

All of it came rushing out of her heart and onto page after page— the courage of the women she'd come to know, why the government had left them no other choice but to risk prison, why she, too, would risk prison again if she had to. She loved him—and Mother—she said. But she had to remain in Washington to do what she could for the cause, for all American women. If that sounded overly grand, so be it. But it was what she was about. She'd be staying with her friend, Millie, at least for now. She dipped the pen in the inkwell one last time and signed her name, with love.

It wasn't until she was blotting the last page that she saw the three twenties, propped up against the telephone, as if her father had read her mind. And she slipped the money she considered a loan into her purse, snapped off the lamp, and groped her way to the door.

It was one o'clock when Kate walked out of the hotel and made her way on foot along all-but-deserted streets past Dupont Circle and along Massachusetts to Millie's apartment in a red brick row house that she shared with her aunt, away with friends for the summer on Chesapeake Bay. Not really to Kate's surprise, Millie didn't answer the bell, and Kate went back downstairs and outside to sit in the dark on the top step and wait.

She'd first met Millie in the Dean's office at college where they'd been sent one month into their freshman year to be disciplined for smoking on campus. Then and there, she and Millie agreed they'd been destined for each other. By the next semester, they were roommates. Kate, the westerner; Millie, the scholarship student—both outsiders, they gladly put up with each other's bad habits.

Millie's father had been a loan officer at a bank in a small Ohio town. Halfway through her junior year, he'd died of a heart attack. Her mother took to baking fruitcakes for the local bakery, and Millie quit college, took the train to Washington and in less than a week had a job as a receptionist with the Department of the Army. Now that Kate thought about it, she didn't see any reason she couldn't do the same.

She was growing tired of waiting. She guessed it must be at least two. Yet, up and down the block, there was a restless feel to the night, as if everyone had decided it was too hot to sleep. From an open window came the strains of someone playing jazz on an out-of-tune piano. Close by, a child cried. A man and woman argued. Her elbows on her knees, her hands cupping her chin, Kate gazed into an open window on the first floor of the house directly across the street. The shades were up, and she could see a man and woman sitting beneath a floor lamp, reading. After some time, one of them looked up and said something; the other nodded. The ordinary scene was so intimate Kate felt like a voyeur, and she glanced away.

Then, from down the street, she heard laughter, and she looked to see Millie leaning on the arm of a tall, broad-shouldered man, coming this way. When they reached the bottom of the steps, they stopped. The man, who wore an army officer's uniform, pulled Millie close and fondled her rear as he kissed her.

Kate decided she'd better say something, and she stood and started down the stone steps. "I hate to interrupt, but—"

Millie and the man loosened their hold on one another, looked up at her.

"It's me again, Millie. And I need a place to stay."

"Try a hotel," the man said and turned his attention back to Millie.

Kate ignored the soldier. "I hope it's okay because I told my father I'd be staying with you."

"Get lost, whoever you are," the fellow said.

"Oh, shut up," Millie said, slowly shifting her gaze, as if it took her total concentration, to her date. "Who asked you anyway?"

"Baby, come on. Don't be that way," he cajoled.

"Don't baby me, buster." She stepped back, groping for the railing, gazed up at Kate. "Where've you been? Your father telegrammed and I said. . . ."

"It's a long story." She watched Millie stagger up the steps, not sure she'd make it.

Still standing on the sidewalk, the soldier yelled up at Millie. "Hey, what about me?"

"Go away." She climbed one more step, paused. Leaning against the railing, she looked up at Kate, a crooked smile on her lips. "Ya know somethin'?"

"You're drunk."

"You guessed it." She slid down onto the stone step. "I think I may even throw up."

Kate went down to her friend. "Give me your key."

But it was too late. Leaning through the railing's rungs, Millie began to vomit.

"You've seen the last of me, doll face," called the soldier in a disgusted tone.

"I sure hope so," Kate said, rummaging in her purse for a handkerchief.

"Witch."

Kate put an arm around Millie's waist, and as they started up the last stairs to the entrance door, she noticed the soldier was already halfway to the corner, weaving down the center of the street.

Millie's apartment was on the second floor, and the climb was slow. After several tries, Kate managed to fit the key in the notch. And the moment they stepped inside, Millie made a beeline for the bathroom. About ten minutes later, pasty faced, she came into the small living room and plunked down onto an easy chair covered with faded chintz. "Lord, what a dunce." She leaned her head back, closed her eyes.

"You or that guy?"

"Both." Millie opened her eyes. "I actually thought I liked him."

"It happens." Kate handed her friend a glass of water. "Sip, don't gulp."

"So what's the long story?" she asked over the rim of the glass.

"Tomorrow."

Chapter 7

The crash of garbage cans cut through Kate's sleep and she opened her eyes, turned her head, and saw the chintz curtains hanging limply at the guest room window. Her skin felt clammy with perspiration and she decided the temperature must already be in the high eighties. She listened for signs of Millie, but heard only quiet. Millie must be at work, which meant it had to be at least nine o'clock.

Kate wanted to surprise Lucy, even impress her when she showed up at headquarters today. She scrambled out of bed. Standing at the bathroom sink, she decided that after last night's bath, a slapdash wash job on her face and under her arms would do. She dressed in the clothes her father had left her, then searched Millie's closets for a hat and found a navy straw. Not until she headed toward the front door did she see the note propped up against the telephone in the alcove.

Kate—cheers! I should be back from work by six. Help yourself to whatever you need. An extra door key is in the drawer of the hall table. Can't wait to hear the story. Your hung-over pal.

Kate smiled. Millie. Easy come, easy go, she took life as it came—the kind of friend who accepted you for what you were, warts and all. Whether that included Kate working for the NWP now, she'd soon find out.

⁂

Kate saw the White House through a screen of trees as she entered Lafayette Park. On the other side, at right angles to Pennsylvania Avenue, she could just make out a line of houses built in the Federal style. One of them, she knew, was NWP headquarters.

Excited, filled with a sense of urgency, she strode along a pathway that cut through the park, dodging a little boy rolling a hoop, passing beds of yellow and white roses and squares of lawn, still green in spite of the heat. Up ahead, she spotted an American flag flying from the rooftop of a cream-colored, white-trimmed house in the middle of the block. Even through the trees, she could see a purple-and-gold banner hanging above the porte-cochere, and she thought of the one torn from Lydie's hands.

Her heart pounding, Kate crossed the street and walked up to the house. A bulletin board framed in glass next to the front door caught her attention, and she paused to read the headlines from *The Suffragist*. In the center of the page were announcements of various kinds, but it was the notice of a congressional committee meeting where Alice Paul, NWP President, was to testify that caught Kate's attention.

She started toward the entrance again just as four or five women in dresses of soft-colored lawn and stylish hats came out, so deep in conversation they almost bumped into her as they passed and, as if in afterthought, waved a brief apology before hurrying on. And Kate stepped inside.

As she stood in the small foyer, gaining her bearings, she watched women bustling up and down a broad, mahogany paneled staircase, heard voices swirl around her, telephones ring. From somewhere above her, a disembodied voice hollered for anyone who had a car.

The entire house seemed to be on the move, alive with urgency. And she shivered in anticipation as she went upstairs to the main floor.

Walking down the central hallway, she inspected the rooms on either side—work rooms that had once been the living room, dining room, the library, she thought. Not seeing a familiar face, she leaned into one room where four women were seated at a table, licking envelopes, asked them where she might find Lucy Burns.

"Upstairs. If she's there," one said. "First door to the right."

Kate smiled her thanks and, staying close to the banister to keep out of the way of a woman carrying a large, brown carton, she went up. She heard high heels clicking against bare floor above, and she looked up, saw a door open. A moment later a small, slender, dark-haired woman came out.

"Excuse me." Kate hurried up the last few stairs. "I'm looking for Lucy Burns."

Huge, deep-set brown eyes regarded Kate with interest. "And you are?"

"Kate Brennan."

The edges of the woman's lips curled slightly. "The girl at Occoquan. Lucy told me about you."

Kate wondered what Lucy might have said as she watched the slender woman begin to pull on white gloves.

"I'm Alice Paul."

Kate's eyes widened, speechless at meeting the president of the NWP like this, out of the blue.

"I'm afraid Lucy's not here." Her voice was pleasant, but formal: a voice to keep strangers at bay. "I told her to take a few days off."

"Maybe Olivia Melborn?"

"She's gone back home for a week. But if you're looking for something to do—"

"Actually . . ." Kate drew herself up a little taller. "I don't know what qualifications you're looking for, Miss Paul, but, in addition to being at Occoquan, I—"

"You can start by helping with the mailing downstairs." A voice from below called Miss Paul to the telephone, and she leaned over the banister. "Thanks. I'll take it up here," she said, then glanced back at Kate. "You'll have to excuse me." She took a few steps backward. "About the mailing. It needs to get out tonight."

Kate stared at the closed door, embarrassed at how poorly her first meeting with Miss Paul had gone. And disappointed. What she'd expected she wasn't quite sure. But it wasn't to be dismissed and sent off to help with a mailing. At a loss, not knowing what else to do, Kate went downstairs to the room where she'd seen the women stuffing envelopes.

❧❧❧

Kate reached for another rubber band and twisted it around the last of her batch of mail destined for Charlotte, North Carolina. It was three o'clock. She'd been working all day, and now her only company was the neat stacks of banded envelopes, arranged by city and state, lining four long tables.

She sank back in the chair, dispirited. She'd seen herself assigned to join a picket or at the very least confront a senator or two. Yet the women stuffing the envelopes had been so earnest, Kate wouldn't have dared complain. Even when someone had brought in sandwiches and iced tea, not a soul stopped working.

The talk, she admitted, had made up for the tedious chore. Maybe because she'd grown up in a family where politics were the center of dinner table conversation, she'd become intrigued. Mostly it was speculation about the Senate and whether or not it finally seemed in a mood to follow the House's example and debate the suffrage amendment—the reason why, a girl from Virginia told Kate, today's mailing to local constituents was so important. Guesses as to how individual senators might vote flew around the room, but, at the moment, Kate couldn't remember a single senator's name.

Now, tired of sitting, she got to her feet, stretched, and walked over to the bay window with a view of the park. She thought about her father, wondered if he'd taken the afternoon train or was still in

66

the hotel only a block away, a five-minute walk at most, but one she wouldn't take.

She returned to the table of envelopes. Until Lucy came back and they talked, she was stuck. In the meantime, she had to figure out how to support herself. Until she ran out of her father's sixty dollars, a part-time job would get her through. She supposed Millie might give her a lead, but most of the government jobs girls had involved typing, and Kate had never advanced past the hunt-and-peck method. A clerk at a shop was the likeliest possibility. One within easy walking distance of headquarters would be best. With the shortage of help, she shouldn't have a bit of trouble.

⁕

Kate strode down F Street, her eyes prowling the rows of buildings for a likely shop, when she saw the sign above a store front: "Weintraub's Dress Shop," and she paused to inspect the display in the window. The mannequins wore the usual summer fare—shin-length cotton and rayon dresses, pale blues or greens, small prints, belted at the waist, the bodices loose. The dresses looked cheaply made, the kind that might appeal to clerks and secretaries on a budget. She imagined chatting with customers, maybe mentioning the NWP as she made out the sales slips.

Kate went in, waited while a young woman at the cash register rang up a sale, and asked to speak to the manager. The girl pointed to a glass-walled office at the back of the store. As Kate passed a counter with a display of scarves, she caught her reflection in the nearby mirror. Beneath the blue straw, she saw chin-length, bobbed, dark hair, eyebrows that could stand plucking, lips brightened by just a hint of rouge. On the whole, the girl looking back at her appeared neat, sure of herself, and competent, exactly how a clerk should look, Kate decided, if she were doing the hiring.

Kate had nearly reached the manager's office when the matter of experience occurred to her. Except for volunteering during Christmas vacation at the second-hand store run by St. Luke's Hospital when she was in high school, she had no sales experience at all. But in a lower-class store like this one, she guessed experience probably wouldn't be required.

The door to the glass-walled office was open, and she tapped on the frame. A stout man in a rumpled tan summer suit, his tie askew, looked up from the papers on his desk.

Straightening slightly, putting a smile on her face, she went up to the desk and introduced herself. "I've come about a part-time position as a clerk," she said in what she considered a bright, positive tone.

The man regarded her with dull eyes and blotted the sweat from his forehead with a rumpled handkerchief. "Sorry, part-time is against company policy."

The immediate turndown surprised her and it took her a moment to react. "I do war work," *the truth*, "and—"

"Sorry. No exceptions. Just never seems to work out," he said, and went back to his paperwork.

She stared at him, wanting to argue the point but the telephone on his desk rang and she turned and left.

Standing under the awning, out of the way of the passersby, she regained her composure and decided there were more fish out there than this tadpole. Chin up, she went into the next store, Parkinson's Shoe Store. The only customer was a young woman trying on a pair of brown, canvas-topped shoes with black rubber soles Kate knew were all the rage.

Kate approached the clerk, a gray-haired man with stooped shoulders, who said he would be with her after he finished with the customer. But when the customer finally left and Kate asked him about part-time employment, he said they weren't hiring. She heard the same story at the Fabric Emporium across the street. In the next block, she tackled two more dress shops and a jewelry store. One of the dress shops was hiring, though for Saturdays only. None used part-time help.

Standing on the corner as she waited for the police to stop the traffic and allow pedestrians to cross, beginning to panic, she noticed a four-story department store in the next block. The large sign on the roof said "Hechts." Its windows on the street level were large, the entrance doors bronze. It had the elegant look of a store on New York's Fifth Avenue that catered to the wealthy. Kate crossed the street and headed toward it. This was her kind of store, a place she'd feel at home. Her confidence returned.

The personnel office was on the fourth floor. Her smile was a bit forced by now, but she had her query down pat. Yet, as soon as she uttered the words "part-time," the gaunt receptionist told Kate it was pointless to fill out an application. In the elevator on the way down, she was close to tears.

The seats on the streetcar back to Millie's were taken and she had to stand. Hanging from the leather strap, she surveyed the women around her and absently wondered where they worked. Several got off at her stop and she almost went up to them to ask but something—call it pride—stopped her, and she turned onto Massachusetts Avenue. Her feet hurt. She longed for a cool bath to wash away the discouragement. Yet as she walked along, she became aware of a friendliness about the neighborhood she hadn't noticed before. A man winding up the awning over the five-and-dime smiled at her as she paused, and she smiled back. Across the street, customers outside a grocery store were chatting with each other as they picked through boxes of fruits and vegetables on display. Her spirits rose a notch, and, for a moment, before she remembered her financial straits, she almost bought a half-dozen oranges to take to Millie.

Ahead, on the corner, a group of laughing men and women in light, summer clothes spilled out of a restaurant she hadn't noticed before. Perelli's Family Café, according to the sign in the spotless front window. But what caught her eye was the "help wanted" sign in the door. Visions of greasy dishes and complaining customers loomed. But the money her father had given her wouldn't last forever. And staring back at her was a possibility she hadn't come across all afternoon. It was either that or go home.

A bell tinkled overhead as Kate closed the door. Glancing around her, breathing in the smell of garlic, she counted eight tables covered with red-and-white checked cloths. Off to the side, next to a cash register, was a tray piled high with glasses, coffee cups, dirty plates—perhaps remnants from the recent customers. Framed photographs of men and women grouped in front of the restaurant covered the far wall.

A heavyset woman with an immense bosom, thick black hair fastened in a knot at the nape of her neck, and dressed in black emerged through a doorway in the rear. "Sit anywhere you want. I bring a menu," she said in a lilting Italian accent.

Kate smiled. "Actually, I've come about the help wanted sign."

The woman arched a dark eyebrow, gave her a discerning look. "No offense, but you don't look like no waitress."

"True. But I'm a fast learner. Ask anyone."

A hint of a smile worked at the edges of the woman's generous mouth. "All's we need is somebody to cover the breakfast shift."

"Perfect," Kate said, and she brightened her smile. "I can start tomorrow."

"It's just tips to start."

"But once I prove myself, there'd be a salary, right?" Kate could hardly believe her bravado.

The woman folded her arms over her large breasts, pursed her lips. "What did you say your name is?"

"Kate Brennan."

"Brennan."

"It's Irish." Emboldened now, Kate seized the moment. "My granddad came over during the Famine."

Smiling broadly, the woman nodded. "A good Catholic girl. I should have seen it the minute you walked in."

Kate met the woman's approving gaze, smiled. Truth came in various shades. Being a high Episcopalian wasn't the same as being a Catholic. But with all the incense and kneeling, it was as close as a person could get and not be one. Just last Christmas Kate had argued the point with her mother when Tom had written of his intention to marry Miriam Savage, a Catholic.

"I got two girls about your age. Married with bambini and husbands in the army. My son, Vic, he's in the infantry."

Kate waited a respectful moment before she asked, "Did I mention that I can start tomorrow?"

"I dunno." The woman glanced over her shoulder toward the kitchen. "Wait a minute and I go talk to the mister."

"Or you could give me a try and then decide," Kate said. "What time do you open?"

"Five thirty, but—"

Kate turned toward the door. "I'll be here."

Chapter 8

The windows open, Mary Daly was standing in her stocking feet at the sink, enjoying the cool of a Colorado summer evening as she dried the last of the few supper dishes she'd used, when she heard cries and the crash of things breaking next door. She'd heard the sounds twice before since a man and his wife and teenage girl—the Gillians, she thought the name was—had moved in a month ago. She could have called the cops. But she knew they wouldn't lift a finger. A man's home is his castle. Hadn't she heard that enough to make her puke? And she'd decided to stay out of whatever had been going on.

Shawn Hegarty, who owned the place, had made his money buying and renting rundown houses all over town. He never fixed them up. Mary hated to think what the places were like inside. Not that Hegarty cared. These days he lived on the other side of town in a mansion, too good for the likes of the people he milked for rent money. So renters came and went, some better than others. As for this house, ever since she'd walked out on Gino and come back to live with her brother, Rob, the two of them took pride in keeping it shipshape.

Mary walked to the screened door, listened. The noise had stopped. With a shrug, she sat down at the kitchen table, where the light was good, and opened the paper. Slowly turning the pages, reading the war news but only skimming the Neighborhood Doings section, she became conscious of the quiet. Her eyelids grew heavy. She glanced over at the clock above the stove. Half-past eleven.

She folded the paper, placed it on Rob's chair where he'd find it in the morning, pushed herself to her feet. A bit of a breeze was coming through the window, and she walked over to open it a little wider. She was turning away when, out of the corner of her eye, she noticed a shadowy figure in the back yard.

Curious, Mary opened the screened door and stepped outside. Only then did she realize the figure was a woman and a smaller figure—a girl—was behind her . . . She thought of the family next door. As the two figures walked toward the light, Mary noticed the woman was cradling her left arm with her right hand.

Mary stepped onto the stubbly grass her brother Rob had mowed that morning and ducked beneath the clothesline. "Is there something I can do for you?" she asked in a low voice.

In spite of the heat, the woman was shivering.

"Come in, why don't you? You and your girl. I'll fix us some coffee." Without hesitating, Mary put an arm around the woman's shoulders. "And I've got a bit of sheeting to make a sling for that arm."

Once in the kitchen, Mary pulled down the window shades, and the three women sat around the table. Slight, and stoop-shouldered, as if she'd spent her life apologizing, the woman squinted at Mary with small, ferrety eyes. The girl was sturdier, with a ruddy complexion, her breasts small mounds. Her light brown hair had been worked into corkscrew curls and she sat with her hands clutched in her lap, her eyes on the floor.

Mary eyed the woman's arm, saw the bump of a bone beneath

the skin. She leaned across the table, felt the lump gingerly. "You need a doctor to set this break, Mrs. Gillian," she said. "It is Gillian, isn't it?"

The woman said nothing.

"I'll go with you." Mary smiled. "It's not that far. Six blocks. Dr. Maloy is his name. He's used to patients comin' at all hours."

Mary saw the darkness of an old bruise along one side of the woman's pale face. Her eyes were getting a wild look, and Mary went to the cupboard over the sink, reached in the back, and pulled out a bottle half-full of whiskey. She poured a finger's worth in the bottom of a glass, took it over to the woman. "Sip on that. A little whiskey will get the color back in your cheeks quick as a wink."

But the woman shook her head, so Mary set the glass down before her on the kitchen table.

"It's Annie here that needs help," the woman finally said, so softly Mary could barely hear her.

Mary looked over at the girl, her head still bowed, and felt a flash of intuition as the mother kept talking.

"I caught her heaving up her supper. And she told me how her dad came to her bed." Tears filled the woman's eyes, spilled down her cheeks. "After supper, I put it to him and he came at me with a two-by-four. He said Annie was a liar and a whore. That he was going to throw her out."

Listening to her, Mary heard the half-truth and the self-pity beneath the cry for help. She didn't doubt the woman's story or that her daughter was pregnant. But she suspected it wasn't the first time and that this time they thought they'd found someone who might find a way to an abortionist on the cheap.

"I shouldn't have come and bothered you this way, but . . ." She shot a teary look at her daughter, sniffed. "When he finds we're gone, he'll know I told and he'll come after us, sure."

"If he does, we'll call the police," Mary said. "But right now the three of us are goin' to pay a call on Dr. Maloy, have him set that arm or yours, and—"

"You tell him my girl ain't quick."

"You're her mother. You tell him, Mrs. Gillian. Now I gotta get on some shoes."

In her bedroom, sitting on the edge of her bed and tying her shoes, Mary remembered how her Ma had teased her about always dragging in the halt and the blind. A bird with a broken wing, once a sad yellow dog with a back leg cut off when a beer truck had run over it. Mary couldn't help herself. Not when a pregnant girl and her Ma with a broken arm came for help. If it were up to her, she'd cut off the bastard's dick and leave him to bleed to death.

❧

Josie Rowland's office was on the north end of downtown Denver in a neighborhood of duplexes and small stores, nothing fancy. The small brass plate above the doorbell said J. Rowland, Attorney at Law. Not that Josie wanted to hide her sex behind a sign. That much Mary knew. It just made good business sense. Get them in the door, and Josie would have a better-than-even chance of convincing clients a woman could represent them as well as a man—as long as it was about real estate and other minor civil suits that would come before a justice of the peace. Josie had her law degree and the paper to prove she was a certified lawyer. But there were ways, Josie said, a judge could make certain she'd lose any case she defended when it dealt with a felony.

Mary had met Josie two years ago at a meeting of the Woman's Party. Now she needed Josie's advice. And over coffee, Mary said, "I have a funny feelin' about the mother. I wouldn't be surprised if she and that husband farm their girl out for money."

"Where are they now?"

"At Doc Malloy's. I'd put them up but I don't want the husband bustin' in. Rob wouldn't like the mess."

"They can stay here. I have a couple of cots in the attic." Josie took a sip of coffee. "The law won't protect her. Or the girl. As far as that goes, if she were on the up-and-up, the mother would charge her husband with her daughter's rape. At the very least, she should charge him with taking indecent liberties with a child under the age of sixteen, which is considered a felony. And if her husband is found guilty, he can be sent to the penitentiary for up to ten years."

"And while all this is goin' on, the girl is scared out of her wits."

"In either case, there would have to be a trial first, where I'd have to prove the father did, in fact, rape her. Difficult to do because, in the end, it is the daughter's word against her father's."

"What about the mother's broken arm?"

"What about it?" Josie refilled Mary's cup. "What her husband did to her was a case of assault and battery, which involves provocation. It would be entirely possible for his attorney to convince the jury that his wife egged him on, made his life so miserable that he was driven to physical violence. Even if the jury found him guilty, the most we could expect would be a two-thousand dollar fine and a year in prison."

Mary rose and walked to the window. "So what happens to them?"

"I'll look the other way and you find a doctor to help the girl and hope the police don't catch up with you."

"The Church says abortion's a sin."

"Then convince the mother to take her daughter and disappear. Move to another state."

Mary turned back. "What you're tellin' me is a woman's still got no choice at all."

"It depends on how much money she has. Even then . . ." Josie shrugged. "But women are beginning to fight back, Mary. Things are about to change."

Mary looked at her friend, the memory of the long-ago night when she lay on a table covered with a blood-stained sheet, a mere girl, as she clutched her cross, her life in the hands of a man who fixed automobile engines by day and removed fetuses by night. "I'd like to believe it, but I'm a doubter by nature," she said.

"And a fighter," Josie said, with a crooked smile and a look of admiration in her green eyes.

Chapter 9 ———————————————————————

The first day back on the job after five days, Lucy leaned back in her office chair and breathed in the mixture of scents from the roses and magnolia trees that grew in the park across the street, glad to be back. She'd walked the six blocks from her apartment in the gray dawn, the streets empty of traffic. Yet she knew she wasn't her old self, and she blamed it on the dreams of that prim-faced prison doctor bending over her, telling her to hold still while he jammed a tube down her throat, that everything would be all right. All right? For whom?

Swallowing was still a problem but milk had a soothing effect, and she finished off the glass she'd poured herself in the kitchen below, put it aside, and returned to the pile of letters containing reports and newspaper clippings from field workers around the country. Over the years, she learned to trust the rumors picked up by field workers. Often they were the first hints of a senator's stand on an upcoming vote. Armed with such inside information, she and Alice stood an even chance of uncovering the truth when they confronted a senator or his aide.

At her elbow was yesterday morning's edition of the *Chicago Tribune* and she put aside the files and turned to it, hoping to find an article about Occoquan. Most of the front page was taken up by a dark photo of men in helmets and grimy fatigues, trudging past the remains of a church, and a caption that read: "American troops dig in northwest of Chateau Thierry." Staring at the faceless figures, she tried to imagine their misery, the danger they faced—not the same, yet endured for the same reason women—she—accepted prison. There were times when she wondered what it would take for them to make the headlines.

She flipped to the next page and the page after that. But it wasn't until the bottom of the fifth page that she spotted the meager, two-paragraph report of thirteen members of the National Woman's Party who had been released from Occoquan Prison in Virginia after serving a sentence—its length wasn't mentioned—for obstructing a public sidewalk in front of the White House.

She tore out the article she'd paste in her personal scrapbook later. Strictly speaking, to arrive at the number thirteen, the reporter had included Kate Brennan, not a member and now, Lucy presumed, back in Colorado. Yet what difference did a number make? The results were what counted.

Lucy picked up the second section, pleased to find a lengthy interview with Mrs. Carrie Chapman Catt, president of the National American Woman's Suffrage Association. According to the article, she was predicting the passage of the Susan B. Anthony Amendment in the Senate on Thursday. Lucy reread the statement. Odd. Alice hadn't said a word about an upcoming vote.

Yet, as prominent as she was, Mrs. Catt wouldn't have spoken to the press about something as important as the Senate vote if weren't true. The NAWSA—National, as most called it—carried a certain respect. Most members were highly thought of in the community—intelligent, if a bit stodgy. And, like all proper ladies, patience was their by-word, which had gotten them nowhere. It didn't help that thousands of women still cherished the status quo, feared what they might lose with the vote. So it should come as no surprise that after one hundred years well-intentioned women like Mrs. Catt were still begging like so many orphans in a Dicken's almshouse for a right that was already theirs.

Ten years ago, when she and Alice were recuperating from a lengthy stint in England's Victorian monstrosity, otherwise known as Holloway Prison, they realized what English women had already figured out. First and foremost, patience was a waste of time because the very intransigence of those in great power made compromise on the vote impossible. Women had no choice but to snatch it away, even if it meant fighting tooth and nail, which also tended to get a good play in the newspapers. The key to success was to learn the political process and beat the men at their own game. Once back in the United States, she and Alice had started plotting. Their coming-out party had been the massive march deliberately planned to coincide with Woodrow Wilson's first inauguration. And they had been at it ever since.

Lucy lowered the paper, still perplexed by the *Tribune* article. Alice was sure to know the truth behind it. When she arrived a half hour later, Lucy went next door, paper in hand, tapping lightly on the doorframe as she entered.

"What's this about Mrs. Catt?" Lucy handed the paper to Alice seated at her desk.

"Lucy Burns, you're supposed to be in bed."

"Too much to do." She perched on the edge of the desk. "Since when has the amendment been scheduled for debate?"

"For a week." Alice spread the paper out on her desk. "I guess we have our friend, Senator Jones, the chairman of the suffrage committee, to thank."

Lucy caught the cynicism in her friend's voice. The senator from New Mexico was a decent enough man, but with little clout. And she suspected that the Democratic Senate leadership giving him the chairmanship of the Senate Committee on the Suffrage Amendment was a sop to keep the small western contingent—where most women could already vote—happy. "Then tell me why Jones conferred with Carrie and not with you."

"Perhaps because Carrie Catt is easier to hoodwink," Alice answered. "Still, her statement about a vote is astounding. Surely, she knows the leadership has purposely held off approving the military spending bill until the last moment, conveniently leaving no time for debate on the amendment."

"Agreed. So why bother with the mailings in the making that I saw when I came in?"

"Lucy, you know perfectly well why. The old boys in the Senate need their constituents at home to remind them that they're being watched. That they can't wiggle off the hook, no matter what tricks they dream up."

Lucy rubbed the back of her neck. "Lord, nothing changes, does it? Go away for a few weeks and you come back to find the same games still going on."

Alice frowned. "Luce, are you sure you're all right?"

"Could I win a foot race? No. But I'm well enough to do what needs doing at my desk." Lucy saw the doubt in her friend's eyes. "Really."

"You're sure?"

"Alice, drop it. We need to talk about what to do about Jones. In fact, maybe I'll go over to talk to him today and see what else the Senate has up its collective sleeve."

"You're going nowhere today. I'll go."

"Take someone from New Mexico with you."

"I don't know that there is anyone unless . . . What about that new girl who was at Occoquan with you. Isn't she from the West?"

"Kate Brennan. She went home."

"Au contraire. I bumped into her the other day. Eager as a puppy. I told her to help with the mailing."

"Kate Brennan, here?" Lucy laughed, imagining her encounter with Alice and pleased that the girl hadn't disappointed her after all. "I'll bet you scared her half to death."

"I did no such thing."

Still laughing, Lucy started toward the door. "If she's who you want, I better find her."

"When you get hold of her, tell her to meet me here by one thirty."

"And if I can't reach her in time?"

"Find someone else."

On the way downstairs, Lucy decided that maybe Kate Brennan showing up at headquarters wasn't that surprising after all. But once the newness wore off, what then?

Chapter 10

Kate unlocked the door to Millie's apartment, went in, untied the sensible, black oxfords she'd bought in place of the white high heels, and kicked them off. She still considered it nothing short of a miracle Mr. Perelli was keeping her on. On her first two days, she had mixed up orders and dropped a tray of dishes. And this morning, just as she was beginning to get the hang of it, she dumped a plate of scrambled eggs into the lap of Mr. Rinaldo, one of the café's best customers.

Kate fumbled in her purse, pulled a cigarette out of the box of Lord Salisburys, and lit it. Collapsing into the easy chair, she stretched out her legs, let her head drop back against the chintz slipcover, and took in a long drag. Another morning like this one and she'd be out of a job. And she was running out patience.

She wasn't sure what she'd expected to do for the cause when she got out of Occoquan but it certainly wasn't licking stamps. If it weren't for the political gossip, she'd die of boredom. A snake pit was how one woman described the Capitol. But Kate wanted to see for herself.

She sat up and was reaching for the glass ashtray on the coffee table when the phone rang. She tapped the ash off her cigarette. The phone rang again. One of Millie's boyfriends. Kate stayed put, took another drag. Two more rings. Annoyed, she put her cigarette down in the ashtray, went to answer it.

"Kate?"

She'd know the voice anywhere. "Lucy! How are you?"

"I thought you had gone back to Colorado. But Alice tells me you are helping with the mailings."

"I am, yes. But—"

"Listen, Kate, I'm sorry for this last-minute call, but Alice needs someone to go with her to call on Senator Jones of New Mexico. You'll need to be at headquarters by one-thirty. Can you make it?"

Kate's heart skipped a beat.

"Kate, are you there?"

"Sorry. Yes. Tell Miss Paul yes, I'll be there. Oh, and, Lucy, if you had a hand in this, thank you." She could hear herself babbling.

"Don't thank me. Thank Alice."

❧

Fifteen minutes early, Kate straightened her shoulders, tapped lightly on Miss Paul's open office door.

"Come."

Kate stepped inside. Miss Paul had impressed her as an elegant person and the starkness of the room, devoid of even a painting on the wall, took Kate by surprise.

Alice Paul, who was putting on her hat, glanced at her. If she detected Kate's reaction, she gave no sign of it. "Ah. Kate Brennan. Good." She glanced at her watch. "Right on time. I'd prefer to walk, but I don't want to be late, so we'll take the streetcar." She tucked her purse under one arm. "Follow me."

Nearly running to keep up with her, Kate followed Miss Paul down the two flights of stairs, out the front door, through the park, and along Pennsylvania Avenue to the streetcar stop. They had to wait only a few minutes before one rolled up. The door opened, and Miss Paul climbed the two steep stairs, Kate right behind her.

The car was crowded with servicemen. But two sailors stood and offered their seats. Miss Paul smiled her thanks, slid in first. Sitting beside her, Kate stole glances at Miss Paul's profile—the straight nose, arched eyebrows, flawless skin, deep-set eyes. Kate wanted to ask what Miss Paul expected her to do once they reached the senator's office. But she sensed Miss Paul wouldn't want to discuss their business in a public place.

They got off at First and with Miss Paul leading the way walked to the Senate office building. Entering by a side door, they hurried down a long, cool marble hallway lined with tall, dark mahogany doors and took the elevator to the second floor. Once its door slid closed and they were beyond the hearing of the uniformed operator, Miss Paul glanced up the hallway and said, "Here is the situation. Senator Jones is a good friend and chairman of the Senate Suffrage Amendment Committee. Even so, I'm afraid he lacks the necessary influence to move the amendment along at this critical time.

"I will introduce you, of course. It is unfortunate that you are not from New Mexico. But so be it. Colorado will have to do. A show of back home interest is vital, and we have a standing rule that in order to guard against future denials of what was said, no one calls on a senator or congressman alone. Your job is very simple: sit there, listen and say nothing. Understood?"

Kate nodded, almost literally quaking in her boots, and Miss Paul led the way to the door marked "Senator Andrieus Jones" on a discreet brass nameplate and waited for Kate to open it.

The reception room was small, darkly paneled. An oil painting of a desert scene in a gilt frame hung above a brown leather couch. Miss Paul addressed the receptionist by name as Miss Carlson, who looked up from her typewriter. "The senator is expecting me," Miss Paul said, presenting her card. "And I've asked Miss Kate Brennan from Colorado to join us."

Kate attempted a smile, but the secretary had already glanced away. Like a child on her first day at school, she didn't know what to do next. Take the chair in the corner or sit with Miss Paul on the couch? Should she remove her gloves now or later? She was still hesitating when a man in a light brown, three-piece summer suit and stiff collar entered. Of a stocky build, he had thick reddish hair and a mustache flecked with gray. Kate guessed he might be about her father's age.

"Miss Paul." He offered his hand. "Good to see you."

Alice Paul rose in a single, graceful movement and smiled the barest of smiles as she took his hand. "Senator." She turned to Kate. "I'd like to introduce Miss Kate Brennan. From Colorado."

"A pleasure." Above his smile, his eyes shifted to his reception-ist. "Hold all my calls, will you, Miss Carlson?" And with another smile and a courtly sweep of his arm, he invited the women into his office.

The room was good-sized, perhaps twenty by twenty, its view a block of souvenir shops and lunchrooms. A scattering of photo-graphs dotted two of the cream-colored walls. Hanging on the wall behind the senator's oversized walnut desk was another large oil painting, this one a scene of an Indian pueblo. On the desk were piles of letters and documents, a large family photograph next to the ink well. Off to one side was a small table that held a telephone and a framed photograph of the senator, smiling and shaking hands with President Wilson.

"Please. Make yourselves comfortable." He went around the desk, placed a square hand on the back of the high-backed brown leather upholstered chair. "Excellent to see you, Miss Paul." He glanced at Kate. "And—"

"Miss Brennan," Miss Paul said briskly as she settled into one of the dark brown leather barrel chairs in front of the desk and indi-cated that Kate should take the chair next to her.

"Of course." The senator sat down behind his desk and wiped his perspiring forehead with a snowy handkerchief, unbuttoned the top two buttons of his vest. "This Washington heat is going to kill us all."

Alice Paul offered a smile, took off her gloves and arranged them on her purse in her lap in a way that left no doubt she'd had enough small talk. And Kate did the same.

"Senator, we appreciate your time," Miss Paul said, "We know how busy you are. Perhaps we should get down to business."

The senator shifted in his chair. "By all means."

"We understand the Anthony Amendment is to be brought before the Senate for debate this week. On Saturday, to be specific," she said crisply.

Kate glanced at the senator for his reaction as she might an actor in a stage play but he was absorbed in refolding his handkerchief and returning it to his jacket pocket.

"As it happens, our information comes from a statement that appeared in the *Chicago Tribune* attributed to Mrs. Carrie Chapman Catt, who also indicated there was a good likelihood the amendment would pass."

The senator sat back. "You don't say? Well, now. I'm afraid you know more than I do. I haven't had the pleasure of speaking with Mrs. Catt for several months."

"So you know nothing of this matter firsthand?"

The senator shook his head. "I must confess, no." But Kate who had followed the plot carefully had the distinct feeling he was lying and that Alice Paul knew it.

"You have no idea, then, how Mrs. Catt came by that impression?"

"There are many of us who are hopeful, of course." Beads of perspiration trickled down the sides of the senator's face.

"Votes, not hope, are what we're after, Senator," Alice Paul replied.

"Of course."

"You do know that former president Theodore Roosevelt has thrown his support behind the amendment," she said.

He nodded then added. "Though I'm sad to report several other distinguished Republicans—Herbert Hoover, for one—are point-blank against it."

Kate shot a glance at Miss Paul, fearing the information would throw her off balance. Instead, in a voice as smooth as silk, she said, "I also understand there are no plans for a caucus."

"Not on the matter of the woman's vote, no."

"Except, as chairman of the Senate Woman's Suffrage Committee, you may move for consideration."

"I can do that, yes." Kate watched the senator contemplate his thick hands clasped on the desk as if deciding how best to respond. Finally, he looked up. "However, may I remind you Sunday marks the end of the fiscal year."

"Indeed. With grave matters to deal with such as the army budget that cannot be postponed and take precedence over the Amendment," Miss Paul said, her tone cool.

"Exactly," he said, all but sighing in relief, Kate thought, at the out Miss Paul seemed to have given him.

"Senator, we would not in any way jeopardize our troops' well-being," she said, evenly.

The senator nodded.

"However, I'm certain I don't have to remind you that, regardless of budget matters, the fall elections are only four months off. Three of the senators up for reelection in the West are Democrats—as well as one Republican, Senator Borah from Idaho." Sitting with the grace and straight back of a ballerina, Miss Paul gave him a steady look. "So, at the very least, I would like to think you will do everything in your power to assist your Democratic colleagues in what could prove to be difficult campaigns."

"A difficult campaign?" he repeated. "I'm not sure of your meaning."

"Oh, come now, Senator. Should the amendment fail to pass this time, the National Woman's Party will have no choice but to work for their defeat and replace them. You can count on it."

Kate could almost reach out and stroke the tension in the air as she glanced from Miss Paul to the senator.

"Miss Paul, let me assure you such a step is not necessary. I will do everything in my power on your behalf. Surely, you recall that I was one of the first to inspect the deplorable conditions you experienced at Occoquan Workhouse last year."

"Ah, yes. Occoquan." Miss Paul glanced at Kate. "Perhaps Miss Brennan would care to speak to that. She and Miss Burns and a dozen other women from our organization were recently released from Occoquan, where they had been held without previous benefit of lawyer or trial for fourteen days."

Kate flushed with surprise. She hadn't expected to be called on. She had no idea what Miss Paul wanted her to say. So the truth would have to do. In a voice that she hoped sounded authoritative, she said, "I'm afraid to report, Senator, conditions are deplorable. The women have to endure rats and cockroaches in the cells, and work under inhumane conditions, some in the hot sun without water."

The senator made a tent of his fingers, pursed his lips and scowled. "Most distressing."

"To put it mildly," Miss Paul said and rose. "So you understand, Senator, why the women of this nation cannot—will not—wait any longer. We are counting on you and on the amendment's passage this Thursday."

The senator got to his feet. "And shall I expect your presence in the gallery?"

"I'm surprised you would have to ask, Senator."

Once out in the hall, Miss Paul set out at her usual pace. Heels clicking against the white marble floor, she strode along the corridor and down the stairs, Kate again taking up the rear, racing to catch up. Not until they stood outside, pulling on their gloves and blinking in the sunshine did she have the chance to ask why the senator had been so careful to dodge around bringing up the amendment when he was the chairman of the Suffrage Committee.

"If you do not understand the situation, how can you be of help?" Miss Paul said by way of an answer, and started off toward a streetcar stop.

Cheeks blazing in embarrassment, Kate followed. "It was what wasn't said that I don't understand."

Alice Paul stopped. "And that's at the crux of the matter. Let's just say that Senator Jones knew perfectly well that the only reason the amendment was to be brought to the floor for discussion was because its opponents had already arranged for its defeat, and he didn't want to admit it."

"Which is where the military budget comes in," Kate said.

The edges of Miss Paul's mouth twitched ever so slightly in what Kate thought might be a smile. "Well, then, you do understand after all. And, yes, the military budget is a convenient excuse because it must be passed before July 1st. The Southern Democrats are undoubtedly responsible for this maneuver. No matter how passionately Jones may plead for consideration, another Democrat will filibuster against it. And the amendment will be postponed indefinitely which, if you are unfamiliar with the process, means the amendment will die in committee." Miss Paul walked on.

Trotting after her, Kate noticed two men coming toward them. Neither wore a hat as if they might have just come from the Capitol and were heading for a nearby office, and as they passed Miss Paul, they exchanged knowing glances as if they recognized her. Kate caught up, matching Miss Paul's stride, anxious to be seen with her.

Seemingly oblivious, Miss Paul picked up where she had left off. "Mind you, it isn't as though the members of NWP are indifferent to the needs of the military. Whether you believe in the war or not—as in my case—the fact remains that nearly every woman has a brother or husband, or a son, in France. Yet if the purpose of the war is to make the world safe for democracy, wouldn't you think it logical for the government to address the home front, where one-half of the population is still denied the vote?"

They had reached the streetcar stop.

"Which brings us back to the amendment," she said. "It can be brought up again, of course. But, as I reminded the senator, it best be soon. Our members helped defeat nearly all the Democrats up for reelection two years ago, and he knows we can do it again." She checked her wristwatch, shot a glance down the empty tracks. "Let's walk. Exercise helps one's circulation."

Kate followed, the heat radiating from the sidewalk through the soles of her shoes. "Miss Paul, there's one more thing."

"Which is?"

"I'm not quite clear how defeating Democratic senators up for reelection will help pass the amendment."

Miss Paul took Kate's arm and led her off to the side of the walk to let a woman pushing a baby carriage go by. "I explained that to the Senator. But, obviously, you weren't paying attention. So . . . At the present time, the Democrats control the Senate. A Democrat—President Wilson—also occupies the White House. The Democrats, therefore, determine the political agenda, which includes what items will be placed on the calendar for debate and when a vote will be taken. Clear?"

Kate nodded.

"However, if a sufficient number of Democratic senators lose their bid for reelection, that could tip the control of the Senate to the Republicans who—"

"But even if that happens, how can we trust the Republicans any more than the Democrats?" Kate asked.

"Excellent question," Miss Paul said, suddenly stopping to look up at something. "Good heavens. Look there." She pointed at a long-tailed triangle of brilliant color bobbing in the blue sky. "A kite. Amazing it stays up on a day as still as this." She eyed Kate. "A bit like our campaign, isn't it?" And, as they walked on, she would glance over her shoulder several times to look at it again.

Finally, within sight of the White House, Kate dared to ask what would happen should the amendment be postponed. Miss Paul didn't answer at first but when she did her voice had a tired sound to it.

"There are parliamentary ways around it if our friends in the Senate choose to use them. And the President also has the power and influence to get the votes we need—if he chooses to use it. Though after six years of hemming and hawing, giving us one excuse after another, I have few hopes."

"Wouldn't you think he'd worry more about his fellow Democrats up for election?" Kate asked.

"The President or Senator Jones?"

"Both, I guess."

Alice Paul gave her an amused look. "Indeed, you would. So we must make them worry—worry so much that they see no other course than to vote for the amendment."

They cut across Lafayette Park, and Miss Paul switched to accounts of the Senate campaigns in the last election. Kate nodded at what she hoped were appropriate times but she was only half-listening as she tried to sort out the various pieces of what she was beginning to understand as a high-stakes political game.

⁙

It was nearly six when Kate paused in the entryway of the row house to check Millie's mailbox. Not even Miss Paul's final putdown had dampened her excitement over sitting in on the parry-and-thrust in the senator's office. Kate could hardly wait to tell Millie every detail whether she wanted to hear it or not.

The mailbox was full, which meant that Millie was still at work and Kate emptied it and climbed the stairs. She worked her key into the notch, opened the apartment door. The windows had been open all day, but the place felt like an oven as she stepped inside. She dropped the mail on the kitchen table, unpinned her hat, tossed it and her purse onto the guestroom bed, and took off everything down to her slip, brassiere, and panties . . . Back in the kitchen, arranging the mail against the salt-and-pepper shakers on the table, she was surprised to see one piece of mail was addressed to her, and that it was in her mother's handwriting.

Kate picked it up, staring for a moment at the graceful Spencerian script. Her mother had always been the letter writer in the family. Through Kate's college years, two pages had arrived regular as clockwork each Wednesday. No ink blots, no lines that climbed uphill, no crowded margins. The weather was invariably the first topic, then the family's state of health, and finally the events—a board meeting of the Denver Orphanage, a tea, a dinner party. Always included was Kate's last letter with spelling errors circled in red ink. The first time such a letter had been returned, when Kate was a freshman, she couldn't stop tears from welling up in her eyes. That her spelling was more important to her mother than the message had hurt. After a while, she got used to the criticisms, chalked them up to her mother's penchant for self-improvement, and barely glanced at them.

Kate worked her thumb slowly under the flap, drew out two sheets of engraved vellum, unfolded them. Sucking in a deep breath against the lecture in store for her, Kate began to read.

Dear Kate,
*   Of course you know of my relief when your father returned home with the news that you are all right in spite of your terrible ordeal. But you must also know how disappointed we are that you decided to stay in Washington.*

Kate could almost hear her mother say the words, calmly, deliberately. *Your father and I* were code words, the result of days of discussion. She wondered if her father had brought home the letter she'd left at the hotel, if her mother had read it.

The discussion would have started in the car on the way home from the station and gone on all day, ending that evening on the porch that overlooked the garden, bricked off from the neighboring house for privacy. The grass, cut short as a putting green, bordered by white and yellow tea roses, citron colored asters and bright-faced daisies made a quiet retreat. A pleasant place where the family could spend a warm evening, though she doubted her younger sister, Lizzie would be there. Parties with friends, not home with parents, were her cup of tea.

By seven or so, Christine, now the family's only household servant, would be in the kitchen, putting the finishing touches on a cold dinner that she would carry to the porch on trays. Chicken salad flavored with a hint of curry, hot rolls small enough to eat in a single bite. Baby rolls, Christine used to call them. But before dinner, her father might have brought out the single malt Scotch, left from their stash before Colorado went dry, and poured a splash into each of the two glasses her mother would have brought from the pantry. By the time Christine came with the salad, they would have been so distracted over the problem of how to manage their strong-willed daughter, they might not have eaten more than a few bites. Wasn't it enough, they would have said to each other, to worry about a son who faced death every day?

We understand your change of heart regarding law school. Frankly, we have never been clear as to when law school became an interest of yours. Because we believe that young women these days who have the aptitude should have the opportunity to pursue a profession, we certainly don't object. But if the law is not for you, that is for you to decide. You are now an adult, after all.

Kate grimaced at the condescension behind her mother's word.

Regarding your joining the National Woman's Party, I believe your father explained our long support of women's suffrage. While I applaud the NWP's intentions, their methods can only result in failure. I know from experience that success in gaining the women's vote comes not from picketing the White House and being thrown into jail but from building coalitions, convincing the men who make the decisions as to the logic and the merits of the cause. Men like our dear friend, John Shaffroth. Naturally, this takes time and patience, not a trait you are known for, Kate, but one I had hoped you had acquired during your college years.

Another little jab.

You are a fine, intelligent young woman with much to offer the world. We don't want to see you hurt, and we urge you to reconsider—not only for your future's sake, but also for the sake of your younger sister, Lizzie, who looks to you as a model. Come home until you have found a more appropriate path to follow.

Kate looked up, the pages dangling between her fingers, annoyed at her reaction—the feeling of inadequacy, the need to explain herself—that always came with her mother's letters. Most of the time Kate tried to please her mother. After today, this was not one of them.

❦

It was nearly seven before Millie came home from work. Kate didn't mention her mother's letter as they went about putting a supper of leftover roast chicken and potato salad on the kitchen table. But she did tell her about the excitement of lobbying the chairman of the Senate Woman's Suffrage Amendment Committee.

"I thought you were stuffing envelopes," Millie said, putting the plates on the table.

"I was. But after today . . ." Kate paused in the middle of arranging the forks and knives. "I think Miss Paul trusts me."

Millie gave her a quizzical look. "You're really caught up in this, aren't you?"

"Of course, I am. You should be, too."

"And go to prison in the bargain? No thanks." Millie reached for two glasses on the top shelf of the cupboard and Kate took the pitcher of tea out of the icebox.

"Don't you want the right to vote?"

"I guess so. But I've lived this long without it and survived."

"You're from Ohio. What do you think the chances are of men in Ohio giving women the vote?"

Millie laughed, picked up her fork. "Not great. It's been tried. Nothing came of it."

"Which is why we have to get the federal amendment passed. We're Americans as much as men are—and we deserve the same rights. Don't you see that?"

Millie stuck a forkful of potato salad in her mouth, chewed. "I believe in fair as much as the next person," she said, her mouth full. "But even if the amendment passes, three-fourths of the states have to okay it." She wiped her mouth with her napkin. "And that'll never happen. You can bank on it."

The telephone rang, and Millie ran to get it. A few minutes later she came back, a grin on her face.

"That was Phil. He's bringing a pal. They called from a place on the corner. They'll be here in a minute." Millie stuck a piece of chicken in her mouth and picked up her plate. "I said you were gorgeous."

"Count me out. I'm bushed."

"A little music and you'll revive."

"I'm serious."

They argued the point a little more, but Millie was in a hurry to dress, leaving Kate to wash the dishes. She was filling the sink with hot water when she heard a knock on the door and Millie dashing out of her room. A moment later, Millie entered the kitchen with two fellows in tow, one in an army officer's uniform, the silver bar of a second lieutenant on his shoulders, the other in a rumpled summer suit.

"Kate, meet Phil." Millie threw a smiling glance at the lieutenant, a broad-shouldered fellow with thick brown hair and heavy eyebrows. "And . . ." She grinned up at the civilian, taller than Phil, but on the lanky side, with thinning blond hair.

"The name's Charlie. Charlie Harrison," he said.

Kate smiled.

"Chuck works for that outfit that puts out news about the war," Millie said.

She looked over at Kate, gave a little shooing motion. "Go comb your hair, girl, and get your dancing shoes on. Phil has to get back to the fort by midnight."

"I told you, Millie—"

"You're bushed. I know. Aren't we all?"

"Truth is I'm not such a hot dancer," the blond fellow said.

Kate smiled at him, grateful for the out he'd given her. She'd have the apartment to herself after all.

"Party poopers," Millie said, leaning against the lieutenant. "But if that's the way you want it, far be it from me. Chuck, you can stay here and gab with Kate."

And before Kate could object, Millie and Phil, his army cap on her head, were half way out the door.

Kate stared after them, angry with Millie, when she remembered the blond fellow and she gathered her manners. "Well. I guess it's just the two of us."

They exchanged awkward smiles.

"I guess I better be going," he said.

"I have some iced tea. Would you like some?"

His smile brightened.

"I just made some before supper." She backed into the kitchen. "But we're low on ice so it might be awfully strong."

"Just the way I like it," he said, following her.

As she reached up into the cupboard for glasses, she noticed the dishes in the sink, soaking in the cold water. She was on the verge of apologizing for the mess when she saw him take off his jacket, toss it over the back of one of the chairs, and roll up his shirt sleeves.

"Why don't I take care of these while you pour us that tea?" he said, going over to the sink.

Kate stared at him, tongue-tied as she watched him feel around in the murky water and remove the stopper. She'd never seen a man wash dishes. "You really don't need to—"

"If you're worried I'll break something, rest easy. I've had lots of experience at this. Shouldn't take five minutes."

Later, Kate might cringe at how easily she'd agreed. But right now it made sense to have the dishes out of sight when they'd be sitting not three feet away at the kitchen table. She pulled out the soap powder from below the sink and handed it to him. As quickly as he'd predicted, the plates and glasses were stowed in the cupboard and Kate and Charlie were looking across the table at each other, glasses of iced tea at their elbows.

"So . . ." She took a sip of tea and reached for a conversation opener. "Millie said you work for—is it a newspaper?"

"Not quite." Charlie rolled down his shirtsleeves, buttoned the cuffs. "I work for what's called the Committee on Public Information. The CPI. We put out patriotic stuff local newspapers can use. Some call it propaganda. But, lately, the job's changed."

"And before the war?" she asked, noticing how intensely blue his eyes were.

"I was a reporter, and before that a jack-of-all-trades—set type, operated the press, anything that needed doing. My Dad put out a weekly in a coal mining berg in southern Colorado and since it was just the two of us—"

"Colorado? I can't believe this. I'm from Denver." She shook her head at the coincidence, laughed. "I'll bet your father really misses you, back here, so far from home."

"I'm afraid he's dead," he said, his tone neutral, without feeling, which Kate suspected had taken time to achieve.

"I'm sorry." She took another sip of tea, thinking how inadequate "sorry" was when it came to death. "Who runs the paper now?"

"I sold it. After that, I bummed around until George Creel, an old friend of Dad's, caught up with me last year in Pueblo where I was working for the daily. The war had just started. I wasn't eligible for the draft because of a busted eardrum. Creel offered me the job at the CPI. And here I am."

"Do you like it?"

"Living in Washington?" He shook his head. "I'm not a city boy. As to the job. . . . I look at it as my chance to help the war effort." He took a sip of tea. "How about you?"

"Me? I love Washington. Millie was my roommate at Bryn Mawr—maybe you've heard of it—outside of Philadelphia—a women's college. When I graduated in May and stopped by to visit her, I decided to stay on to work for the National Woman's Party," Kate said, amazed at how she'd edited the truth.

"The NWP. Sure. The ladies who picket the White House."

"You know about us then," she said, pleased.

"Do indeed. But you're the first real, live member I've ever met."

She laughed. "Now you can tell people we don't even bite."

"I hope you weren't with the bunch that got hauled off to jail a couple of weeks back."

"Correction: hauled off to prison. Occoquan Workhouse. And, yes, thanks to our president, I was one of the thirteen who were sent there."

"Wow," he said, softly.

"Unfortunately, it seems to be the government's only answer to dissent." She forced a smile and stood up. "I don't know about you, but I'm about to die of the heat in here. Why don't we go into the living room. Millie has some records. . . ."

He pushed to his feet. "Sounds good, but I think I'd better be on my way. I've horned in on your evening enough as it is."

"I'm glad you stayed," she said, watching him as he lifted his jacket off the back of the chair and walked into the hall.

"Maybe I could come by another time," he said not to her surprise.

"That'd be nice."

He retrieved his hat from the alcove table.

"I'll call." He took her hand and held it a long moment before he let it go, and Kate felt her face flush.

"I'm usually home by six," she said, opening the door.

"Six, it is." He smiled, his eyes crinkling in the way she'd noticed before, and walked past her, pausing at the top of the stairs to lift his hand in a kind of wave good-bye.

Kate stood in the doorway until she heard the front door open and close. She had almost forgotten how to act with a "date." Yet it hadn't seemed to matter. He'd literally rolled up his sleeves and made himself at home. In some ways, their conversation had been frank enough for them to be longtime friends. She liked that. She guess he was twenty-six, give or take a year, a little older than the boys who had invited her to dances on weekends at college—and he was more serious. If he did telephone, he'd probably take her to a play instead of, say, a music hall. Kate stepped back into the apartment and closed the door.

Kate left the light on for Millie in the little hall alcove, undressed, and climbed into bed. She was just closing her eyes when she heard a key in the lock, then a man's deep voice and a giggle. She rose quietly and closed the bedroom door.

After a few minutes, even with the door closed, she could hear the sound of bedsprings creaking, followed by more giggles. Kate pulled the sheet up over her head and held her hands over her ears. She must have dozed off because she was awakened by footsteps in the hall, whispers, and the sound of the front door closing.

Desperate for cross ventilation, Kate flung off the sheet and opened the guest room door. "I'm dying in here," she said as Millie, naked beneath a loosely tied red silk kimono, lounged in the doorway.

"I wouldn't wonder. I'd offer you a beer, but we drank it all."

Kate switched on the hall light and started toward the kitchen, stopped. "I'm sorry."

"Because you were in the next room? Fiddle. Anyway, Aunt Lou isn't here to disapprove and we're friends." Millie followed Kate into the kitchen. "Which reminds me . . . You don't happen to have a cigarette, would you?"

Kate noticed a nickel-sized bruise mark on Millie's neck, a love mark, she'd heard it called. "There's a box of Lord Salisbury's in my purse."

A moment later, Millie came back with the box, a cigarette already lit in her hand. "So did Chuck stick around?" She pulled out one of the kitchen chairs, sat down and blew a smoke ring toward the ceiling.

"For a while." Kate took a cigarette and looked at Millie. "You and Phil are—serious?"

Millie got up and tapped the ash from the end of her cigarette into the sink. "Serious, no. But he's fun." She turned, leaned against the sink, a grin on her face. "Besides, it's my patriotic duty. You tramp around and lobby for women. I sleep with the doughboys."

Kate couldn't help laughing.

"And if you're worried I'll get pregnant, don't. I'm a big girl."

"Whatever that means," Kate said. In a way, she envied Millie's lack of concern about her reputation or the consequences. Who cares what "they" think was her attitude, so different from how the Brennan household looked at the world, especially her mother. In her view, life was something to be used and shaped. Millie simply enjoyed the moment.

"But enough of my love life." Millie drew in deeply on her cigarette. "Tell me about yours."

"There's nothing to tell. We talked."

Millie arched an eyebrow.

"That was it."

Millie blew a smoke ring toward the ceiling. "Why am I not surprised? If I could talk you out of this NWP stuff, I would. And you know why? Because it's not going to change a thing. Not a living soul is going to thank you for whatever you do, least of all most women, even if you go to prison twenty times. Go home, Kate. Go to law school like you were talking about once if you're so intent on breaking the rules. Better yet, get married. Have a bunch of kids. If you're so hell-bent on changing the world, that's the way you'll do some good. Chuck will tell you that."

"His name is Charlie. And I can't."

"Can't? Or won't?" Millie jabbed her cigarette out in the ashtray and looked at her with that same unflinching flash of indignation that Kate remembered from the day they first met in the Dean's office. "Well?"

Kate's first impulse was not to answer. "Both," she said, quietly.

Millie pushed slowly to her feet and walked to the doorway before she glanced back and answered. "I never should have asked." And she disappeared down the hall and into her room.

Chapter 12

Two days later, Kate stood at the window in her slip and surveyed the early morning overcast sky, the raindrops glistening on the wrought iron gate by the alley. She'd need an umbrella. This noon, if Senator Jones lived up to his promise to Miss Paul, the Senate would discuss the Anthony Amendment and maybe—maybe—bring it to a vote. A notice had been posted at headquarters that all those planning to monitor the proceedings should meet at eleven. She would have to rush straight from work to make it on time.

Turning to the closet, she pulled out a clean white blouse and her navy skirt, put them on, found her hat, and dashed downstairs. Outside, she hurried down the steps and, ducking beneath store awnings and dodging the puddles, she ran down the nearly empty streets toward Perelli's.

The regulars—mostly old men, mostly Italian—were filing in the door and she called out a "good morning" to them. They waved, smiled at her as they might a daughter or granddaughter. When they'd discovered she came from out West, they'd kidded her about cowboys and Indians. With a few exceptions she knew how each man liked his eggs and whether he took sugar and cream in his coffee.

Following them inside, she breathed in the rich aroma of freshly baked bread and headed toward the back room where the supplies were kept, calling a *buon giorno* to the Perellis as she passed the kitchen. She took one of the aprons, sparkling white and crisp with starch that Mrs. Perelli always had ready, off the hook and, tying it around her waist, gazed at the framed photo of a dark-haired, handsome young man in a khaki uniform. Vic Perelli: a sergeant in the artillery, somewhere on the Western Front, the light of his parents' lives, who was facing God knows what today. Just for luck, she kissed her fingertips and touched them to the glass.

In the few weeks she'd worked for the Perellis, they had come to treat her like family. Worrying about how little she ate, urging her to forget politics and find a nice young man. Often when Kate stayed after her shift to scrub vegetables for the lunch crowd, the talk would turn to the war. Mr. Perelli raged over the stupidity of the higher-ups who allowed the French General Foch to continue as the supreme commander when American boys were doing the worst of the fighting. Only yesterday he'd told her about a friend whose nephew was with the Marine Brigade of the Second Division and had just lost a leg at Belleau Wood.

But today she snatched the last customer's cup of coffee from him, scribbled out his bill, took his money, tossed her apron in the laundry basket in the back room, and dashed out the door, waving a hasty good-bye to Mrs. Perelli. A half hour later, out of breath and damp with perspiration, she hurried through the front door of headquarters and into the small office on the ground floor where Paula was going over lists of names.

"Miss Paul and Lucy have gone on ahead," she said as an automobile horn sounded, and she dashed into the hall, pulled open the door. "That's the first of our transportation," she said to Kate over her shoulder. "Run upstairs, will you, and tell whoever's up there to hurry?"

Before Kate was halfway up the stairs, women were coming down, and she watched them rush outside and pile into the three touring cars. Paula motioned to her, and Kate followed her outside. They checked off the occupants of each car against a list. As soon as the cars pulled away from the curb, three cabs drew up. More women came out of the house, pinning on hats, carrying umbrellas. Paula and Kate climbed into the last cab.

Sitting on the jump seat next to Virginia, whose mother had volunteered to care for her two kids for the day, Kate joined in the laughter as someone in the back seat complained the breeze was ruining her hairdo. But the laughter disappeared as quickly as it had erupted and the women went back to nervously twisting the handles of their purses, chewing on their lips, rhythmically patting their gloved hands together.

The convoy drew up at the east side of the Capitol, where a dozen women were already waiting. Paula gathered the group together, and the women followed her up the broad stone steps and into the marbled rotunda, out of the rain.

This was Kate's first time in the Capitol, and she gawked like a tourist at the frescos lining the inside of the dome towering overhead, squinted at the huge oils depicting historic moments along the walls. Someone grabbed her hand, pulled her along through a blur of Williamsburg blue and green halls, more frescoed ceilings, then up a narrow staircase, down another hall until they came to a door guarded by a uniformed man with gray hair. Paula spoke to him. He nodded, opened the door, and gestured for the women to enter.

Kate stood on the top step, gazed down at the Senate Chamber. The walls appeared to be covered by tan, drab-looking damask and were divided into panels by tall columns and pilasters of dull, reddish-gray marble. Below, the rows of the senators' cherry wood desks were arranged in semicircles so that they faced the dais, which was framed by marble columns. The only light came from chandeliers high above the Senate floor, giving it a shadowy appearance. As she started down the stairs to join Paula and Olivia, already seated in the front row, she was surprised to see that, except for her group and a dozen other women whom she didn't recognize, the gallery was all but empty.

Kate sat at the end of the row, next to an aisle. Removing her gloves, she leaned over the railing to see what was going on. So far only a few senators were at their desks, most of them reading newspapers. She saw two men in the back, talking—one of them Senator Jones, the other a slim, gray-haired man in a dark blue, cutaway jacket and stiff round collar. Kate leaned toward Paula. "Who's the man with Jones?"

"Reed from Missouri. A 'no' vote. Claims suffrage is strictly a state issue," she said.

Behind the two men, other senators were coming through double doors in the rear of the Chamber, and Kate was astonished when she realized one of them was Mr. Shafroth. Senator Shafroth, whom her father had said had worked for her release from Occoquan. Except for a bit of a paunch, he looked just as she remembered him from last summer at the Grand Lake regatta: slightly over six feet, broad shouldered with a thick shock of unruly, sandy hair. She'd always thought of him as the uncle she'd never had. He played tennis with her father, had been a pallbearer at Granddad's funeral. She'd played croquet with his sons. When she was little, he used to hoist her on his shoulders and parade her around. She elbowed Paula, pointed him out. "There's a 'yes' vote for sure. I grew up with his kids."

Paula's eyes flashed with amusement. "You don't say. I'll have to add that to his file. Up to now, it only lists Shafroth as a lawyer, former governor, two-term congressman, co-sponsor of the Shafroth/Palmer Amendment. Now we can add the interesting fact that Kate Brennan grew up with his kids."

Kate flushed. She'd seen the file boxes containing cards on every congressman and senator: names of family members, religious preference, schools attended, income, voting record—particularly regarding suffrage and temperance. It was all there. A few cards were said to contain notations of extramarital love affairs. But she'd never bothered to look at a one of them.

Paula leaned closer. "And I presume you know he's one of the senators up for reelection and one of our targets. I'd like to think he'll vote 'yes' today. But I wouldn't be surprised if the pressure from the leadership is enough to make him back down. Give a little here, get a little there. These fellows are masters at it."

Kate studied John Shafroth as he talked with several senators. She'd heard her mother describe him as a diamond in the rough, one of those people who earned your trust instinctively. Kate hoped Paula was wrong about his giving in to political pressure.

A half-dozen more senators wandered in and made their way to their desks. Newspapers were put aside. Kate became aware of latecomers taking their seats across the aisle, and she turned, looking for Miss Paul and Lucy and saw them sitting toward the top of the gallery. A moment later, conversations stopped as a large, heavy man with silver hair started toward the podium. A gavel sounded. The mood in the high-ceilinged room tensed. Kate and every other woman in the gallery hunched forward as the Senate was called to order.

After the invocation, seats were resumed, the Chamber settled itself. As a clerk read the journal of yesterday's proceedings, Senator Jones, seated in the second row, twisted around and whispered to the man directly behind him. Mr. Shafroth strolled to the back of the room. Across the aisle, Senator Reed from Missouri concentrated on his newspaper. Kate wondered what was actually going on as the journal was approved by a voice vote.

Her frustration only grew as one piece of minutia after another was taken up: a one week leave of absence for two senators whose names Kate didn't catch, one to attend to pressing personal business, the other to engage in the Liberty Loan campaign. A letter from the Provost Marshall was read into the record, regarding the status of young men between the ages of eighteen and twenty-one appointed to West Point and Annapolis.

Kate crossed and recrossed her legs, surveyed the room. Mr. Shafroth had returned to his desk and was doodling on the margins of a newspaper. Jones was nowhere in sight. An hour passed. Jones had returned but made no move to ask to be recognized. Another senator moved for consideration of Senate Bill 712 for the purpose of amending the act that regulated the construction of dams across waterways used for interstate commerce.

Kate felt the boredom settle over the Chamber. Perhaps Miss Paul and Lucy Burns had been misinformed about the prospect for debate. The only sign of things to come was when Senator Jones glanced up and scanned the faces in the gallery, perhaps searching for Miss Paul, then look away.

Finally, a few minutes past three, he rose and was recognized. "Mr. President, I move that Joint Resolution 200, proposing an amendment to the Constitution of the United States extending the right of suffrage to women be placed on the calendar."

The gallery stirred. Kate sat forward again.

Senator Reed gave the lapels of his suit jacket a tug, pushed to his feet. "Point of order, Mr. President."

Kate felt an elbow in her side, glanced at Paula who whispered in her ear. "Here we go. Reed's the leader of the opposition."

"The chair recognizes Senator Reed."

Kate held her breath as the handsome senator glanced about the Chamber. "Mr. President, with all due respect to the esteemed senator from New Mexico, I believe H.B. Bill 1432, which holds the fate of millions of America's finest men risking their lives daily on our behalf, stands before the Senate as unfinished business."

Senator Jones stepped forward "Mr. President—"

"The chair recognizes Senator Jones."

"Mr. President, I assure the honorable senator from Missouri I am not ignorant of—"

"Mr. President," Senator Reed interrupted. "I am sure I do not have to remind the honorable senator from New Mexico that at this moment we are within one day of the end of the fiscal year. More importantly, we stand at a crossroads in our battle against the Hun. To give precedence to any other matter when monies for our armed services are in jeopardy . . ." He paused as if for dramatic effect.

Kate shot a glance toward Senator Jones, held her breath. Not a woman in the gallery moved.

"Mr. President, I move to postpone indefinitely consideration of the amendment for woman's suffrage," said the senator from Missouri. The question was called. The ayes had it. Senator Reed nodded and went back to the matter of the appropriation bill.

Kate sat back, stunned. From gavel to vote, the suffrage amendment had been dispensed with in less than five minutes. How Mr. Shafroth or any of the other senators might have voted had they been given the chance, she would never know. Apparently, nothing Lucy and Miss Paul had said, none of the mailings sent to constituents, none of the picketing, not even their imprisonment had made a difference or changed a single mind. A rage began to build inside her, rising with the steadiness of mercury in a thermometer. She'd been a naïve, trusting fool—a child. Never again would she believe that the justice of the amendment was enough for it to carry the day.

Chapter 13

Lucy and Alice chose to walk back to the headquarters. Over the years they'd discovered the calming influence of the wooded Mall. They didn't talk. There was no need. They both knew the decision to bury the amendment once again had been made days ago in the smoke-filled back rooms. Aside from Senator Jones, not a single "yes" vote had stood to demand the floor to object. Not one.

As they approached the house, they knew the women who'd witnessed the debacle were waiting for them. No matter how many battles were fought, defeat was hard to take. Following Alice in through the front door to the empty foyer, Lucy wasn't surprised to hear the angry voices from the floor above.

She and Alice exchanged glances, and Alice moved to the stairs. She paused for a moment, one hand on the newel post, and glanced at Lucy before she started up the stairs. Lucy couldn't remember how many times she'd seen Alice pull her shoulders back, as she was doing now, and go at it again. Before she reached the second floor, she was already ordering food to be brought in, the dining room table to be cleared of the latest mailing.

Lucy followed. Silverware and napkins and clothes were already on the tables, chairs placed around. She saw Kate and waved for her to help move two more tables together. All the while, arms folded, Alice stood by the fireplace like a pint-sized general, urging on her troops. In a matter of a few moments, she had transformed a room full of anger into resolve. The NWP was back on track.

Within half an hour, the meal appeared. Deviled ham sandwiches, hard-boiled eggs, potato salad, celery, carrot sticks. Eyes blazed anew as the women Lucy had come to know ate, sipped at wine intended for a celebration, and made plans. She knew the next move was hers, and she stood. "Well." She surveyed the room with what she hoped was a triumphant smile. "I think it's safe to say Mr. Jones botched his chance."

Clapping, laughter. As if on cue, heads automatically turned to Alice. Not moving from where she stood, she pushed back the sleeves of her French blue chiffon dress and leaned her elbows on the table. "If the Senate Democrats cannot see the value of moving on the amendment, we have no choice but to take the next step."

Wine glasses paused midair.

"For a beginning, it's high time our senators received their fair share of picketing and newspaper attention." Alice glanced around the room. She had everyone's attention.

"But the central focus will be on the home front—" She turned to Lucy and smiled.

Lucy had seen that smile work its magic hundreds of times. Turned on and off as easily as an electric light. Even on her. There had been times when Lucy had felt used as a trusted servant was used. But Alice seemed oblivious.

"This is Lucy's bailiwick, of course. The state committee chairmen will be the key. It is through them that we will organize for the primaries and the general elections."

"What about mailings?" Paula asked as she passed a platter of lemon cake slices around the table.

"Of course. Mailings must continue. And as you may have noticed, the articles in *The Suffragist* are more and more frequently picked up by newspapers across the country." Alice wiped her fingers on her napkin and smoothed it across her lap. "Ladies, I cannot emphasize strongly enough that you must not allow today to discourage you." Her brown eyes traveled from one face to the next. "Men like Reed are counting on that. But surrender is out of the question because we are the ones with right on our side."

"And Jesus Christ," someone said.

Lucy caught Alice's reaction, the cool eyes above the smile. She didn't like to be upstaged. "I'm sure we can use any help that comes our way," Alice said—a Quaker, who Lucy guessed had never spent much time on Jesus. "But, tonight, let's relax a little. We've got a first-class battle ahead of us."

Conversation started up, the click of silverware in the background. Then chairs scraping against wood flooring. Plates and leftover food were taken to the kitchen. By nine o'clock, aside from Alice, who had gone up to her office, Lucy and Kate were the only women in the house. And together they moved the last of the tables and chairs back to their usual places.

Lucy walked over to the staircase to the third floor, eased down onto the bottom step, closed her eyes, and leaned her head against the rungs of the railing. The muscles along the base of her neck ached with exhaustion. Just the thought of walking back to her apartment made her decide to treat herself to a cab if she could find one.

"Can I get you something, Lucy?" Kate's voice.

Lucy opened her eyes, summoned a smile. "Thanks, but I was just getting my energy together to go home."

Kate sat down cross-legged on the floor before her. "You knew, didn't you? You and Miss Paul. You knew nothing would happen today."

"Strongly suspected. But hope springs eternal."

Kate leaned forward, her elbows on her knees, intense. "How can you be so calm?"

"Who says I'm calm. Tired, yes. Calm, no." She got up slowly and brushed off the back of her skirt. "Right now, I'm going to find myself a cab and go home and I suggest you do the same."

"I'll walk out with you," Kate said.

Outside, standing with Kate in the growing dark, the hum of the city in the background, Lucy glanced up the street, empty but for a single pair of headlights and decided to walk over to the Hay-Adam where she was bound to find a cab.

"What I don't understand is how you can keep on, Lucy? I mean, after all these years . . ."

Lucy glanced at Kate, laughed. "My Lord, you make me sound like Methuselah." Lucy put a hand on Kate's slender arm. "What you need to do is cheer up. Tomorrow will look a lot brighter." But even as she said it, Lucy wasn't totally sure she believed it.

❧⚜❧

As Lucy let herself in her apartment, she thought of Kate's remark about her age, the inference that Lucy was an ancient, battle-scarred warrior. She told herself that at forty, she still had the energy she'd had at twenty. And most days she did. But one good look in the mirror at the strands of gray in with the red and she knew better. And her attitude had changed. She'd become cynical, frustrated lately. For more years than she cared to remember, she had been battling wrongs with a vengeance. There were times when she wondered if she—and Alice—had offered more than they could deliver. Still, wasn't that better than offering nothing at all?

What the NWP needed was new blood—girls like Kate, young enough to flaunt the rules and let the Devil take the hindmost. Like when all those years ago she'd kicked the bobby in his privates when she and Alice and the Pankhursts were picketing Parliament.

Lucy felt for the switch on the wall just inside the door and flicked it on. On the hall table was a small pile of mail left by Mrs. Ells, her colored housekeeper who came in three times a week to clean and take care of the laundry. Not much older than Lucy. A grandmother, somehow bringing up four grandchildren on her small salary.

Last Christmas Edith Houghton, one of Lucy's friends from Oxford wrote a card with news that she was soon to be a grandmother. It had come as a shock, a reminder of the years that had passed. She and Edith had gone separate ways: Edith to marriage and family, Lucy to fighting the good fight. If she had any regret it was John Chandler.

With his chiseled face set off by a short-cropped black beard and brilliant dark brown eyes, he'd had had the looks of a matinee idol. She had met him at a party given by the Pankhursts. Then, she'd been ten pounds slimmer but with the same clear, fresh skin, minus the freckles that plagued redheads. That night she'd worn a deep-necked green dinner dress that showed off her hair and her breasts.

Emmeline had seated her next to John. From the start, they'd fallen into easy conversation. He told her he was a graduate of Eton, with a first from Oxford in early French literature, that he had a passion for opera. That night he asked her opinion of the new opera, "Le Jongleur de Notre Dame," by Massenat and, by dessert, they were debating reviewers' comments that had appeared in *The London Times*.

It wasn't until the men excused themselves for cigars and brandy and the ladies repaired to the drawing room to sip their coffee, that Lucy had a chance to corner Emmeline and ask her about this John Chandler. They sat on a loveseat off to themselves and Lucy learned that he was the only child of an eccentric widower who had made his fortune in shipbuilding and was a member of Parliament. With his father's failing health, John was expected to stand in his father's place at the next election, and Emmeline wanted his support for the cause of women's suffrage.

"So you see, my dear, as delighted as I am that you find John Chandler attractive," Emmeline had said smiling over the rim of her gold-rimmed Lemoges demi-tasse cup. "Your job this weekend is to work on him."

During the next three days with John Chandler, Lucy had talked up the importance of the woman's vote and fallen in love with him, and he with her. The memories of that weekend would haunt her forever: laughing in pure joy as they strode, hand in hand, her skirt trailing in the sopping grass through a meadow edged with cowslip and wood violets, the ride in the donkey cart into the village for afternoon tea at the hotel, so ancient its wide-planked floors tilted at an angle.

The following four months became a blur. Lucy went back to her studies. Christmas was spent with John and the Pankhursts in London. There were late dinners after the theater, the opera. John proposed marriage and talked of sailing the family yacht to southern Spain for their honeymoon. Yet he never mentioned taking her to meet his father. She supposed John feared a confrontation over an American girl who had no fortune and took an interest in women's suffrage would shatter the old man's frail health. A month passed, then two. Their letters to one another became less frequent, and Lucy prepared herself for disappointment, as if all along, she'd had a sixth sense that their marriage was not to be.

That same spring the Pankhursts formed the Woman's Social and Political Union. When Lucy received Winnie's note that a march was scheduled for London in the working-class district of Dalston, Lucy wanted to be part of it. She hadn't expected the fierce reaction. The police stepped in quickly and forcefully. That was the night she met Alice.

The next day the arrests hit the headlines, just as Emmeline Pankhurst had hoped they might. After that notoriety, Lucy saw John only two other times—once in Edinburgh, where she was organizing a chapter of the WSPU. He had been friendly enough, polite, but she wasn't surprised six months later when she read of his betrothal to a Lady Sarah Crossen, whose family supposedly traced its roots back to Henry II. Lucy still thought of him. Yet she could no longer remember the feel of his lips on hers.

Lucy walked into the kitchen, switched on the light, and reached in the icebox for the glass pitcher of water she kept there in preference to the lukewarm stuff that came out of the tap. She took a glass out of the cupboard above the sink, filled it full, and took several large swallows.

As she stood at the sink and stared out into the dark beyond the open kitchen window, she thought about her family, but, mostly her sisters. Though they watched their words on the few occasions they were together these days, she knew they harbored doubts about her work. *Lucy always was the impatient one, wasn't she? Any other woman with her education would be tickled pink to have snagged a good teaching position. But, no, off she goes to Europe for more studies and ends up doing Lord only knows what?* Except they knew all too well what she was doing. That was the problem.

Next summer, if the elections went according to her plan, she'd rent a place on the Maine coast. Her younger sisters would come. They liked the ocean and were strong swimmers. Or perhaps she should spend the time with her mother at the old house in Brooklyn. She was getting on in years. The servants weren't always reliable. And the house reeked of old age and African violets.

For months now, Lucy had been toying with the idea of arranging for the entire family to come to Washington over the Christmas recess, maybe stay until the inauguration of the new Congress. They'd go to concerts, a play or two. The zoo would be open. Yet that didn't solve the problem of her mother. If she moved here, Lucy would have to find a bigger apartment, perhaps a house. Georgetown might be perfect. Not city, but not country either. Reasonably close to headquarters. She'd ask Mrs. Ells to live in.

Buoyed by the possibilities, Lucy put her glass in the sink, turned off the light, and headed for bed.

Chapter 14 ———————————————

Monday morning the air was fresh and blessedly cooler as Kate washed and dressed. After two nights of tossing and turning, unable to let go of her anger over the tabling of the amendment, she could do with a good dose of the jokes and neighborhood gossip the regulars at Perelli's always passed along.

Outside, the milkman waved and smiled as he deposited milk bottles on the front stoop, and her spirits rose. She realized how hungry she was as she walked toward the café. Her mouth watered at the thought of a plate of sausage, eggs, and a thick slice of fresh bread after the first rush of customers was over. Up ahead were the usual three early customers waiting out, but as she came closer, instead of smiles, she saw tears brimming in their eyes.

"The boy," they said in unison.

She looked from one to the other. "Vic? Vic Perelli?"

"Anthony says the telegram come last night," one man said, glancing toward Mr. Glorioso who nodded.

"Dominic and I were playing chess like always when it comes. From Victor's captain." The small, white-haired man drew a large, snowy handkerchief out of a back pant's pocket and gave his nose a good blow. "It says how Victor died. In the Battle of Chateau Thierry."

The grieving old man looked at her as if she would know what to do next, and she gave him a hug, opened the door and held it to let them all file slowly past her, hats clutched in their hands. In the kitchen Mr. Perelli was standing over his wife, hunched in a battered chair by the stove. Both were sobbing.

Kate glanced around the kitchen. On the stove, the oversized frying pan filled with sausage was sizzling. The huge blackened coffee pot was boiling over. The aroma of the baking bread warned her that it was ready to come out of the oven. She walked to the stove, reached for one of the spatulas that dangled among assorted forks and spoons over the stove, flipped the sausages, and shoved the pan off the heat. As she was taking the four pans of bread from the oven and placing them to cool on racks, she heard the sound of a door opening and closing. She left the kitchen to tell customers that no breakfast would be served and why, then returned and arranged the food on plates for the Perellis and the three early customers.

That done, Kate was at a loss. The sight of the weeping Perellis made her uneasy. She'd never seen other adults weep in public, particularly not a man. If Tom, God forbid, was killed, her parents would offer callers solemn smiles, thank them for coming, and retreat to their bedroom for their grieving. She didn't know how to handle the emotion that overwhelmed the steamy kitchen. Against her will, Kate felt tears welling in her eyes, and she blinked them back.

Once the three customers said their good-byes, she forced herself to go over to the Perellis, hug them, feeling awkward as she mumbled inadequate sorries. When Mr. Perelli finally guided his wife up the steep stairs to their apartment above the café, Kate put the food away in the icebox, washed the few dishes, the pots and pans. As she went out the door, she hung the Closed sign in the window.

Not to her surprise, she found Mr. Glorioso waiting for her. "You are a good girl, Kate. You are family."

He cupped his work-worn hands lightly around her face, his dark eyes glistening with tears, and she offered a weak smile, said, "Did I ever tell you that I have a brother in France who's a flier?"

Mr. Glorioso shook his head. "You worry about him?"

Kate nodded, not mentioning the dream she had that Tom was flying at night and lost his way, ran out of gas before he found a field, crashed. "Will the Perellis reopen, do you think?"

"What else is there to do but work?"

"If you see them, please tell them—"

"That you will be here next Monday just like always. They know already." And with a little wave, he shuffled off down the street. Watching him, the image of the Perellis in their grief returned and she had the same empty feeling she'd had when her granddad died.

❦

Kate dragged into headquarters. The fewer people she had to talk to the better. As she'd been riding over on the streetcar, she'd had the growing feeling that Victor's death was an omen that the life she'd put together in the last two months was about to change. But she needed time by herself to figure it out and, with a stack of the latest issue of *The Suffragist* and a box of envelopes to stuff them in, she headed toward a corner of the mailroom. She was just untying the string around the papers when Virginia Swift leaned through the doorway with the news that Miss Paul was looking for her.

"Any idea why?" Kate asked.

"All she said was that you were to meet her and Lucy at Senator Jones's office at ten-thirty."

Kate glanced at her watch. She had twenty-five minutes. After Saturday's debacle on the Senate floor, Miss Paul probably wanted to strike while the shame of what Senator Jones had failed to do for the amendment was still fresh in his mind. Kate guessed the reason she'd been summoned was that she was still the only member at headquarters who hailed from west of the Mississippi. Straightening her hat as she dashed outside again, Kate decided that the only way she could be on time was to part with the cost of a cab.

Kate pushed open the heavy doors to the Senate office building, ran down the marble hall. Holding her skirt out of the way, she took the stairs two at a time to the second floor where she found Miss Paul and Lucy waiting outside the entrance to Senator Jones's office. Kate barely had a chance to catch her breath before Miss Paul pulled open the door, gave only the barest of nods to the receptionist, and led them down the hall and into the senator's office.

The robust senator rose as they entered and smiled as if unsurprised by their sudden appearance, as if Saturday had never happened. "Miss Paul, Miss Burns. Miss—"

"Brennan," Kate said.

"Of course." He glanced from Miss Paul and Lucy. "An unexpected pleasure," he said, busying himself with drawing three chairs up to his desk.

Once seated, Alice Paul fixed him with a steely look. "Senator, I'm sure you know why we are here."

"I understand your disappointment," he said, sweat trickling down the sides of his square face as he settled in his high-backed chair. "Yet, surely, you realize the turn of events was unavoidable."

Without comment, Miss Paul met his gaze. "How soon do you anticipate bringing the amendment to the floor again?"

He pulled at his mustache. "A difficult question."

"It seems pretty straightforward to me."

"You must understand how these things work. The measure on curbing war profiteering that will be coming out of committee and—"

Alice Paul recrossed her legs. "To be sure. Nevertheless, the question remains. How soon do you anticipate bringing the amendment to the floor again?"

The senator sat forward, rested his clasped hands on the desk. "May I be frank?"

"We wouldn't have it any other way."

"I have just been told that the amendment will not be placed on the Senate calendar again during this session."

Kate sucked in a quick breath, shot a look toward Miss Paul and waited for her response. "That is the final word?" Her voice was cool, controlled.

"I'm afraid so. Yes."

"Even though the President is now pushing for the amendment?" Miss Paul said.

Kate stared at her, wondering if she'd heard right. The president pushing for the amendment? Since when? Kate wondered how she could have missed gossip as important as that.

"You do realize, Senator, that such inaction is unacceptable."

"Ladies, I can understand your disappointment, which I share. But what with the war, the way of politics . . ." He looked anxiously from Lucy to Kate and back to Miss Paul.

"Disappointment has nothing to do with it, sir," she said. "The vote is what women in this country deserve and expect to have. Not next year or the year after, but this year. 1918. Election year. If the Senate refuses to act, the voters will." Miss Paul glanced at Lucy and Kate, and they rose as one. "Now you will have to excuse us, Senator. We have work to do."

Kate followed Miss Paul and Lucy out of the office and down the hallway. To passersby, Miss Paul and Lucy—one barely five feet, the other a good head taller—might have looked like tourists. Yet, to Kate, the sound of their heels clicking in synchrony against the marble was clearly the sound of soldiers marching into battle. Two women with hearts strong enough and hides thick enough to go after the most powerful men the country had to offer. Some day, years from now, she'd be able to tell how she'd known them, witnessed their courage first-hand.

❦

Kate didn't get back to Millie's until nearly six thirty that night. She threw her hat in the guestroom and was starting for the kitchen, wondering what to fix for supper, when she heard a knock and went back to the door, opened it.

Facing her was Charlie Harrison, a shy kind of smile on his face. "I was in the neighborhood so I thought I'd stop by."

"Well, hi," she said, not that surprised to see him. "Come in." And she led him into the living room.

Seeing him, standing in the center of the slightly worn carpet, his hands thrust deep into his trouser pockets, his enamel-blue eyes squinting a little, a hopeful look on his face, she decided he was better looking than she remembered.

"I know it's last minute, but I was wondering if you'd like to go to dinner."

She met his smile. "Actually, I'd like that a lot."

"Great! They say Harvey's is good. But any place you want to go is okay with me."

"You choose. I'll get my hat."

One of the newer spots in town, Harvey's was crowded, mostly with men in uniform. She and Charlie had to wait just to reach the mâitre d', who raised an eyebrow as he took in Charlie's civilian clothes and led them to a table next to the kitchen's swinging doors.

"Sorry about this," Charlie said as he seated her. "Sometimes I'm asked for my draft card."

"This is fine. Maybe you ought to wear a badge that says 'government worker,'" Kate said, and he laughed.

They settled their napkins on their laps, looked at each other, smiled. Kate was reaching for a topic of conversation when Charlie placed his elbows on the table, leaned toward her. "I was wondering . . . The other night you said you worked for the NWP but you didn't say what you do there."

She grinned. "Between the two of us, I mostly stuff envelopes."

"Seriously?"

"But recently I did tag along with Miss Paul and Miss Burns when they tried to convince what I'd call a lily-livered senator to do his duty by the amendment."

"Lily-livered? I like it!" He threw back his head, guffawed, and, the ice broken, they sat back and picked up their menus. Kate was deciding among the entrees that were the least expensive when Charlie said, "I remember you said you were at Occoquan."

She lowered the menu. "For fourteen days. Filthy. Cruel. It ought to be wiped off the face of the earth. Prisoners are treated like animals. No one sent there could come out and still believe in justice."

He looked at her hard as if trying to see inside her.

"The worst of it was being sent there in the first place. The judge denied us an attorney. We were given no trial. Our civil rights were tossed aside as if they didn't exist. And I seriously doubt obstructing a public sidewalk—that was the charge—warrants a prison sentence." Shaken by her vehemence, she turned back to the menu, noticing that her hands were shaking, and the conversation turned to the weather.

By the time their dinner of pork chops, mashed potatoes, and green beans—completely covered with congealed milk gravy—arrived, a small band made up of a saxophone, a violin, and a bass had assembled and was playing a tango. An older couple stepped onto the tiny dance floor, laughing as they attempted the dance. Kate and Charlie watched them as they ate. There was no point in trying to talk over the music.

After dinner, they stood outside in the fading evening light, out of the way of passersby. Kate pulled on her gloves, enjoying the breeze that had come up and might relieve the sultry heat, and Charlie settled his fedora on his head. Frowning, he apologized for the terrible dinner, the service, the noise. When she said it didn't matter, that she'd enjoyed herself, he smiled at her with something like gratitude and suggested Charlie Chaplin's new movie *A Dog's Life*, which had just opened at the Orpheum, though he was afraid the theater might be hot.

"Then, how about a walk?" Kate glanced up at the darkening sky and the sheet-like look of the clouds, heavy and leaden. "It might rain later, but, at least, there's a breeze. And the Mall is only a block away."

Crossing the street, Charlie took her hand as if it were the most natural thing in the world to do, then let it go as they stepped up onto the curb again. She felt easy with him and still a little guilty about her outburst when he'd asked about Occoquan. Side by side, they slowly wound through the block of dingy brown, rectangular buildings, some of the temporary space for the burgeoning Washington bureaucracy that had sprung up with the war. When they came to one in the center, no different from the others, he pointed it out as the place where he worked.

Looking at it, she said, "Am I wrong or did you say your job had changed lately?"

"It has, yeah. Now with the Espionage Act, seems they want us to gather material about groups dangerous to the war effort."

"Like Germans."

"Germans and pacifists. Socialists. People who speak out against the government. We monitor German newspapers, for instance." He took her arm, and they walked on toward the trees. "My boss might send me to Wisconsin or South Dakota to check out reports of what a group with members who are German-born has been up to. I write it up, hand it on to my boss, who decides what to pass on to the newspapers or the higher-ups."

"I had no idea," Kate said, placing a hand on her skirt to keep it from being whipped by the wind that had come up. "Or that you understood German."

"I don't, but a couple of guys in the department do."

Bits of trash mixed with leaves from the beech trees lining the pathway filled the air, and Kate used her other hand to clutch her hat. "Maybe this wasn't such a good idea after all," she said with a laugh.

Charlie held out his hand, palm up. "Rain. Looks like we ought to head back to Millie's before this storm breaks. Our best bet for a cab is probably Harvey's." He took her arm again. "Come on. Let's make a run for it."

By the time they reached the restaurant, the rain was coming down in sheets. Charlie told her to stand beneath the overhang, and he sprinted down the sidewalk, signaling cabs that drove by as he went—but with no success—until he rounded the corner and disappeared from view.

Still out of breath, Kate hugged herself against the damp and thought of their conversation. If she had understood what he'd said, his office investigated—*he* investigated—anyone who took exception with the government. The NWP certainly qualified. For all she knew, he might have told his boss that he'd met a member of the NWP and had been assigned to find out what he could from her that might be useful. The realization bothered her more than a little and she was trying to decide whether to say anything about it when a cab drew up, sending a whoosh of water up over the curb. A door opened, and Charlie climbed out. Rain streaming off the brim of his hat, a pleased grin on his face, he ran over to her.

Inside the cab, they took off their hats, shook them. Charlie gave the cabbie Millie's address, folded his coat collar back in place, sat back. "Boy! What a night!"

She glanced at him. "Charlie, while I was waiting, I thought about what you said, about your job—how you investigate people who take exception to the government—and I was wondering—does that include the NWP?"

He looked at her as he slicked back his wet hair with both hands. "I can't say."

"You mean you're not allowed to say," and, before he could comment she added, "But it's entirely possible that one of your people—you—could have been watching the mob that attacked the picketers in front of the White House that Sunday in June. Could have been in the back of the room at the police station and witnessed the joke of a hearing."

Charlie shook his head. "I was in Baltimore that day."

"So you weren't involved in any way?"

"No."

Kate shifted her gaze to the rain-spattered window for a moment, vaguely conscious of the odor of wet clothes and hair. She wanted to believe him. She could tolerate being perceived as unpatriotic and subverting the war effort by senators or even the President. But for this man whom she liked—liked quite a lot—to be the equivalent of a spy, part of the system that had sent her and the women who had become her friends to Occoquan was another matter. She looked back at him. "Nevertheless, someone else from the CPI might have been there."

"Anything is possible."

The cab slowed, pulled over to the curb. Kate glanced out the window, saw Millie's row house. "This is it," she said to the cabbie, and Charlie dug into his pant's pocket, drew out several coins, handed them to the cabbie, and pushed open the door. He climbed out, extended his hand to Kate who took it, and they dashed up the stone steps, slick with rain, and into the foyer.

Upstairs, Kate handed Charlie the key and he opened the door. But she didn't go in right away.

"It's hard to believe, isn't it?" she said, raising her chin, fighting to hide her emotions and keep her voice under control.

He looked down at her, waited.

"I mean what strange times these are when perfectly decent Americans keep track of other decent Americans solely because they question the government."

"We're at war, Kate."

"As well I know. Not just in France, Charlie, but here at home—the war the NWP is fighting—and it's every bit as important."

"Kate—"

She held up her hand. "No. Please. You have your job. I have mine. So let's call it a night." And she stepped backward into the apartment, thanked him for dinner, and said good-bye.

Chapter 15

The next day Lucy strode through the headquarters' front door at 14 Jackson Place, waved a hello to Paula Jacobi bent over a table strewn with mailing lists, and climbed the stairs to the second floor. A board meeting was scheduled for ten in Alice's office. Lucy had just enough time to check in with the Maryland committee chairman, who was supposed to have arrived yesterday by train.

Last night's rain had finally broken the heat, and Lucy had had her first decent night's sleep in a week. She felt rejuvenated, like her old self. Her mind brimmed with strategies. Yesterday when Jones claimed the Amendment wouldn't come up again this session was the last straw. Not even Alice's veiled promise to replace Democrats seemed to faze him. It was time for action.

Walking down the hall, Lucy waved to the girls typing out press releases in what had been a music room. Next door, the long worktables in the living room, whose walls still held the French Directoire mirrors from earlier days, were stacked with literature, ready for the state committees. A familiar figure, standing at the far end of the room where the Senate file information was kept, was staring at the oversized poster filled with photos of the members of the Senate. "Kate?"

She turned, a distracted yet intent look on her face and came over to where Lucy was standing. "I was doing some homework."

"I can see that." Lucy studied the young woman Alice had described as "having potential, if a little vague on issues." Alice was wrong. Kate knew the issues. She was even getting a handle on the nuances behind them. And today there was a special urgency about her.

Lucy eyed the display of senators' solemn faces on the wall behind them. "Looks like a rogues' gallery, doesn't it?"

"As of this morning, I've memorized everyone up to the P's. The next time you and Miss Paul visit another senator and want me to come along, I intend to be prepared."

"You do know there'll be an exam first."

Kate hesitated for only a second before she laughed. Yet the dark green eyes above her generous mouth flashed with such determination that Lucy almost felt sorry for those senators.

"Or consider this." Lucy put her arm around Kate's shoulders. "I've come up with a new plan to attract the newspapers' attention. Five or six of us will dress up in those horrible outfits we wore in prison and stand on a flatbed decorated with our banners. We're going to call it the Occoquan Prison Express. First stop: Baltimore. Then we'll branch out to Pittsburgh, head west, hit the state fairs and assemblies. What do you think?"

Kate nodded but without much enthusiasm, Lucy thought.

"From that look on your face, I'm guessing a parade's not what you had in mind."

"Now that we're about to picket the Senate—if I had my choice— I'd rather not leave Washington," Kate said.

"You realize we can be hauled off to prison again."

"If we are, we are," Kate said matter-of-factly.

"But why risk prison when nothing may come of it, which, you have to admit, it didn't this last time?" Lucy asked, pushing her.

"I'm not sure I'd agree."

"Oh?" Lucy leaned against the doorframe and eyed her speculatively.

"Last night, I discovered that the Committee on Public Information could have us under surveillance. Every time we picket, one of their investigators is snooping around, watching and taking notes. I wouldn't be surprised if those reports land on the President's desk. That may be one reason the President hasn't changed his mind."

"Could be."

"You're not surprised? You knew about them?" Kate asked, wide-eyed.

"The CPI? Sure. They think of themselves as counterespionage."

"And you're not outraged?" Kate asked.

Lucy gestured with her head toward the poster board of photographs. "Aren't we doing the same thing with our file?"

"Absolutely not. We simply want to know whom we're dealing with. It's not the same at all. We have no power. The government does, and it's out to deny us our civil rights."

"Kate, if we lived in a just world, the amendment would have passed years ago." Lucy placed a hand on the slender girl's shoulder. A newcomer with a great deal to learn. Yet the necessary passion was there in spades. And she seemed to have a relish for the political game, an attribute too valuable to overlook. Now might be the right time to fill her in on some thoughts she'd had about organizing the state committees. She was about to suggest coffee and a talk when a voice from upstairs called her name, summoning her to the meeting. And the moment was gone.

❧

Alice was already holding court when Lucy walked into the small office and found a seat by the window.

"As we are all fully aware, it all comes down to finding two votes to give us that two-thirds majority," said Alice, pouring herself a glass of pale iced tea.

"How about stepping up the pressure on the Senate with some picketing?" Lucy threw out.

"I think we ought to concentrate on the local level," the woman next to her said.

Other ideas circled the room. All the while, Alice sat there, arranging and rearranging the folds of her dusty rose, organdy skirt. Lucy knew that only after everyone else had voiced opinions would Alice speak. Coming from good Quaker stock, she'd been raised that way. But Lucy also knew that Alice used the practice to her advantage, like a whale ingesting schools of fish, she was an expert at using what her lessers could bring her.

"You're right about picketing the Senate, Lucy," Alice said. "But the timing's off. We need to wait until October, just before the elections. What we must do now is put pressure on the President."

"By doing what?" Lucy recrossed her legs and frowned at the dark circles under her friend's eyes. It was hard to remember the Alice Paul of ten years ago with rosy cheeks, before the stints in the London prisons.

"I can't prove it," Alice said, "but I believe that when Jones told us the amendment will not be reconsidered until after the recess, he was delivering a message straight from the White House. That's why we have to put on a full-fledged rally with at least one hundred women from as many states as we can muster."

"In front of the White House again?" Lucy asked.

"I was thinking across the street in the park might be better—at the Lafayette Monument. Close enough to the White House to get good press coverage and far enough to avoid being accused of obstructing a sidewalk." Alice's gaze traveled from one woman to the next as if checking for disagreement, but there were only nods. "At least one hundred members, I think. The first week in August sounds right, giving us nearly a month."

"Still not much time to get something that big together," Lucy put in, just for the record, because she, not Alice, would be held accountable for the organization.

"In the meantime," Alice continued as if she hadn't heard, "we'll push the Republicans to come out for the amendment."

Eyebrows shot up.

"Oh, I know: Senator Lodge is opposed to the amendment," Alice said. "But, in this case, we will approach him as the Senate minority leader, and ask him to call for a caucus. Lodge is a practical man. I'm confident he will see that it is in the best interests of his party to come out in support of the amendment."

Lucy watched the other women, eyes fixed on Alice, listening to her with all their hearts. They would follow her into Hell if she asked them.

"So." Alice pushed back from her desk, rose. "We're in agreement. Now let's get back to work."

After everyone had left, Lucy sat back, stretched. "Went well, don't you think?'"

"M-m-m."

Lucy shot a glance toward her friend at the lukewarm response. "You sound worn out. Where's that fan of yours?" She could feel the sweat running down between her breasts.

Alice reached beneath a pile of papers on her desk, plucked up the folded paper fan and handed it to her.

Sitting down heavily on the window seat next to the open window, fanning herself, Lucy eyed her friend again. "Okay, it's time to tell me what's bothering you."

"I'm worried, Luce. The next few weeks are crucial."

"Agreed. According to the morning papers, the Germans think so, too. Right now, the war is the biggest obstacle to passing the amendment. The Senate will do its best to continue to use it as an excuse." Lucy shifted to the Morris chair someone had donated that was closer to Alice, propped her feet on the footstool, and continued to fan herself. "So what to do?"

"I don't know. That's the worst of it." Alice slumped against the back of the high-backed swivel chair, her slender arms on the wooden armrests. "At least, the money's coming in. Mrs. Belmont is doing wonders for us." She sighed. "The trouble is, you can't depend on them—the Democrats or the Republicans. Least of all, Lodge. What I said earlier to the contrary, the southerners are the worst. Change isn't a word in their vocabulary. Think of how many bills have died at their hands, including denying the Negro his civil rights. It's no wonder we're at a stalemate. The Confederacy lost the Civil War, but the South rules the country today."

She tilted back. "As if we don't have enough to handle, there's the women's peace delegation to deal with. Jane Addams, Miss Rankin, Mrs. Catt. They tell me there's to be a meeting. I'm for peace and they know it. But first things first. Why can't they wait until the amendment is passed to tackle the peace? Everything else comes second. Don't they see that?" Alice closed her eyes.

Lucy regarded her friend she'd shared so much with. "Can I get you an aspirin?"

Alice opened her eyes. "You tend to fuss too much, Luce. Did I ever tell you that?"

"Once or twice, yes. But this is no time to cave in on me, friend." Lucy got up and went over to pat Alice on the shoulder. There were days when she felt like a sturdy Mother Superior, except Alice wasn't a novice who could be told what to do. One way or the other, they were joined at the hip: two not-very-old maids with a cause that left no room in their lives for anything else. "If you're up to it, we should go over that list of Democrats up for reelection." She walked into the hall. "I'll get it."

In her office, Lucy pulled open the file drawer that contained the list, her mind still on Alice. To anyone else, she appeared the tower of strength, undaunted by the mounting pressure to produce the Promise. Yet Lucy knew about the headaches and the demons that hounded her friend. Whatever she did, Alice viewed it as never good enough. It was a sickness. Another bout of depression like the one that hit her last year could be a disaster.

Chapter 16 ⸙

Her father's note still in her hands, a cigarette dangling from her lips, Kate stopped prowling around the apartment and gazed out the open window to the nearly deserted street. Across the way, an American flag flown in honor of the Fourth of July hung from the roof of Ripley's meat market, limp in the heavy air. Millie had left an hour ago, with bathing suit and towel in a canvas bag, headed for the beach along the Tidal Basin where she was to meet Joe somebody, another lieutenant—presumably, a replacement for Phil, who had been ordered to Boston before being shipped overseas.

Kate turned, stabbed her cigarette out in the Coney Island ashtray on the end table, frowned at the yellowing ivy leaves dangling from the pot on the table by the couch—Millie persisted in over-watering—and resumed her pacing. Since it had arrived in yesterday's mail, the note had become a thorn in her side. She unfolded it again, glanced at the check.

> *Dear Kate,*
>   *Your mother wonders if you received her letter.*

Kate sighed.

> *Enclosed is enough for a ticket home if you've changed your mind.*

One hundred dollars. Written on his business account at Denver's International Trust Company. Twice the price of a train ticket even with the cost of a lower berth, if one could be had—the balance way more than what she would make for the rest of the summer at

Perelli's once they reopened. In case I've decided to give up. But he knows better than that.

Otherwise, all is well in the mile high city.

Otherwise covered a lot of territory.

Take care of yourself and keep your nose clean.

Your loving, Dad

She fingered the check. Her father's original sixty dollars was gone, spent for clothes, half the groceries and room rent, carfare. One hundred dollars would go a long way: allow her the luxury of some fall clothes, a decent haircut, a dinner out now and then. She could even make a small donation to NWP. No more worrying about every nickel and dime. The women at headquarters who had a husband or a father—a trust fund—and didn't have to work could afford to give the kind of time Lucy and Miss Paul expected.

Kate put the note back in its envelope, returned to the guest bedroom and tucked it underneath her extra nightgown in the top dresser drawer. Her father had said the money was for a train ticket, which could mean he'd given in to her mother's edict—because that's what it was, though she'd taken pains to cloak it in other words—that Kate was to come home. Or it could be his way of saying he understood—or giving her the rope to hang herself so that she couldn't blame them for holding her back. If she kept the money. And she might.

As it was, the last thing she had time for was fretting about her father. According to the notice posted yesterday, the biggest rally in six years was scheduled for the first Tuesday in August. This is what she'd been waiting for, and Lucy had asked her and Lydie, veterans of Occoquan, to organize it.

Last night, wanting to brag to someone just a little, Kate had told Millie about the plan and Millie just shook her head.

"For God's sake, Kate, what's it going to take, a smack between the eyes with a two-by-four before you smarten up?"

They'd argued. Millie had gone out; Kate had washed a blouse and underthings in the kitchen sink—something Millie hated her doing—and hung them on a piece of clothesline strung from the kitchen window to the edge of the fire escape.

She'd gone to bed, but she hadn't slept. Now, taking her underwear from the line, she found it was still damp. She set up the ironing board, spread her one clean blouse over it, and managed to singe the tail. The day was off to a miserable start, and she left for headquarters in a foul mood.

⁕

The office she and Lydie were to share was the small room on the first floor just off the front door. Lydie had already taken the desk by the window, and Kate had to bite her tongue to keep from asking why she hadn't been consulted about who was to work where. To make matters worse, Lydie informed her cheerily that it would be her job to go through the mailing lists and gather names and addresses and telephone numbers.

"And what will you be doing?" Kate snapped.

If Lydie noticed Kate's bad humor, she ignored it. "Contacting the big shots. Unless you'd rather do that."

Kate pulled in her horns a bit. "No, I'll do the lists."

"You're sure?" Lydie asked.

"Of course, I'm sure. I love lists. All that detail. What could be more thrilling?"

Lydie eyed her. "Have you been drinking? You hate detail." And Kate started to giggle.

Still friends, they ended up splitting the responsibility. One week, then two went by. Lydie, Miss Efficiency herself, went over sheet after sheet of lists, knowing from experience which members to contact first. Notes arrived offering help from women who worked in munitions plants and those just returned from working for the

Red Cross in France. Kate suggested they should lead the rally. The details fell into place. Because Miss Paul wanted at least one hundred women to take part, Kate had contacted every state committee chairman and pleaded for warm bodies. Judging by the promises that poured in, Miss Paul wouldn't be disappointed.

The end of the second week of July, the Perellis reopened the café and Kate went back to work. Vic's photograph, framed in black, was on display on the wall behind the cash register. Mrs. Perelli had lost weight; her husband had aged. Both had large circles beneath their eyes. At first, the old customers were unusually quiet, almost shy, as if uncertain about how to behave around such grief. But, gradually, the laughter returned.

At headquarters, Kate was reminded all over again of Lydie's kindness at Occoquan. Always a ready smile, quick to compliment. No one thought twice about working well past the dinner hour when Lydie asked. Yet she had a sense of when it was time to rest, and she'd insist the two of them take an hour off, and they'd walk to a nearby restaurant for lunch. The proprietors would greet her with open arms and drop everything to serve Lydie first—fussing over her, refilling her coffee cup every other minute. To them, she might as well be a princess. One day, over turkey sandwiches, Kate told her about her adventures learning to wait tables at the Perelli café, and Lydie came back with a long story about an aunt who was remarrying at the age of seventy and insisted on having bridesmaids. Kate thought of Lydie as a sister.

But what had gone so smoothly began to have problems. They hadn't counted on the difficulty of transportation, of trains clogged with troops. And there were mothers, at the last minute, unable to find anyone to care for their children. Some confessed they didn't have the money to make the trip. On the night before the rally, after Kate and Lydie had finished yet another count, the totals came up two shy of Miss Paul's minimum.

Though nearly eleven at night—if the thermometer in the headquarters' kitchen was to be believed—the temperature still hovered in the mid-eighties. The women who had been assembling the banners for the picketers had gone home. Neither Kate nor Lydie had eaten since breakfast. Lydie was upstairs, giving Lucy the final numbers. When she finally came back, she had a distracted look that Kate hadn't seen before.

"What's up?"

"Not a thing." Lydie sat down at the desk, shuffled through some papers.

Kate eyed her friend. "Was Lucy disappointed about the numbers?"

"No."

They worked in silence for several minutes until Lydie asked casually. "So, how do you think it will go tomorrow?"

Kate glanced at her. Not once had the subject of prison had ever been mentioned, but, from the first moment Lucy had called them to her office about organizing the rally, they both knew the possibility was there.

"Lydie, if it's being arrested you're worried about, don't. Miss Paul says the President will be too embarrassed after what happened to us in June."

"Could be." Lydie stood, wandered over to the window, and stared toward the lights of the White House. Minutes went by, a cricket's chirp beyond the open window the only sound.

"It's going to be okay," Kate said. "Miss Paul's in New York to raise money. You know she wouldn't have gone if she expected trouble."

Lydie turned. "Lucy wants me to lead the rally."

There it was. Out in the open. Lydie was one of the bravest women she knew, but she wasn't a Lucy who could face down a prison superintendent or guard and never blink. "Why, that's wonderful!" Kate forced herself to say with a smile.

"Is it?" Lydie held herself stiff, as if against tears.

"Of course, it is. You deserve the honor. Besides, we have everything organized. It'll go like clockwork."

Lydie bit her lip, glanced away. "I asked her, 'Lucy, why don't you do it, like you did before?' But she said she couldn't. She'd finally wangled an appointment with Senator Lodge to discuss a Republican caucus on the amendment."

Kate got to her feet, went over and put her arm around Lydie's waist. "I repeat. If Lucy and Miss Paul aren't worried, you shouldn't be either."

Lydie looked up at her. "They're both so brave, Kate. They don't understand." Her lips quavered. "But you know Lucy. How could I say no?"

⁕

The next morning dawned clear and surprisingly fresh for early August. A good day for the rally. Dressed in Millie's new white dotted Swiss she'd insisted Kate wear, she took special care with her hair, rouged her lips. If it weren't for her worry about Lydie's reaction to leading the rally, the day would be off to a perfect start.

Last night as Kate lay in bed, she'd recalled the conversation with Lydie. She had gone over the lists so often she knew every name, yet few old-timers she'd worked with before were among them. Not Olivia or Paula Jacobi whose aging father was in the hospital. One after the other, on down the line. Leaving only Lydie. At Occoquan, with Olivia by her side, Lydie had stood up against a matron about dressing in prison clothes, but leading a rally alone and across the street from the White House was another matter.

Yet Kate realized she shouldn't have worried. For as she walked up to headquarters at nine sharp, there was Lydie, calmly smiling, in charge, supervising the women in white, banners in hand, gathered in front of the headquarters and spilling out into the street and over to the park just as if she were organizing a church picnic. On the dot of ten, one hundred women were ready to move. All of them white, because Miss Paul believed, as she had in the past, that a public appearance of Negro members might provide more fodder for the opposition.

According to plan, Lydie—carrying a banner that read "How Long Must Women Wait for Liberty?"—led off; Kate took up the rear.

Under the curious gaze of people crowding the sidewalks on either side of Pennsylvania Avenue, the line of women moved down the side of the street close to the parked cars. Kate eyed the faces uneasily as she passed, remembering the past explosion of jeers. This time she saw only smiles. A few bystanders waved, and the picketers waved back.

The morning's newspapers were full of the war taking a turn for the better. Two weeks ago the Germans had abandoned the trenches and gone on the offensive around Reims, not fifty miles south of Chateau Thierry, where Vic Perelli had been killed. For several days, the war had hung in the balance. Now, the Allies had gained the upper hand, and rumors persisted that America's General Pershing would soon head up an independent American force, apart from the French General Foch.

Kate wondered if the turn of events with peace in the offing had been responsible for the president taking to his own typewriter in his sitting room as Lucy claimed he had and typing out letters to key senators, urging their support of the amendment. He hadn't yet come out with a strong public statement of support, but the rally might be just the push he needed.

At the north end of the park, Lydie led the line of women through the crowd to gather around the base of the statue of Lafayette. From where Kate stood, she could see the lower portion of the sculpture—a graceful, bare-breasted woman cast in bronze lying along the marble base, her hand outstretched toward Lafayette above her, as if appealing for help—perhaps the reason Miss Paul had chosen this spot.

Kate took her post at one end of the line and watched Lydie make certain every woman held her banner so that it might be seen from the White House. Cars rolled past along Pennsylvania, often stopping for a few moments. Banners fluttered in the light breeze. The crowds pressed closer. Two White House guards, caps pushed back, watched from the doorway of the guardhouse.

Kate scanned the hats of the men in the crowd, disappointed not to see a Press sign stuck in a single hatband. She signaled Lydie. Reporters or not, the time had come for the speeches to begin.

Dora Lewis, in her late fifties, a fearless member of the Pennsylvania committee, stepped in front of the group. Facing the White House, she began. "We are here because when our country is at war for liberty and democracy—"

The scream of approaching police car sirens drowned her words. The women near Kate shot her fearful looks. She told them not to worry. The sirens grew louder. Heads in the crowd turned. Kate looked to her left, saw three police cars and four paddy wagons draw up in front of the White House. At least a dozen policemen spilled out, crossed the street, and pushed their way through the crowd to where Dora stood. One of the cops grabbed her and pulled her roughly off to one side, announcing she was under arrest.

Hazel Hunkins from Montana, who had arrived late last night, took her place. "Here at the statue of Lafayette who fought for the liberty of this county and under the American flag, I am asking for—"

Another cop stepped up. The process was repeated. Kate shot a hopeful glance at the White House guards, but neither moved. The crowd had grown. Fragments of the nightmare of that hot June day flashed through Kate's mind.

A third woman came forward. "We protest against the continued disenfranchisement of American women, for which the president . . ." was as far as she got before she, too, was dragged off.

Her heart pounding, Kate broke ranks and ran over to Lydie, wide-eyed with fear. "Let's pull back."

"It's too late."

Out of desperation, Kate pushed through the crowd to where the cops were holding the three speakers. "Officers, we have a right to assemble. This is a public park."

A big cop with sergeant's stripes on the arm of his blue uniform gave her a dismissive glance, nodded his men. "Okay, boys, let's get this over with. Round 'em up and take 'em down to the station."

After everyone had climbed down from the paddy wagons, Kate counted forty-eight women. Inside the police station, the procedure was the same as she remembered it. The women were booked, fingerprinted, led into the room that served as a courtroom. The only change was the judge—this time tall and black-haired with thin lips, who sat behind the bench, drumming his fingers. And Lydie.

Though she stood beside Kate, walked with her, leading the group to the first two benches to face the judge, it was as if she had detached herself from the here and now. And Kate held her hand as the magistrate said, "So that you will know, you have been arrested under the orders of Colonel C. Ridley, the president's military aide. However, you will be released immediately on your own recognizance, pending trial, to appear tomorrow in this court at eleven o'clock."

Puzzled, Kate got to her feet. "Your Honor, what is the charge?'"

"You will be informed of the charge tomorrow. Until then you are free to go." And with a brisk rap of the gavel, giving them no chance to object, the magistrate rose and disappeared through the side door.

Kate stared at the magistrate's receding figure, trying to make sense of what she had experienced. The proceedings, such as they were, had lasted less than five minutes. Maybe Miss Paul and Lucy understood their ramifications. She didn't.

Two hours later, Kate stood at one side of the mantelpiece of the headquarters' living room, Lydie beside her. Forty-eight women filled the room. Their mood was somber, full of apprehension. They spoke in low voices, puzzled by why the magistrate had openly declared the President had been behind the arrests.

Then, in walked Lucy, flashing a smile, grasping a shoulder here, a hand there as she headed for the fireplace. The women, even Lydie, perked up, some laughing out loud. All but Kate. If anything was patently clear it was that Lucy and Miss Paul had called for a demonstration based on wrong information and had left her and Lydie and one hundred women in the lurch, of which forty-eight would go to jail. This when Lucy had assured them it would never happen. She had even convinced Kate.

"Well." Still smiling, Lucy surveyed the upturned faces. "It's been quite a day, hasn't it? Certainly not what we'd expected. But then the president hasn't yet let the Bill of Rights interfere with his plans for us. Why did we believe he might this time?"

A few rueful chuckles. Kate never failed to be amazed at Lucy's magic touch.

"I've talked to our attorney, Douglas McBride, and he tells me the government attorney will postpone the trial to allow him time to examine witnesses to determine, and I quote, 'what offenses, if any, the women would be charged with.' Seems the attorney believes he cannot go on with the case until he has received orders from the president." More chuckles. "The poor man claims there is no precedent for a case like this. And, indeed, there isn't. That's why Mr. McBride will be there with those of you who must appear in court tomorrow. Then we'll see what develops."

A strapping woman with bobbed brown hair got to her feet. "Lucy, this stinks. I can't wait around to go to court. I gotta get back to work."

Heads nodded, grumbling broke out until Lucy asked for quiet. "Give your names to Kate after we adjourn. I'll make phone calls. See what I can do. In the meantime, how about a song?"

"Forward into Light," someone called out. A woman who wore glasses and her hair tied in a bun, produced a pitch pipe. Everyone scrambled to her feet and, in unison forty-eight women, even Kate, burst into song.

> *Forward, out of error*
> *Leave behind the night*
> *Forward, through the darkness*
> *Forward into light.*

By six that evening, Lucy supposedly closeted in her office, Kate and Lydie sat in the little, first-floor office, silent and self-absorbed when Lucy walked in.

"Don't leave until Alice calls, will you?" She started to turn away, stopped. "Better yet, why don't you both come upstairs and we can wait together?" And she was gone before Kate could respond.

Whatever Kate felt about Lucy, she was still in charge and, with Lydie beside her, they climbed the stairs to the small room at the top of the house and waited for Miss Paul's phone call. And when the phone finally rang, the conversation was brief, Lucy giving only the sketchiest mention of the morning's debacle before she hung up.

Kate sat beside Lydie and watched Lucy gather herself together before she said, "Alice says she's coming back from Newport on the morning train. Between now and then, she wants me to get to the President somehow and find out what's going on."

Kate and Lydie got to their feet.

"Hold on a minute," Lucy said. "I need supper before I tackle the White House. We all do. Let's go to Reeves. My treat."

Three abreast, they walked the four blocks through the fading light, their seemingly companionable silence covering the un-answered questions about what had gone wrong. Reeves Bakery was closing when they arrived, but the manager recognized Lucy and waved them inside. The place was still jammed, mostly with ser-vicemen, who eyed the three women with good-natured leers. The manager showed them to a small table at the back by an open win-dow. Without bothering to take their orders, he brought them the house specialty, chicken salad sandwiches.

The round table was so small their knees touched. This close, even in the bad light, Kate could see the effects of the day in sharp relief. Did she imagine guilt in Lucy's eyes? Was that fear of what was to come in Lydie's weak smile? The manager brought glasses of sweetened iced tea and told a bad joke about two doughboys get-ting lost in Paris.

As the women ate the sandwiches and, for dessert, huge slabs of strawberry pie, Lucy fell into reminiscing. The time she stole her brother's firecrackers and set them off by accident, her penchant for climbing trees and ruining her dresses in the process, how she'd buried every doll she was given in the backyard because she hated them so. After she paid the check, they walked to the corner, hugged and parted, the questions still unasked and unanswered.

It was midnight by the time Kate slowly climbed the stairs to Millie's apartment. Her arm felt like a heavy weight as she inserted the key in the lock. Inside, she touched the walls, feeling her way down the dark hall to the tiny alcove where she switched on the lamp. A note in Millie's handwriting was propped up against the telephone. "I bought a steak to celebrate the rally. According to tonight's papers, guess you got tied up."

Kate smiled, touched by Millie's backhanded apology, her thoughtfulness. At the moment, Kate would like to forget the entire day. She undressed and went into the bathroom, filled the tub. With a delicious sense of anticipation, she sank into the cool water, rested her head against the hard porcelain wall of the small claw foot tub, propped her feet on either side of the faucets at the other end.

Submerged up to her chin in a tub of water, she always felt safe, protected, nearly weightless, as if she'd entered an altered state of mind. She closed her eyes, and, against her will, thoughts of the day—the injustice of it—poured into her mind. And thoughts of Lucy.

Had buying Kate and Lydie supper been her way of apologizing for taking too much for granted? Serious picketing had been going on for nearly two years. Everything about it had become almost pro forma. The picketers knew what to expect. Yet, lately, the political scene had changed. Even as a newcomer, Kate had picked up on the President's fixation over what would happen after the armistice when it came, the upcoming election, and a possible Republican takeover. The President had become a desperate man.

Kate hated to let go of her heroines, but whatever was going on,

Miss Paul and Lucy had failed to pick up on it, and, in the process, had sent a woman who was losing her nerve to lead the fray.

Not that Lydie was the only one who was afraid. What Kate had felt as she'd seen the police cars draw up was close to terror because now she knew what might follow. She thought of her brother, Tom. Their mother used to say his crazy antics would land him in the hospital, and now he was climbing into planes, no better than flimsy pieces of cardboard, flying them over enemy territory into a sky exploding with machine gun fire. She'd heard that some men shit in their pants with fright. It drove them to madness. War could change a person in unimaginable ways, and she believed it.

Chapter 17

The next morning, back from work, Kate stood in the guestroom, her mind full of the day ahead. In a few hours the magistrate would announce the charges against her. Anticipating that Lydie wouldn't be up to taking the lead, Kate wanted to look her best, and she changed her clothes, put on a fresh blouse and skirt, even screwing on the small faux pearl earrings she'd bought in the neighborhood dress shop. Yesterday she had told the Perellis she might not be back at work for a while. Politics was how she explained it and they had said okay but looked confused. Now, just before she left the apartment, she wrote a note to her sister, Lizzie, urging her to stay in school, and to her father, thanking him for the check, for his faith in her. If someone had told her she was carrying on like someone about to be condemned to life in prison, she'd laugh.

Kate wasn't due at the police court until noon, and she decided to stop off at the headquarters in hopes of talking to Lucy. But, except for a girl at the telephone and one of the Maryland workers pounding out a press release on a typewriter, the place was deserted. Kate paused at the bulletin board beneath the porte-cochere, astonished to see a front-page article clipped from this morning's *Post* and a large photograph of white-clad women carrying banners as they stood beneath the Lafayette statue. The caption read "Suffragists in a demonstration at the Lafayette Monument." Next to the photo ran the article with headlines in large type. "Women Suffragists Arrested Under Order of President's Aide."

The article that followed said that leaders of the National Woman's Party were arrested as they spoke yesterday before a crowd of several hundred at Lafayette Park on behalf of the suffrage amendment. They were arrested under orders of Colonel C. Ridley, President Wilson's military aide. The article went on to state that forty-six other NWP members from among the one hundred attending the rally were also arrested. All were taken by police wagon to the District police station where they were subsequently released and ordered to appear in court today. Kate reread the article, pleased that it was brief and almost accurate and readable, but puzzled because she couldn't remember seeing any reporters there.

Perhaps the information had come from Lucy. Kate wanted to believe the front-page placement had been the editor's deliberate intent to embarrass the president. Yet there was no use kidding herself. One newspaper article did not a change in government policy make. The hearing today was undoubtedly fixed.

⚬⚬⚬

Doug McBride was waiting for Kate and Lydie as they walked into the police station a few minutes before twelve. The air was hot and the wooden blades of the ceiling fan seemed only to circulate the rancid odor of stale sweat. A pale man in his forties, medium height, clean shaven, with a lock of light brown hair combed across his forehead came out through the door Kate knew led to the magistrate's office and sat down at the far end. A moment later a paunchy policeman called for everyone to rise, and the tall magistrate entered.

Once settled in his high-backed chair, he surveyed the waiting women, then looked at Mr. McBride. "I presume you're the attorney for the defense."

The attorney rose. "I am, Your Honor. Douglas McBride. If it pleases the Court, I respectfully request that the case against my clients be dismissed or that specific charges be made against them."

"Later." The magistrate looked over at the pale man Kate guessed must be the government attorney. "Mr. Stevens?"

The man got to his feet. "Your Honor, the People still request time to examine witnesses."

The magistrate frowned. "Yes, yes, but the charge, Mr. Stevens."

He cleared his throat. "Holding a meeting on public grounds or climbing on a statue."

Kate stifled a cynical smile.

"Your Honor, which is it to be?" Doug McBride asked.

The magistrate returned his gaze toward the sickly attorney as if looking for guidance.

"As I was attempting to explain, Your Honor, the charge will depend on the result of my examination of witnesses."

Doug McBride stepped forward. "Your Honor, my clients have a constitutional right to know the charges levied against them."

The magistrate glared. "Counselor, I do not need you to remind me of the law." He shifted his gaze back to the government attorney. "Two weeks is my limit, Mr. Stevens." He glanced at the bailiff. "Give me an open morning on the calendar, bailiff."

Kate stared at him, wondering what kind of game he was playing. Sitting forward, about to get up and ask him, she felt a restraining hand on her arm as Mr. McBride rose.

"Your Honor—"

"Sit down, Mr. McBride, or I will hold you in contempt." He glanced back at the bailiff.

"Monday, August nineteenth is open, Your Honor."

The magistrate nodded, looked from one attorney to the other.

"You heard it. Monday, August 19th. Ten o'clock sharp." And, with a brisk rap of his gavel, he called the court adjourned.

No sooner had he disappeared into his chambers than Dora Lewis rose and marched over to Mr. McBride. "Young man, this entire business is an outrage." Not only an outrage, Kate thought, but a farce, like a scene in a Gilbert and Sullivan operetta, except what was going on was real.

That night as Millie fried the steak meant for a celebration, they talked about the injustice of what was going on. Millie likened it to the day when kings threw people in dungeons just because they felt like it, and Kate confessed she'd mistakenly thought the President was coming around.

"If you ask me, your sacred Alice Paul and Lucy Burns don't know as much as they think they do," Millie remarked, helping herself to the last of the steak, and, as she started to eat, she added, "By the way, Chuck called. Said he was sorry about the arrests."

Kate said nothing.

"You're a fool, you know that? You oughta grab him and run to the nearest preacher."

Kate shrugged. What was there to say that Millie would understand? That she was glad Charlie called when she suspected he had been behind the arrests?

Millie rested her fork and knife on her dinner plate, looked straight at Kate. "But I forgot. You want to get us the vote. And by the time that happens—if it ever does—a fat lot of good it will do us. And, in the meantime, any man worth his salt will already be taken and you'll end up an old maid, taking care of doddering parents or typing letters for some idiot at a bank or answering telephones. Like Aunt Jan. Well, you can have it."

That night Kate lay in bed with the feeling that the world was coming apart at the seams, and she with it. Keeping busy was her salvation and for the next two days she worked nonstop. She volunteered to take the lunch shift at Perelli's, and, at least for those hours, the musical sounds of Mr. Perelli "*grazie*'s," the "*a piu tardi*'s" as his

Italian customers left helped her forget the District of Columbia's version of justice. And at headquarters, she buried herself in any kind of work that needed doing.

It was afternoon when she was pecking out a lengthy article for the *Suffragist* when Lucy walked into the newsroom. "What would you say to a little good news?"

Kate lifted her fingers from the typewriter keys, sat back heavily. "How good is good?"

"Wait and see," Lucy said with an air of mystery, the hint of a smile in her eyes. "But you have to come upstairs." She beckoned to Kate.

In her office, Lucy strode to her desk and picked a sheet of paper from the top of one of the piles. "Read this and tell me what you think."

At first glance, Kate saw only a press release on the official letterhead of a senator. Then she read more carefully. The senator was Charles Curtis of Kansas, a Republican and the Senate minority whip. The date was August 9th, the day after the farce of the hearing. She looked over at Lucy.

"Read."

The admission by the court that the forty-eight suffragists are arrested upon absolutely no charges and that these women, among them munitions and Red Cross workers, are held in Washington until next Tuesday, under arrest, while the United States Attorney for the District of Columbia decides for what offense, "if any," they were arrested is unacceptable.

The meeting was called (in Lafayette Park) to make a justified protest against constitutional blocking of the suffrage amendment by the Democratic majority of the Senate. It is well known that three-fourths of the Republican membership in the Senate are ready to vote for the amendment. Yet, under the control of the Democratic majority, the Senate has recessed for six weeks without naming any provision for action on this important amendment. In justice to the women who have been working so hard for the amendment, it should be passed at the earliest date.

Kate looked up and matched Lucy's grin. "Miss Paul is responsible for this, isn't she?"

"Partly. It's also good politics on the part of Senator Curtis. What matters, however, is its timing. We couldn't have ordered any better press to suit our needs. This is like throwing down the gauntlet, challenging the President to put his weight behind the amendment."

"Then how do you explain the orders from Colonel Ridley to have us arrested?"

"A bad case of an overzealous aide. That's all."

That's all? But Kate held her tongue. "If you really want to cheer me up, Lucy, tell me Senator Curtis's pronouncement will guarantee us a trial and a not-guilty verdict."

Chapter 18 ————————————————————

Monday, August 19th—the day Kate and Lydie and the others were to learn the charges against them—was overcast, the sky coated with flat clouds thick as cotton batting. Across the street from headquarters, after weeks in the mid-90s, the leaves on the tulip poplars in Lafayette Park were turning brown. When Kate had left the apartment, not even the usually smiling milkman seemed up to waving a hello. The timing for the trial, presuming there was a trial, couldn't be worse.

Yet just yesterday Lucy had been upbeat. The political maneuvering since Miss Paul's telephone call to the president's aide would work in their favor. She'd said Kate and Lydie shouldn't worry. But Kate was dubious. Call it cynical of her but even after Doug McBride called his witnesses from among the crowd at the rally and they substantiated how the women's right to free speech had been denied, there was no guarantee the jury would find them innocent.

⸎

The room that served as a courtroom was nearly full when Kate walked in. At Mr. McBride's direction, she and the others were to take the two front benches, and as she waited her turn, she scanned the faces of the spectators: Lucy and Alice Paul were there, several girls from headquarters, and, lounging against the back wall, were three men who might be reporters and another man with thinning blond hair—Charlie. He was standing off to the side as if deliberately separating himself from the others. Their gazes met. He smiled, and as she nodded, against her will, she felt her heart speed up. Had he offered to tell her why he was here, she wasn't sure she would want to know. She took her seat on the front bench and smoothed her skirt with shaking hands.

Five minutes later, on the dot of ten, according to the clock on the wall behind the bench, the bailiff ordered everyone to rise, the courtroom got to its collective feet, and the magistrate appeared. The cast of characters assembled, the bailiff called the roll. One by one, the forty-eight women rose, gave their names; the magistrate called on the government attorney. The stage was set for the hearing to begin.

With a brisk tug to the lapels of the jacket of his obviously new Palm Beach suit, the pasty-faced government attorney rose, addressed the bench. "Your Honor, as I indicated at the hearing, it was necessary for me to determine the appropriate charge to be made against each of the defendants. I believe you have a copy of my findings before you. As does the defense."

Doug McBride shot to his feet. "Your Honor, I must lodge a protest. I was given a copy of the charges only moments ago. Further, with no previous knowledge of the charges, the defendants—"

"Hold your horses, counselor," the magistrate said. He studied a folder, glanced from the government attorney to Mr. McBride before he eyed the women seated on the benches before him. "Now, I shall go down the list, call the name of each of the accused. As I read the charge or charges, the defendant will inform the court as to her plea."

Kate cringed inside as visions of the day she'd first stood in this courtroom returned in a rush. She touched Doug McBride's arm, whispered the word "railroad" and he got to his feet. "Your Honor, request permission to approach the bench."

"Granted." He motioned to the prosecutor.

Staring at the backs of the two attorneys with a sense of foreboding, Kate strained to pick up the words, but heard only Mr. McBride's urgent tones. After a few minutes, the attorneys returned to their seats.

"Upon a request from the defense," the magistrate said, "I will call a thirty-minute recess. We will reconvene at eleven o'clock."

Squeezed into a small room, probably used for interrogations, Kate and Lydie and the others strained to hear Doug McBride read the list of charges against them. Unexplainably, nearly half would be free to go. But others, like Kate and Lydie and the speakers, were accused of both charges: holding a meeting in a public place and climbing on a statue.

"Now what?" someone in the back of the room asked.

Doug McBride blotted his perspiring face with a folded handkerchief. "For those facing charges, the magistrate will read your names, the charge or charges, and you will enter your plea. I will then ask for a delay to give me time to prepare your cases for trial."

Dora Lewis raised her hand. "Mr. McBride, what would you say—realistically—are your chances of having that delay granted?"

"Fair."

"In other words, after we enter our plea, we will be put on trial, minus a jury, completely in the hands of a man who is blatantly violating the Constitution."

Doug McBride offered a weak smile. "More or less, yes."

Standing at the back of the room, Kate spoke up. "Mr. McBride, what if we enter a not guilty plea and demand a trial by jury?"

"In ordinary circumstances, that is exactly what you should do."

"But since these aren't ordinary circumstances . . ."

"The magistrate could well turn down your request and let you go to jail."

"And your role in this is what, Mr. McBride?" Kate asked.

"I would file an appeal."

Kate looked into the faces of the women around her. A few were old enough to be her mother. She wasn't sure how Lydie would hold up. "I realize what I'm going to propose is asking a great deal, but we have come too far to play into the hands of the administration now. I don't see any other choice but to plead not guilty and demand a jury trial. I could be wrong, but I think a jury would find the charges absurd.

"However, if the magistrate denies us our rights and sends us to prison, the onus is squarely on his shoulders. There are reporters out there today. A year ago, when Lucy and Miss Paul and many of you were sent to prison, barely a mention was made of it in the papers. But that's changed. Just think of the crowd gathered the day we were picked up. They were for us. If the magistrate throws us into prison, it's going to make front-page news. The last thing in the world the magistrate or Colonel Ridley or, most importantly, the President wants."

Mr. McBride scowled. "Miss Brennan, I must advise that you will be taking a grave risk."

Kate had to smile. "I think you'd agree, risk is nothing new to us."

"I understand how you feel, Miss Brennan. But my job is to represent you, and I can't allow you to do this."

"With all due respect, sir, you are not the one to decide," she said and turned toward the other women. "Shall we take a vote? To make this work it must be unanimous, one way or the other."

"Let's do it," someone said. Again, heads nodded, and they filed out of the room and back into the courtroom, their attorney following behind.

Almost immediately, the magistrate gaveled the courtroom back to order. Kate was the first to have her name called and her charges read: standing on a statue and holding a meeting in a public place. She rose, shoulders back, hands clasped, and looked the magistrate in the eyes.

For a moment, the slow creak of the fan overhead was the only sound in the courtroom.

"Miss Brennan, how do you plead? Guilty or not guilty?" the magistrate demanded.

"Not guilty, Your Honor. And I demand a trial by jury."

The magistrate shot a furious glance at Mr. McBride, who raised his eyebrows, shrugged.

The next name and charge were called. The woman stood, pleaded not guilty, and demanded a trial by jury. And so it went, one woman after the other, all the while the pasty-faced government attorney conferring frantically with his aide and the judge's face turning a deeper shade of red. Kate counted twenty of the forty-eight women who would face the possibility of jail if the magistrate denied a trial.

After the last woman sat down, Kate looked at the magistrate. The sight of the clenched jaws, the cold eyes, tightly clasped hands were clues she didn't need, and she was not surprised when all requests for trial by jury were denied. "Furthermore," intoned the magistrate, "the defendants will be incarcerated in the District workhouse for from ten to fifteen days, depending on the seriousness of the charge."

Kate sucked in a sharp breath. Lydie shivered. From behind them, gasps erupted. And Doug McBride sprang to his feet. Yet, even as he was announcing his intention to file an appeal, the magistrate rapped his gavel, called the court adjourned, and swept out of the courtroom. Staring at the closed door, preparing herself for the police who would descend momentarily, Kate tried to find some consolation at the thought of the pasty-faced government attorney groveling later before Colonel Ridley, the President's hired gun, as he tried to explain what went wrong with the plan to force the NWP, once and for all, to back down and admit their guilt.

⁓⁓⁓⁓

Less than an hour later Kate and Lydie and the others stumbled out of paddy wagons and walked into a damp, crumbling building that had once been the men's workhouse. Rising from the swamps of the District's prison ground, to Kate it looked like something out of the Dark Ages.

Guards came toward them, their heavy footsteps echoing as they walked along the cracked concrete floor in the vast and seemingly empty space. Kate shivered, breathed in the stink of decay and gazed up at the tiers of cells, the rusting bars of the half-open cell doors. The silence puzzled her. She looked around uneasily, listening for the sound of voices, some sign of other prisoners, and it began to dawn on her that there weren't any. She and the others—twenty women in all—were alone with how many guards she couldn't tell.

As she expected, one of guards, a stringy-necked man with immense ears who must be in charge, ordered them to line up so they could be processed. Kate glanced at Lydie. Ordinarily, according to seniority, Lydie would be the official spokesman. But the Lydie standing next to her, eyes focused on something no one else could see, was in a daze.

Kate stepped forward. "Sir, we will not be processed. We are political prisoners and expect to be treated as such."

The guard planted his fists on his hips, guffawed.

Dora Lewis left her place in line to stand next to Kate. "Listen here, Mr. Whatever-your-name-is, you and your people either treat us humanely, or we shall go on a hunger strike."

"No, you listen, lady. We run this place, and as long as you're here, you'll do what you're told."

Lydie moved closer to Kate.

"So line up, give the guard over there at the table your name and no monkey business." The guard beckoned to Kate with a fat finger. "You first."

Kate weighed her next step. Dora Lewis wasn't up to violent treatment. Still . . . "I repeat: we demand to be treated like political prisoners."

Instantly, six guards stepped forward, and Kate sank to the concrete floor, arms folded, sitting cross-legged as she'd seen Lucy do at Occoquan. But as the other women followed her lead, the guards immediately moved in to grab them. Dora Lewis kicked her attacker in the shins. Helen Monk from Tennessee clawed at a guard's eyes. But the protest was over almost before it had begun as, one by one, with Kate the last, they were dragged up the iron stairs and thrown into cells.

Kate squinted in the cell's dim light at the usual cot with its stained mattress, the wooden slop bucket in the corner. If she looked closely, she'd probably see cockroaches lurking in the shadows. Soon a rat would appear. She thought about the article she'd read, announcing the opening of a freshly painted, newly furnished correction facility, and decided this wasn't it. She was mildly surprised that she was the sole occupant. On second thought, since they were the only prisoners, there was no shortage of cells. Furthermore, she couldn't recall the guard locking the cell door. She went over to it, gave it a push, and it creaked open.

She peered out. Not a guard in sight. Wherever they were, they obviously weren't concerned about their prisoners, and why should they be? They'd stripped them of their valuables. With no other prisoners to worry about, it was twenty unarmed women against a dozen guards with nightsticks and probably revolvers as backups. Not much of a contest.

Kate stepped onto the walkway. Moving from one cell to the next, she checked to see if everyone was accounted for. Not until she came to the last cell at the end of the tier did she find Lydie, huddled in the corner.

Kate went over and put her arms around her.

"Oh, Kate, how are we going to manage?" Lydie whispered.

"Just fine. But first, we're getting out of these cells."

"But without Lucy . . ."

Kate yanked the mattress off Lydie's cot. "Look, we know how to do this. So take hold of the other side of this mattress. We're going to drag it downstairs where we can all be together."

Lydie didn't move.

"Lydie, trust me. Grab hold of the mattress and, between us, we'll get it downstairs."

Lydie looked at Kate uncertainly.

"There's not a guard out there who is going to stop us. I checked. Come on." But not until Kate had dragged the mattress off the cot and halfway through the open cell door did Lydie pick up the other end.

Once out on the walkway, dragging the mattress, they stopped at each cell and Kate explained the plan. Listening to herself, she almost laughed at how much she sounded like a housemother at college, gathering her charges together.

She and Lydie started down the stairs. Still no sign of guards, but Kate knew they were out there somewhere. The mattress bumping awkwardly down the metal stairs behind her, she became increasingly uneasy. But she wasn't about to turn back. Whatever happened would happen.

Once on the main floor, Kate looked up at the tier of cells, ready to help anyone who couldn't manage her mattress alone, but saw no one. "Hey, up there!"

One by one, the women emerged from their cells, peered down at her from the catwalk.

"Come on! Move!" Kate shouted, now sounding like a field commander—or a cop.

The women disappeared into their cells and came out with their mattresses.

"Anyone who needs help, give a holler, but get going," Kate called up as she glanced nervously toward a massive door at the far end of the room.

Gradually, after what seemed like an hour, Kate helped the last of the picketers—Clare Allen from New Hampshire—to maneuver her mattress in place beside the others along the cracked concrete floor, and surveyed the lineup.

The sound of a door opening came from behind her, then a gruff male voice, "And what do you people think you're doin'?"

Kate turned slowly, looked at the guard, a tall, loose-limbed man with craggy features, as he came closer. "We are getting resettled. Next, we will be bringing down the empty buckets that I presume are for urinating. However, we will also need water."

The guard shifted his glance to the row of mattresses. "You can't do this. It's against rules."

"That may be. But this is where we intend to stay as long as we are in this abominable place." And to Kate's amazement, he simply walked away.

Left alone, one day passed into another, gradually taking on a surreal quality, perhaps because of the hunger. By unspoken agreement, they ate nothing and drank only water, red with rust from the ancient pipes after years of disuse and a taste that, to say the least, took getting used to. To conserve their strength, they lay on the bare mattresses, the dampness gradually seeping up from the concrete and through the straw. Rats scampered around them at night. But the guards left them alone.

After the first encounter with the guard, Kate lost her fear. She devised word games. They sang a little. But after six days, most of the women spent the hours dozing. Kate kept a close watch on Lydie, lying curled into a fetal position on the cot next to hers. Her forehead felt clammy to the touch, and Kate wondered about demanding a doctor.

The light and dark framed by the small, grimy windows against the ceiling became her clock. On day seven, lying on her back on the mattress, Kate was debating whether or not it was worth it to make the fifteen-foot journey to the water bucket when a guard walked down the line of women, stopped, and kicked her feet. "Up. You got a visitor."

Kate stared at him, not certain she'd heard right. The guard repeated himself, and she slowly sat up, smoothed her hair, struggled to her feet. The shaft of sunlight filtering through the narrow windows above gave her the feeling of being underwater, or maybe she was just a little faint. She tried to concentrate on who the visitor could be. Perhaps Doug McBride. If not, who? The guard gave an abrupt jerk of his head, indicating that she walk ahead of him toward the door that she had stared at for so many hours, the door they had entered an eternity ago. Out of habit, she tucked her blouse into her rumpled skirt.

Her legs were so stiff she walked with a disjointed gait. She passed Dora Lewis, who had been moaning in her sleep recently. Whoever the visitor was, Kate had to convince him that if he couldn't secure their release, a doctor had to be allowed to examine the women who were most affected by the fasting. Only as Kate passed through the steel door toward a small room did she think about how bad she must smell.

"Kate?" she heard a man's stunned voice ask.

She started. The voice didn't sound like Mr. McBride. Looking more closely, she saw a good-sized, thickset man filling the doorway. But the light was such she couldn't tell who it was.

"Kate, it's Mr. Shafroth." He strode toward her, put a comforting arm around her shoulders, and led her gently into the room, the guard right behind them. "Here." He led Kate to one of the two straight-backed, wooden chairs in the room. "Sit down. I came the instant I got the call. Strangely enough, it was from a reporter." He glanced at the guard. "Leave us, please."

"Sorry. Can't do that, Senator."

"At least have the decency to stand outside the door."

The guard hesitated for an instant before he shrugged, stepped just outside the door.

Mr. Shafroth drew up the other chair, sat down. He leaned toward Kate, his elbows on his knees, his thick fingers laced. His expression was intense, his blue eyes dark. "You look terrible, dear."

Kate managed a smile. "I wouldn't doubt it."

He frowned. "They tell me you've been on a hunger strike."

She looked at the man she'd seen from the gallery the day the amendment was never debated, the man she remembered from hot summer nights years ago during the croquet games when he'd sent the ball of a hapless player out into the rose bushes with a hard, sure shot of his mallet. "Daddy said you were the one who found out I was at Occoquan. I should have come by to thank you for letting him know."

"Your father would do the same for my boys." He smiled. "Happily, I can report we're in the process of getting you out of here."

Kate wondered whom he meant by "we." "Some of the women are in bad shape, Mr. Shafroth." She could not bring herself to call him senator. "If there's anything you can do to have them released . . . They'll need an ambulance and a doctor."

"Senator Curtis is also on his way over. Seems a Miss Archibald from Kansas City is in here."

"Virginia is her name," Kate said, though her mind was still back on what Shafroth had said about being alerted by a reporter. She could almost see the line of what had undoubtedly been reporters—and Charlie—along the back wall of the courtroom. "Mr. Shafroth, the call you said you received from a reporter—was he from one of the dailies?"

"He didn't say, and I'm afraid I didn't think to ask." John Shafroth took her hands in his. "The main thing now is to get you out of here."

Resisting the urge to withdraw her hands, she said, "I can't leave without the others."

"I understand. But once we have you out, Mrs. Shafroth insists you come stay with us until you get your strength back."

"Please tell her thank you," Kate said. "She's very kind, but I've been staying in the city with a friend."

"I'll make arrangements for Dr. Barker—he's our family doctor—to come see you."

"That really won't be necessary. A decent meal, a good night's sleep, and I'll be back on track."

"None of this should have happened."

She met his gaze. "The president was responsible."

"I believe Colonel Ridley's the one to blame," he said.

"Is there a difference?"

"Let's say it was an unfortunate case of bad judgment," he said.

"It was unconstitutional."

For a split second, his eyes flashed, like a blade caught in the sun with the implication of danger. But he'd caught her meaning, she was sure. "That, too," he said.

She cocked her head. "After all, this is a war, isn't it? People die in war. Except this one is between American women and their president."

He gave her a fatherly, condescending smile, and she imagined his thoughts. Men in France were dying for the cause of democracy and freedom while the picketers—most well-heeled from the looks of them and unpatriotically strident—were interested only in interrupting the conduct of a government that had real issues on its hands. Or was the smile a matter of self-protection? To say anything was too dangerous and might open himself up to admitting the leader of his party was at fault.

With nothing else to discuss, she thanked him, got to her feet. "I need to get back to the others and tell them the good news," she said. And, the guard beside her, she walked away until the steel door clanked shut, leaving behind a man who had become just another piece of her childhood she'd put aside two months ago.

Chapter 19

Lucy put her half-eaten egg salad sandwich aside to take a better look at the photo of Dora Lewis—gray hair hanging in limp strands, a nurse helping her into an ambulance. The caption identified her as an elderly suffragist released yesterday from the District prison. The article beside the photo listed Kate Brennan as the spokesman for the National Woman's Party members incarcerated for picketing the White House.

Lucy held up the paper and glanced over at Alice seated behind her desk. "Did you see this picture of Dora Lewis in the *Post*?" Lucy held up the paper. "She looks like the walking dead."

Alice glanced up from the letter she was writing out in long hand, which would later be typed by one of the girls downstairs. "Are you surprised, after a week in that old place they threw them in?"

"Still better than the initial ten-day sentence," Lucy mused, staring at the photo. She still regretted what had happened at the park. Yet even the best laid plans went astray, and, unfortunately, this had been one of them. She put the newspaper aside, took another bite of her sandwich. She'd like to think the news of the picketers' plight had been behind the Senate Republican first-ever decision to caucus and force a vote on the amendment. More likely, it was the word about the NWP gearing up to defeat every Senate Democrat up for reelection. Suddenly, the Republicans realized that supporting the amendment made political sense.

Alice sat back and regarded Lucy. "It may sound cold, but that photo of poor, dear Dora is worth ten times more than all the press releases we've put out for the last six months. First the Senate Republicans come out for us. Next may even be the President."

"Does that mean he's agreed to see you again?" Lucy asked.

"That's what I'm told."

"After the stupidity of his aide, I'd say it was high time. And take Olivia. Wilson has met her before, and it won't hurt to remind him that a southern woman from an old North Carolina family is one of the leaders of the NWP."

Alice shook her head. "A New Jersey connection would be better. Billie Logan should do nicely. She can recall the days when she and her husband worked to elect him governor."

"And when you're sitting in the Oval Office, then what?" Lucy asked, already anticipating the scene in the making.

"I'll simply ask the President point blank what he's doing to force his fellow Democrats to match the Republicans."

Lucy grinned at the thought of the encounter. "And, in the meantime, I suppose I'm to get in touch with the state committees and tell them to gear up for action."

"Of course." Alice swung her swivel chair around and plucked a folder from the shelf of the small, wooden bookcase beneath the window and opened it. "Our targets are Ashhurst, Arizona; Shafroth, Colorado; Walsh, Montana; Key Pittman, Nevada. And then there's Borah from Idaho." She looked up from the file. "The way I see it, when you talk to the committees, tell them the first thing they must do is remind local politicos how we defeated five senators and more than twenty congressmen two years ago and that we can do it again. Simply put: our five senators in the West have a choice: either they find the two votes we need, or they're out and Republicans will take their place."

Lucy glanced at the calendar on the wall. The end of September was the last possibility for a Senate vote before the recess, giving the state committees and their senators up for reelection less than a month to convince two more of their fellow senators to come up with the necessary votes.

She got up, wandered to the window and looked down at the park bathed in the afternoon sunshine. A uniformed nursemaid pushed a carriage. An elderly man sat on a bench in the shade of a tulip tree, reading. So peaceful; a typical scene in the park. Without a hint that forty-eight women had been arrested just yards away less than two weeks earlier or of the struggle that had been waged within the walls of this house—and for years before—across the country.

Lately, there had been days when she could almost reach out and hold success in her hands, only to have it slip away like sand through her fingers. Intuition told her that this might be their last chance. Too much was at stake to fail.

⚜

That night, determined to leave nothing to chance, Lucy carried home the folders of each state committee to decide which ones would need help. Letters had their limits, and she hoped to gather most of the chairmen to Washington for a meeting in two weeks. Wartime travel would make it difficult but it was doable. And while they were here, she wanted them to visit their senators.

She'd been told that one—Iris Calderhead from Colorado—was already in town, visiting her father, a former congressman from Kansas. Lucy remembered how well she handled the difficult Colorado race in '16 and was glad she was still at the helm.

Lucy unlocked the door to her apartment, stepped in, and turned on the entryway's light. As she unpinned her hat and checked the mail, she was conscious of the smell in the air, as if the apartment had been empty for some time. Or was what she smelled loneliness?

She pulled in a long breath and walked down the hall to the kitchen. Peering in the icebox, she found the salad and lemonade Mrs. Ells had left her. She took them out and placed them on a tray, carrying it to her desk in the alcove off the living room.

Nibbling absently as she worked, she slowly made her way through the pile of folders. Dark settled over the room, and she switched on the desk lamp. The dishes and tray were in the way, and she carried them back to the kitchen.

After a time she became aware of the growing quiet beyond the open windows, and she glanced at the antique clock on the desk, not too surprised to see that it was twelve thirty. She stretched. Another hour and she'd be finished. She reordered the folders alphabetically, paused at Colorado.

When Iris called on her state's two senators, Kate should go with her. Fresh from prison—her second stint in as many months—she'd make a dramatic impression. And Lucy knew of the connection between Kate and Senator Shafroth from the files, one that could be convenient. In this business, anything and anyone was fair game.

Iris and Kate: a formidable team. Iris was a stunner, and Kate not bad looking. And in recent weeks Kate had developed a toughness. Men could smell it in a woman. They didn't like it, but they paid attention to it. Even a family friend like Senator Shafroth.

⁕

The next day, Lucy watched Kate—a little thinner and paler from her bout in the workhouse—as she shook Iris Calderhead's hand, taking her in, top to toe, as only a woman can do. She wouldn't miss a detail of the erect, slim Iris in the pastel green linen dress, her artfully waved strawberry blond hair banded by a matching green silk scarf, the lips with just a touch of rouge in a shade that would emphasize her green eyes. Guessing a woman's age was tricky. Lucy happened to know that Iris was twenty-nine. And, like Kate, she wore no ring on her third finger. Marriage and the amendment were often a poor mix.

"Lucy's been telling me all about you," Iris said.

Kate answered her smile, took a chair nearby. "From what I've read, your work in the '16 Colorado campaign was amazing."

Lucy hid a smile at the genteel sparring between the two young women.

"And I understand you're one of the Richard Brennans who own the *Rocky Mountain News*," Iris said.

"Owned. Past tense."

"Still, it's a great contact, isn't it?" Iris said.

When Kate didn't reply, Lucy decided it was time to move on. "With two of you from Colorado now, I want you to see Shafroth right away. Tomorrow, if possible. After that, Thomas. Such as it is, Shafroth has a history with suffrage and he's respected among the western senators. Not to mention that he's up for reelection." She glanced from Iris to Kate who looked back at her with a gaze that told Lucy that something was bothering her—something beyond her lukewarm reaction to Iris and the emphasis on her family. Lucy had felt it for days. *Whatever is eating you, get over it,* she wanted to say.

Chapter 20

The next day Kate was filled with uneasiness about the coming meeting as she and Iris stepped into the small reception area of Shafroth's office. Lucy obviously counted on the Brennan connection. What she didn't know and Kate should have told her about was the encounter she had had with the senator at the workhouse, which could undo it all.

Iris gave their names to the receptionist, and she and Kate sat down. She had never been to the office before. Glancing around, she was struck by the old-fashioned tone of the pine furniture and the black horsehair couch. The look was an unpretentious, small-town lawyer's office. A person could be caught off guard in surroundings like these.

Kate picked up a magazine from the nearby table and flipped idly through the pages, her mind on Mr. Shafroth—father and husband, good provider, public office holder for twenty years. The kids in the neighborhood had always envied the Shafroth boys their easygoing father. But, occasionally, like the night Tom and Will, the youngest of the Shafroth boys, set off fire crackers that started a small fire in the alley, Mr. Shafroth applied the belt to both their rear ends. Like her father, he had his limits.

Kate heard footsteps, and glanced up to see John Shafroth standing in the doorway. She and Iris rose. "Good afternoon, Senator. Good of you to see us," Iris said, extending her hand.

"Miss Calderhead. As always, a pleasure. Last time I saw you was in Denver." He turned to Kate, a broad smile wrinkling the tanned skin around his blue eyes. "Well, how about this! Kate. You look a whale of lot better than you did last week. I dropped a note to your parents to tell them you'd been released."

Kate forced a smile, thanked him. The greeting seemed genuinely cordial. So far, so good.

"But, say, now." Mr. Shafroth stood aside. "No sense standing out here all day. Come on in."

As Kate had expected, his office had the same down-home feel as the reception room. With its large, rolltop desk and Mission style chairs, their cushions upholstered in brown leather, a man could put his feet up, loosen his tie, make a deal here.

Once seated and assuring Shafroth they didn't care for iced tea but thank you very much, Iris as the chairman for the Colorado committee took the lead. "Senator, I'm sure you will recall the campaign we waged against your colleague and fellow Democrat, Charles Thomas, two years ago."

The senator tipped back in his swivel chair, eyed them pleasantly. "Do indeed."

"Had it not been for the assistance that came from the President's promise to keep the country out of the war, Mr. Thomas would have been defeated."

"It's hard telling," Senator Shafroth said carefully though seemingly relaxed.

"In the interim, the situation has changed. The primary issue now is the federal suffrage amendment. And, if you will permit me to be blunt, sir, though the Republicans have come out for the amendment, Democratic efforts have been less than forthcoming."

Kate caught the same flick of wariness in his eyes she'd seen at the workhouse. "I think you're off base on that, Miss Calderhead. My record speaks for itself, and it's as sound as it gets on that important subject. If you recall, fifteen days after Senator Palmer and I introduced the Shafroth-Palmer amendment in 1914, the Senate took its first vote on the Anthony Amendment. The vote was thirty-six ayes, thirty-four nays. And the record will show that I was one of those who cast a favorable vote." He ran his square hands along the chair's varnished arms. "I feel as bad as you do that the final tally fell short for passage."

Kate watched as Iris met his gaze without so much as a blink and changed her opinion about her. Iris knew her politics. "And from there it was sent to the Rules Committee, where it languished," she said. "Though, if memory serves, one of your favorite issues—greater freedom for the Philippines—was reported out favorably."

The senator scowled slightly. "Miss Calderhead, I don't want to be rude, but tell me where you're going with this."

"Our point, Senator, is that unless you make certain the Democrats come up with the required votes necessary to approve the Anthony Amendment before the end of this session, the National Woman's Party will work for the election of your Republican opponent."

He chuckled. "I must say I'm flattered you think I am in a position of such power to pull off something like that."

Iris arched an eyebrow, plainly annoyed. "You seem to find the idea amusing. Let me assure you, we are contacting every Democrat up for reelection to convey the same message, Senator. Whatever connections you may have with the President, I would advise you use them and urge him, for the Party's sake if not for women, to come out for suffrage."

"My, you people never miss a trick." The smile held as he tipped back in his chair. "And you, Miss Kate? Where do you fit into all this skullduggery?"

The condescension again. "I will do whatever I can to be of assistance."

He gave a nod. "Well said, Kate. Well said. You sound just like your mother."

She didn't reply.

"In any case, we trust you will give due consideration to the matter." Iris rose, and Kate did the same.

"I can't promise anything," he said as he stood. "But I'll do my darnedst." He came around the desk.

"I certainly hope you will, Senator," Kate said, whatever uneasiness she'd felt when she'd walked in the office gone.

"Senator, is it? Well now." One corner of his generous mouth twisted into a little smile. "Last time, at the prison, it was just plain Mister."

Kate forced a smile. "This is business, Senator. As you know, we are neither pro-Republican nor pro-Democrat. Our only interest is in national woman's suffrage. It's that simple."

❦

Two days later Kate sat in the headquarters' newsroom, unable to concentrate. A cigarette was in order if she could find one. She paused from her hunt-and-peck typing of the report she would take to Lucy and pawed through the stacks of papers on the desk and finally found a slightly mashed package of cigarettes. Two left. She took one out, lit it.

Iris had left yesterday, before the crucial meeting with all the state committee chairmen. Family responsibilities was all Lucy had said by way of explanation, which could have something to do with the fiancé Iris had mentioned in casual conversation. A widower with two teenage children, she'd said. Kate didn't approve. Either you were the chairman or you weren't. She tapped the ash from her cigarette on a cracked butter plate that served as an ashtray. Enough of Iris. Who ran the Colorado committee was Lucy's business.

Labor Day was coming up on Monday. Millie's aunt would be back the next week. Till now, Kate had used lack of time as an excuse for not searching out a place of her own to live. Several people had urged her to look into the government dormitories. The price at fifteen dollars a month was reasonable. The rooms were said to be clean, and they were safe. But there was a waiting list, and the dormitories were a long hike or several streetcar changes from both Perelli's and headquarters.

With a sigh, Kate stubbed out her cigarette and tried to focus on the lines of type on the page, only to give up. Everyone at headquarters who had the chance would be spending the weekend in the country: a final hurrah to summer. Not that the heat would go away, because it wouldn't. Washington was south, some of the women kept reminding her. Kate pushed back her chair, got up and went down to the kitchen for a fresh glass of iced tea.

Three girls from the Maryland committee stopped in the hall on their way out, peered in and asked if they could give her a lift somewhere. "No, but you could tell me where I can find a place to live."

A blond girl from Annapolis—Beverly Ashland, Kate thought her name was—said she might have a connection that would help. A friend of her mother's was a housemother in one of the women's dorms. Everyone laughed at the typical Washington solution, but Kate grabbed a slip of paper, scribbled down the woman's name and address. Tonight she'd write her a note.

Kate leaned against the sink, sipping her tea, and, against her will, she thought of Iris again. It wasn't exaggerating by much to say the effectiveness of the Colorado committee could determine the outcome of the Senate vote that might—just might—be brought up the end of September. Yet there was Iris, tending to family responsibilities, whatever that meant, as though there was all the time in the world to come up with those two crucial votes. Kate poured what was left of her tea down the drain, left the glass in the sink and went in search of Lucy.

Kate tapped on the open door to Lucy's office, and leaned in. "Can I talk to you a minute?"

Lucy looked up from something she was writing, and motioned to her.

"I'm worried."

"That makes two of us." Lucy replaced her pen on the inkstand. "Let's hear yours first." She waved toward the chair near her desk, and Kate sat down.

"It's about Iris stepping down."

"Her fiancé has the flu."

"I didn't realize," Kate said. She'd heard it was going around. Spanish Influenza, it was called. She was a little ashamed now of her poor opinion of Iris leaving. "Is he in the hospital?"

"I have no idea. Iris simply said we shouldn't count on her."

"What about the Colorado vice-chairman? Doris Stevens, I think it is."

"A good person but no Iris and not the kind who works well alone."

"There has to be someone else."

Lucy laced her fingers behind her head, leaned back and gazed at Kate for a minute. "Tell me about this family connection of yours with Shafroth."

Her family, always her family. Where did this obsession of Lucy's come from? Kate swallowed her annoyance. "What's to tell? We live on the same block in Denver. I grew up with his boys."

"But it's true that the connection is strong enough that Shafroth went to the District prison and tried to get you out."

Kate looked at Lucy hard. "If you're thinking I should take Iris's place, I'm not the one to do it and I'll tell you why."

"Shoot."

"For starts, I've never been involved with a state campaign."

"And?"

Kate leaned forward. How would Lucy who had traveled the world, been brought up in New York, whose home was in Washington ever understand the culture of a city like Denver? The big social event of the summer was the *Post* operetta. The state fair wasn't far behind.

Everyone knew everyone else, or, at least, had heard of them. The men who ran the newspapers would remember her as a child, not take her seriously. As to the leaders of the Democratic Party, she'd cut her teeth going to Democratic functions. She could almost feel them pat her on the head as they might a niece or granddaughter. "I'm just the wrong person, Lucy. It wouldn't work. There's too little time. The campaign is too important to botch it. Anything else, I'll do in a minute."

❧

Kate let herself into the apartment and was taking off her hat when she saw Millie in the living room, yanking the cushions off the couch. Curly brown hair tied up in a scarf, a cigarette dangling from her lips, barefoot, wearing only a slip. Kate thought she might be drunk.

"About time!" Millie said. "Aunt Jan sees the filth in this place, and she'll have my hide."

Kate surveyed the chaos of chintz curtains now draped over chairs, gilt-framed landscapes off the walls. "I guess I didn't realize this was the night to clean. Since that's the plan, why don't I take the bedrooms and stay out of your way?"

"Fine. Perfect. Just get busy."

Kate took a few steps backwards toward the hall, giving her friend a closer look. "Millie, are you drunk?"

"What do you care?" Millie said, pounding a seat cushion.

"Did you get fired?"

"No." Millie held the pillow to her breasts.

"What then?"

Millie's eyes filled with tears. "Phil is dead." She let the pillow drop back onto the overstuffed chair.

For an instant, Kate couldn't think who Phil was. Then she remembered the dark-haired second lieutenant who had brought Charlie to the apartment.

"Dead." Through her tears, Millie picked up a small ashtray and stubbed out her cigarette in a single, vicious gesture. "In an army hospital. In France." She glanced at Kate. "And you want to hear a good joke? He didn't die of wounds. He died of influenza."

Kate stared at her.

"You heard right." Millie wiped at her tears with the back of her hand, sniffed. The flu's the Krauts' latest weapon."

"Sit down. You're talking gibberish."

"Am I?" Millie sank into the chintz-covered chair. "Damn it, Kate. It isn't fair. He was such a nice guy. We talked about getting married and how he'd go into his father's business. Ladies' notions." She closed her eyes.

"How about some iced tea?"

"Whiskey. Please."

Kate went to the kitchen, got the bottle of bourbon from the cupboard by the sink and poured a generous amount into one glass, a splash in another. Back in the living room, she handed Millie the fuller of the two. "How did you find out?"

"In a letter. It came today. From a chaplain at the hospital. There was no postmark, but the letter was dated August 10th. Phil talked about me before he died. My address was in his wallet." Millie took a big swallow of bourbon, shook her head. "Lord, what a waste."

Kate sat cross-legged on the floor in front of Millie, and took a sip of her bourbon, feeling its warmth as it snaked its way down into her stomach and the thought came to her that in a single day the flu had touched both her life and Millie's. Maybe it was spreading. She hadn't paid any attention to the papers lately.

Millie looked up from her glass. "Spanish influenza. No one tells us anything. For all we know, the Krauts are winning."

Kate reached up and placed her empty glass on the side table, stood and held out her hand to her friend. "Enough. We've got work to do."

It was eleven o'clock before Millie finished scrubbing the kitchen floor and Kate had washed the last window. The work had calmed

Millie down enough for her to suggest they go out to a kosher grocery store and get something from their delicatessen for a late supper. Back at the apartment, they were unwrapping the pastrami and cutting dark pumpernickel bread in thick slices when the telephone rang. Few people called this late, and Millie and Kate exchanged quick glances.

"You get it, will you?" Millie said. "I've had enough bad news for today."

When Kate picked up the receiver, she was astonished to hear Lucy's voice at the other end of the line.

"Hope you weren't asleep, Kate, but I have something to ask you that won't wait."

Kate gazed at the flowered pattern of the lampshade, golden from the bulb beneath, and felt a premonition of what was to come.

"I received a telegram this afternoon from Iris, telling me that Doris Steven just resigned, too. Seems her father is gravely ill," Lucy said.

"That's too bad," Kate said automatically.

"We need you out there, Kate."

"The last time I looked, the Colorado committee had close to one hundred members."

"That's stretching it and it includes the entire state. I'm talking about leadership."

Kate leaned against the wall. She thought she'd gone all through all the reasons why chairing the Colorado group was a bad idea. Closing her eyes, she could see herself at seven, the Kate Brennan people would remember. A large bow in her bobbed black hair, sucking a lollypop, her short legs swinging impatiently, scrunched down in her seat beside her parents, wishing away the time when the boring man on the platform bedecked with American flags would stop talking. And there was the business of her family's relationship with John Shafroth. Taken together, she was the worst possible choice.

"Kate? Are you there?"

The insistent tone reverberated in her head.

"Kate?"

"Still here." There was too much at stake. Yet Lydie was right. It was impossible to say no to Lucy. "When do you want me to leave?"

Chapter 21

Mary Daly walked past parked cars and up the front walk toward the substantial two-storied, light-colored brick. From the moment the letter came last week, she'd wondered how many women would show up. There was Labor Day coming up and school starting and the way the flu was spreading around Denver, people were too scared to do much more than go to work and back. But Iris Calderhead must have decided she had to take the chance and rally the troops.

Mary was about to press the doorbell when she saw the sign. "NWP: please go around to the garden." She went back down the stone steps, walked along the path. Hearing women's voices, she found the garden gate and pushed down the latch.

In the shade of a large elm, two dozen women were seated on lawn chairs. Facing them was Iris Calderhead—hair finger-waved, pale blue dress, white shoes. Done up for giving a tea party.

Mary walked over, the other women looking her over from the tip of her black oxfords to her black hat, and Iris turned to greet her. The back door opened, and an older woman in a maid's gray uniform with starched white collar and cuffs came out and put a tray of cookies down on a glass-topped table, next to a row of glasses filled with orange juice.

Mary chose one of the metal garden chairs at the back of the group, felt the narrow legs sink into the lush grass as she sat down. The women here were young, new since '16—housewives with kids and a hired girl to help, she guessed. From the look of them, not one a workingwoman like herself.

The maid offered the juice. Iris produced a folder from under her chair, stood, and asked for their attention. The chatter stopped.

"First, I apologize for our having to meet outside. Because of the flu, it seemed the best thing to do." The women murmured, nodded heads, and Iris opened the manila folders. "So to business." She pulled back her shoulders beneath the silk bodice of her dress. "Recently, I had the privilege of meeting with Miss Paul and Miss Burns at our NWP headquarters in Washington. I also called on our senators—both Democrats, as you know—to remind them that our party will campaign for Republican candidates if the amendment is not passed out of the Senate.

"Though Senator Thomas is a lost cause, Senator Shafroth has always been with us. Now we will see just how firm his commitment is." She blessed the gathering with a solemn look. "We do not care how he does it, but either he manages to guarantee two more votes in the 'yes' column or we will be obliged to defeat him for reelection."

Mary let the words sink in. The gist was that Shafroth could whine that he was only one man among ninety-six, but it wouldn't work this time. It was put-up-or-be-shut-out time in the holy-of-holy Senate. Mary approved of the plan, but doubted the women around her understood what was involved in such a campaign.

"I hope the Senator will cooperate fully," Iris was saying. "However, if he does not and we find we must work against him, you should be aware that, as always, he will be a formidable candidate." Iris removed several sheets from the folder. "These are lists. The top sheet contains the name and address and telephone number, if there is one, of every NWP member in Denver. Please find your name and check the entry for accuracy. If you are a Democrat, please place a D next to your name because we will expect your particular help."

Mary saw several women frown.

"Also check to make certain the area of town where you live is noted," continued Iris. "We want every section of the city covered." She paused. "Which brings me to the next reason for this meeting. Namely, that it is with great regret that I must report Miss Doris Stevens, due to the illness of her father, will no longer be able to serve as vice chairman. However, I am pleased to report that Miss Kate Brennan, whom some of you may know, has been assigned as my assistant."

Mary stared at Iris, not hearing what else she said. Kate Brennan, the vice chairman? A girl whose family was known to be a close friend of the Senator working against him? The damp air in Washington must be turning the minds at headquarters to mush.

The woman in front of Mary passed her the sheets, and she checked the squares that applied, her mind was on Kate Brennan. How long had it been since she'd worked for that family? Fifteen years, at least. Kate was just a child. Bobbed hair, stubby legs. Mary had been with the family temporarily while the regular upstairs girl's broken leg healed.

Beyond her thoughts, Mary heard Iris finish off the meeting with a thank you. Everyone stood, and Mary wandered over to the table with the refreshments, took a cookie. She wanted to talk to Iris about Kate Brennan, but Iris had been buttonholed by two women—both talking animatedly at the same time—and Mary decided the less she knew about the mess the better off she'd be.

Standing outside the gate, she breathed in the pungent scent of mock orange. The peace of the neighborhood was hard to resist. No mothers hollering at their kids, no old men hawking their wares off pushcarts. A place walled off from the rest of the world where kids worked twelve-hour days alongside their mothers, who earned half the wages of a man. As fine as the flag-waving part of NWP was, it was the power that would come from every woman across the country voting that would turn the tide so other women might have a chance at a life like this.

As to Shafroth, she had mixed feelings. A decent enough fellow. She'd always voted for him. He was a Democrat, after all. If, by some miracle, Kate Brennan proved to be more than a spoiled girl who never took off her white gloves, this election could be the political fight of his life.

❦

It was dark, a half-moon hanging in the black sky, when Mary walked up to the wire gate Da had built for the dog they'd had once. She felt for the latch. The small, one-story board house beyond was dark. Her brother, Rob, a fireman for the Burlington Northern, was on a run up to Casper. He'd never asked why she'd come back to the house that day in June; she'd never said. He let her be, and she loved him for it.

A board creaked beneath her feet as she stepped on the porch. As she reached out for the screened door, she heard the squeak of the swing, smelled the tobacco. And she turned, saw the dark form sprawled on the wood swing. "What do you think you're doin' here, Gino?"

"You stiffed me for the rent."

"Hah! And I found where you pawned Ma's earrings."

He gave himself a little push, moving the swing back and forth. "Where you been? I'm hungry."

"At work."

"That's what you say." He tipped his head back, smoking, the tip of his cigarette glowing red.

"We're gonna beat Shafroth if the Senate doesn't pass the woman's vote amendment."

He snorted.

"The NWP. Better go tell your buddies."

"I do, and you know what'll happen."

"I'm tremblin' all over."

"The downtown boys—Tim Delaney over in the fifth—the

heavy hitters. Shafroth's their man." Gino tossed his cigarette over his shoulder, got to his feet. "You gonna invite me in?"

"Nope."

He came toward her, beckoning to her like she was a dog. "It ain't no fun without you, baby."

"Get out."

"I know you want it. I can smell you, like a bitch in heat."

"You put a hand on me and I'll stab you through the heart. Self defense."

"With what?"

"Don't push me, Gino. I mean it."

He hesitated. She could sense his eyes, heavy-lidded, sizing up his odds. "Knowin' you, you'd probably put rat poison in my food."

She said nothing.

"I got better things to do anyway." He stepped off the porch. "Next time I see the senator, I'll tell him you're workin' for the enemy."

"Do that."

Not until she saw his form disappear around the corner did she go inside and lock the door.

Chapter 22   ❧

Lugging her suitcase, Kate wound her way through the crowd of Denver's Union Station with the sureness of someone familiar with her surroundings. The only food she'd had all day was an oversized pretzel she'd bought from a vendor who had come through the train in Fort Morgan, and she looked forward to a decent dinner.

Three days earlier, she'd said a tearful good-bye to the Perellis, promising she'd be back in no time, told Millie to look for an apartment they could share, and watched Washington recede in the distance. The hours since then, sitting up in an ancient coach and gazing out at endless fields, broken only by occasional farmhouses, had given her time to size up the battle.

She had three and a half weeks before the last possibility of a vote on the amendment in the Senate. Colorado's women had been voting for nearly two generations. Why should they or the men in the state care whether or not the women east of Colorado had the vote? Worse, it was the Colorado power brokers she had to convince. Either the popular Shafroth got a commitment from two senators who had voted no on the amendment in the past to switch their votes, or the NWP would work for his defeat in November. The way she saw it at the moment, unless a miracle occurred, she had as much chance of success as Sisyphus with that infernal rock making it to the top of the hill.

Kate pushed open the station's large exit door, crossed Wynkoop Street, and walked up Seventeenth Avenue, the only traffic a yellow streetcar. The familiar stone buildings were shut down in the growing dark. Four blocks ahead, past the Colorado National Bank, now occupying the corner where her family's newspaper had first stood, was the Albany Hotel. A four-story red brick with turret windows trimmed with Victorian bric-a-brac, it was one of those old time, respectable drummers' hotels that specialized in cheap rooms, decent food, and, until Denver had gone dry two years ago, a bar that had been a watering hole for all of downtown. A place where she knew she'd be safe and probably never see a soul she knew.

Kate entered the hotel lobby and walked up to the front desk. Calmly asking for a single room with a bath, she ignored the desk clerk's arched eyebrow and filled out the register. Key in one hand, her suitcase in the other, she climbed the stairs to the second floor and unlocked the door. Once she found the light switch, she saw a room barely big enough for the bed, a chest of drawers and flat-topped desk and chair. Not much, but it would do. She hoisted her suitcase onto the bed and headed for the bathroom.

She'd been dreaming about a bath for days, and, as the tub filled, she unpacked what little she'd brought with her: three blouses, a skirt and a dress suitable for dinner, two changes of underwear, and a nightgown. Finally, easing into the warm water, she sighed in relief and thought how odd it was to be staying in a hotel in her hometown.

The alternative was her parents' house, which she considered no alternative at all. Yet she felt an obligation to let them know she was in town and staying at a hotel before they heard it from friends. Her mother wouldn't understand, but it couldn't be helped. She would go by the house first thing in the morning.

But when Kate woke the next morning, energized after a good night's sleep and the sight of the clear blue sky, she decided her first obligation was to visit Iris. Kate had a check in her purse for one hundred dollars as her monthly salary, proof she was on the NWP payroll. What she didn't have was Iris's experience running a campaign, and she badly needed her advice. But when Kate closed the door to the lobby's telephone booth and asked the hotel operator to ring Iris's number, there was no answer. And a call an hour later produced no better results.

Frustrated, Kate returned to her room. Perhaps she should call Iris at her fiancé's home, but she didn't even have his name. Pacing the floor, conscious of the room's faint odor of cheap cigars, she thought of the next three weeks ahead and all that she was expected to do. The official state plan made the job sound so straightforward: call on the editors of newspapers and important political figures who influenced John Shafroth's opinion and convince them that if the Senator wished to be reelected, he must find two fellow Democrats willing to commit to joining him in a "yes" vote. Left unsaid was how to get past the gatekeepers, like secretaries and aides. In Washington, that job had been done for her by headquarters.

Overwhelmed, she flopped down on the bed, and stared up at the water-stained ceiling. And she still hadn't tackled her parents.

❦

The house Kate had grown up in was on a quiet street six blocks from the state capitol. Three stories, built of red sandstone, with a turret. She used to think it looked like a castle. Seeing it now, she was surprised that it looked smaller than she remembered. But the lawn in front was still a perfect carpet of green, the windows still sparkled, no weed spoiled the loveliness of the beds of white rose bushes. Behind the house and a brick wall was the garden shaded by elms and a willow. And to the right, next to the alley, was the carriage house that had been converted into a garage. As far as she knew, Will, the chauffeur, who had enlisted in the army last year, hadn't been replaced. The overall effect, she decided, was understated good taste.

Squaring her shoulders, Kate started up the walk to the front door when she heard women's voices coming from the direction of the open living room windows.

"Forget it, Mother. I don't care if Daddy has paid the tuition for ninety-nine years and bought the train tickets. I would rather die than be stuck with those stupid little ninnies who wouldn't know fashion if they saw it. I've told you a million times I'm not going, and I'm not." Kate smiled at her sister's fervor.

"Young lady, you will do what you're told." Their mother.

"You'll have to carry me bodily onto the train, and you know I won't go quietly."

"I simply don't understand you, Elizabeth. Most girls would—"

"I am not most girls."

"Elizabeth, where are you going? Come back here this instant. I will not tolerate this impertinence."

Kate heard a door slam. She had almost forgotten Lizzie's outbursts. Her father used to joke that his youngest child should go on the stage. Her mother called her scenes pure willfulness. Kate had always chalked the performances up to what came naturally to little sisters. Whatever the case, from the conversation—if it could be called that—the fight was over Lizzie's going to boarding school, something Kate understood because she'd refused to go herself.

Given that it was already September, most school terms would have already started. What Kate had heard obviously was a last-ditch stand for both Lizzie and her mother.

Kate eyed the front door. The timing of her arrival certainly wasn't the best. She wondered if she should wait a few hours for tempers to cool or come back tomorrow. But now that she was here . . . She pressed down on the door latch and stepped inside.

Standing in the entrance hall, Kate glanced toward the living room and saw her mother next to the gleaming ebony baby grand, her hands to her mouth, gazing out the window. "Mother?"

Margaret Brennan started, turned and stared. "Kate!"

Smiling, she walked into the living room. "In the flesh." Her mother looked a little heavier than last summer. But the way she carried herself, her marvelous posture, no one else would probably notice.

"You should have told us you were coming. Dad would have met you at the station." She gave Kate a hug, stepped back, and frowned. "Kate, you're like a stick. Haven't you been eating?"

"It's the Washington heat," Kate said, still smiling.

"Well, it doesn't matter." Her mother gave Kate's arms a brisk pat. "You're home now."

"Mother—"

"I'm afraid Dad's still at the office, but Christine's in the kitchen. She'll want to see you." She tucked her arm through Kate's, leading her toward the pantry. "I knew you'd eventually come to your senses and see what a mistake all that business with those picketers was. Dad and I always said you had a good head on your shoulders."

"Mother, I'm here on NWP business."

She stopped, let go of Kate's arm. "Which entails what exactly?" Gone was the warmth from her voice.

"I'll explain later," Kate said and walked past her mother through the pantry and into the kitchen toward the slight, pale figure in a white uniform and sturdy black shoes that looked too big for her. "Christine?"

The old woman brushed an errant strand of white hair off her lined face, glanced over her shoulder. "Katie. God in heaven, it's true," she murmured, putting aside the ball of dough she'd been shaping, and smiled at Kate's mother. "It's her."

"So it is," her mother said coolly.

"I don't get a hug now that you're the big college graduate?" Christine asked in a tone of mock seriousness, and Kate went over to the tiny woman, put her arms around her. Christine Anderson had been a fixture in the house for sixty years. According to family stories, she'd stepped into the kitchen at eighteen, not a month after leaving Sweden, and never looked back. She'd baked Kate's mother's wedding cake, helped raise her children. Not even Christine's marriage had dimmed her devotion to the family.

"So now." The old woman's keen blue eyes inspected Kate as they had when she'd been a kid coming in from play, all dirt and grime. "I bring your suitcase upstairs. You get cleaned up nice before your father comes home. You can sit out on the porch if you want and have a nice chat with your parents while I fix dinner." She dusted off her hands and started toward the door to the hallway.

"Actually, my things are at the Albany," Kate said.

Christine paused, glanced back at Kate, a confused look on her wrinkled face.

"I'm here on business. I'll be coming and going to meetings and other appointments. I need to be downtown."

Christine shot a glance at Kate's mother. "Mr. Brennan can go get the suitcase after dinner. *Ja?*"

Kate's mother looked at Christine. "We'll see," she said with a determined brightness reserved for servants not privy to private family matters, and gave Christine's arm a pat.

⁂

Kate agreed to stay for supper and took a walk around the neighborhood to pass the time until then. Next door the Dennis house, after that the Millers'. Across the street was the Shafroth house, gray stone with a wide porch. But the vacant lot where her brother Tom and his friends had built forts was gone. In its place was a large house, white clapboard with black shutters and a garage. She wandered east another dozen blocks to Cheesman Park and sat in the sun on the edge of one of the fountains next to the marble pavilion, gazing at the distant mountains, readying herself for the confrontation she would soon have with, if not her father, certainly with her mother.

Back home, Kate tiptoed up the backstairs reserved for the servants and down the hall to Lizzie's room, entered without knocking, and closed the door behind her. With a magenta skirt spread around her, Lizzie who was sitting cross-legged on the floor, hunched over a pile of magazines.

"What's the latest thing these days?" Kate asked and her sister glanced up.

"Kate!" Her green eyes went wide. And, in the next instant, Lizzie was on her feet and they hugged each other. "I wondered when you'd screw up your nerve and come home to breech the gates."

Kate laughed. "When I was coming up the walk earlier, I heard you and Mother going at it."

Lizzie plunked down on her bed. "She wants to ship me off. Out of sight, out of mind."

Kate sat down next to her sister. "Boarding school might not be so bad."

"How would you know?"

Kate shrugged. "A lot of girls at college went to boarding school. They seemed to have survived."

"Good for them." Lizzie leaned back against her elbows. "So tell me what you're doing?"

"Trying to get the suffrage amendment passed."

"Oh, pooh! I know that. That's all Mother and Daddy talk about. What else?"

Outside, a car door slammed, and Kate exchanged a quick glance with her sister. "Must be Daddy." She gave Lizzie's leg a pat. "I better go downstairs and face the music. See you later."

At dinner, Lizzie took her usual place at one side of the table, Kate across from her, their father at the head of the table, her mother at the foot. If it hadn't been for the silence, an onlooker would think it an ordinary family gathering. All the while, Christine came in and out to serve, her eyes blinking back tears. At dessert, Kate's mother told Christine not to bother with coffee. Once napkins were folded and Kate's mother got to her feet, Lizzie excused herself. As she passed Kate, she lifted her eyebrows and went upstairs.

The library was Kate's favorite room: comfortable looking and good-sized, with a southern exposure and more light than most of the other rooms in the house. All of the windows were open to the warm September night. The overstuffed couch and two large deep blue leather chairs on either side of the fireplace had a welcoming feel to them, more informal than the living room. Bookshelves, overflowing with biographies and ancient history that her parents shared a penchant for, lined two walls. Framed photographs of the family and friends in scenes captured during happy times were arranged on the slender cherry wood table set against the back of the couch.

Kate moved toward one end of the couch at her mother's beckoning. Her father settled into his favorite chair by the fireplace, stuck his feet on the footstool.

"All right." Her mother arranged the skirt of her flowered print silk. "No more avoiding the subject. Christine is in the kitchen, out of earshot. I want to know exactly what you intend to do here. Exactly."

Kate pulled in a deep breath, and let it out. "It's not easy to explain. I'll only be here for three weeks then Iris Calderhead will take over again."

Her mother glanced at her father. "Do we know a Calderhead, Dick?"

"Iris's father was a congressman from Kansas," Kate said.

Her mother arched a qualifying eyebrow as if to indicate Iris had passed some kind of preliminary test. She folded her hands. "All right. Out with it."

"Briefly, our objective is to persuade the press and others to put pressure on Mr. Shafroth to force the Anthony Amendment out of the Senate."

"Miss Calderhead will do that?" her mother asked.

"I will."

Her mother sat back, arms across her chest. "That done, you will go back to Washington. Is that it?"

"Unless the Senate fails to approve the amendment. In which case, we will work to defeat Mr. Shafroth for reelection."

Her mother sucked in a quick breath, stared at Kate. "Say that again."

"We will defeat Mr. Shafroth for reelection."

A moment passed, then two, before her mother said, "You sit here in this house, *my* daughter, and tell me that you intend to work against a man who might as well be part of this family."

"Mother—"

"I can't believe this. Have you lost your mind? Have you no sense of loyalty?"

Kate shot a glance toward her father, hands still clasped over his stomach, a closed look on his face, well out of harm's way, or so he probably hoped. He had spent his entire married life in this house, which, until four years ago, had been under the control of his father-in-law, a fifth wheel, trying to accommodate, to keep the peace. Even as a child, Kate had realized his impossible role: the head of a family but master of nothing.

"Mother, I'm not working for or against anyone right now. It's up to Mr. Shafroth. If he can get the two votes we need by the first of October . . ."

Her father recrossed his legs, cleared his throat. "Might I remind you, Kate, that one man does not a majority make."

"You're wrong on that, Daddy."

Her father gazed at Kate with half-closed eyes. "And if it isn't enough, you and your pals are going to crucify him."

"I think that's a little extreme," she said, quietly. "What we will do is elect his opponent, Lawrence Phipps, because his party, the Republicans, already supports the amendment."

Her mother let out a little gasp. "You will work for a Republican? Vote for a Republican?"

"If I have to."

Her mother sighed, massaged her temples with her fingertips, as if willing away a headache. "Your grandfather is turning over in his grave."

"Not every Republican wears horns, Mother."

"Don't be smart. This is principle we're talking about. Your great grandfather was a Jackson man. Your grandfather went to his grave a Democrat. The Brennans are Democrats. Period."

"Mother—"

"Show me a Republican who ever stood up for the little man?"

"Lincoln?" Kate caught the shadow of a smile on her father's face.

"Nonsense."

"He freed the slaves." Kate clasped her hands tight to keep them from shaking. "Yet the President of the United States who is a Democrat has had women thrown in prison—I was one of them— without benefit of a trial, just because he doesn't like our message."

"You are deliberately missing the point. We are talking about John Shafroth. Who lives on this very block. You grew up with his boys." Twisting, her mother reached in back of her for a silver framed photograph on the table behind the couch. "Look at this, Kate." She held it out. "There he is, holding you when you were six months old, his own little Morey right beside him." She turned the photograph as if to see it better. "We were all at the lake." There was a wistful tone in her voice.

"Mother, this is about the guarantees promised by the Bill of Rights and the Constitution. If the Democratic members of the Senate can't do what's right for the women of this country, then those senators who are up for reelection have to be replaced with those who will."

Her mother continued to stare at the photograph.

"Mr. Shafroth isn't the great supporter of woman's suffrage you may think he is, Mother. His version of the amendment he sponsored is just a sop to appease the Southern Democrats who can only think about states' rights." Kate slid a glance toward her father who was contemplating the toes of his shoes.

"I suppose your NWP friends told you that," her mother said icily.

"What I'm saying is true."

"Well, you are quite mistaken." Her chin high, her mother smoothed her dark hair. "I simply don't understand your thinking. Your family stands by its friends, and John Shafroth is a very dear friend. He even went to that prison to make sure you were all right and saw to your release."

"The District jail. Yes. He had a hand in our release."

"Exactly. Whenever we've needed him, he's been there."

Out of the corner of her eye, Kate saw her father lower his chin, draw further inside himself and close an invisible door as if anticipating what was coming.

"Before you were born, when your grandmother Brennan died and your father had to go back to West Virginia, who was it that dropped everything and looked after me and your brother? Your grandfather had gone to Chicago. I was alone, caring for baby Tom who was down with scarlet fever. I couldn't have gone on without John's help." Kate's mother laid her hands gently over the glass covering the photograph.

Kate eyed her and saw something in her mother she'd never noticed before. To Kate, she'd always been the one person who always knew what to do, when to do it, and how. Kate tried to imagine her mother at twenty or twenty-one—her age—running this big house. Her father's house. Entertaining his cronies and political friends. Always there for everyone, night and day. An expert at coping. But even she had had her limits. Being alone with a desperately sick toddler was one. No wonder she had a soft spot in her heart for John

Shafroth. Or was there more to it? But she let go of the thought and said, "Mother, this is about party politics."

Her mother's lips were pursed as she carefully replaced the framed photograph on the table. "Never in my life have I heard such stupid, unfeeling drivel." She stood, looked down at Kate. "You do as you wish. You are of age. What your family stands for apparently is of no importance to you." She drew herself up taller. "I cannot speak for your father, but as far as I'm concerned, as long as you pursue this course, you are no longer welcome in this house." With that, she turned and left the room.

Chapter 23 ————————————————————

Kate lay awake for hours after her father had dropped her off in front of the Albany. Neither had spoken during the short ride downtown. Kate knew how much he hated arguments, but she had hoped that, because of the letter she'd left for him in Washington, he would say he understood.

The sounds outside her room's window were muffled versions of Washington—police sirens, the wail of a fire engine, car horns—sounds that reminded her she had a serious job to do, and very little time to do it. When the morning light finally filled the room, Kate sat up, threw off the sheet, and squinted at her watch. A few minutes before six. Too early to telephone Iris, though the dining room might be open.

Kate chose a table by a window and ordered a fried egg and toast and coffee, strong, the way she liked it. But it was still only seven thirty by the time she finished the last of her coffee so, to kill time, she bought a paper at the newsstand outside the hotel and chose a spot by the window in the lobby to read. On the dot of nine she tossed the paper aside, walked over to the telephone room, no bigger than a closet, just off the dining room, and gave the operator Iris's number. This time, she heard the receiver lift. But when she asked to speak to Miss Calderhead, Kate was told she could not be disturbed. Let down, Kate left her name and the hotel's number.

Opening the booth's door for air, wondering what to do next, she yearned to talk to someone. Anyone. And she thought of Doris Stevens, the vice chairman whose father was sick, and Kate closed the booth door again and placed another call.

The Stevens house was in east Denver and only a short walk from the streetcar line. A two-story beige brick with dark brown trim and a covered porch, it was shaded by a large weeping willow. The tiny lawn was filled with weeds and needed cutting. The only spot of color was a red-leafed barberry bush planted against the base of the porch. Except for the distant bark of a dog, the neighborhood was quiet, sleepy in the warmth of the early fall day.

The moment Kate stepped onto the porch, the front door opened, and a full-figured woman who looked to be in her late thirties stepped out. "Kate Brennan. I'd recognize you anywhere. Iris couldn't rave enough about you, and she's not the raving type." Doris glanced behind her toward the screened door. "I wonder if you'd mind sitting out here. I try to keep it quiet inside for Dad." She nodded toward two slat-backed wooden chairs at the far end of the porch. "I've made coffee. We can have a cup and talk."

Sipping at the rich, strong coffee, Kate asked a litany of questions—which of the members whose names appeared on the list Lucy had given her were the best workers, how many had worked on the last campaign. Doris gave her a list Iris had created of key women to contact outside of Denver. "And, as big a state as Colorado is and as little time as you have, I'd stick to the biggest towns that have dailies. The editors are generally decent about talking to us. Of course, in Denver, you have to get to the ward bosses. They like to ignore us. So you have to keep after them."

The gentle tinkle of a bell sounded. Doris tensed, excused herself, and disappeared into the house. Ten minutes later she was back, and Kate asked specific questions about the women on the list Doris had given her. In the middle of the discussion, a black roadster pulled up and parked, and Doris jumped up as a white-haired man, thin and slightly stooped, wearing a serviceable dark suit and fedora got out. He was carrying a black medical bag. Kate started to gather up her notes.

"No, wait a minute. Dr. Neal never stays long."

She and the doctor went inside. When the two came out again, Doris's face was drained of color. Kate looked away and tried not to eavesdrop on their conversation. Death was a private matter, not easily shared, and Kate sat quietly, not wanting to call attention to herself.

After a while, Doris walked the doctor to his car, where they continued to talk until the doctor climbed into his car and drove off. Back on the porch steps, Doris stared at the screened door for a moment, pulled in a deep breath.

"I have to go in. The doctor says Dad may not make it through the next couple of days," she said, her voice breaking. "I'm afraid I won't be able to help much."

"Please. Lucy Burns mentioned your situation. I understand," Kate said.

"Call me if you get in a pinch," Doris said and Kate nodded, though she knew she never would. "And, of course, you have Iris as a backup."

"I'll be fine. This is my hometown, remember?" Kate slid the sheets of paper into the folder and tucked it under one arm. She wished she could say she'd be praying for Doris' father, but praying had never been part of her family tradition and she didn't really know how.

On the streetcar ride back to the hotel, Kate reviewed the lists and picked out a key town in each area of the state to visit after she talked to the ward bosses. The only Colorado she knew was limited to Denver and the village near Grand Lake, high in the mountains, a hundred miles to the north, where her family had a cabin. The thought of venturing out onto the High Plains and over the mountain passes to the little towns west of the Divide excited her.

After a supper of soup and a pot roast sandwich, Kate put in another call to Iris. Full of apologies, Iris explained her fiancé's condition had taken a turn for the worse. "Finding nurses is impossible. I want to help, of course, but I simply can't leave him. I'll send over my materials," she said. "And you have Lucy's, of course. Plus, our experienced members will be a great help. I can't tell you how sorry I am. But if anyone can handle it, you can."

After she hung up, Kate slumped against the back of the small chair, overwhelmed. All the reasons she'd given Lucy about why she wasn't the person to do the job still held true. And here she was with only three weeks to do it.

Upstairs in her room, she switched on the desk lamp, slid Lucy's state committee file onto the desk, sat down, and removed the list of Colorado NWP members. Reasoning that all of them were experienced, that all had worked for the '16 campaign and were seasoned troops, she had to figure out how to use them to full advantage. So, one at a time, she examined each sheet of names, looking for a pattern—something she could use immediately.

Running a finger down the columns, she noticed the D's for Democrat by various names with Denver addresses. Twenty of them. She'd guess most knew their state legislators personally. A plan came to her. She would ask each Democratic member to contact her representative or senator and urge him to immediately write or telegraph Shafroth, a man who put party above all else. He'd pay attention, she was sure. Then faced with appeals from newspaper editors and ward bosses she planned to line up, he would be forced to do his duty.

Kate gazed across the dreary room, letting the plan sink in. Too much was at stake not to give it a try, and she reached in the drawer again for stationery.

⁂

The next morning was Friday, September 6th—Kate's first full day as Colorado's NWP chairman *pro tem*, and she marked it on the calendar she'd found in the desk. Not counting Sunday, she had sixteen days to do her job.

She had chosen to start her campaign with the *Denver Post*, the state's largest Democratic newspaper, and she dressed with particular care, made certain her stocking seams were straight, her gloves were clean. The publisher, Fred Bonfils, had founded the paper with a former curio seller, Harry Tammen. But Bonfils was the man who set the paper's policy and the man to see.

As Kate left the hotel, she imagined her grandfather's reaction to what she was about to do. Once the owner of the *Rocky Mountain News*—the *Post*'s competition—he'd always considered Bonfils a complete fraud. But the *Post* was a strong Shafroth supporter. If anyone could persuade the senator of the importance to twist his fellow senators' arms, Fred Bonfils was the man.

The office was on the second floor of a red stone building in the middle of the block on Champa Street, a short walk. The rather plump secretary showed Kate in, and Mr. Bonfils rose from his high-backed black leather chair, invited her to sit down. Dark hair graying at the temples, impeccably dressed in a lightweight brown wool suit and crisp white shirt and beige, silk tie, he was the picture of a wealthy businessman.

The publisher sank into his chair behind his large, mahogany desk. Resting his elbows on the gleaming oak arms of the chair, he placed his fingertips together, eyed her. "If you don't mind my saying so, Kate—I hope I may call you Kate—I'd never thought I'd see the day a Brennan would darken my door."

Reminding herself that he was only another man, she answered his Cheshire cat smile with as much aplomb as she could muster. To be sitting here with this smooth talking, former carnival barker was a test of her commitment. "This is not a personal visit, Mr. Bonfils, and, if I may, I'd like to get down to the reason why I'm taking your time today."

The steel-blue eyes above his smile openly focused on her breasts. "By all means."

Kate swallowed hard and started in to explain how important it was for him—a supporter of Senator Shafroth with a great deal of political influence—to encourage the Senator to push harder for the amendment. "Otherwise, I'm afraid the NWP will be forced to back Lawrence Phipps, the Republican candidate," she said. And Bonfils laughed.

His reaction shouldn't have surprised her, but it did. She tried to think of what Miss Paul might say. "You do know the Republicans have endorsed the amendment?"

"So I've heard."

"Then you understand that the possibility of our backing Phipps is not an idle threat."

Bonfils tipped back, chuckled. "What does your Daddy say to all this?"

Kate fought to keep her composure. "That's beside the point, Mr. Bonfils. What you are going to say to Senator Shafroth and how soon you reach him are all that matters."

Bonfils, still grinning, rose from his chair. "I'll give it some thought," he said, and walked her to the door.

Once outside again, still shaking, Kate tried to tell herself that once Bonfils had time to think about her message, he'd take her seriously and come around. The *News* was only two blocks away. She didn't have an appointment, but she decided to take the chance that the new publisher would see her, and he did.

A slender man, nearly bald, with thick black eyebrows and a prominent nose, John Shaffer reminded her that they had met at the reception after her grandfather's funeral. He talked about what a fine man her grandfather had been, and Kate agreed.

After a few minutes of polite conversation, she set her purse aside, removed her gloves. "Mr. Shaffer, I'm here about the Anthony Amendment. The National Woman's Party has reason to believe it will be brought up before the Senate for debate the end of the month.

Two additional votes are needed if a two-thirds favorable vote is to be achieved. We hope you will do everything possible to persuade Senator Shafroth to do his part in procuring those votes."

He listened to her politely, nodded. And why wouldn't he? The *News* was now a Republican paper. She was preaching to the choir. After repeating her plea, she thanked him for his time, and left.

The next day, Saturday, Kate shifted her attention to the weeklies. She began by marking their locations on the map Doris Stevens had given her. Two longtime papers were in central Denver. The other six were out toward the suburbs. Most of them probably favored Republican candidates. Though it might be a waste of time to bother with them, she couldn't afford to take anything for granted. She set out, buoyed by the brilliant blue sky, determined to make headway.

But the plan met with defeat from the start. The harried editors, always frantic about looming deadlines, barely listened to her. By the following Wednesday, Kate was glad her appointment with the *Montclair Enterprise* was the last. Located east of City Park in one of the newer neighborhoods, the newspaper was tucked in among a row of small stores and difficult to find. She'd had to transfer three times to reach it. The weather had turned cold and windy. The editor kept her waiting for nearly an hour and then told her she "was whistling Dixie" if she thought he'd waste a two-cent stamp to write to John Shafroth.

Sitting in the hotel dining room that night, picking at her ham steak, Kate reviewed the last week and wondered what—if anything—she'd accomplished. Not a single editor had given her a commitment. Her next task—to tackle the ward bosses—would be even tougher.

Perhaps she ought to use a different approach, though at the moment she couldn't think of one. Down in the dumps, she reached for the latest edition of the *News* she'd bought in the lobby and began to read as she ate. As always, the war dominated the front page. Seven American divisions had taken the lead in smashing the German-held St. Mihiel along the Meuse River. Kate found no mention of flyers, and she turned to the next page, skimming a story about the president visiting wounded soldiers. She was about to flip to page three when her eyes caught the headline "Keating Scheduled to Speak" above a one-paragraph story tucked next to an ad for Bishops Liver Pills.

Congressman Keating. An affable Irishman who had once worked as a copy boy for her grandfather at the *News*. Years later he had continued to honor the man, had wept openly at his funeral. More to the point, she remembered that Ed Keating had grown up in the Fifth Ward. In fact, he'd been ward boss for five years. And the congressman was to address the United Mine Workers tonight at a location across the Platte, in the Irish part of town. Kate smiled at the possibility. A word from the congressman might get the campaign back on track. She checked her watch. She could make it if she hurried.

⁕

Fifteen minutes before eight, Kate stood at the foot of the stairs leading to the hall. Men's voices drifted down from above. She took in a quick breath, adjusted the collar of her jacket, preparing herself for storming the lion's den. A union hall was off-limits to women, that much she knew from the stories her grandfather used to tell when he defended the mine workers. But the meeting was her best chance of talking to Mr. Keating, and she went up.

The pea green paint peeling off the walls of the large, high-ceilinged room gave it a forlorn look. Men had already started to fill the rows of battered wooden chairs. A lectern had been placed at the front of the room. Behind it was a large white sateen banner with UMWA lettered in red, white, and blue. Next to it was an American flag. A couple dozen men—most gray-haired, too old to serve in the army, were clustered around a man of medium height, whom she recognized immediately as Ed Keating. He hadn't changed much. His dark hair combed straight back, stocky build. A smile filled his broad, open face. Unlike the men around him dressed in work clothes, he wore a shirt and tie. But the shirt collar was unbuttoned, the tie loosened.

Heads turned as she started to walk down the aisle between the rows of chairs. A man came up to her and was asking her business when Mr. Keating glanced her way. She smiled, continued walking toward him. Not certain that he remembered her, she gave her name.

His dark brown eyes instantly widened, and his broad face broke into a wide grin. "Kate Brennan, as lovely as your sainted mother. How long has it been?"

She met his smile. "Just two years, at granddad's funeral."

"A lot of water's gone under the bridge since then," he said, a little wistfully Kate thought. "Unless I miss my bet, I'd say you didn't come to talk about old times."

She nodded. "I have a favor to ask."

"Just name it. But first . . ." He glanced at the men around him. "Lads, I'd like you to meet Miss Kate Brennan, granddaughter of none other than Tom Kerrigan, one of the finest men God ever created. Worked his way to the top by the sweat of his brow. A senator, a rich man. But he never forgot where he came from. Always a friend of the workingman. The Lord only knows how many times he defended the likes of you and me."

Kate watched the gray heads nod, the approving glances sent her way. The ice had been broken.

Mr. Keating took her arm. "If you'll excuse us, boys, Miss Brennan and I need to catch up on old times. I'll be back with you in a few minutes."

He dragged over two chairs, ignoring the voices around them as men continued to enter the hall. Kate explained why she was in Denver, all the while watching for his reaction. Word of his help was bound to spread through local political circles and open important doors. It might even get back to her parents, proof that a man they respected took her seriously.

"Mr. Keating, I can't emphasize enough how important it is for Senator Shafroth to do everything he can to force the amendment out of committee and gain approval before the end of the session. I spoke with the senator in Washington, but he needs to hear from a fellow Democrat in Congress." She leaned forward. "Almost as important, he has to hear from men here in Denver, like the boss of the fifth Ward. Your old stomping grounds."

Ed Keating nodded, sat back, spilling over the straight-backed chair. "That'd be Tim Delaney."

"I realize you no longer represent Denver's congressional district, but a word from you . . . For old times' sake . . ." She flashed what she hoped was a dazzling smile. "A telephone call . . ."

"Why not?" Ed Keating chuckled. "Your Granddad would get a kick out of this."

Kate smiled. "There are only two weeks before Congress recesses," she said at the risk of pushing her luck.

Mr. Keating got to his feet, touched her shoulder. "John Shafroth's a good man. He and I go back aways. Still and all, the Senate operates on another planet. As to Delaney in the Fifth, that I can do. I'll call first thing in the morning."

Kate surveyed the narrow staircase leading to the Fifth Ward headquarters. Every step was occupied by someone apparently waiting his or her turn to exchange a vote for a favor—money to cover funeral expenses, a word to the right person for a city job. She had to believe Ed Keating had kept his promise to contact Tom Delaney in charge of dispensing such favors. Squaring her shoulders, she picked her way around those waiting, so intent on her mission that she felt only the slightest twinge of guilt over butting in ahead of them.

The room at the top was small, crowded. Two doors on either side of the room opened and closed with regularity as people came and went. A woman with wiry blond hair, sitting at a battered desk, seemed to be in charge of taking supplicants' names. Kate went up to her and said she had an appointment with Mr. Delaney.

"Don't know nothin' about it, honey," the woman said distractedly as she pawed through a pile of papers on her desk.

"Congressman Keating called Mr. Delaney yesterday," Kate said, hoping it was true.

"Just wait your turn." The blond snatched a paper, waved it toward a woman seated nearby who held a baby in her lap.

One of the doors opened. A man appeared, beckoned to the woman with the child to come in. Kate regarded the door as it closed. Somewhere beyond it had to be Mr. Delaney. The blond was busy with a short man in overalls. With nothing to lose, Kate went over to the door and opened it, ready to say she was after the bathroom if anyone stopped her.

She found herself in a hallway. A moment later, the woman with the baby stepped out of a door at the far end and came toward her. Behind them was a thickset man with graying hair and a ruddy complexion. "You let me know if the doc gives you any trouble, Mrs. Haley."

The woman gave a respectful bob of her head, mumbled her thanks, and slid past Kate and down the hall.

Guessing he was Tim Delaney, Kate walked toward him. "Mr. Delaney, I'm Kate Brennan. Congressman Keating told you about me?"

"Did he now?" He ran a finger around the inside of his shirt collar as he eyed her, perhaps weighing whether she was worth his time. "Well, then, come in. Have a seat."

The office was a corner one, enabling the occupants a view of Twenty-seventh Street below and the South Platte River to the west. A bank of wood filing cabinets lined two walls. Four chairs for visitors, an ancient swivel chair next to an equally aged, rolltop desk filled the rest of the room. Framed photographs of men Kate presumed were political luminaries hung on the wall.

Mr. Delaney picked up a half-smoked cigar, its tip still glowing, from a heavy glass ashtray, stuck it in his mouth, and sat down. "What can I do for ya?"

The question made Kate suspect Ed Keating had said nothing about the reason for the appointment, which meant she was on her own. Making a show of taking off her gloves and arranging them alongside her purse on her lap—signs, she hoped, that what she had to say was important enough to require his attention for more than a moment, she got right to the point. "Mr. Delaney, Senator Shafroth needs your help. Unless you can persuade him of the importance of urging his fellow senators to come up with the necessary two votes to pass the suffrage amendment out of the Senate, he will be defeated for reelection."

The Ward boss stared at her out of hooded eyes as he chewed on his cigar. "And what is your business with all this?"

"I'm representing the National Woman's Party."

"The ladies with the banners."

She met his amused gaze. "May I remind you we almost defeated Senator Thomas two years ago."

"Not in this ward, you didn't."

"The President's promise to keep us out of the war was all that saved him from defeat. Fifty more votes, Mr. Delaney. Right here in the Fifth Ward. The figures are in the election office." She hadn't actually seen them. Iris had noted the figures in a report. "Fifty votes and Senator Thomas would have been back in Denver practicing law, and a Republican would have replaced him in the Senate."

Delaney removed the cigar from his mouth, studied it for a moment before he put the soggy end back in his mouth. "You're givin' this story to the boys in the other wards?"

"I am. But you're the key. As the boss of the Fifth Ward, you have a great deal of influence." She straightened slightly. "Senator Shafroth needs a push from home to do what's right, and he needs it now."

One corner of his mouth twisted into a lopsided smile. "Little lady, you talk real nice. But here's how it is." He leaned forward, lowered his voice, as if for emphasis. "The Fifth votes Democratic. Always has, always will. As to Old John, he's been around the political racetrack more than a time or two. He can take care of himself."

"If you believe that, sir, you are underestimating the women of Denver who vote." She gathered her gloves and purse, terrified he would notice her shaky hands. "This time there will be no issue like the war appealing to voters' heartstrings to save him." She stood. "For your sake and the senator's, I hope you will bring your considerable influence to bear."

Letting herself out, her heart thumping nearly out of her chest, she made her way back down the stairs, past supplicants and out into the blinding sunshine. As she paused for a moment to pull on her gloves, she sensed someone's eyes upon her. She glanced up at the rounded windows of the corner room on the second floor and saw a man looking down at her. She smiled, gave him what she hoped was a casual wave, and walked off, not too fast, but with a purposeful stride.

Excluding Sunday when the offices were closed, Kate's visits to the other Democratic ward bosses over the next ten days went about the same. Not a one was even mildly concerned about the senator's political future. Old John could take care of himself. He was a shoe-in. None offered the slightest indication he would contact Shafroth.

Today's call to the Tenth Ward had been the worst. The secretary ignored Kate's attempt at using her connection to Ed Keating. Her boss, Mr. Talbot, would be out all day. Kate had waited for his return, just in case, but he'd never appeared. Now as she crossed the hotel lobby to the front desk, Kate knew that, another day like this one, and she'd begin feeling sorry for herself. If she were in Washington, she'd have Lucy to turn to. As it was, she had no one. She'd had no word from the NWP members she'd written. Since she'd arrived in Denver, she hadn't run into a single girl she knew. Not that she'd expected a welcoming committee, but, at this moment, she yearned for company or a little good news, and she didn't have either.

The desk clerk named Joey—a gangly kid with a deformed left hand that must have kept him out of the army—smiled as Kate approached and handed her a letter and a telegram along with her key. With a nod of thanks, she turned toward the staircase, studied the envelopes. Though the telegram's bland, buff-colored envelope gave no hint of its contents, in her present mood, she feared the worst. The letter, on the other hand, was in Millie's handwriting, and Kate opened it as soon as she entered her room and switched on the light.

Kate. Miss you. Aunt Jan has slowed my love life. Your Chuck came by a few days ago to ask for your address and I gave it to him. Hope that was okay. Still hot. Work is boring. Don't see anything in the papers about your amendment. Write and tell all.

Love, your pal, Millie.

Kate smiled. She missed Millie, too. Missed her irreverent view of life that belied a passion Kate admired. And ever the matchmaker, referring to Charlie as *your Chuck* when she knew the situation perfectly well. Kate wondered what he'd do with her address. Would he write? Or was he simply keeping track of her as part of his job—coming to the hearings as he had, telephoning Shafroth about her being in prison? At the moment, she didn't want to think about it, couldn't think about it, and she returned Millie's note to its envelope, and opened the telegram.

Amendment rescheduled STOP September 26 STOP Full speed ahead STOP Lucy. Kate reread the words. Today was Friday, the 20th. Until now, the work of the state committees—her work—had been based more on hope than reality that Senator Jones could maneuver the Democratic leadership into allowing debate on the amendment before Congress recessed. But he'd done it! And this time, the Senate would pass the amendment.

Grinning, Kate was suddenly ravenous. She decided to treat herself to a steak somewhere other than the hotel dining room. First thing in the morning, beginning with the *Post*, she'd start making the rounds again to reinforce the message that Senator Shafroth better have pulled in every favor owed him and found two more votes to add to the "aye" column or he wouldn't be coming back to the Senate next spring.

Chapter 24

Lucy opened her eyes to the pale, pre-dawn light and rolled onto her side. The air in her bedroom was cool with the promise of fall. Last week she'd glimpsed bits of gold among the leaves in the park, hints of the burst of color that would soon fill the woods. Yet she hadn't slept well last night. The ever-lasting lists of names, people to contact, things to do that should have been done days or weeks ago, packed her brain. She wished the human mind were like a gramophone that one could just turn off. And what sleep she had managed had been filled with dreams of Senator Reed rallying the troops to hold off debate on the amendment today.

At this moment, NWP members were lighting fires in the urns at the base of the Lafayette memorial, fueling them with copies of the president's speeches. Arrests would follow. But given the Senate's scheduled debate this afternoon, she hoped the White House had called the police off that detail for the day.

The women around the country had been hard at work trying to cement the two needed votes. Yet conditions had changed since last May's vote. Fuel shortages, trains at a near standstill, war profiteering scandals, and looming peace negotiations provided distractions for a Congress too easily distracted.

She turned over onto her back, flung an arm over her eyes. How naïve she and Alice had once been when they set out on this cause. So impatient, so sure they could do what thousands of women before them hadn't and outmaneuver the politicians. Stints in prison had taught them important lessons, had hardened them. The naiveté had vanished long ago, but the impatience still held.

As of this spring, eleven states—ten western states and New York—enjoyed full suffrage, still a far cry from forty-eight. Alice blamed it on the liquor lobby, which had opposed suffrage from the beginning. For Lucy, the major disappointment still was the South. The impenetrable, reactionary Democratic South. Other than winning the primary vote in Arkansas, the South remained solid enough to sink the ship. Unless the rumors were true.

Talk swirling through the Capitol was that Secretary of the Treasury McAdoo, the president's son-in-law, was deeply concerned about the consequences should the Democratic Party lose control of Congress. He had pleaded with Wilson to make a personal appeal to his fellow Democrats that they put aside their objections to the suffrage amendment. She envisioned the President sitting in his bathrobe, bleary-eyed from a night back at his typewriter, pecking out letters to the malcontents—beseeching them to put aside their rhetoric about how the vote would ruin a woman's femininity and do the right thing, for the Party.

Lucy thought of all the occasions since Wilson's inauguration when every suffrage group in the country had begged him to come out for the amendment. And now, ironically, he might do it, but only because he needed votes for his peace plan.

Yet there was always the chance the southerners might still balk. And if they did, the state committees would go into phase two. Aside from the Republican Borah, the target senators would all be Democrats: Walsh of Montana, Warren of Wyoming, Pittman of Nevada, Lane of Oregon, Thompson of Kansas, and Shafroth of Colorado. In the East, there was Saulsbury of Delaware and Baird of New Jersey. Neither man would be missed. While not southerners, they might as well be for all their backpedaling. Republicans Weeks of Massachusetts and Moses of New Hampshire were no better. But some of the others were decent senators, the sacrificial lambs.

Lucy threw off the covers and sat up. Of all the committees, Colorado's worried her the most. Every other state had a veteran of earlier campaigns at the helm. At first, Kate's family connections with Shafroth seemed like an advantage. Now Lucy wasn't so sure. What lay ahead in the next weeks would tell the tale.

Lucy shook her head, shrugged on her bathrobe. What was the saying? Worry was like a rocking chair: it gives you something to do but doesn't get you anywhere. It was time to tackle the day.

After a quick bath, she took the dark green silk suit—always her best color—with its deep pleated skirt and jacket trimmed with braid that she'd bought for the occasion out of the closet, slipped it on. She sat at her dressing table and managed to pin her wiry, red hair into place. And, as a finishing touch, she dabbed a powder puff over her face and applied a light touch of lip rouge. She slid the hatbox from Hechts off the closet shelf, lifted the lid, folded back the tissue, and removed her hat with its fashionable deep crown and wide brim, made of the same green silk as her dress, and put it on. Picking up her purse and gloves, she returned to her dressing table and cast a discerning glance in the mirror. Gazing back at her was a reasonably attractive, well-dressed woman with an air of business about her. She gave a little shrug. She was as ready as she was going to get.

Lucy and Alice strode down the hallway toward the Democratic Senate cloakroom. Time was short, but Senator Jones needed a last-minute reminder that they would be watching him carefully. Exchanging smiles of recognition with the doorkeeper, they went in. L-shaped, the main part of the room was narrow and drab. The walls were tan, the draperies a dull green. A half-dozen senators were seated on the couches and chairs of cracked brown leather, arranged along one wall. Senator Jones was huddled with the senator from

Missouri at the far end of the room, and Lucy and Alice went over to them.

"Senators." Alice glanced from Jones to Reed. "We trust we can count on your votes for the amendment."

"You may be sure the matter will be given due consideration," Reed said gravely.

Lucy gave him a level look. She wouldn't believe James Reed if he were pledging allegiance to the United States.

"And you, Senator Jones?" Alice asked smoothly.

"Senator Reed couldn't have expressed it better." Jones nodded earnestly. "A fair hearing. That's what we're all after."

As she and Alice excused themselves, Lucy noticed beads of sweat along Jones's upper lip, whether from nerves or the heat, she wasn't sure. But his false heartiness betrayed nerves, and she suspected the votes he'd lined up were not as sure as he might want.

❧

The invocation had already been given and the preliminaries were underway when Lucy and Alice took their seats in the front row of the gallery. Lucy peered over the railing just as Senator Jones got to his feet. She sucked in a quick breath. The fat was in the fire. All that could be done had been done. A nod to her Catholic upbringing, she offered a quick prayer to St. Jude, patron saint of the impossible.

"Mr. President," called the familiar baritone voice.

"The chair recognizes the senator from New Mexico."

Jones squared his shoulders. "Mr. President, I move the Senate proceed to the consideration of unfinished business."

A rap of the gavel. The motion was agreed to. The chair declared that the Senate as a whole would resume consideration of Joint Resolution 200 proposing an amendment to the Constitution of the United States, extending the right of suffrage to women. Eighty-three senators answered the roll call. A quorum was declared present.

Lucy and Alice exchanged glances, nodded. So far so good.

Senator Pittman, a rough-around-the-edges man with thinning brown hair, a Democratic from Nevada, was the first to be recognized.

Lucy had wondered whom the Democratic leadership would choose to nitpick the Amendment and now she knew. Pittman, the westerner, was willing to trade his soul to be recognized by the eastern movers and shakers, and he was about to do so by castigating the NWP.

"Mr. President, I am not a member of the Committee on Woman's Suffrage, but I have made every effort to bring this matter to a vote and see to its passage. Thus, it is important for me to say as an opening statement that the National Woman's Party has conducted campaigns throughout the suffrage states, saying that not only has the Woman's Suffrage Committee, a majority of whom are Democrats, obstructed this vote but that the President of the United States himself was responsible for the obstruction of it."

The Nevada senator went on. It seemed, he said, that the Republican Party—that is, the Republican members of the Senate—had held a caucus on August 24, the result of which was to support the amendment. He wasn't sure of the date but the 24th had been reported in *The Suffragist*, a paper run by the Woman's Party, which supported the Republican Party throughout the equal suffrage states.

A senator at the rear of the Chamber asked if the Woman's Party was the one that has been picketing in Washington, and Pittman said it was. He rambled on about how the other group, the National American Woman's Suffrage Association, which never mixed in politics, had everyone's complete confidence.

Alice leaned toward Lucy, whispered, "If I were Mrs. Catt, I'd take that comment as a mixed blessing."

Lucy grinned, enjoying the picture of the grande dame of the old guard's reaction to words of approval from a crude pipsqueak like Pittman.

Senator Smoot, a Republican from Utah, rose. "I believe, Mr. President, that if the honorable Senator from Nevada is in favor of woman suffrage, I do not think he is making any headway in securing the passage of the joint resolution by trying to inject politics into the question."

The Nevada senator looked injured, protested. Smoot waded in again.

"The honorable Senator is well aware that all but twelve votes on the Republican side of this Chamber will be cast for the suffrage resolution, which is more than he can say for his own party," he said. "Further, that to say that the Republican Party is responsible in any way for the picketing is false."

The finger-pointing went on.

Henry Cabot Lodge of Massachusetts, the newly elected Republican floor leader and one of the coldest fishes Lucy had ever had the dubious honor of dealing with, shot to his feet and said, "Mr. President, I presided at the conference, and there was no opposition to the resolution whatever. It passed unanimously."

Lucy turned toward Alice, said sotto voce, "Unanimous, my foot! It never ceases to amaze how easily the lies roll off their tongues. Every one of these blokes knows Lodge refused to go along with the resolution."

The ball was passed from one senator to the other. A Republican senator asked Pittman whether it was true that a larger proportion of Republican senators were in favor of the amendment than Democratic senators. The issue of the pickets was brought up again, though, this time, Pittman dodged it nicely and returned to urging that the vote be postponed in order that full suffrage might be saved.

Lucy gazed down at the top of his balding head, tempted to hoot. Save full suffrage by postponing the vote? To postpone was to kill the amendment, and he knew it.

Pittman and Smoot went on to argue over the number of votes for and against the measure. Lucy was close to despair when Miles Poindexter, a Republican and long supporter of full suffrage, was finally recognized.

"Is the honorable Senator from Nevada bragging about the fact that his side has only thirty-one votes in favor of the resolution?"

Senator Pittman looked wounded. "Mr. President, I do not think this is a matter of levity. But then I suppose it is rather a good joke to those who thoroughly enjoy it," he said. "Indeed, a magnificent joke upon the leading suffrage women of the country who depended on you, sir. Why, you have done wonders! You have brought the joint resolution forward for defeat!"

Poindexter raised his chin ever so slightly. "To whom is the honorable Senator from Nevada referring when he says, 'You have brought the joint resolution forward for defeat'?" he asked, evenly.

Lucy felt the tension between the two men crackle. If this were a saloon out West, guns would be drawn.

"Mr. President, I am referring to the proceedings of the Republican caucus," Pittman said.

Poindexter again: "Is the distinguished Senator from New Mexico, the chairman of the Woman's Suffrage Committee, a member of the Republican caucus?"

Pittman was red in the face. "Mr. President, my answer is in the negative."

"The honorable Senator from Nevada told me some time ago he would bring the Resolution forward," Poindexter said. "Yet now he appears to be opposing a vote on the matter."

The focus of the debate returned to the NWP, beginning with a jibe from Senator Reed from Missouri. "Mr. President, I am shocked that some of our esteemed colleagues have become mere pawns in the hands of damsels of uncertain age."

Lucy smiled to herself at what she was sure was intended to put her and Alice in their places. If thirty-eight was an uncertain age, what did that make Reed at sixty-some?

"Mr. President!" called the senator from Illinois, signaling frantically for recognition. "Has it come to pass that a distinguished Senator can, on the floor, indict these women for coming to us and seeking to protect their rights when every railroad lobbyist in America in the past could, with freedom, haunt this capitol?"

Reed refused to answer. Next, Thomas, a Democrat from Colorado, who Lucy had always thought looked as if he were sucking a lemon, stepped in to make a plea on behalf of suffrage, despite "the neurotic behavior of the women who burn the President's words."

Lucy sat back, folded her arms, only half-listening to The National Woman's Party being raked over more coals. Finally, the senior senator from Virginia rose. White-haired, impeccably dressed in high wing collar and buttoned waistcoat, always smiling, he was the kind of courtly looking man who would lock his wife in her house supposedly for her own protection. "Mr. President, I move for adjournment until twelve o'clock on Monday so that some of the senators absent today might be present."

Lucy cocked an eyebrow at the attempt to allow more Southern Democrats to be present and defeat the measure. She sat up, shot a glance toward Senator Jones. Would he let the motion ride or . . . That's when she saw Shafroth stand.

"Mr. President." The Vice President recognized the senator. "I move for immediate adjournment."

Everyone in the Chamber knew the motion took precedence over the Virginian's. A vote was taken, passed. Thanks to Shafroth's quick thinking, the Senate would reconvene the next day on Saturday, September 28th, at noon—minus the absent southern senators. If the junior senator from Colorado had been after credit in the eyes of the NWP, he had it, at least for today. Kate had been doing her job.

The next morning was cloudy, the air heavy. On the way back to headquarters last night, Lucy and Alice had agreed that the hours of speechifying had been pure show with no evidence that Wilson was putting pressure on his fellow Democrats. Today the gallery was packed, and Lucy wanted to believe it was a good omen.

The proceedings began well enough as Senator Jones started out by moving for consideration of unfinished business. But when the first speaker, the newly appointed senator from Tennessee, rose and spent nearly an hour equivocating about his position, Lucy changed her mind. She recognized a "no" vote when she heard it.

John Shafroth got the floor. Lucy's hopes rose. But Shafroth hadn't said more than a paragraph's worth when a message from the House about the dangers of Spanish Influenza was introduced, and he was forced to yield. Not until thirty minutes later was the Committee of the Whole finally able to resume debate on H.J.R 200.

Once again, Senator Shafroth stepped forward. "Mr. President, it has been said that senators have been influenced politically to change their views upon the subject of the woman's vote; but, so far as I am concerned, that charge does not lie at my door. Forty-odd years ago I made a speech in a debating society in favor of woman's suffrage, and there never has been an hour since that time when I did not feel that it was an outrage for man to deprive woman of the right to vote. I introduced this identical joint resolution in five successive Congresses when I was a member of the House of Representatives, and yet its passage was always refused.

"Is it possible that any person can fairly reason that a woman is not entitled to this right when that declaration has been accepted by all republics except Great Britain throughout the world, and when it is supposed to be acquiesced to by every man on the floor of this body? Our forefathers said it was so. Clearly, it was a self-evident truth."

Lucy found herself unable to resist this sturdy man, the sincerity of his plea for the amendment. If she were a tourist who had happened by and was sitting in the gallery, she would be completely taken in by his ringing words. Yet were they a sign of expediency or conviction? In his six years in the Senate, in spite of his own version of a suffrage amendment, his support had been indifferent. Politicians always wanted to have it both ways. If it hadn't been for pressure from home, she suspected he might never have said a word today.

The debate went on. A Republican senator rambled on about

women in ancient Rome. Lucy felt her eyes grow heavy. She started to doze off when, out of half-closed eyes, she noticed a senator enter from a side door, mount the steps to the dais to speak to the vice president, followed by a short whispered conference. She sat up. The vice president adjusted his cuffs, smoothed his tie. Something was up. The doors to the Chamber opened. All heads turned. Mouths gaped at the intruder.

"Senators, the President of the United States."

Chapter 25

On her feet, as was the entire Chamber, Lucy looked down on the slender figure of the president as he strode down the aisle to the rostrum, accompanied by a committee of leading senators and much applause. Just behind him was his Cabinet, who took seats that had been hastily provided. Aside from the members of the Senate, she wondered how many in the room realized that Wilson was setting an historic precedent.

Applause still ringing through the chamber, he solemnly shook hands with the vice president, went to the podium and held up his hands for quiet. Lucy glanced at her watch: one o'clock.

"Mr. Vice President, gentlemen of the Senate, the unusual circumstances of a world war in which we stand and will be judged in the view not only of our own people and of our consciences but also in view of all nations and people will, I hope, justify, in your thought as it does in mine, the message I have come to bring you."

Lucy surveyed the faces of the men seated at their rosewood desks, looked for a lift of an eyebrow, a frown, some hint of reaction to the president daring to flout Senate tradition, but saw only stoic expressions.

"I assumed the Senate would concur in the amendment because no disputable principle is involved, that the only question was the method by which the suffrage is to be extended to women. Certainly, there is and can be no party issue involved in it. Both of our national parties are pledged, explicitly pledged, to equality of suffrage for the women of the country."

Lucy had to admire how smoothly he'd put his own party members on the spot. The Democrats had included a suffrage plank in their platform at the last national convention all right, but that's where they'd stopped.

The president glanced down at the text of speech. "Neither Party, therefore, it seems to me, can justify hesitating as to the method of obtaining it, can rightly hesitate to substitute federal initiative for state initiative if the early adoption of this measure is necessary to the successful prosecution of the war.

"This is a people's war, and the people's thinking constitutes its atmosphere and morale. They think in their logical simplicity that democracy means that women shall play their part in affairs alongside men, and upon equal footing with them. I tell you plainly that this measure which I urge upon you is vital to the winning of the war and to the energies alike of preparation and of battle. And not in the winning of the war only. It is vital to the right solution of the great problems which we must settle, and settle immediately, when the war is over."

Lucy pursed her lips. "And not in the winning of the war only," the president had said, code words for how much he feared losing a Democratic congress, which was essential to his peace measures.

For an instant, Wilson surveyed the faces before him then looked back at the text. "I tell you this measure which I urge upon you is vital to the end of the war. It is vital to the right of the great problems, which we must settle when the war is over. We shall need then a vision of the women as we have never needed it before. Many may deny its value but no one can brush aside or answer the principle upon which it is based. This is my appeal. The executive tasks to this end are many. I ask that you lighten them and place in my hands the spiritual instruments which I do not now have and surely need."

The president glanced up, gathered his speech, gave a slight nod to the assembly, and left the Chamber, his Cabinet behind him. Lucy checked her watch again. One fifteen. Fifteen minutes, from start to finish. If his words accomplished their purpose, Lucy didn't care a whit about his motives.

⁓⁂⁓

The doors had hardly closed behind the president, the senators were still settling in their seats, when the vice president entertained a motion to stand as a Committee of the Whole and resume debate on the amendment.

Shafroth took the lead again, and urged immediate approval. As if they'd heard a warning bell, the states' right men—most, but not all, southerners—immediately stepped forward. Was it the esteemed senator's intention to rob the states of their sovereign power, which they reserved to themselves when the Federal government was formed, asked the senior senator from Georgia. Shafroth started to rebut when another senator reminded the assembly that there were eight states where men with nothing more than first citizenship papers were allowed to vote. Shafroth deplored the situation. Another senator proposed an amendment to the amendment outlawing such fraud.

John Shafroth, who had become the lone warrior, drew a hand slowly over his mouth as if to hide his exasperation. "Sir, I cannot consent to any amendment being attached. Not even the Ten Commandments, although every one of them is good. Why? Because the House of Representatives by a bare two-thirds majority—not one vote over—passed this joint resolution. If we send this resolution back with amendments attached to it, no matter what kind of an amendment, it will never be considered by the House of Representatives, and the change of the votes of one or two Representatives might defeat the entire measure."

Borah, a fellow westerner and a Republican, waded in with the states' rights issue again. Pittman from Nevada joined him, again quoting from *The Suffragist* in disparaging tones. A southern senator feared for the safety of delicate womanhood. Then Borah again. A speech he'd made on the income tax was entered into the record. Lucy sighed, smelled a filibuster in the making.

Six o'clock came and went. Lucy's stomach growled. She wished she'd had more than coffee for breakfast. She and Alice took turns going to the public restroom. Only NWP members and those from National remained in the gallery. The vice president had been relieved by a president pro-tem. The number of senators in the Chamber was down to six. Jones from New Mexico and Shafroth and Poindexter lounged in their chairs, letting the endless words of Borah and Pittman and a lone senator from Alabama wash over them. The moment the southerner finally left the room, presumably to answer nature's call, Jones made a motion to stand in recess until Tuesday, October 1st. The ayes had it. Hope was still alive.

The gallery stirred, gloves and coats were gathered. A soft undercurrent of voices started up. Alice paused to speak to Mrs. Catt, and Lucy went on, meeting smiles with a nod, for she was too caught up in the events of the afternoon for conversation. What, finally, would the president's appearance mean to the outcome? Had he crashed the venerable Porcellian Club at Harvard, he might be forgiven. But the Senate? She wasn't so sure.

Tuesday, October 1st, dawned clear and cool, with no hint of rain. The Senate was scheduled to take up the amendment at noon. More than enough time for Lucy to eat a leisurely breakfast, and she fixed herself a boiled egg and a piece of toast along with her coffee, leaving the dishes in the sink for Mrs. Ells to wash. Back in her bedroom to dress, Lucy decided on something a little less showy than the green silk to wear and chose the deep russet suit with a brown hat trimmed in quail feathers.

Alice decided they should part with the money for a cab. Neither spoke on the drive over to the Capitol. Alice's eyes had a distant look about them that Lucy had seen before in times of crisis. And she tried to remind herself that what was about to unfold was beyond her control.

Leaning down from the gallery, Lucy noted a dozen desks still vacant when the vice president called the assembly to order. The invocation given, various memorials were presented. Four more senators drifted in. A conference committee was requested to come to agreement on a House bill to regulate the hours of the officers and members of the fire department of the District of Columbia. All the while, Reed of Missouri stood talking to Henry Cabot Lodge, no friend of suffrage.

The Vice President declared the morning business closed. Senator Jones, the floor leader of the amendment, asked unanimous consent that the Senate proceed to the consideration of the unfinished business of the amendment. No one voiced an objection. Jones took the floor.

For a man who had never impressed Lucy with his speaking abilities, his speech, listing every objection to woman suffrage and why each was ill conceived, was one of his best. Senator Walsh took up where Jones left off. Lucy scanned the Chamber for reaction, distressed at the number of senators reading newspapers and whispering together in the back of the room.

Reed was recognized next and returned to his usual diatribe about woman suffrage being a states' rights issue. Shafroth doodled on the newspaper on his desk. The senior senator from South Carolina offered an amendment to restrict the amendment to white women. Instantly, Shafroth sprang to his feet. The Resolution would not pass with an amendment, he maintained.

Yet more amendments followed; each was voted on; each was barely defeated. John Shafroth got to his feet again, signaled the vice president who had a whispered consultation with the clerk. With a slight nod of his head toward Shafroth and a rap of the gavel, the vice president declared the Joint Resolution was without amendment and ordered a third reading. Senator Jones asked for the ayes and nays.

This was the moment of reckoning. Lucy could almost hear every woman in the gallery suck in her breath. She pulled the list of Senate members from her purse, checked the names as, one by one, they were called out. Fifty-four yeas—including Senator Pittman, who at the last moment must have decided he'd be wise to avoid the wrath of the Nevada women voters. Thirty nays. The vice president took the tally sheet from the clerk and announced that, not having a sufficient two-thirds majority, the Joint Resolution did not pass.

Lucy sat back, sick inside. Among the twelve abstentions were Borah from Idaho and Fall from Arizona, western senators. Two votes. Lucy had never held any illusions about Borah. Fall, however, had been on the fence. Her mother used to say that adversity built character. At this rate, Lucy knew a good many women who qualified for sainthood.

Yet the drama wasn't over. Before the president of the Senate had time to move on, Senator Jones asked to change his vote from yea to nay. Alice shot Lucy a glance, nodded approvingly at the parliamentary move, which left the way open for reconsideration at some future date. A small, but faint, light remained at the end of an otherwise dark tunnel.

Chapter 26

Kate came out of the bathroom, buttoning her blouse, anxious to check the morning papers for word of the vote. The debate on the amendment had been scheduled to begin last Friday. When she hadn't heard from Lucy over the weekend and there had been no news in the papers, she couldn't decide whether to be worried or hopeful. She was about to reach in the closet for her skirt when out of the corner of her eye she noticed the Western Union envelope on the carpet where it had been shoved under the door.

With a sense of trepidation, she walked over, picked the telegram up, and, working her thumb under the flap she pulled out the telegram and unfolded it. "*54 yeas STOP 30 nayes STOP 12 abstentions STOP Letter follows STOP Lucy.*" Translated: without the necessary two-thirds affirmative vote, the amendment had failed.

Kate reread the words again and then again in the vain hope that the numbers might change. And when they didn't, her anger kicked in and she crushed the sheet into a ball and hurled it into the wastebasket. The stupidity of the men who ran the country knew no bounds. Good Lord, it might as well be the Middle Ages. Not that she'd actually believed the Southern Democrats and men like Reed would come around. And the vote probably meant Borah, ever the equivocator, had probably abstained. Yet she had so hoped.

Her heartbeat slowed. The reality behind Lucy's telegram took hold. Now every Democratic senator up for reelection had to be defeated. Including John Shafroth. In four weeks—four short weeks—she had to persuade the majority of Colorado voters to mark their ballots for Lawrence Phipps, a man who, from what she knew, had little to offer beyond being a Republican with a great deal of money. She sank onto the edge of the bed, trying to digest the enormity of what lay ahead.

If it wasn't for the flu epidemic and the ban against public meetings, she could hire a hall and use prominent speakers as Iris had done during the '16 campaign against Senator Thomas. Kate lay back, closed her eyes, feeling like the captain of a rudderless ship.

Up until this moment, she hadn't allowed herself to think about the next step, how she would manage without Iris and Doris. All she had now were names of members on typed sheets of paper to help her. She sat up, stared across the room until slowly an idea came to her. If a public meeting was out, she and the women on those sheets would use stores to spread the word about Shafroth.

Neighborhood stores where people tended to be friendlier than they were downtown. Their spiel couldn't be long. People shopping were too impatient to listen. So each member would need pamphlets to hand out, the kind that door-to-door salesmen left—the message brief and to the point: "Women of Colorado: The Democrats have Betrayed Your Trust. Vote for Lawrence Phipps for U.S. Senate, Republican, the Party FOR national woman's suffrage."

The idea of the pamphlet grew in her mind. There was sure to be a printer within an easy walk. But before she did anything else, she had to get a copy of the *Post* or the *News* and see what their take was on the vote—more to the point, what John Shafroth had said.

※

Kate chose a table by one of the dining room windows and asked the waitress for coffee before she unfolded the morning edition of the *Post.* Staring back at her was the banner headline. "Shafroth Makes Valiant Senate fight for Democracy," and, below it, a two-column story about Monday's Senate vote on the woman's suffrage amendment.

Kate glanced up as the waitress returned with the steaming cup of coffee, nodded her thanks. She took a sip and began to read. From the excerpts of Shafroth's speech that were quoted, the casual reader would think the senator was nothing short of a knight in shining armor, the supreme defender of a woman's right to vote. When, all along it wasn't speeches that had been needed, but two measly votes. That's all he had been asked to produce. One could have been Senator Borah's.

She looked up. The problem was to get beyond the John Shafroth who said he believed in women's right to vote and the politician. Handing out polite pamphlets was fine. But Colorado voters also had to hear the truth—one on one—from women they knew who also knew about Senator Shaffroth, the Democrat.

But to spread the word took people. The last time she had gone over the lists, she'd counted fifty-one Denver members, twenty of them Democrats. And an equal number scattered around the state.

All received *The Suffragist* so they'd be armed with the details of the vote. Forget the stores. She'd have members work in pairs, going door to door, in their neighborhoods.

Kate shoved aside her coffee and hurried upstairs for the list and the map of Denver. Sitting cross-legged on the bed, the list in her lap, she found each address on the map and made a note of its precinct and ward next to each member's name. A pattern began to emerge, one she didn't like. Most members lived east and south, where the wards were predominantly Republican. There, they'd be talking to the choir. Only one member lived in a Democratic ward along the South Platte River, where the Italians and Irish lived, and none north of the Capitol. At the very least, Kate needed three members to do double duty, which would involve their taking long streetcar rides into unfamiliar neighborhoods.

The list in hand, she got to her feet, and walked over to the desk. Uneasiness nagged at her. Inventing a campaign at the last minute was risky. She had no idea of the pitfalls. She should probably check with Lucy, but there wasn't time. She sat down, trying to see all sides, until with one swift motion she pulled open the drawer and removed the sheets of hotel stationery inside. She would need more but this was enough for a start. She began to write a note to every woman on the list, detailing the plan. Pamphlets, she added in the postscript, would arrive under separate cover.

Two hours later, her hand aching, she stuffed the last of the letters in envelopes, sealed them, and set off for the post office. At a print shop, she ordered five thousand pamphlets. She knew it was far from an ideal plan. The number of members needed didn't match the number of critical precincts in Democratic wards. But every member had more than she could probably handle—everyone except her. She'd forgotten to add her own name to the list.

❧

The next morning, Kate strode east along Seventeenth Street, past delivery boys and men in somber business suits and hats, energized by the challenge of the day ahead. The oversized thermometer in the corner window of First National bank registered seventy degrees, warm for early October, and Kate was glad she'd decided to leave her sweater at the hotel. She crossed Broadway, walked south two blocks and then east again up Capitol Hill, all the while rehearsing in her mind a version of the message she'd used for the pamphlet. By the end of the day, she'd have firsthand knowledge of what tack worked best and be able to pass on suggestions to the other members.

Just ahead was the Immaculate Conception Cathedral, a handsome Gothic city landmark. A side door opened, and a priest in a flowing black cassock, a black fedora on his head, came out and hurried down the stone steps. Watching him, Kate realized she'd never been inside a Catholic church.

She gazed up at the huge rose window above the central doors. Stretching behind the church was the Ninth Ward. If this was the neighborhood church, it might be useful to become acquainted with it, and she mounted the stone steps. Standing just inside the entrance, she gazed toward the front of the church. Behind the marble altar was a larger-than-life figure of Jesus hanging from a gold cross. The quiet of the stone interior wrapped around her, and she felt an unexpected sense of peace.

As her eyes adjusted to the dim light, she saw a woman, head and shoulders covered by a black shawl, her head bowed, on her knees in one of the front pews, perhaps praying for her son in France as Mrs. Perelli might have prayed. Kate felt like an interloper. Yet it seemed all right somehow to whisper a message to God to watch over Tom and ask His help with the amendment.

Outside again in the bright light, Kate turned the corner, ready to begin. The neat, sturdy, two-story red brick houses looked friendly enough. No different from hundreds of others around the city. Some had front porches; all were set close together, their only distinguishing mark an occasional different color of trim. Each had a small front yard. Most had pfitzers or lilac bushes planted against the house. A few elms and cottonwoods had been planted in the patch of grass next to the street.

Pulling herself tall, Kate marched up the nearest front walk, mounted the steps to the porch, rang the doorbell. After a few minutes the door opened and a broad-faced woman in a flowered cotton housedress looked out. "Yes?"

Kate smiled. "Good morning."

The woman eyed her. "If you're sellin' Bibles . . ."

"Actually, I'm not selling anything," Kate said brightly. "I've come on behalf of the National Woman's Party and—"

"I'm awful sorry but it's Wednesday."

"Oh," was all Kate could think to say. Then she remembered the woman in the Cathedral. Perhaps it was a religious feast day.

"The water bath's just come to a boil."

Thoroughly confused, Kate could only nod. "I'd like to talk to you about the upcoming election. It won't take but a few minutes."

The woman started to close the door. "I'm sure it's all very interesting, but I really gotta go. The tomatoes, you know."

The door closed. Kate pulled in a deep breath, eyed the house next door. She wondered if a water bath was boiling there, too. She shrugged. An hour passed, and she'd talked with only five women out of the dozen houses in the block, and they weren't interested in the November election. Excuses ranged from baking bread to lack of trust in any politician no matter what party he came from to railing at Kate for electioneering when she should be doing war work. Two houses had quarantine signs posted on the front door.

A few blocks north, she found a lunchroom on the corner and ordered a ham sandwich and a cup of coffee. Complimenting the waitress on the frilly white curtains in the window, she was about to slide into her pitch about voting Republican when two women came in and took the table next to hers. The waitress excused herself. As Kate went back to her sandwich, she overhead the women's conversation—a sale was on at Denver Dry Goods, one of the children was down with chicken pox. She could find no opening to bring up a discussion of the election. So she paid her bill and left without approaching them.

She started her routine again. Ring the doorbell, wait, ring again, wait. Tap on the window, wait. Ten minutes later go to the next house, perform the same ritual, and, later, the house after that. Cross the street and repeat the process. In the middle of the afternoon, the routine had a slight alteration. The "lady of the house" was a white-haired widow as desperate to talk to someone as Kate was. But she no sooner began to explain the purpose of her call when the woman let lose with a full family history. Kate tried to listen, but the house smelled of cat urine. She began to sneeze. Twenty minutes later, she managed to escape.

By six, men occasionally came to the door. Suspenders over work shirts, faces drawn with fatigue, they eyed her with suspicion and told her they weren't buying whatever it was she was selling. Some asked if she knew it was suppertime. She trudged back to the hotel, ate a bowl of soup and a slice of apple pie in the nearly empty dining room, went upstairs and fell into bed.

The next day, she shifted to older, but also heavily Democratic neighborhoods clustered closer to the east side of the South Platte River, and met with no more success. She came back to the hotel exhausted and frustrated. Tomorrow was Friday, the end of the first week of her campaign. Three weeks remained before the election. She had to face facts. Unless she found someone to get her into the Democratic wards, Shafroth would carry every one of them by such a large margin that he could overcome any losses elsewhere in the state and win.

❧

Mary Daly looked to be about thirty, Kate guessed. Rangy, with full breasts beneath a faded blue man's work shirt, and wild black hair tamed into a braid that hung down her back. A strong nose and heavy eyebrows that had never been plucked. A wide, curving mouth minus any lip rouge. Her fair skin had the weathered look of the outdoors. And she had the darkest eyes Kate had ever seen, so deep set it was as if they must view the world from caves.

"So you're takin' Iris's place?" Mary asked in a husky voice.

"That's the idea."

They stood on the front porch of the small weather-beaten house in the Fourth Ward in north Denver, the same part of town where she'd met with Ed Keating and where many men worked for the railroad. "I wish I could have explained more in the telegram."

"That's where a phone comes in handy, but my brother Bob thinks it's not worth the money." The woman reached for the screened door, gave a nod of her head. "Come in. I'll make some coffee and we can talk about what's to be done. Bob's asleep, so keep it down. He works for the Burlington Northern, and he's just come in from a long run."

They walked single file down the narrow hall and entered the small kitchen that held the odor of fried bacon. The woman closed the door softly behind her, filled a blackened coffeepot with water and coffee grounds, and put it on the stove, then added several pieces of coal to the firebox. "On second thought, let's sit out back," she said in a low voice, pointing to the screened door.

Kate squinted in the sunlight as they stepped outside and settled on the back stoop. White sheets hung, slightly puffed like sails in the breeze, from a wire clothesline that extended from the back of the house to the wide board fence next to the alley. Only the steady yap of a dog from down the block interrupted the neighborhood quiet.

"Iris's fiancé and his children have the flu," Kate said.

The woman named Mary shielded her eyes with one hand, looked at her. "Some say it's our penance for past sins. But I think it's the ignorant who're doin' the talkin.'"

Kate smiled uncertainly, thinking she'd made a mistake, that she should excuse herself and leave, find another woman to help. But there wasn't one.

"So is working for the Party all you do?" Mary asked.

"I waited tables in Washington."

"Did you now?"

Kate winced at the disdain in the woman's voice and came to her own defense. "I just graduated from college in June."

"Ah, sure. I can see that." See what, Kate wondered as she met Mary's eyes that seemed to mock her. "Me, I get housekeeping jobs for women and run a union I started up a couple of years ago. Domestic Workers of America, it's called. The boys don't like it. Women gettin' into unions, I mean. But that's too bad, because there's another one in Duluth now. And Seattle." Mary leaned back on her elbows, one eye closed against the glare. "We clean up other people's messes. For all you know, your mother's upstairs maid might belong."

"Nobody has upstairs maids these days," Kate said, more testily than she intended.

Mary laughed. "And, sure, nothin's the same, is it? Look at us: a union member and a college girl about to go out and tell the lot to vote Republican. My old Da wouldn't believe it." Mary got to her feet. "I'll take a look at the coffee."

As she waited, Kate gazed across the yard, heard the screen door close. She didn't much like Mary Daly or her crack about upstairs maids. But the campaign wouldn't last forever.

Five minutes later, Mary reappeared, carrying two steaming mugs. She handed one to Kate.

Smiling a stiff thank you, Kate said, "As I said in the telegram, there's been a change of plans. The way I see it, the Fifth and the Ninth wards—and this one we're in now—are key. I don't know how much chance you've had to talk to people around here, but I worked the Ninth and part of the fifth by myself without much success. That's where I thought you could help."

"Sure." Mary settled on the step next to Kate. "But what about the other neighborhoods?"

"We have about twenty members to cover those in south Denver and east of the Capitol. One—Jew Town where member by the name of Ethel Steinberg lives—also goes Democratic. Whether we have time to make it out there . . ." Kate shrugged. "I know we can't convert every voter, but if we can convince a few and they spread the word—"

"And the rest of the state?"

"I'm going to have to write the members on the western slope and up north and tell them they're on their own." Kate paused, took a tentative a sip of coffee. "Then there's Pueblo. As the second largest city in the state and the most heavily Democratic, it could make the difference of a win or a loss for Shafroth."

"Let it go," Mary said. "It's a hundred miles south. We'll waste a good day just gettin' down there. And a lot of the Italian ladies aren't citizens."

Kate put her cup down. "But some of them are, and if the election is close and we can swing a hundred votes to Phipps, those votes could do the trick."

"And when do you see us doin' this?"

"The last week before the election. Only two-and-a-half weeks from now."

Mary stared down at the coffee for a moment, looked up. "Pueblo's a tough steel town, Kate. A union town before the war during the last coal strike. But when it lost, the company blacklisted every member. Still, there's a rumor goin' around that another strike's in the offing once the war's over. At least, if the Mine Workers have their way."

"What's your point?" Kate asked.

"The point is the union and the Democrats are thick as thieves. One washes the other's hands when it suits 'em. It wouldn't surprise me if a fellah I know who's a union organizer is down there this minute. And he'll be greasing palms and twistin' arms to keep the Democratic vote in line. In other words, we'll be up against the union as well as the Democratic Party."

Kate shrugged. "You could be right, but we can't let that concern us."

Mary leaned her forearms on her knees, eyeing Kate in a speculative way as if trying to make up her mind. "I'll have to make arrangements with Mrs. Griffin at the agency for time off."

"Of course." Likeable or not, Kate sensed a fearlessness about this woman that she needed. "What about money? I can't pay you for the time you'll be losing from work."

"I've got a stash under my mattress that'll see me through." Mary pushed to her feet. "So that does it. Name the time and place where you want to meet and I'll be there."

"On a field of snow at dawn?"

Mary gave Kate a quizzical look.

"An old pioneer expression my grandfather used," Kate said, suddenly reenergized. "How about nine A.M. tomorrow—here?"

Chapter 27

The next morning, waiting with Kate on the front porch of the one-story red brick house for Mrs. Gilleland to come to the door, Mary thought about her brother's words of warning when she'd told him she was joining up with Kate Brennan for "the cause," as Mary called it.

"Oh, for the Lord's sake, girl. You can't trust a one of their kind. Take is all they know," he'd said. She hoped he was wrong.

Finally, the door opened, and a young woman's face appeared.

"It's Mary Daly, Mrs. Gilleland. From across the street."

The door opened wider, and a round-faced girl with dark brown hair pulled away from her face, dressed in a cotton housedress, stepped out, a baby on one hip. Mary glanced toward Kate and back again at her neighbor. "I'd like you to know my friend, Kate Brennan." Before the young woman could say anything, Mary had turned back to Kate. "Did I tell you, Kate, that Tim Gilleland works with my brother Bob?"

The young woman's baby began to squirm, and Mary reached

in the pocket of her dress, pulled out her house keys and dangled them before the baby's pale blue eyes. "And, sure, I've forgotten the child's name."

"Timmy. After his Dad."

Mary nodded, frowned. "If you think he's hungry, we should go in and sit with you a while."

The kitchen was small, but neatly kept—the worn linoleum rug swept, the breakfast dishes drying on the drain board. On the wall by the back door was a framed picture of Jesus Christ in flowing white robes, tiny birds perched on his outstretched hands. The girl settled in a wooden rocker, unbuttoned the bodice of her dress, and offered the child an engorged nipple. Mary hid a smile when she saw Kate glance away, as if embarrassed.

To Kate, this neighborhood must seem like a foreign country. But when Mary eased into the business of voting for the Republican candidate for Senate, Kate jumped right in with how important it was for every woman in the country to be able to vote. She could see Nora Gilleland take it in, nodding, as she settled the baby on her shoulder to burp him.

By the fourth house, Mary was pleased to hear Kate saying things like how she hoped no one in the household had had the flu or, pointing to a cup and saucer on display in the front room, say how pretty they were.

If the woman's husband was in the army, Mary asked after him and always turned to Kate. "Kate, here, has a brother over there in France. Mind you, I never was keen on us gettin' into it. No Irishman worth his salt would be fightin' on the side of the English. But then I said to myself: Mary, those people over there are no different than you and Bob. They have feelin's after all. The Germans started the fight. And now that we're Americans, the least we can do is help out. No different than why us women in Colorado who can vote must reach out to those who can't."

At this, the woman on the receiving end often looked confused.

"How can you not feel for the millions of women back east who don't have that right? I mean, this is a democracy, isn't it?" Here she might coo at the baby. "It's our duty to help them. And we can do that by votin' Republican."

The eyes always went wide at the word Republican, as if it were a curse word. But Mary pretended not to notice. "The way I see it, it's our chance to strike out for the liberty of these poor souls." She'd smile. "But we've got to be goin.' Just remember now: November third. Our chance to help our sisters. Vote Phipps for Senate."

The weather was fine, warm yet not hot. Mary didn't bother with a hat, and Kate had taken to leaving hers at the hotel. The golden cottonwood leaves crunched beneath their feet as they walked and talked. Before Mary realized it, Kate was pouring her heart out to her—her hopes for the success of the amendment, her terror in prison, the women she'd met there—things, Kate claimed, she'd never told anyone else. Once she spoke of a fellow named Charlie. She seemed to have feelings for him but had pushed them aside. And all the while, Mary listened.

Occasionally, she'd part with a bit of her own life: going to work as a dishwasher in a saloon when she was ten, being hired as the upstairs maid of the saloon owner and fighting off his advances, and when she quit, the problem of finding another position without references. Back into a household on Capitol Hill, wiser now. At that, Mary had seen the question in Kate's eyes, as if wanting to know where on Capitol Hill, but she said nothing.

One day toward the end of the second week—Thursday, it was— they stopped at a shop for coffee and donuts. They talked about canvassing the neighborhoods near the smelters where so many Germans lived before the war. "A shame, don't ya think, scarin' them off like the government's done so they had to sell their businesses?" Mary said, licking bits of cinnamon sugar off her fingers.

"There's an agency in Washington called the Committee on Public Information that keeps track of them."

Mary caught the bitterness in Kate's voice. "Snakes of the human race, some call people who do that. Spies, I say. Let the poor souls who live in America alone. They don't like the war over there no more than the rest of us."

That afternoon, they came upon a woman hanging out the wash. Mary greeted her. She and Kate stepped into the back yard, grabbed a handful of clothespins and helped her hang up the socks and shirts while they chatted about the election. Before they finished, the woman had promised to vote for Phipps. They were on the move.

Until Saturday. At a small house, when they felt their welcome slip away. Mary chalked it up to a husband who'd spent his entire paycheck the night before on bootleg booze and needed someone to blame. Whatever the reason, the woman, whose name was Dot, was reluctant to let them in. They stood on the porch, the woman in the shadow of the open door, her arms folded over her breasts, not warming to Mary's friendly remarks.

"Jim says we vote Democrat."

"And what do you say?" Mary asked.

The woman fixed her gaze on the porch floor. Studying her, Mary noticed the bruise on the woman's left cheek.

"Jim's gettin' pressure at work, is he?" Mary asked kindly.

The woman glanced up, a sharp, nervous, bird-like look in her eyes.

"Ah, sure, I can see why you want to watch your step, Dot. Still and all, it is a secret ballot."

But that was as far as they got. The door closed. The scene was repeated at every house on the block.

"You'd think we were spreading the flu," Kate said.

"The word's out. That much is plain."

"What word?"

"About what we're up to."

"But you said it, Mary: it's a secret ballot. There's no law a person has to vote the straight ticket. Women have a right to vote any way they want."

"Fine if they're livin' alone, though maybe even not then," Mary said as they reached the end of the block. "You live with a man and you get to know his ways. And he knows yours. If the election comes up, most men say how they're plannin' to vote, meanin' how you're to vote, too. If you don't agree and you're smart, you keep your trap shut. But chances are he knows anyway. Go your own way, and you pay a price."

"Like what?"

"A cuff. Worse, a beatin'. Or little things. He don't come home nights or drinks up all his pay. Or he goes at the kids." Mary eyed the low stone wall that bordered the house on the corner, suggested they sit down for a minute. "There's more to life than the vote."

"What do you mean?"

"For starts, bein' protected against your Da."

"You're not serious."

"Dead serious, am I, and if you're wonderin' did it happen to me, the answer is, yes. So I cleared out at sixteen. I know the fear. As does the girl who lives next door to me. I helped put the law on her dad. Now she and her Ma are havin' to live out of state to keep him from goin' at her again." Mary shook her head. "Besides, it's not just the fear of beatin's, but takin' the risk of thinkin' for themselves. It's not what people are used to."

❧

The next Thursday morning, Mary stood at the stove and pressed the spatula down on the two sausage patties sputtering in the frying pan. She worked out of habit, her mind still full of the campaign. What if Shafroth won the election and the Democrats kept the control of the Senate? What if the amendment lost again and the eastern ladies like the Alice Paul and the Lucy Burns gave up, turned their energy to the peace? What would happen to the Domestic Workers Union?

A deep voice brought her up short. "Mary girl, I'm half-starved and I have to get to work."

"Hold your horses. It's comin'." And, with one hand, she scooped up the patties, letting the grease drain into the skillet. With the other, she took the plate with two biscuits from the warming shelf and added the patties. Turning, she put the plate down in front of her brother, then reached back for the coffeepot and filled two cups with coffee.

Her brother took a sip, looked at her over the rim of his steaming cup. "Spit it out. Somethin' is stickin' in your craw." When she didn't answer, he said, "If I was a bettin' man, I'd bet on the election."

"And what if it is?"

Bob shrugged his wide, muscled shoulders.

Easing down in the chair across the table, Mary watched him pick up his fork, cut one of the sausage patties in half and stick it his mouth. Her brother was a good man with a good heart. He didn't deserve her sharp tongue.

"That high-flown friend of yours is gettin' to you, is she?" he asked through the food in his mouth.

"Her name's Kate Brennan, Bob Daly. And we're goin' to Jew Town, if you must know."

At that, his eyes went wide. He let go of his fork. "Jesus, Mary. What are you thinkin'?"

"And what's wrong with Jew Town?"

"Ask the Father."

"I'll not be goin' to Hell if that's what you're het up about." Mary took a swallow of her coffee, got to her feet and snatched her brother's plate away. "As for that, I don't have time to wait around while you mind my business and me with ironin' to do before I leave."

Later, as she and Kate were climbing on a number forty streetcar, Mary felt bad about her fit of temper, defending the Jews. But unlike most she knew, she had a soft spot in her heart for them and for Jew Town, located on the other side of the tracks and the South Platte, out of the reach of the city's ruling Protestants. It was there that old man Lipinski, the rag picker, lived—the man who had hired her when no one else would, and for a decent wage at that. Like Mr. Lipinski, most Jews she knew were hard workers. She'd always wondered what the world had against them.

Most important was that Denver Jews, like the Irish, were

Democrats she and Kate hoped to convert, if only for the Senate race. As for Bob, he was right about Father O'Shea's reaction, but not for the right reason. The full vote for women was not a cause the Church looked kindly on.

Their contact this afternoon was Ethel Steinberg. An NWP member, she'd volunteered to ask a few friends over to hear the pitch. Mary had high hopes they'd see the logic of Shafroth's defeat.

The streetcar was nearly empty, and they chose two seats near the back. Mary settled next to the window, glanced over at Kate who seemed wrapped up in her own thoughts. A strange one, Kate Brennan. At this very minute, she could be back in that grand house on Capitol Hill or in one of those fancy places in the newer part of town, married to one of those muckety-mucks making a killing on selling coal to the army. Yet here she was, on a streetcar headed for Jew Town.

Aside from mentioning her sister and brother, Kate had kept to herself about the rest of the family, with not a mention of how she'd grown up in the same neighborhood as the Senator. And not another word about Charlie. Not that a woman had to have a man. From her experience, to put a man with a woman who had a mind of her own was like mixing oil with water. Like her and Gino.

Even now, against her will, she felt a stirring at the thought of him. Except for that bump on his nose from being at the wrong end of a cop's nightstick once, he had a body and a face that could melt most women's hearts. God in Heaven, the way he could make love. Sinewy hands kneading every inch of her body until she pleaded for him to have done with it, but he'd keep at it until she was half out of her head with her passion.

"Penny for your thoughts," she heard Kate say.

Mary smiled. "Just day-dreamin' about an old boyfriend."

"Handsome?"

"You could say that."

"What does he do?"

"Organizes strikes," Mary said.

"The man you mentioned who might be in Pueblo?"

"That's the one" Mary said. "How 'bout you?"

Kate shook her head. "When is there time?"

The Steinberg house was a sturdy, two-story brick, a bit of a porch, and a neat-as-a-pin front yard. Large balls of deep purple and gold chrysanthemums, like so many fat jewels, lined the walk. She and Kate approached the front door, and Mary rang the bell, crossing her fingers for luck. Almost instantly, the door opened and a short, thickset woman with huge bosoms and iron-gray hair looked out at them.

Mary summoned a bright smile. "Mrs. Steinberg? Mary Daly and Kate Brennan."

"It's nice to meet you, though I feel as though I know Kate a little from her letter." Mrs. Steinberg stepped back. "Please come in. I managed to gather a few friends. They're in the front room, waiting for you."

As they entered, Mary sniffed at the musty smell she recognized came from a room being closed up most of the time. Dark, heavy furniture that gleamed with layers of wax filled the room. Bric-a-brac lined the mantle above the gas fireplace. Over it was a painting of a fearsome-looking, white-haired gent with a full beard.

Ethel Steinberg introduced them to eight ladies, brought them tea. Cookies were passed. As Mary and Kate sipped at their tea, other women talked about the war. Mary asked her usual question about whether any of the women had sons or grandsons overseas. A small, white-haired woman seated in a straight-backed chair in the corner said a nephew had been killed in the Battle of Lodz along the Russian front. Tears welled in her eyes, and the room went quiet.

Mrs. Steinberg brought the teapot over to refill Mary and Kate's cups, and said in a low voice, "Mrs. Belinsky speaks of the eastern front. Her family still lives in Poland. She does not know how many are alive."

One of the women near Mary mentioned a coming Bar Mitzvah, and the conversation began again. Mary sipped at her tea, impatient to get started even as she listened to the ebb and flow of the voices and picked out what was important to these women—the flu, the high price of food, the shortage of fuel, the candidates' stands on the peace. The amendment wasn't on their minds, but she was determined to give it her best shot. A long twenty minutes later, Mrs. Steinberg collected empty cups. Three women picked up knitting—army green yarn for socks and scarves—that Mary suspected they brought with them everywhere to work on. When the room quieted again, the hostess returned from the kitchen to introduce the topic of the afternoon.

Mary gave a quick glance of encouragement to Kate, who was to talk first. Kate rose, walked to the fireplace and turned to face her audience, smiled. According to their plan, she was to begin with a short history of women's suffrage, then a quick review of how Colorado women got the vote. But, given the general age of the audience, Mary was afraid they might nod off and she coughed lightly as a signal to Kate who shifted to her first experience with the National Woman's Party, picketing in front of the White House, the bedlam that she tried to persuade the police to break up. "But instead they arrested me along with the picketers and we were thrown into a filthy prison for fifteen days."

At that, women lowered their knitting needles. Kate told them about the horrible conditions, Lucy Burns's fasting. "Which brings us to the election," she said, finally. "And why Miss Daly and I are here to ask your help and the help of every woman in Colorado."

Looks were exchanged, eyes widened expectantly. Mary watched their expressions as Kate tossed out the bomb. "To help women across this country win the right to vote, you must vote for Lawrence Phipps, the Republican candidate for the Senate."

The ladies gasped in unison.

"It's asking a great deal, I know. I'm a Democrat myself, as is my family. But the Democrats in the Senate have refused to support the amendment. As much as I'd like to be loyal to the Party, my heart tells me that the basic right of women in this country to vote is more important." The only sound, the steady tick of the grandfather clock in the hall, Kate moved her gaze from one woman to the next.

A long minute passed before a gaunt woman, her face flushed, turned to Mrs. Steinberg. "Ethel, you should have told us. If we'd known . . ." She glanced at the other women and back at her hostess. "We have been friends for years. But voting Republican?" Her gray eyes teared, and Mary felt the first of nine votes slip away. She rose to her feet.

"Ladies, I can tell just by lookin' at you that you're good people. I'd guess a good many of you are like Mrs. Kassel who came over from the old country not that long ago, same as my Da." She looked from woman to woman. "He came here because people have a chance to make somethin' of themselves. To have a say in what goes on. Hard as it is to believe, millions of women in this country aren't so lucky as we are in Colorado. So if it takes holdin' our noses and votin' for the likes of Republicans to set things right, then that's what we must do."

Another silence. Mary glanced at their hostess, read the embarrassment on her face. Plainly, neither she nor her guests would bring themselves to put an "x" next to the name of a Republican. Traditions died hard.

Once outside again, she and Kate silently walked toward the streetcar stop. Mary could shrug off the cool good-byes. It was what they represented that weighed on her, and she said so to Kate.

"Maybe we should have gone to the rabbi of that big temple first. His support might have softened those ladies a bit," she said.

Mary only grunted.

"And there are still the colored women. I think I can find a contact."

Mary shot Kate a disgusted look. "If you knew anythin', you'd know they're already Republicans, still votin' for Abe Lincoln."

"How about Little Italy?"

Mary shook her head. "You're jokin'. Just thinkin' about votin'

Republican there is reason for a roughin' up, or worse." Mary glanced down the street for a sign of a streetcar, but saw only empty tracks. The business of begging votes depressed her. If only they could rent a hall or . . . She stopped, turned to Kate. "I just thought of somethin'."

Kate eyed her.

"Every election, the Democratic boys put on a picnic at Highland Park, not a dozen blocks from my house, the last Sunday in October."

"Not this year, they won't. Not with the flu."

"Maybe, maybe not. See, it's outdoors, which is bound to make a difference. And the weather bein' nice as it is . . ."

Kate didn't reply.

"I say we give it a try."

"It doesn't sound worth bothering with to me," Kate said. "We'd have to leave for Pueblo by early afternoon. We only have four days down there and we can't risk missing the train."

"We don't have to stay at the park for long. Just stop by for an hour, maybe. Hand out pamphlets, talk to a few people," Mary said.

"If there's a picnic, and if there's a crowd—two big ifs."

Mary went back to staring down the tracks. For the first time since they'd been together, the setback of the afternoon had taken the starch out of the both of them. They were verging on bad tempers, and nitpicking. If they couldn't hang together, the whole blessed thing they'd been wearing their shoes and brains out for would fall apart.

The streetcar came into view. "We've agreed then," Mary said, opening her purse and pulling out a nickel. "We'll meet at St. Catharine's at ten A.M. on Sunday with our suitcases, so we can head straight to the station at noon." She gently shoved Kate ahead of her onto the streetcar. "And I can hardly wait to see the look on the good old boys' faces when they figure out we're crashin' their party."

Chapter 28

The next day, returning from canvassing the Park Hill area, Kate pulled open the heavy entrance door to the Albany and walked slowly across the lobby to the front desk. Her feet hurt. She was sick to death of tramping around the treeless suburban wilds with no results to show for it, tired of wasting half the day waiting for streetcars. But because the politicos hadn't yet locked the new precincts at the east edge of Denver into one party or the other, she and Mary had decided the residents might be open to persuasion. What they hadn't counted on was how few people lived in each block that sometimes contained no more than a house or two.

When she asked the desk clerk for her key, he handed her not only the key, but a letter. The postmark was Washington, the handwriting Lucy's rolling script. Kate wavered between ripping open the envelope or waiting for the privacy of her room, and she finally chose privacy where she could savor every word.

Once in her room, without bothering to take off her hat, she sat on the edge of the bed and tore open the precious envelope.

Dear Kate,

I hope you are well. This flu has everyone thoroughly frightened. The theaters here are closed. I have not heard from Iris but trust her fiancé is on the mend.

In case your papers have not carried the stories, I wanted you to know that we have not been idle since you left. Most of our time is now spent at the Capitol. Two weeks ago Olivia and Sarah Stillman led the charge with a marvelous banner.

Kate read on, imagining the scene. The purple-and-gold banner, fluttering in the breeze, held high over Olivia and Sarah's heads, the rush of police. A few hours later more women, just as fearless, storming up the Capitol steps, just as men had charged across No Man's Land. Her heart lightened at the thought of it.

> *Before I forget, a word of warning that Mrs. Catt is coming out for John Shafroth. A not unexpected move, for she is very strong on Wilson's plans for peace and believes they will not have a chance in a Republican congress.*
> *Much to be done. I am off to New Jersey for what had been planned as a rally but, with the flu epidemic, will be held in a member's house, though a big one.*
> *Alice sends her best wishes.*
>
> *Your friend, Lucy*

Returning the letter to its envelope, Kate felt comforted by the intimate feel of the letter. Gone was the resentment she'd harbored after Lucy had insisted she go to Colorado. *Your friend,* she'd said, as if Kate was her equal.

As for the details, particularly Mrs. Catt's coming out for John Shafroth, that might boomerang and work in the NWP's favor, Kate thought. Coloradoans were a clannish bunch who resented the East. She felt her spirits rise, and she got up and went over to the desk and pulled the folder with her campaign notes out of the drawer.

On the inside cover was the calendar with the days of the month crossed off. Not counting today, there were exactly nine days until the election. Monday through Saturday in Pueblo, Sunday for the train ride back to Denver, leaving Monday to take care of loose ends, and it would be over.

If she'd given any part of the campaign short shrift, it was help to the outlying little towns. True, most tended to vote Republican but Shafroth was popular with voters on both sides of the political aisle. The best she could do now was to urge the NWP members to spread the word. She sat at the desk and wrote to each committee. The difference between victory and defeat could well be in your hands, she wrote them. Talk to neighbors and friends, tell them how urgent their vote was. Before she sealed the eight envelopes, she slipped a few flyers in each. In the morning she'd leave them with the desk clerk to mail.

Kate sat back. She still had her notes about the Denver precincts to go over. She felt like a rubber band stretched to the breaking point. Her stomach rumbled, and she realized she was starved. She glanced at her watch. Eight o'clock. If the dining room was still open, she might splurge and order steak. She got to her feet and had just picked up her purse when she heard a knock. Thinking it might be the desk clerk with a telegram, perhaps from Lucy, she dug a nickel out of her change purse for a tip. But instead of the skinny desk clerk, what stood before her was a vision of purple, carrying a suitcase.

"Lizzie! What on earth are you doing here?"

Her sister stepped past her into the room. "A hello might be nice."

"Does Dad or Mother know you're here?"

"They will when they get back home. Mother's up in Boulder, spending the weekend with that friend who collects butterflies. Dad is duck hunting. When I told Christine where I was going, she almost helped me pack. Our dear parents may not agree, but Christine thinks you walk on water." Lizzie put her suitcase down, looked around. "Aren't you going to ask me to sit down?"

Kate eyed her sister in exasperation. "It's the desk chair or the bed. Take your pick." She loved Lizzie. Any other time, she'd be glad to see her, but not now, not tonight. "Judging from the suitcase, I gather you're going somewhere."

Straight-backed, perched on the edge of the bed, Lizzie looked up at Kate with a smile. "Actually, I'm running away."

Kate noted her sister's pout. "You and Mother had another fight."

"How did you guess?"

"What was it this time? A boy she doesn't approve of or a new dress she won't let you have?"

Lizzie narrowed her eyes. "Okay. Belittle me if you want. After all, I'm just the little sister. No one worth worrying about, not like you in Washington or Tom in France."

"Lizzie—"

"You don't have the slightest idea what I care about and neither do Daddy and Mother."

Kate knew the feeling, at least as it concerned their mother. Seeing the spark in her sister's green eyes, she imagined herself only three months ago. "So your solution is to run away. Is that it?"

Lizzie gazed up at her soulfully. Kate had grown up with little Miss Sarah Bernhardt, as their father used to call Lizzie. Dramatics were her stock-in-trade. "May I remind you that you're only sixteen."

"Oh, please! If I closed my eyes, I'd think it was Mother talking."

Kate shrugged. "True, nonetheless."

Lizzie got up, circled the room. "Anyway, what difference does it make? Mother and Daddy will never miss me."

"What about school?" Kate asked, reaching for anything to diffuse Lizzie's determination.

"Who needs it? Anyway, I'm at least a year ahead of the other girls." Lizzie tucked her long, black hair behind her ears.

"If that's the case, maybe Mother would let you get a job of some sort."

"What dream world do you live in?" Lizzie scoffed.

"How do you know if you haven't asked her."

"Because I have an even better idea."

Kate arched an eyebrow.

"I'll come with you."

Kate narrowed her eyes at her sister's ploy. "This was your plan all along, wasn't it?"

Lizzie shrugged, smirked.

"For your information, I'm going to Pueblo tomorrow afternoon and won't be back until election day. And you are not—I repeat—not coming with me."

"You're going to Pueblo?" Lizzie made a face.

"I take it you don't approve. All the more reason to pick up that suitcase and go home." Kate was losing patience.

"Okay. I'll go to Pueblo."

Kate shook her head. "Wrong. You'll go home."

"Not a chance."

"Lizzie, I don't blame you for resenting me and Tom. I know it's hard to be the youngest."

"You don't know one single thing about being the youngest. So you can give me all the soft soap you want, but I'm not leaving."

Kate recognized stubbornness when she saw it. It might as well be the middle name of every woman in the Brennan household. "Okay. I'm willing to compromise. You can spend the night. And then I'm taking you home."

Chapter 29 ————————————————————

Kate watched for her reaction as Mary walked down the steps of St. Catharine's, suitcase in hand, and spotted Lizzie, done up in purple, carrying a suitcase. Mary wouldn't have to be a mind reader to figure out that Lizzie would be joining them and, from her stony expression, Kate saw she wasn't pleased. But by the time Mary had reached them, she had pasted a smile on her face.

Kate had barely introduced the two and explained Lizzie would help hand out pamphlets at the picnic when Mary took Kate by the arm. "You'll excuse us for a minute," she said to Lizzie. And they walked back toward the entrance to the church. "Tell me about that suitcase she's carryin'."

"She came to the hotel last night and said she was running away. My parents are out of town. I let her spend the night. When she found out about the picnic at the park, she insisted on helping."

"Doin' what, pray tell?"

"Handing out pamphlets. Whatever we need."

"And then she's goin' home?"

Kate nodded.

"She's not comin' with us to Pueblo?"

"Absolutely not. She almost gagged when I mentioned Pueblo last night."

"Good."

Kate caught Mary's appraising glance toward Lizzie and imagined her thoughts about one Brennan being more than enough in her life. On the other hand, Kate knew Mary put great stock in family, and Lizzie was family. "The picnic, then," Mary said.

Kate nodded. "The picnic."

❦

Kate remembered Highland Park as a child, when she'd come here with her grandfather during campaigns for other Democrats. The size of a city block, it was a grassy square with a drinking fountain and a couple of horseshoe pits, elms and cottonwoods for shade, in the center of a neighborhood of modest houses and a library at one end, with enough grass for kids to play ball without the risk of a broken window.

Even with no sign of the Colorado Democrats' banner, the moment Kate saw the American flag hung from a rope stretched between two trees she knew the picnic was getting under way. Mary put down her suitcase, looked around. "And where is everyone, pray tell? Mass is over. If they're comin', they should be here."

Kate did a quick count. No more than two dozen men were smoking and talking by the trees and, off a ways, five women were arranging covered dishes along makeshift tables. Chatting together as they worked, the women wore men's sweaters against the cool air over what must be their Sunday best black dresses.

Kate and Mary—Lizzie right behind them—entered the park, surveying the tables where most people would gather. Kate dug into her handbag and gave Lizzie a handful of pamphlets. "You take these over to the ladies at the food table and watch our suitcases. Mary and I will go talk to the men over there for a while and then we'll be back."

But they hadn't gone twenty feet when Kate heard the toot of automobile horns, and she glanced over her shoulder to see two Cadillac open cars, their tops down, decorated with red-white-and-blue banners, pull up to the curb. Tied to the bumpers were "Shafroth for Senate" signs. A moment later, the Senator himself climbed out of the back seat of the lead car.

Kate tapped Mary on the shoulder. "Look who's here." She watched four men walk over, apparently the greeting committee.

"Let's go say hello," said Kate.

"You, not me."

Kate raised her chin, squared her shoulders and followed the growing group of men trailing after the senator and his greeters, headed toward a makeshift podium beneath the trees. She decided to stand on the perimeter of the crowd and wait for the right moment, but the senator saw her, beckoned to her. The men stepped aside so she could move closer.

"Gentlemen, if you haven't already met Miss Brennan, you're in for a treat. She grew up with my boys." He took her by the arm. "Good to see you again, Kate. What brings you to this fine occasion?"

"To speak about the importance of the national suffrage amendment, as I'm sure you would expect, Senator," Kate said, as she carefully removed his proprietary hand. This was the first time she'd seen John Shafroth since their meeting in his office. For a man in the last, usually frantic days of a reelection campaign, he looked distressingly relaxed. "In fact, I'd like you to meet another NWP member working with me who might be new to you." She glanced over the men's head toward Mary a few feet away, motioned to her. "Senator, this is Miss Mary Daly."

"A pleasure," he said.

"Happy to meet ya, Senator," Mary said.

"Do my ears deceive me, or do I hear the lilt of the Irish in your voice, Miss Daly?"

"You do indeed, sir. We Irish women take our politics and our rights seriously."

"So you two ladies are checking up on me, are you?" he said, looking directly at Kate.

A few of the men around him chuckled.

"We're here about the amendment, Senator," Kate answered, handing him a pamphlet. "Our only purpose is to ensure that all women in this country have the vote."

"As I have, for many years," returned the senator, handing the pamphlet on to an aide.

"But do your supporters know the Democrat Party has refused to come out for the amendment? Instead, we women have had to rely on the Republicans," Kate prompted.

"A slight exaggeration, wouldn't you say?"

Kate caught an edge to Shafroth's voice, saw the shift in the men's shoulders, heard the low grumbles. The women were horning in on their turf. Knowing his upbringing would prevent him from abruptly cutting her off, Kate plunged on. "As the pamphlet says . . ." She eyed the folded pamphlet sticking out from the aide's shirt pocket. "If the amendment is to succeed, the women of Colorado have no other choice but to turn to the Republican candidate for Senate."

The crowd had grown to nearly a hundred by now. "Throw 'em out," a man in the back shouted over the laughter and the hoots.

The senator held up his hand. "No, no. This is a free country with free speech."

"They're daft, is what they are," someone yelled.

"Wait now." The Senator held up a hand. "The ladies have a right to be heard. What they haven't told you is that a federal amendment for the woman's vote is only one of dozens of issues facing this country." The smile gone, his expression had turned serious. He talked about the brave boys in France, three of them his own. Every man was listening, nodding agreement. This could be the war to end all wars, he said, but it would take a Democratic Congress to give the president the backing he needed in order to lead the way.

"So let's hear it, boys! Three cheers for Shafroth for Senate," a man in a billed cap shouted. The senator beamed as the cheers turned to a chant until, finally, he held up his hand for quiet. By this time Kate had been jostled away from the senator, and Shafroth went into his spiel, promising lower prices and higher wages. Fifteen minutes later, after a final cheer, the senator shook hands all around, went over to the ladies at the food table to sample a piece of cake and shake more hands before he climbed back in the campaign car where the driver and an underling had been waiting, and they sped away.

Once the car was out of sight, Mary turned to Kate and asked, "It's none of my business, but what happened between you and him? I got the feelin' he was sendin' you a message."

"He helped get me out of prison."

"Sounds like more than a bit of a favor to me."

"The only reason he did it was to please my parents," Kate said, still shaken from the meeting. Talking to him, seeing him here—not two miles from his home and hers, as opposed to the Senate office building or the floor of the Senate Chamber or even the District workhouse, reminded her that no matter how she might deny it, this campaign was personal. Taking in a deep breath, she glanced toward the food tables. In the confrontation with Shafroth, she'd completely forgotten her sister. "Where's Lizzie?"

"Beats me. I expect she got her fill of politics and went home all on her own."

Chapter 30 ꙮ

Two hours later, Kate and Mary pushed through the crowd gathered along the platform at Union Station toward their train. Considered a local run, the 4:50 for Colorado Springs with a change to Pueblo consisted of a mail car and three passenger cars. As they climbed up into the last car, Kate decided that with the mob around them, she and Mary would be lucky to find seats.

The air reeked of tobacco and unwashed bodies. Babies howled. Kate spied two vacant seats down the aisle across from an elderly couple. Motioning to Mary with her head, she pushed past two men in bowler hats, and shoved her case up onto the overhead rack. "All aboard" was called. A blast of steam. The screech of a whistle.

Kate sat down, pulled in a deep breath of relief as the train jerked and slowly began to move. The last two days of tying up loose ends in Denver had almost done her in. After a moment, she folded her arms, closed her eyes, determined to nap through the two-hour trip when Mary gave her a nudge. "Don't look now, but we got company."

Kate opened her eyes, glanced around.

"Lizzie. At the far end of the car."

Kate craned her neck, sighed at the sight of her willowy sister. "Damn. It's too late to have her thrown off." She glanced at Mary. "I'll send her home when we get to Colorado Springs."

"Easier said than done."

Kate watched with dismay as Lizzie moved down the aisle toward them, carrying a sack, smiling, just as if Kate had expected her.

"Phew! I barely made it. I had to call Christine to tell her where I'd be, and the line at the lunch counter was forever long." She reached over Mary, seated on the aisle, and handed Kate the bulging paper bag. "I hope you and Mary like ham and cheese. That's all there was. Whatever you don't want, I'll be sitting back there by the door."

Giving the bag to Mary, Kate stepped over her feet and into the aisle, and said to Lizzie, "We need to talk."

"Too noisy in here," came Lizzie's glib reply.

"Then we'll go outside." She took Lizzie's elbow and shoved her along the aisle.

Standing on the small platform that joined their car with the next, balancing against the sway of the train, Kate clung to the railing, shouted, "This isn't a game, Lizzie."

"Never thought it was," she said, holding her blowing hair away from her face.

"You promised you would go home."

"Did I?"

"Look here. I love you, Lizzie. You're my sister. But I cannot risk having you mess up the campaign, not now. There's too much at stake."

"You think that's what I'll do: mess up the campaign?"

"You might."

"Kate, listen—"

"I'm through talking about it. As soon as we get to Colorado Springs, I expect you to take the next train back to Denver. I can't wait around to make sure you do it, but I hope you will. For both our sakes." Without waiting for Lizzie to object, Kate pushed against the heavy door, held it open for her sister, and they went inside.

Back at her seat, Kate took the sandwich Mary handed her.

"Who's this Christine?" Mary asked.

"The housekeeper."

"Ah." Kate never ceased to be amazed at how much ground Mary's *ahs* covered. "As to Lizzie, I've been thinkin.' We'll only be there four days."

Kate eyed her.

"While you and her were out there, I was sittin' here, rememberin' when I was younger 'n her, how I walked my first picket line alongside my Da, and—"

"May I remind you that we are not walking a picket line during the next four days but trying to convince women—Democrats whose husbands and fathers may throw us out of their houses—that they should vote for the Republican candidate for Senate. What Lizzie knows about politics wouldn't fill a thimble. And she could get hurt."

"Three would be harder to throw out than two," Mary said, not looking at Kate.

"Whose side are you on?"

"Kate, she's here, and an extra pair of hands can't hurt."

"I'll think about it." Kate turned to the window as the train moved slowly past lines of empty freight cars and warehouses along the Platte River, its still, shallow water like a brown mirror. She weighed the sense of what Mary suggested as she watched the city turn to treeless, rolling brown grassland and scattered farmhouses, where ruby-leafed sumac bushes clustered along the fence lines. She leaned her head against the thick windowpane, and gave in to the rhythm of the train.

Her thoughts drifted to all the other NWP members working in Wyoming and Montana, Arizona, Idaho, frantically trying to convince Democrats to switch parties. Were some of them on a train, too—in the middle of nowhere, rolling toward yet another town? Did they ever feel as disconnected as she did sometimes, wondering whether Lucy and Miss Paul, sitting in their offices at headquarters, two thousands miles east, ever thought of them as more than names?

At twenty minutes to eight, the train pulled into Colorado Springs' red sandstone station one hour late. Kate tried not to worry about making the connection to Pueblo. Every train was late these days. Taking no chances, Kate grabbed Mary's arm and the two went in search of the train schedule posted next to the ticket windows. To her consternation, Kate saw a line drawn through the departure to Pueblo. The train had been sidelined for a troop train. There wouldn't be another until morning, the lone man behind the grill-work of the ticket window said.

As they stood by the window, gazing out at the empty train tracks beyond the platform, wondering what their next move should be, Kate realized she hadn't seen Lizzie. With luck she might be on the other side of the depot where the northbound trains came in. But then she heard Lizzie's high voice, calling her, and she turned to see her emerge from the ladies' restroom.

"When does our train leave?" Lizzie said, putting her suitcase down beside her.

"I thought I told you to go back to Denver."

"But I already told Christine I'd be in Pueblo with you. So Mother and Daddy won't worry." Lizzie glanced at Mary who winked. "So when DOES our train leave?"

Kate caught the "our." "It doesn't. At least, not until tomorrow morning. A troop train gets priority."

"We'll have to find a hotel," Lizzie said.

Kate felt her resistance wane, not because she was any more enthu-siastic about Lizzie coming along, but because she had other, more important things on her mind. Like this delay that would cost them nearly a full day in Pueblo. Mary was right: an extra pair of hands could be valuable. Lizzie was trying to be responsible, though she would have to prove herself. Plus, Kate admitted grudgingly, Lizzie's sense of adventure could help keep their spirits up in a town that might be difficult to crack.

As it turned out, the few hotels along the street near the station were beyond their pocketbook, and all of them shabby. Lizzie went off to find a restaurant and discovered a Chinese place. As they waited in the nearly empty restaurant for the chow mein they'd ordered, they debated about broadening their search for a hotel and decided against it. They would wait out the night in the train sta-tion. Kate was glad there would be three of them after all.

Dark with a cold wind that had come up out of the west, they shivered as they started back to the station. Lizzie ran ahead, her purple silk skirt swirling around her, Kate and Mary, like sedate elders, followed behind.

"Feels like snow, doesn't it?" Kate asked, drawing her sweater around her.

"Once we get in the station, best pick a spot near the stove," Mary said.

For safety's sake, they chose a bench in full view of the man at the ticket window, slid their suitcases beneath their feet and tried to make themselves comfortable on the hard surface.

Some time in the middle of the night, stiff with the chill of the waiting room, Kate went in search of the ladies room. The tiled floor was filthy. Bits of trash lay collected in the corners. A wide yellow stain led from the faucet to the drain in the sink. In the dim light, she squatted over the cracked toilet, washed her hands in cold water, and dried them on the hem of her slip. Staring back at her haggard face in the cracked mirror, she tried to remember herself at sixteen. Her cheeks had been plumper. Not bad looking. A decent figure; she'd developed breasts early. There'd been a boy she'd met at cotillion who always stared at them when they danced. Freckles and flame-red hair, sweaty palms. Sid Halloran, she thought his name was. Or was it Halley? She hadn't thought of him in years. Back then beating her brother Tom at tennis had been her only goal.

Kate tucked her blouse in her skirt, glanced at her watch. Three o'clock. Another six hours and they'd hopefully be in Pueblo. She thought of the four days ahead. Neither she nor Mary knew the people or the town. Mary might feel at home with the Irish, but Pueblo Democrats were primarily Italians who, according to Mary, considered Republicans a close second to heretics. To urge them to vote for the same could be dangerous, and that's what she and Mary—and now Lizzie—were about to do. Still, there was Phoebe Atwood, the Pueblo committee chairman. A local, undoubtedly with important ties.

It was nearly ten, mid-morning, before they boarded the train to Pueblo, already an hour behind, thought Kate with irritation. After the long night, the hour and a half trip seemed endless. Too impatient to sit, Kate left Mary and Lizzie and stood at the back of the last car and gazed out at mile after mile of treeless plains, dry land farms with meager houses and unpainted barns. As the train neared Pueblo, the fields gave way to small, unkempt houses along dirt roads, lining the track. What trees she saw were spindly, leafless. To the east, the landscape was cut by arroyos, the desert-like acres covered with strange, blackened, twisted cactus. Gradually, more prosperous looking, even grand, stone and a few frame houses with cupolas and bay windows came into view; then sturdy, red brick buildings, church spires. The train whistle howled. Kate leaned out and saw a red stone station with an imposing clock tower down the track. Yet, for all its air of respectability, the town gave her an uneasy feeling.

The train lurched to a stop; steam whooshed out from beneath its cars. She went back inside, and she and Mary and Lizzie pulled their suitcases from the overhead rack and followed the other passengers out the door. The sunshine momentarily blinding her as she waited her turn to descend the steep steps, she thought she heard a man call her name. She cupped her eyes and looked down at the platform, craning her neck to see who it was. And then she saw him, standing beneath the eaves of the station. Charlie Harrison. Not fifteen feet away.

He was smiling up at her, and she was helpless to stop her heart from rising at the sight of him. He called to her again and came to the bottom of the steps, held out a hand, and she took it, felt its warmth as she climbed down.

"What are you doing here?" was all she could think to say.

"I live here now," he said as he let go of her hand and turned to help Mary and Lizzie down. "Work for *The Pueblo Chieftain*. I'm covering the Senate race at the moment. Every once in a while I pick up an article about the NWP. I heard from Millie you were back in Colorado, and I figured you'd be down here eventually."

"But how did you know what train we'd be on?"

"Didn't. I was supposed to meet one of Phipps's henchmen, but I don't see him. This is the only train that comes in from up north carrying regular passengers these days." He looked back at Mary and Lizzie, and Kate introduced them and they shook hands. "You ladies just missed Phipps himself. Left two days ago. I'm trying to follow up on the rumor he's buying votes."

Kate simply nodded and watched him pick up the suitcases the conductor had placed at the bottom of the steps. Except for Millie's note about his asking for her address, Kate wasn't aware he knew what she was doing in Colorado. Yet here he was, and she had to fight off an unfamiliar warm glow that already was distracting.

"Wherever you're headed, my car's out front. It'll be a squeeze. But there's no cab. I can tie the suitcases on the back if I have to."

Mary and Lizzie behind, Kate walked beside Charlie. "What happened to the CPI?"

"With the war almost over, Mr. Creel didn't mind when I quit. I told him I had some unfinished business in this part of the state. I telegraphed my former boss, and he rehired me." Charlie stopped by a four-door Dodge parked by the main entrance to the station, and put down the suitcases.

Kate wanted to ask him what kind of unfinished business. Instead, she said, "I don't think I ever thanked you for what you did, getting us out of prison."

"How do you mean?"

"Senator Shafroth told me a reporter—though not anyone from the District papers—had tipped him off. You're the only person I could think . . ."

But Charlie had turned his attention to Mary and Lizzie and was helping them get settled in the back seat.

Still standing on the sidewalk, Kate waited as Charlie maneuvered the suitcases so they'd have room to sit.

248

"Where does Miss Daly come in? And Lizzie?" he asked once he'd finished and had closed the back doors.

"Mary's from Denver. That's where we met. She's a member. We're friends." Kate drew her coat sweater around her. The sun wasn't as warm as she'd thought. "Lizzie is my sister who invited herself." She looked up at him. "You said you had unfinished business to attend to here."

"It has to do with my Dad," he said in a tone that left no doubt the subject was closed, and he held the passenger door open. "Where are we headed?"

Kate gave him Phoebe Atwood's address. He closed the door and walked around to the driver's side. She wished she could figure out what was going on. That first instant when she'd stepped off the train and seen him at the foot of the steps, she'd thought maybe he'd followed her. But she'd known down deep that was absurd. It was a case of sheer coincidence. He was just what he'd said: a reporter, assigned to cover the Senate race. Charlie was doing his job when he met the train that she just happened to be on. Or had it been fate? Until this morning, she'd had no contacts with the local press. And now she did.

Chapter 31 ———————————————

Kate gazed at Phoebe Atwood's house, set on the corner of a block on the hill just north of downtown. A neat two-story brick with a broad front porch, its trim had been painted pale blue. The neighborhood had the well-cared-for, almost smug look of a place where families who weren't rich but didn't worry much about money lived. She was sure discussion of election issues stopped after the morning paper was put down, the husband went off to work and the wife planned the day's menus. Certainly not the kind of place, Kate thought, where women would think to join the NWP. She wondered about Phoebe.

It wasn't until Charlie pulled up to the curb that she saw the swing dangling from the huge cottonwood tree in the yard and the bright green scooter lying on its side in the leaf-blanketed front yard. Children. Of course. But the possibility had never occurred to her. Kate felt her plans for the next three days fade before her eyes.

The dry air held the faint smell of burning leaves as Kate and Mary and Lizzie climbed out. Charlie drew a package of cigarettes out of his pocket, said he'd wait. Walking up to the porch, Kate heard children's high squeals. She gave the brass handle on the doorbell a twist. The door opened a crack, and a small face peered out at them. Kate smiled. The door opened a little wider to reveal a girl of about five in a pale blue smock dress smudged with what looked like streaks of chocolate. Ringlets of golden hair covered her head. She was barefoot.

"Is your mother home?" Kate asked.

The child peered at Kate and Mary. "She's giving Jimmy a bath."

From inside the house a woman's voice called, "Who is it, Laura?"

"Some ladies."

"I'll be right down."

A few minutes later a slender woman with short reddish hair, holding a child wrapped in a bath towel, stood at the door.

Kate introduced herself and Mary. "And Lizzie. My sister," she added.

Phoebe smiled. Kate had never seen such deep green eyes. "Come in. Please." She shooed her little girl away and opened the door wider. "I really must apologize. I'd planned to have everything shipshape. But with the children . . ."

She led them into the front room, invited them to sit down, all the while removing pieces of clothing off the chairs and a battered couch. "Laura was playing house," she said, shifting the little boy to the other hip.

"Let me hold the child, why don't you?" Mary said, captivating the boy with her smile, as Kate had seen her do to other children dozens of times.

Phoebe Atwood looked down at her child. "He doesn't take to strangers but if you want . . ."

She handed him to Mary, and, for an instant, his little face screwed up as if preparing to howl in protest. Then he spotted the gold cross that hung around Mary's neck and grabbed for it. The little girl came over, pulled on her skirt. "Do you want to see my playroom?"

Her mother reached for her. "Laura, leave the—"

"A playroom, is it?" Mary asked as if she were impressed.

Nodding eagerly, the little girl looked over at Lizzie. "It's way up in the trees."

"Well, then we should truly like to see it." Mary glanced from the child's mother to Lizzie, and grinned. "Want to come along?" Without waiting for an answer, she said, "We'll be back in a jiff." And, bouncing the baby as she walked, Mary, with Lizzie behind her, followed Laura into the hall.

Phoebe Atwood set the bundle of clothes she'd collected down on the couch. "Dear me. I am sorry. This isn't exactly conducive to politicking, is it?"

Kate struggled for a smile. "They're lovely children."

"I'm afraid the neighbors don't always agree. Jim being a doctor, his children are supposed to behave properly."

Kate let go of her smile. "About the campaign . . ."

"Yes. Well. I thought we could go around the neighborhoods. The women who have worked on the election here have been thorough but I thought a reminder—"

"Ordinarily, I'd agree," Kate interrupted. "But with so little time, we'll need to concentrate on the hardcore Democrats."

Phoebe frowned. "That wouldn't be around here. More south of the river."

"You know the area?"

"I'm afraid not all that well."

Kate stifled a sigh. "Maybe one of your members?"

"Perhaps, though I doubt—" Phoebe Atwood glanced toward the hall. "My goodness, it just occurred to me. Your suitcases."

"Suitcases?" Kate asked, confused for an instant and then remembered Charlie, still sitting out in his car. "A—friend brought them—brought us. He's outside, waiting to hear where we'll be staying."

"I wish we could put you up but . . ." Phoebe smiled apologetically. "The Bristol isn't bad. It's reasonably clean. And cheap. If you want, you could go over, see about a room, then come back."

"I'll let you know in a minute." And Kate ran out onto the front porch and down the front walk to where Charlie was leaning against the hood of his car, smoking.

"Sorry about the wait," Kate said.

"Is she able to put you up?"

"No, there's no room, what with the children. She suggests the Bristol."

"It'll do." She tried not to take Charlie's detached tone personally. "I guess you want me to take you over there now."

"Actually, do you mind waiting a little longer? Or you could come in."

He tossed his cigarette onto the grass, ground it out with the toe of his shoe. "I'll wait."

Kate turned to go back to the house, stopped, and faced Charlie. "She could have warned me that she'd only worked the Republican neighborhoods. I'd been counting on her. Now I'm not sure what we'll do." She shook her head. "And she'd never said a word about kids."

Charlie folded his arms over his chest, his eyes suitably solemn, but there was a smile working at the corners of his mouth.

"It isn't funny. We have four days. Five, if it hadn't been for the train problem." She glanced away then looked back at him. "Let me have one of your cigarettes, will you?"

He dug into his pockets, drew out the package, shook out a cigarette, held it toward her. She took it, put it between her lips.

"Hold on, I've got a match," he said, and he removed a plain kitchen match from another pocket, lit it with his fingernail, held it to the tip of her cigarette.

Kate drew in deeply, exhaled. "Thanks." She waved the smoke away and leaned against the car's front fender, gazing across the street. "Lord save us. Pushing a baby carriage around the neighborhoods that have already been covered and keeping an eye on that wild little girl of hers. That's what we'll be doing."

Charlie squatted and picked up a pebble, lobbed it across the street, as if he was bored.

"I realize this isn't your worry," she said, staring at his broad back. "But do you have any idea how this may affect an entire campaign?"

He tossed another pebble. "What's plan B?"

"I'm thinking about it now," Kate said, out of sorts.

"These days, Pueblo will be a hard nut to crack," he said, standing.

"So my friend, Mary says." Kate smoked for a few minutes, and Charlie came over to lean against the other fender. "The way she explained it most of the Democrats down here are Italians, the majority of whom work at the steel mill. And, apparently, a strike is being planned. All very sub rosa, I guess, because the union has been outlawed, but planned nonetheless with the help of someone named Gino."

Charlie eyed her. "Gino Franchetti. Tough son-of-a-gun."

Kate took another long drag on her cigarette, exhaled as she reviewed the facts as she understood them. "All very grim except for one thing."

"Which is?"

"The majority in Pueblo votes Democratic but I would bet my last dime that the men who own this town—the Mill owners and those who run it—are Republicans." She slid a glance toward Charlie to check his reaction but saw only a deadpan expression. "I presume they also control the police. Which means that the Democratic Party won't like what we're doing but they won't dare give us any grief." She smiled at the thought. "Just think of it, Charlie. For once, we're on the same side as the anointed."

Kate stood outside the dark red brick hotel, eyeing it with little enthusiasm. Situated across the street from the railway station, the two-story building must be a stopping place for traveling salesmen. It had a worn look, probably old enough that the bathroom was added later, perhaps on the first floor behind the kitchen. In comparison, the Albany in Denver looked plush.

Charlie carried in their suitcases and waited with Mary and Lizzie while Kate went in search of a desk clerk. She found a heavyset woman, drinking coffee in the kitchen, who told her the second-floor front was available. The price was five dollars a night. A cot for Lizzie would be fifty cents extra. Kate said she thought it was high. The woman blamed it on the war. Kate asked for the key. Charlie picked up the suitcases and carried them upstairs.

Kate walked over to the room's only window, looking out as she fingered the worn print curtains. The room itself was just big enough for the basics. Twin beds pushed together for lack of space, a dresser with a mirror attached and a nightstand. A chamber pot was in one corner. The cot Kate had arranged for would crowd things even more. But they weren't here to be comfortable. She could put up with almost anything for three days.

Charlie put the suitcases down, and Kate said, "Remember how you asked me about Plan B?"

"I do. And we talked about the connection between the union and the Italians."

Kate shot a glance toward Mary, still in the doorway, her arms folded, her dark, hooded eyes watching Charlie, as if sizing him up. Here in these close quarters with strong morning light from the window, Kate noticed his collar was frayed, and he could do with a haircut.

"I hope Charlie here also told you that parts of this town might be dangerous for us to stick our noses in," Mary said.

"Nothing new there. We're always strangers, always suspect. Except this time we'll have the police on our side."

"Now that I'll have to see to believe," Mary said.

Kate looked back at Charlie. "So let me rephrase the question. Where will we find the most Democrats in Pueblo? Phoebe Atwood seems to think it's south of the river."

"And she's right. But—"

"Where, I gather, most of the Italians also live."

Charlie nodded, and Kate smiled. "Finally. An answer." She glanced at Mary. "Now we know."

Mary bit her lip, stayed silent. Kate glanced over at Charlie and saw a solution. "I have an idea. You're covering the election. How about a story on the NWP trying to convert dyed-in-the-wool Democrats to vote for the Republican candidate? It might even be a day-by-day series. You could follow us around, take pictures."

He cocked an eyebrow, pursed his lips. "It sure is an unusual angle. But my editor might go for it."

Kate clapped her hands together, glanced at Mary. "Terrific!" She checked her watch, looked at Charlie. "It's just past noon. Your editor might be at lunch. So we'll have to wait, but we can use the time to settle in and get organized. How does two sound to meet in front of the hotel?"

⁂

The sweet taste of the apple pie she'd eaten still in her mouth, Kate rolled down the car's window, enjoying the feel of the warm early afternoon air as Charlie drove across the Arkansas River. Under protest, Lizzie had agreed to stay behind and distribute the pamphlets in the neighborhood around the Atwoods. Now Kate inspected the modest homes lining the dirt road with an eye to what she and Mary might encounter. Neat with freshly painted trim and prim mounds of shrubbery below the porches, they had the look of homes belonging to longtime workers, reliable people, company people who valued their jobs too much to give in to union intimidation—much like those she and Mary had visited in the Irish section of Denver.

"Well." She glanced at Charlie and motioned toward the houses. "I don't see any boogie men so far."

Charlie pulled on the brake, cut the engine. "They come later. I thought this might be a good test."

Kate opened the door and climbed out. Stretching, she glanced up through the branches of a cottonwood that still held a few golden leaves toward the blue sky. She felt reinvigorated, ready to tackle any and all Italian Democrats. "What is this place called again?"

"The Groves." Charlie opened one of the back doors and Mary got out.

"Because of all the cottonwoods," Kate said.

"Expect so." Charlie opened the trunk, removed a box Kodak. The trunk closed, he pulled a narrow notebook from his jacket pocket.

Kate smiled at his preparation and turned to glance toward the last house on the block. "Mary, let's start down there. We can take pamphlets with us."

"What about our friend, Charlie, here?" Mary asked.

"I'll be right behind you, taking it all in," he said.

The women who opened the doors smiled, if a little uncertainly, as Kate and Mary introduced themselves—and Charlie. Only a two who were bold enough to take off their aprons, smooth their hair, and step outside to have their pictures taken for tomorrow's edition. After some roundabout questions, it became clear few voted. Those who did looked confused about why they should vote for a Republican candidate.

Three blocks later, the trio paused to decide how many more houses to contact. The sun had taken on that particular brilliance of late afternoon. Mary suggested the women now had other things on their minds: supper to make; men coming home from work. Time to stop canvassing for the night, and they walked back to Charlie's car and drove across the river toward larger, more prosperous houses. At the end of one block, they spotted Lizzie, sitting on a tree stump, a small pile of pamphlets next to her, her purple skirt draped over her crossed legs, chin in hand.

Kate called to her, and she stood, swiped at the back of her skirt. "I hope you're not counting on this part of town. The women who came to the door either wanted to know why I wasn't in school or what a nice girl my age was doing wandering around by herself." She ducked her head, climbed in next to Mary, and tossed the pamphlets on the seat beside her. "These things are a complete waste."

"Don't worry about it, love," Mary said. "Most will probably vote for Phipps because their husbands will. The others—if just one woman in a block reads it, the message'll spread like wild fire."

Kate smiled at her optimism, glanced at Charlie. "What's your impression so far?"

"Out of the bunch you and Mary talked to, maybe four might mark their ballot for Phipps but only if their husband's don't catch on first."

"You're not serious?"

Mary leaned over the seat, placed a hand on Kate's shoulder. "Old-country ways die hard. And, by the way, if Charlie will drop Lizzie and me at the Atwood place, we'll walk back to the hotel. I promised the little girl we'd come by before her bedtime for graham crackers and cocoa."

❧

Mary and Lizzie gone, a deliberate ploy on Mary's part, Kate was sure, in the name of well-meaning if misguided romance, the car seemed suddenly smaller, as if it had shrunk. Each time Charlie shifted gears, his hand grazed her leg. His nearness, the silence between them resurrected memories of their parting she thought she'd buried. She tried to concentrate on the passing houses, to remind herself that she was here to do a job. And that, sitting beside her was someone who could make the job easier and, hopefully, more effective.

So when she saw the hotel, she invited him to come in for coffee. "I'd like to fill you in on some background for your articles while we have the time," she said. "I didn't see a dining room, but I know they have a kitchen. We can sit in the lobby."

Kate bribed the hired girl with a quarter to bring them coffee, and soon they were sitting in the corner of what was little more than an oversized entryway, Charlie's notebook and their coffee cups on the small table between them.

The bulbs in the filigreed, bronze chandelier by the staircase that might have been converted from gas gave off an uneven light, but apparently enough for Charlie to see as he took notes and for Kate to notice his eyes still looked like chips of blue enamel. It wasn't until the clock in the corner sounded the hour that she was aware of the time, and she sat back. "Well, there you have it. Soup to nuts. I hope you'll put some of this in your article. Or have I given you too much?"

They exchanged smiles.

"You never know what you need till you write the story, my Dad used to say."

"This morning at the station you mentioned having unfinished business where he was concerned," Kate said.

"More a debt I've owed him since he died," Charlie said. He drew in a deep breath, let it out slowly, looked at her, his eyes dark. "Six years ago of a bullet from a thirty-thirty in the back. Not ten feet from where he put out the paper." Charlie shifted his gaze for a moment to some point across the room, looked back. "It was black as pitch that night. Whoever did it knew Dad's habits, knew when he'd be coming back from jawing with his friend, Bud Hibbard, who ran the company store, as he did every night." One corner of Charlie's mouth twisted into a little smile. "He and Dad were—how do the Italians say it?—*simpatico*. I was cleaning up when I heard the shot and I ran out to him. But he was already dead."

Kate gazed at him, trying imagine the horror of the scene and couldn't.

"I'd grown up setting type for Dad's editorials. The issue was always the same: conditions in the mines that were killing men every day. He used to kid around about how his words made him a marked man and that one day the big boys would get him." Charlie shook his head. "I thought it was brag."

"And now?" Kate asked, quietly.

"Now I'm spending my off-hours talking to people, retracing steps. But after six years, memories grow fuzzy. Mr. Hibbard died of a heart attack, or that's what the death certificate says. The superintendents of some of the mines around Dove Creek have changed. The old ones moved away or aren't willing to talk. I'd started out determined to find the shooter and who paid him. Now I think that won't happen. So the way I see it, the next best thing—maybe the better thing—is to pick up where Dad left off." Charlie straightened. "Which is where you come in."

She smiled uncertainly, not sure of his meaning.

"It wasn't until that hearing—the one in Washington before they sent you to the Workhouse—that I realized that what you were up against was power. Different situation than Dad's, but power nonetheless. And here I am."

Kate met his gaze, felt its intensity, and smiled. "Thank you."

Charlie stuck his notebook in his coat pocket, rose. "Don't thank me until you see the stories. Which reminds me: I better get back to the paper and write up the afternoon, get the photos developed."

Kate walked him to the door. They agreed he would pick them up at nine the next morning. Upstairs, Kate unlocked the door to her room and entered it without turning on the light. For a moment, she stood quite still, thinking of Charlie. A quiet man, a loner, really. A man eaten by terrible memories who kept his feelings stored deep down inside. Whatever his real reason for helping her and Mary, he had touched her more than she would have ever expected.

Chapter 32

Today was Tuesday, one week until the election and the second day in Pueblo, but the first for a full day of campaigning. A short article below Charlie's byline was in the morning edition of the *Chieftain* about the arrival of "Misses Kate Brennan and Mary Daly of Denver and chairman and vice chairman of the Colorado division of the National Woman's Party for the purpose of campaigning for election of Senate candidate, Lawrence Phipps." Alongside it was a photograph Charlie had taken of Kate and Mary, smiling and holding pamphlets.

Kate had envisioned something more, at least a quarter page, but she was still pleased. And, after Charlie had dropped Lizzie off up the hill from the Atwoods where she had stopped work yesterday, Kate brought the matter up.

"I saw the article, Charlie. And we appreciate it." It was important to phrase the next so he wouldn't be offended. "But I thought there'd be more about the women in the Groves. And some of your photographs which I'm sure were great."

"Ben decided we should work into it."

"Which means what, exactly?"

"That there are three days to go, plus Sunday's edition."

"So why not make it into something like a diary of what we do each day? The people we see, what their reactions are. Kind of like a serial but with bits about the amendment stuck in here and there."

"I could manage that."

Kate's spirits were rising. She twisted around, looked back at Mary. "What do you think?" And her answer was a smile.

Charlie drove across the river, past a filling station where the

American flag atop the roof flapped in the wind. Clouds scudded across the sky with the look of rain or possibly snow. Not a great day for tromping around neighborhoods, but Kate refused to let anything mar her confidence, and she pulled the list of Pueblo Democrats from her purse. Phoebe and Lizzie were bound to come up with at least fifty votes among women who ordinarily didn't bother to vote, leaving it up to her and Mary to persuade the eligible hardcore. Another fifty votes. She wasn't greedy. With Charlie's articles and the power structure on their side, how difficult could that be?

⁕

Dried leaves swirling around their ankles, the wind whipping at their skirts, Mary and Kate, with Charlie behind them, walked up to the next house on the block where they had stopped the night before. The woman who came to the door was white-haired and tiny and hunched with age. "*Buon giorno*."

Mary elbowed Kate, whispered, "Try your Italian."

"*Come stai?*" Kate asked.

The old woman's mouth spread into a toothless smile. "*Uno momento*," she said and called to someone in the room behind her, and a bony, black-haired woman appeared, wiping her hands on her apron. "Can I help you?" she asked.

As she had done so often, Kate introduced Mary, who handed the younger woman a pamphlet. Taking turns, she and Kate tried to explain who they were, that they would like her and the old woman to vote for Lawrence Phipps for senator next Tuesday.

As Kate talked, Mary noticed the woman's gaze straying to Charlie, saw the question in her eyes, and Mary introduced him, explaining he was a reporter for the *Chieftain*. "He's doing a story on the election this year and he'd like to take a picture of you and—your mother."

The daughter translated for her mother. There was conversation. In the end, they all exchanged smiles, but neither agreed to have her picture taken. Mary and Kate retraced their steps to the road and continued up the block. The sun had disappeared behind clouds, the wind had grown cold, and Mary hugged herself. "At this rate, if we're lucky and find someone who speaks English each time, we'll get to talk to maybe eight women when suppertime rolls around." She glanced at Kate. "No offense, but what we need is someone along who can really speak Italian."

They continued up the road, all of them staring at the modest houses, as if by some miracle, the solution lay hidden inside and only had to show itself, when Mary stopped, slapped her forehead with the palm of her hand. "Rosalie. Rosalie Nicholetti! Why didn't I think of her before? She lives right here. In Pueblo. Some place called Goat Hill. She's a member of my union. The whole family's union. Her Da used to work in the Ludlow mines down in the southern fields and went out in the '13 strike. As far as I know, he hasn't had a job since."

"You're sure she still lives here?" Kate said.

"Did, the last I knew," Mary said, and turned to Charlie. "Have you ever heard of Goat Hill?"

"It's not a half-mile from here." He motioned with his head. "The other side of the ravine at the end of the street down there."

"Won't your friend be at work this time of day?" Kate said.

"Might and might not." Mary started walking down the road. "Come on. Let's go back to the car and find out."

Chapter 33

The road up Goat Hill was steep and deeply rutted. The houses were smaller than those in the Groves, one no different from the next, board siding in need of paint, a sagging porch, an outhouse in the back. True to the neighborhood's name, a few goats were grazing in weedy lots. The houses bore no numbers, and Charlie drove slowly as they looked for the name "Nicholetti" on a house or a fence.

In spite of the persistent breeze, Mary caught a quiet about the neighborhood that bothered her. No children playing, no women in the yards hanging out laundry, no neighbors calling out to each other. Only an eerie quiet.

"I'd say your friend might have picked a better neighborhood," Kate said, peering at the houses. "This place gives me the creeps."

Charlie leaned over the steering wheel to gaze out the windshield and inspect the houses. "Prime territory, I'd say, for the Republicans offering ten bucks for votes."

Mary let the comments go past her as she continued to scan the houses for signs. She had almost given up hope when she saw it. Nicholetti, the black letters faint but clear enough to make out. She told Charlie to stop.

After he had shifted into neutral and set the brake, he shot a backward glance at Mary. "You want us to come in with you? I'm not sure I like the looks of this place."

"Stay put. You two will scare the poor woman to death." Mary climbed out. "I'll be right back."

Mary walked toward the wire gate, found the latch, pushed against the tangle of weeds until it opened. Walking up the hard-packed dirt path, the crunch of her footsteps against the carpet of dried leaves magnified in the silence, she felt a foreboding she couldn't explain.

As she approached the front door, Mary saw the stir of the curtain at the single window that looked out on the porch. Someone was home. She hoped that someone was Rosalie.

Cheered at the prospect of seeing her friend, Mary gave a brisk knock. Footsteps sounded from inside. The door swung open, and standing in the shadows of the darkened room was a man she knew all too well. The silence around here suddenly made sense. Gino Franchetti was working the neighborhood. With his rasping, bullying voice and his big, unyielding body, the man could frighten the Pope himself if he put his mind to it. You had to be tough to organize. A day didn't go by but your life wasn't on the line. But

Gino was one of those men who didn't mind bleeding. He thrived on danger, on fights, and, even, Mary suspected, on killing.

"Mary Daly in the flesh. I heard you was around." He gave her that crooked smile that had once stirred her into a frenzy, and stepped aside, gesturing for her to come inside. As she passed him, she was aware of the smell of his sweat, and the mixed memories of their lovemaking made her legs weak. Instinct told her to turn and run, but she had faced Gino down enough to know it could be done again.

The room she entered was no more than nine by twelve, a front parlor of sorts. The air was stale and the floorboards creaked beneath her step. In the half-light, the pale sun barely breaking through the opening in the curtain, Mary could not only smell him but also see him. Nearly six feet, slim, that dark hair cut close to his head, those muscled arms as thick as a stevedore's.

"I'm lookin' for Rosalie Nicholetti."

"That a fact?" He stroked his chin, a thin smile on his lips, and then his arm pulled back. Before she could duck, Gino swung at her, hitting her across the side of the head hard enough to make her stagger, nearly fall. "Whore. Sellin' yourself and the union down the river to lie with a rich bitch." He swung at her again, but this time she dodged him.

"Look who's talkin'." Her heart pounded in her ears. She caught in a breath. "Puttin' the fear of God in these poor souls to join your damn union, and them already hangin' onto their jobs for dear life."

They were circling each other now. He took another swipe at her, missed and sent a chair crashing. "Your dear old Dad would roll over in his grave."

"To Hell with him." A wisp of hair fell into her eyes. She brushed it back.

He lunged at her, grabbed hold of her arm and twisted it behind her back, giving it a jerk upward. She cried out, struggled to break loose, tried to kick his shins, but his grip was like iron.

"A woman can walk the picket line for your bunch." She winced against the pain. "Starve through a strike. But where's the union to help get a woman a fit wage?"

He shoved her away, sent her sprawling to the floor, and she scrambled to her feet. "Hope you're ready to die, bitch, cause that's what you're gonna do." He dropped into a crouch, like a great animal stalking his prey, and came toward her. In his hand was a slender knife—the switchblade he always carried in his boot. He held it up, beckoning to her as he might a dog.

Mary backed toward the wall, her gaze fixed on the blade. For a split second, she had the sensation that Gino, the knife, the room were all part of a terrible nightmare. She dodged around a chair, desperate to get past him, to reach the door, but he cut her off. She watched him, her heart nearly beating out of her chest, sure he could smell her fear. He moved toward her again, slowly as if in no hurry. She tensed like a bird ready to take flight, but the next moment he was on her, plunging the knife, deep and sure of its mark, into her gut.

The sudden pain took her breath away. She clutched her middle, gathered her strength, staggered toward the door. But her legs collapsed under her, and she crumpled to the floor. From some place at the edge of her consciousness, she was aware of voices calling her name, the sound of heavy footsteps in another part of the house, then quiet.

Chapter 34

Mary's head in her lap, the car smelling of blood, Kate tried to hold her friend against the sway and bounce of the car as Charlie raced down Goat Hill and along the streets toward the hospital.

"Who did this to you?" she asked, her voice trembling. "Was it Gino?"

Mary's eyelids fluttered, her mouth opened, but no words came out.

Kate placed a hand gently on Mary's forehead, terrified by how cold her skin was. "Just a few more minutes, dear, we'll be there."

Mary's eyes opened, unseeing, her lips moved, and Kate bent over her to catch the words. "Don't ya dare quit." A cough.

"Not a chance," Kate said. "You and I still have the ratification ahead of us." And she thought she saw Mary smile.

Kate glanced anxiously out the window. "Charlie—"

"The hospital's just ahead."

Their hands and clothes covered with their friend's blood, Kate and Charlie managed to carry Mary inside. Nurses converged. A gurney appeared. Mary was whisked away. Two doctors appeared, then vanished inside a room down the hall. A policeman in an officer's uniform questioned Kate and Charlie about "the incident." As they told him what little they knew, she could feel her hands stiffen as the blood dried.

Hours later, after she and Charlie had washed up and gratefully accepted a cup of bitter hospital coffee, one of the doctors emerged from a nearby room. A slender man whose starched white coat seemed several sizes too large, he introduced himself as Dr. Atwood, Phoebe's husband. In a voice hoarse with fatigue, he told them quietly that there was nothing more to be done, that it had been a testimony to Mary's strength she had survived as long as she had. Perhaps they would like to come in to say their last good-byes.

Blindly, Kate took Charlie's hand and they stepped inside and watched a priest give Mary the last rites. His healthy complexion looked oddly out of place against the starkness of the hospital room and Kate inexplicably felt a wave of dislike for the cleric. A nurse glanced at Kate and Charlie expectantly. Kate went to stand by the bed and gazed down at her friend, her eyes closed, her skin pale and delicate as tissue paper. Only her thick hair, which had broken loose of its customary plait, gave a hint of the Mary she had come to love. Kate bent over, touched the cold forehead with her lips, then moved to one side so the doctor could place his stethoscope to Mary's heart. There was only silence in the room that smelled of

266

antiseptic. The nurse took the doctor's place and pulled the sheet over Mary's head.

Perhaps guided by some primordial instinct of what was expected next, Kate returned to Charlie, waiting in the doorway, and they walked down the hall and out a side door, as if life were normal.

The early morning air was cold and he took her in his arms, held her close. She leaned against him, listening to his heartbeat. "What have I done? Dear God, what have I done?"

"Kate, you've done nothing. Mary died because Gino Franchetti stabbed her."

She shook her head, her cheeks wet with the tears. "No. It's my fault. I made her come down here. She warned me about Pueblo. About Gino. I insisted."

She glanced up at Charlie and he brushed the tears gently away with his fingertips. "I'm as much to blame as you are."

She shook her head again. "It's because of me. I knew better. I might just as well have killed Mary with my own hands." Kate leaned against him again and started to sob.

Charlie wrapped his arms around her, stroked her hair until she was able to catch her breath. He handed her his handkerchief. "Darling Kate, Mary came here because she believed it was the right thing to do. You were a team. She loved you as much as you loved her."

Kate blew her nose and he looked down at her. "Don't you dare quit. Isn't that what Mary said?" And they went back inside the hospital to find an office where Kate could send Mary's brother a telegram.

❧

Kate sat by the window of the crowded car, Lizzie beside her, and gazed at the outskirts of Denver rolling by. To the west, the back range of the mountains was touched with snow. There was a strange sort of comfort knowing that Mary lay in her coffin two cars behind them. Bob Daly would meet the train. A Mass for the Dead would be held at St. Catharine's tomorrow, the very church where Mary and Kate had stood on the steps that Sunday and argued about Lizzie coming along to Pueblo.

The Lizzie who sat beside Kate this afternoon was a changed person. Gone was the petulant little sister. In her place, a young woman who had taken charge of packing their suitcases, dealing with the hotel bill, telegraphing their parents. She had even thought to bring along a copy of the *Chieftain*, hot off the press.

Kate reached for it now to reread it. There on the front page, beneath Charlie's byline, was a full account of the tragic death of Mary Daly, vice chairman of the Colorado committee of the National Woman's Party, and an interview with the police chief, describing the all-out search for her alleged murderer, the notorious union organizer, Gino Franchetti. But, according to Lizzie, Charlie's crowning touch was the quote from the telegram sent by Lawrence Phipps to Miss Kate Brennan, expressing his condolences and his appreciation for their work.

Kate leaned her head back against the dusty velour-covered seat. This late in the afternoon, Charlie might be in the city room, hunched over his typewriter, pecking with two fingers, writing up the last of the series, timed to coincide with election day and intended as a memorial for Mary.

Closing her eyes, Kate saw him again as they stood in the shelter of the Pueblo train station early that morning, remembering his words. "I've loved you from the night we met. But the woman I loved then can't hold a candle to the woman I love now and will love for the rest of my life. She is lovelier and braver and more stubborn, if that's possible, and I can't live without her." He had gathered her into his arms and kissed her on the mouth, and when she had pulled back to catch her breath, he had begged her to marry him.

She knew now that what she felt for Charlie had begun as she'd watched him do the dishes in Millie's kitchen. Even at this moment, weighed down by guilt over Mary, her longing for him overwhelmed her. She remembered the stories her parents told of knowing from

268

the first moment they had met that they had been destined for each other. For the first time, she understood what they meant.

For the first time, too, she realized that the hardest part of life, even harder than loss and pain, was living through the paradoxes, the ironies, and ambiguities of it. Life rolled on—over, through, under everything. It could either carry you or crush you. She had always believed in logic and reason and fairness. But it wasn't that simple or that easy. She was beginning to understand that each person's life, each event was simply a crossing of strong fine threads of an enormous web, none of which she could totally grasp. What she could hold onto were what she'd come to know as true. She would not quit. She would mourn Mary. She would respect Lizzie, and she would marry Charlie. It was that simple and would be that hard.

Five days later, Kate sat at the back of the election headquarters in Denver's massive Victorian county courthouse and watched as clerks entered new figures on the chalkboards set up at the front of the room. Off to the right was an oversized calendar with the day's name and date: Thursday, November 7, 1918. Lizzie was back at home. Kate had cast her ballot in the parish house of St. Michael's Episcopal Church, four blocks from her parents' house. She had attended the Mass for Mary, not surprised at how many people were there. When Mary's brother, Bob, had approached her, venting his rage over his sister's death, Kate had decided not to go to the cemetery. And now, three days since the election, the Senate election still hung in the balance.

Beyond Colorado, peace negotiations were going on in France. American flyers—maybe one of them Tom—were dropping rations to hungry French civilians. The number of cases of flu had dropped enough for movie theaters to reopen. A telegram from Lucy yesterday had contained mixed news. Senator Weeks of Massachusetts and Saulsbury of Delaware, both die-hard opponents, had been defeated. Yet most of the Democratic western senators up for reelection had survived. Translated, that meant that even if the Republicans gained control of the Senate and Shafroth lost, the amendment would still need one more yes vote.

Kate turned her thoughts back to the figures on the chalkboard. Phipps was ahead statewide by six thousand votes. Encouraging, but not conclusive, because the final tallies from a number of outlying counties, including Pueblo, and the traditionally Democratic mining towns tucked away in the mountains, were still missing. Until they came in, Shafroth's people refused to concede.

Studying the chalkboard more carefully, Kate noticed a puzzling pattern to the Denver vote. A third of the state's population lived in Denver where the Democrats were at their strongest. Even with the work she and Mary and all the other women had done to counteract Shafroth's popularity, Kate had been prepared for the worst. Why else had she and Mary gone to Pueblo? Yet the totals in the precincts within every Denver Democratic ward gave Shafroth only the slimmest margin, at best. A few, like the Fifth—Tom Delaney's kingdom—had even fallen short.

She glanced at the knot of men, all Democratic ward bosses, still holding vigil as they lolled on the benches or leaned their elbows on their knees, smoking, eyes on the blackboards. But instead of the glum expressions she would have expected, they were trading jokes. They, who had assured her that, "Old John" Shafroth could fend for himself. Were they looking at a different set of numbers than she was?

Then a man with an official-looking paper in hand walked in and strode up to the chalkboard. The conversation in the room stilled. The men with the smug smiles from the Denver ward headquarters sat up. Kate leaned forward, straining for a view of the figures being erased and replaced. Phipps: 42, 664; Shafroth 31,537. Eleven hundred twenty-seven votes, the difference between victory and defeat.

Kate glanced back at the ward bosses, puzzled by their knowing smiles, when it was she who should be smiling. In fact, she should be ecstatic. Now, finally, when the new Congress convened next spring, Phipps would add his vote to those of the other Senate Republicans who would surely be elected, and the amendment would be approved. Women's votes across the country would turn Mary's dreams of laws protecting women against abuse and the eight-hour day into reality. But something about the reaction of the ward bosses bothered her.

Two months ago, Kate had told her mother that working against Shafroth was for the ultimate good, that it was nothing personal. Kate still believed it. She was proud of what she and Mary had had a hand in accomplishing. Yet, down deep, she ached for John Shafroth. She should return home. If anyone could explain those numbers, her father could. As important, she couldn't go back to Washington with her mother hating her.

⚜

Filled with trepidation, Kate pressed down the latch of the front door and stepped into the entryway. In the center of the long, antique sideboard was a large bouquet of dried lemon yellow and orange wild flowers and weeds that she knew her mother had arranged in the brass vase. Kate decided the silence meant that Lizzie was still in school and Christine had gone to market.

Kate glanced toward the living room: no sign of anyone. On the other side of the hall the dining room was also empty. She was about to go upstairs when she heard heavy footsteps and saw her father, in shirtsleeves.

"Hi, Daddy."

"When I heard the door, I'd hoped it was you. Mother's upstairs, resting." He motioned toward the study behind him. "Come in, why don't you? We can talk."

The oak-paneled room was small with a cozy feel to it. A bookcase brimming with adventure stories her father loved to read took up one wall. Two brown leather, well-used chairs had been drawn up to a large desk that her father once used in his office at the paper before it was sold. Beyond the desk was a single window that looked out on the alley and a neighbor's yard beyond. Kate always thought of the room as her father's retreat.

"I take it you know the election results," he said.

"I haven't come home to crow, Daddy."

"Didn't figure you had." Her father sank into one of the leather chairs. "Sit, and tell me why you did come."

"Are Lizzie and Mother on speaking terms yet?" Kate asked.

"Of course. And I'm sorry to hear about your friend, Mary."

Kate drew in a shaky breath, tried for a smile. "Daddy, I just came from the court house." She handed him the figures she had copied down. "Take a look at the Denver results. I can't make sense of them."

He glanced at the paper, then back at her. "Apparently, you didn't see the ad in the *Post* just before the election."

She shook her head, and her father pushed to his feet, went over to his desk, picked up a newspaper and handed it to her. "It's on page five."

Kate turned to the right page. At first glance, she thought she was reading an article. Looking more carefully, she realized it was an ad paid for, the small print at the bottom said, by friends of the recently deceased mayor of Denver, Robert Speer. She read the copy slowly. The ad was a scathing indictment of prominent Democrats who, twelve years earlier, had stood up against the Speer-Democratic machine. Heading the list of culprits was John Shafroth, specifically accused of being "the ultimate party wrecker." Dumbfounded, Kate glanced over at her father, who was back in his chair. "Why?"

Her father stretched out his long legs. "It's called politics." He eyed her. "But you know all about that now, don't you? If memory serves, you said as much to your mother."

"But this . . ." Kate held up the newspaper. "It's downright vicious."

"What the ad alludes to is the fight John got into with some of his fellow Democrats over the issue of home rule for Denver. He knew the risks of standing up against a political boss in his own party, so I wouldn't feel sorry for him." Her father studied the toes of his shoes then looked over at her. "I've known John Shafroth for some thirty years. Politics have been his life. He's honest. He does what he thinks is right"

Unable to sit still, she went around the desk, gazed out the window for a moment before she turned back to her father. "What will he do now?"

"Practice law. The boys will join him eventually. He'll do fine."

"Is Mother upset?"

"She takes her loyalty to friends seriously, in case you haven't noticed. But give her time. She'll come around."

Kate went over to her father, and he stood and wrapped his arms around her, and she surrendered to the feel of them, the smell of his tobacco, and, for a moment, she felt like his little girl again. Pulling away, she said, "I'm going back to Washington on the first train I can get. I don't know where I'll be living yet. Maybe Millie's for a few weeks if her aunt will let me use the couch. Millie and I might share a place. I'll write as soon as I know."

They walked to the front hall and Kate saw her mother coming down the stairs. Facing her now, Kate felt awkward, tongue-tied. "Daddy said you were resting," was all she managed to say.

"I was." Her mother looked down at her. "There'll come a day when you will understand what a tragic day this is for Colorado."

"Mother, this campaign was never about Mr. Shafroth. It was about the suffrage amendment, which was larger than any senator or congressman. It was about achieving the vote for every woman in the country, our right." She met her mother's accusing gaze. "You were my age when you and Aunt Mary walked the streets for the vote as I did these last weeks. Surely, you remember."

"That was a long time ago." Her mother absently ran a hand back and forth along the banister's satiny wood.

"Twenty-some years. But it was the same issue, wasn't it?"

Kate's father went to the stairs and held his hand out for his wife, who took it and came down to stand next to him.

"Will you be back for Christmas?" her mother asked

"I don't think so. Maybe next summer. The amendment will have to be ratified by the states. It depends on where I'm needed." She looked from her mother to her father. "I met someone—Charlie Harrison is his name. I wouldn't be surprised if he calls on you. You'll like him, I know." She hugged her mother, who kissed her lightly on the cheek, then went to her father.

"Take care of yourself, kiddo," he said as he released her.

Kate widened her eyes against tears. "You, too." She turned, opened the door, and closed it behind her.

Chapter 35

Four days later, Kate held her raincoat tight around her as she hurried through the park in the cold Washington rain. Shriveled chrysanthemum bushes lined the walk slick with fallen leaves. For all her anticipation of the work ahead, her heart was heavy with grief. She missed Mary's wry wit, her common sense view of the world.

Directly ahead, through the dripping branches of tulip trees, Kate saw the familiar purple-and-gold banner, drooped forlornly over the headquarters' porte-cochere. She sprinted across the street, gave the bulletin board a cursory glance, pulled open the front door, and went in.

Standing in the foyer, Kate removed her hat and shook off raindrops. From the floor above, she heard women's voices. A telephone rang. She smiled at the familiar hubbub and thought of Mary, wondering what she would make of it. Widening her eyes against tears, Kate mounted the stairs. A girl she didn't recognize, who looked to be about her own age, with brown, bobbed hair, was seated behind a typewriter. She glanced up, smiled. "Can I help you?"

"Is Lucy in her office?"

"Does she expect you?" the girl asked.

Kate smiled. "More or less." And, before the protective girl could stop her, Kate continued on to the third floor. The door to Lucy's office was open. Though Kate had telegraphed she was on her way, she hadn't been specific about the day of her arrival because she couldn't be, as crowded as the trains were. Now that she was here, she could hardly wait to learn about the experiences of the other state committees, the details of every Senate race that only Lucy would know.

Just as Kate was about to knock, Lucy looked up from her desk. "Kate! Oh, my goodness!" She rose, came around her desk, and gave Kate a quick, fierce hug. "You did us proud."

"Thanks, but it was the hundreds of women I never saw who did most of the work. And Mary Daly, of course. I can't remember if I wrote you about her."

"You did, yes. I'm so sorry. Sad to say, she wasn't the first to give her life for the cause." Lucy squeezed her arms and Kate saw the genuine sorrow in her eyes. "But look at you." She grimaced at Kate's soggy raincoat. "Take that thing off, sit, and have some coffee. I'll bet you're exhausted. I hear the trains are jammed." Lucy turned back to the desk, picked up a silver-toned thermos and mugs from a tray half-hidden in the clutter of papers. Shaking it, she grinned at Kate. "Just enough left for two cups."

Smiling, Kate saw the woman with the intense blue eyes and wild red hair pinned off her broad face, who had faced the District police that steamy afternoon, and nothing about her had changed.

"You and Mary Daly and the others did a fine job."

"We managed to raise the issue and some dirty Democratic politics in Denver didn't hurt," Kate said. "But what now?"

"Alice and I decided to give this Congress one last chance. Senator Jones is going to make a try for a vote in early February." Lucy unscrewed the top of the thermos. "It won't work, of course. Still, there's no harm in trying. In the meantime, we have to gear up for the vote after the new Congress is sworn in. We're shooting for late May and early June."

"What's your prediction?" Kate asked.

"We'll carry the House overwhelmingly. No worry there." Lucy poured coffee in two mugs, handed her one. "As to the Senate . . . We'll make the two-thirds majority, but with not a vote to spare."

"Even with the new pro-suffrage men who were elected?"

Lucy nodded. "Even with them." She took a sip of coffee. "After the vote, there's still the ratification hoop to jump through. Some say it'll be a snap. I, for one, am taking nothing for granted.

"Alice and I have already decided you must organize the western states. Not as easy as it sounds, I fear, and we're counting on you." Mug in hand, Lucy sank into the battered swivel chair behind her desk. "We've come too far to let it fall apart now."

Kate couldn't hide her smile. Nothing had changed: no one refused Lucy Burns. "I'll do my best." She took a sip of steaming coffee. "When it's over, when the amendment is finally part of the Constitution . . .What will you do?"

"Will I run for office? No." Lucy's smile had a reflective look to it, Kate thought. "I'm not sure I ever mentioned my two sisters who are unmarried. Occasionally, we've talked of living together. And there's our mother who is alone. I thought I might buy a house, maybe in Georgetown. Some place with a yard big enough for a garden. I thought I'd try my hand at roses. Yellows and corrals are my favorites."

Kate tried to picture Lucy on her hands and knees, a trowel in hand. "But you can't just up and retire from politics."

"Oh, but I can, and will. Though Alice won't, nor should she." Lucy rocked in the swivel chair. "And you?"

Kate tilted her head, smiled. "On the way over, I was thinking how amazing it's all been. And I wouldn't have missed any of it. As to what's ahead?" She smiled, envisioning a Sunday afternoon walking, hand in hand, with Charlie along the Potomac, talking about insignificant things, just happy to be with him. "I'll probably get married."

276

"And have a house full of children."

"Me, with children?" Kate laughed. "Well, maybe one or two."

Smiling, Lucy reached across her desk for the thermos. "More coffee?"

Kate held out her mug. Some day, she'd look back with wonder and, perhaps, with a certain longing for this day with Lucy—for all the days spent within these four walls, once a servant's room but, for two years, the command center of a war as important as any ever waged and won, for Mary and all the other women she had come to know and admire and the thousands who were only names, and the men who had stood with them. Would history remember? She hoped so. Not the details. Those weren't important. What mattered was the result. The vote.

Afterword

꧁꧂

Following the 1918 election, President Wilson devoted most of his time to the League of Nations. Even so, NAWSA President Carrie Chapman Catt was able to persuade him to include a plea for passage of the federal suffrage amendment in his Annual Message to Congress.

The election had produced two new pro-suffrage votes so that when the Sixty-sixth Congress convened and the House was scheduled to repass the amendment in May of 1919, the Senate approval appeared to be a sure thing. Still, Alice Paul and Lucy Burns took no chances, and they continued to shore up shaky votes and encourage stalwart supporters.

They had reason to believe a newly elected senator, William J. Harris, a Democrat from Georgia and a personal friend of the President, could well be the swing vote. Paul sent Maude Younger, a tireless worker known as the "millionaire waitress" who had founded the waitress union in San Francisco, to meet with pro-suffrage Democrats, including Joe Tumulty, the president's chief of staff, in hopes they would urge the president to convince Senator Harris to cast a favorable vote. And they did. Within days, a second uncommitted senator, Henry W. Keyes, a Republican from New Hampshire announced that he, too, would vote in the affirmative. Then another, Senator Frederick Hale, a Republican from Maine, shifted his vote to the suffrage column.

On June 4, 1919, with little debate, the Senate finally passed the Susan B. Anthony Amendment by a vote of fifty-six to twenty-five votes. The Speaker of the House and the Vice President signed the joint resolution later that same day.

The ratification process took only fifteen months to complete. Understandably, most assumed that those states where women had already won the vote would be the first to ratify. But, except for Kansas and Michigan and New York, that was not the case. In fact, those states where women had had the vote longest were the slowest to ratify. On August 26, 1920, when Tennessee signed the certificate of ratification, three-quarters of the states had approved the amendment, finally enfranchising twenty-six million women of voting age.

After the fact, Connecticut and Vermont also ratified the amendment. Missing were the southern states of Virginia, Maryland, North Carolina, South Carolina, Georgia, Alabama, Louisiana, Mississippi, Florida, and Delaware.

In retrospect, Alice Paul and her compatriot, Lucy Burns, who, like others in the Progressive Era had been shaped by their strong religious beliefs and dedication to democracy and reform, seemed destined to found and lead the National Woman's Party. Unlike Lucy Burns, Alice Paul continued her association with the NWP, convinced to the day she died at the age of ninety-three in 1978 the Equal Rights Amendment would be ratified. As to Lucy Burns— ever the superb organizer, she abruptly retired from public view and spent the remainder of her life, unmarried, devoting herself to the Catholic church and the care of her orphaned niece.

Nineteenth Amendment to the Constitution of the United States

Susan B. Anthony Amendment

Section 1. The right of citizens of the United States to vote shall not be denied or abridged by the United States or by any state on account of sex.

Section 2. Congress shall have the power, by appropriate legislation, to enforce the provisions of this article.

Suggested Reading

Catt, Carrie Chapman and Shuler, Nettie Rogers, *Woman Suffrage and Politics: The Inner Story of the Suffrage Movement* (New York, Scribner, 1923).

Flexner, Eleanor and fitzpatrick, Ellen, *Century of Struggle: The Woman's Rights Movement of the United States* (Cambridge, Harvard University Press, 1996).

Fraisse, Genevieve and Perot, Michelle, *A History of Women: Emerging Feminism from Revolution to World War* (Cambridge, Harvard University Press, 1993).

Garner, Les, *Stepping Stones to Women's Liberty: Feminist Idea in the Women's Suffrage Movement, 1910–1918* (Rutherford, N.Y., Fairleigh Dickson University Press, 1984).

Irwin, Inez Hayne, The Story of the Woman's Party (New York: Harcourt, Brace, 1921).

Lunardini, Christine A., *From Equal Suffrage to Equal Rights: Alice Paul and the National Woman's Party, 1910–1928* (New York, toExcel Press, 2000).

Marshall, Susan E., *Splintering Sisterhood: Gender and Class in the Campaign Against Woman Suffrage* (Ann Arbor, University of Wisconsin Press, 1997).

O'Neill, William, *Everyone was Brave: A History of Feminism in America* (Chicago, Quadrangle Books, 1971).

Stanton, Elizabeth Cady, et al, eds., *The History of Woman Suffrage*, 6 vols. (New York, Foster and Wells, 1881–1922).

Stevens, Doris, edited by Carol O'Hare, *Jailed for Freedom: American Women Win the Vote* (Troutdale, Ore., New Sage Press, 1995 and first published in 1920).

Author's Notes

For sheer drama, the long battle waged by American women to gain the precious right to vote has few equals in the nation's story.

Among the actual players during the last months prior to final congressional approval of the Nineteenth Amendment to the Constitution are Alice Paul and Lucy Burns, founders of the National Woman's Party; U.S. Senator Andrieus Jones of New Mexico, Congressman Edward Keating and Senator John Shafroth of Colorado; and all the senators involved in the amendment. Careful research was done to present them accurately with particular care taken regarding Senator Jones and Senator Shafroth, and his bid for reelection in 1918. Only those who knew them at the time, however, can be certain whether the characterization is as precise as it might have been.

About the Author

Sybil Downing is a fourth-generation Coloradoan and the award-winning author of numerous books, including *The Binding Oath*, *Ladies of the Goldfield Stock Exchange*, *Fire in the Hole*, and *Tom Patterson: Colorado Crusader*. Carrying on a family tradition, she has held state and local office. She and her husband live in Boulder, Colorado. Visit her website: www.sybildowning.com.